COHESION AND CHAOS

Shadows of Edros Book #1

Meredith Midnight
Elle Joyner

ABERRANT ARCHIVES

From Meredith Midnight (Effervescent):
To the original team of the Ascender Chronicles.
Thank you for always enjoying my world.

From Elle Joyner:
To my immeasurably patient husband, my two precious gremlins and my parents who read everything I've written since I was ten. I couldn't do this without any of you supporting me. And to my amazing co-author, who let me into her beautiful world so we could write this book together!

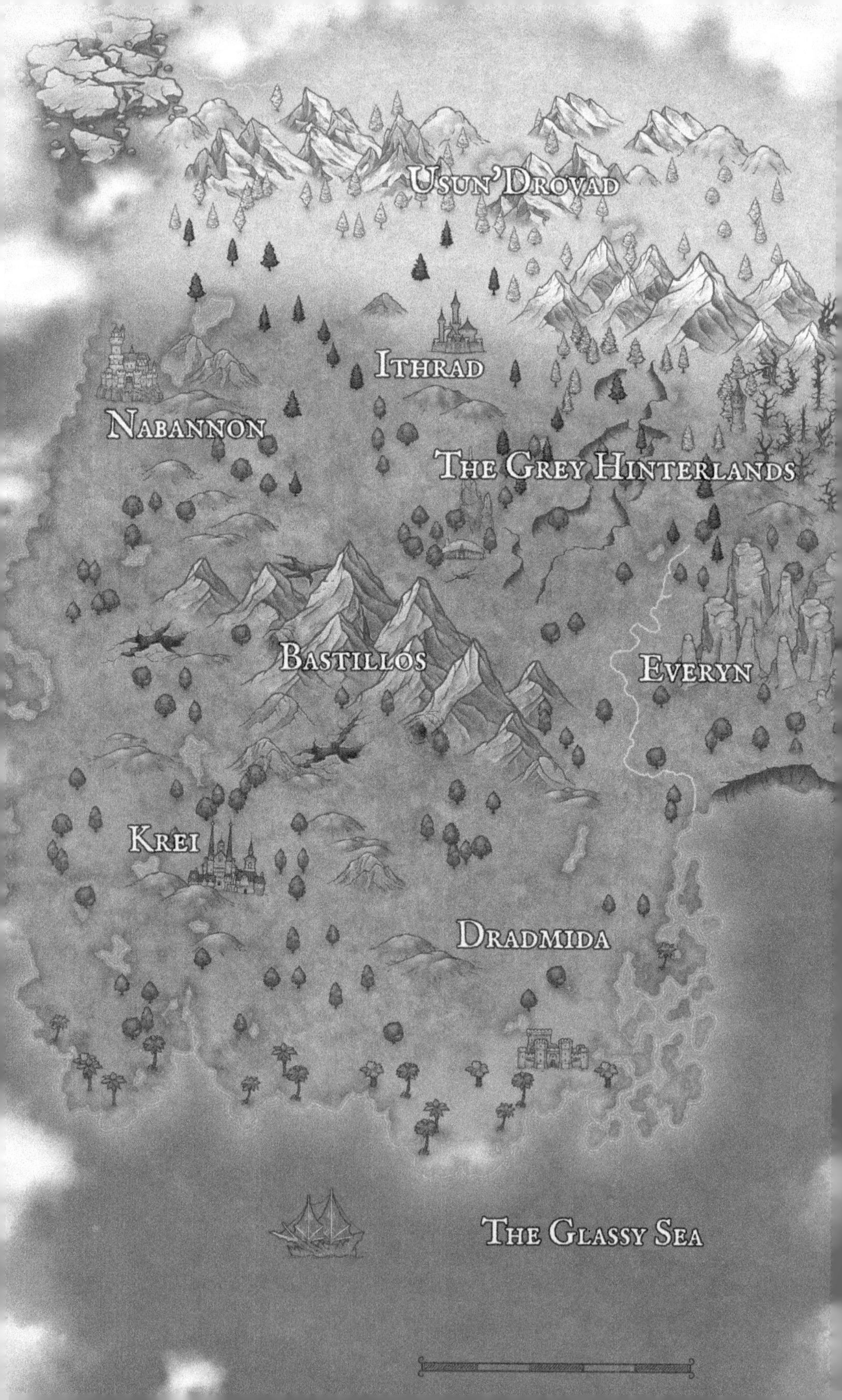

Usun'Drovad
Ithrad
Nabannon
The Grey Hinterlands
Bastillos
Everyn
Krei
Dradmida
The Glassy Sea

CONTENTS

The following is a list of content warnings for Cohesion and Chaos so that you can make an informed decision on whether or not to proceed.

- Mention of slavery

- Bound by chains around the neck

- Human Trafficking

- Giant Spiders

- Mentions of the buying and selling of individuals for the purposes of sex

- Suicidal ideation

- Involuntary Disassociation

Year 1220 of the First Era
Day 68 of Winter

PROLOGUE

Iron figurines dotted the table map before Queen Zalette of House Iliume, her youthful face shielded by a veil of gold and gemstones that jingled as she leaned inward. War was brewing around the mountains of Bastillos — her lands — and all the surrounding kingdoms of Edros was in preparation. General Demonte led the meeting discussing what his scouts had reported regarding the northern kingdoms of Nabannon and Ithrad.

"A battalion has been sent to each of Ithrad's border fortresses," the general said as he pointed to metal cylindrical pieces that resembled a tower. Flag shaped pieces with Ithrad's colors of green and white depicted a battalion next to each tower. "Only the ones to our border. There's activity from Krei that suggests that should things escalate, their forces will join with Nabannon."

"Given they are neighbors, I have no doubts," said the Head of Commerce, Gerand of House Tumould. Men did not wear adornments, but often wore fashionable caps with woven beads. Gerand's cap cuffed behind his ears and sloped to his forehead in a point. "Trade has been sparse from both kingdoms since your ruling, Your Majesty."

The head of the Guild of Architects, Nemmay of House Vertagn pursed her thin lips. Her guild was responsible not only for the buildings within the caverns of Bastillos, but the structural integrity of every tunneled road. She was an intelligent woman, and wise, but silent during these meetings. Zalette had learned in the six years of her reign to read Nemmay's expressions when the woman would not speak. Nemmay's disposition showed displeasure towards the young queen's reign, though not in a personal slight.

"Northern trade was found to be corrupt," Zalette stated. "The monarchs are aware. They were smuggling more than just people."

"Whispers in the air speak of the slight towards orcish merchants in the last six years," Gerand said with a sigh. Further north, beyond the human lands of Edros presided the orcish lands of Usun'Drovad. They hadn't been enemies of Edros in centuries, and in fact had aided the humans in the advancements of their societies. Bastillos would not have thrived without their engineering. Nemmay's operations relied heavily on orcish ingenuity.

The others at the table looked to the empty seat next to the Head of Commerce where Manak, Head of Engineering, would have sat. The orc had stepped away from his position and left Bastillos last Season.

"They think it is a maneuver to control Edros," General Demonte said solemnly.

"It is not," Zalette stated, and clenched her jaw to stave off defense. The table was occupied by men and women three times her years who would barely acknowledge her presence during the meetings. It was as if it were a formality, her title granting her permission to observe the adults debating the lives of her people; her responsibility. The general was the only one to actively address her, and without exasperation.

She was not supposed to be queen of Bastillos so soon. Her mother died six years prior at the culmination of the slave rebellion leaving her with the burden at the age of twelve. They've never stopped viewing her as a child despite her now being of age to marry.

"We should lower the trade regulations," Gerand suggested. He was addressing General Demonte, of course. Had he forgotten the generals of the Bastillosi army deferred to their queen? "Lower tariffs to the north and set up an agreement that can't be misconstrued as a violent takeover."

"People died because of their smuggling operation," the general reminded. "They caused our civil war. And we should reward them for it?"

"It's not a reward, Demonte. Our infrastructure cannot handle the stress of a loss of trade," Gerand reminded. "Especially if war is on the horizon."

"The orcs have been smuggling our slaves out of Bastillos for as long as we've traded with them," Nemmay said, her voice calm and melodic. Her black hair was streaked with grey and pulled back in a sweeping fashionable set of swirls adorned with silver chains. Her ears were cuffed with filigree that matched the silver embroidery of her Krei style dress that held stiff pointed shoulders.

"Yes, but their last operation caused an entire tunnel to collapse with a riot," General Demonte said. Nemmay's painted lips pursed, and she said nothing more. "If our allies believe they need to bolster their borders, trading among the lands will already be strained. We need to regulate what comes in and out of our mountains. There are consequences to every action."

"And what of the consequences of this?" Gerand posed. "If we do not provide some relief, some humility, Bastillos will crumble in more ways than one."

Queen Zalette sat back in her seat, the metal of her headdress delicately clinking, ringed fingers brushing over the plush upholstery of her arm rests. Her council room was once used solely for war, its utilitarian structure built far within the mountain wall and held with thick pillars of metal and stone. A heated everglow stone rested in a hearth that emitted a comfortable warmth, and the mirrorlight tunnels provided bright daylight from the outside.

"I will present the senate with these findings," she said. "We need to get ahead of the escalation. General Demonte, stay aware, but do not assign anyone to the border just yet. I don't want them to think we are preparing for war in response. Tumould, draft a trade proposal you think will be just and have it ready for tonight's senate session. I trust your judgment. Vertagn, if you would remain behind after dismissal, I wish to speak to you regarding the restoration of the collapsed trade route. Everyone else is dismissed."

The men bowed lowly to their queen and exited quietly. Nemmay looked to Zalette expectantly as the door creaked to a close. "Your Majesty, restorations are still underway. We've had some setbacks over the last year as our efforts caused another portion of the tunnel to collapse. We're currently drafting options to reroute the road to avoid further delays."

It was evident on Nemmay's features she knew of the queen's true intent for their private meeting. Nemmay still would not offer her thoughts freely. Zalette respected that, and wished she, too, could remember to hold such commanding air. That was more her mother's demeanor: cold and unapproachable.

"Do you think Edros finds me weak?" Zalette asked. She knew the answer, and fought against the desire to fidget. Slowly, she closed her fingers inward and pressed her nails to her palms.

"Of course," Nemmay stated candidly. "All of this seems an excuse for them to take the mountain kingdom. We're the center of Edros. We are the roads which all must travel for better and safe trade. We own the mountains within and without. They cannot pass through our valleys without our knowing and our permission. To command this kingdom would be to rule Edros."

"Do they think that is what I'm trying to do?"

"Your mother was trying to do so," she answered. Zalette was not sure if she believed that. "It's only natural you would as well. And why not?"

"I only want to rule Bastillos," Zalette said. She looked at the map once again, eyes following the terrain leading to the valleys of her kingdom. The towering mountains undulated at the center proudly. Her fingers traced over the engravings that formed the Dradmidan border leading to the sea.

"Ruling Bastillos could be ruling Edros, even if by mediation among the monarchs," Nemmay said. "You don't need to be a tyrant, but you need to be smart. Bastillos will fall without trade. They know this. Our mountains give us shelter, but it also complicates our economy."

The thought of such perception put Zalette at unease. She did not wish to be viewed like her mother. It was what caused her people to rebel, though perhaps it was for the better. The slaves were now free people who no longer had to flee to the Grey Hinterlands for a better chance at life. They could achieve that here.

"You'll be at the senate tonight?" Zalette asked. The older woman offered a nod, grey eyes trailing over the map.

"Would you like for me to present the proposal for the new route?" Nemmay asked.

"Yes, that would be helpful, thank you. You may go, Vertagn."

The Head of the Guild of Architects rose gracefully, her adornments tinking as she bowed to her queen.

The queen sat as still as stone during the senate's closed session. The slightest movement could cause her royal adornments to clang like bells of gold medallions, which was only acceptable in private. It was proper for a princess to keep her body still in public, and it was expected for a queen to be statuesque. Her people had to see the regality, and know she was in complete control.

Queen Zalette felt the weight of her adornments on her head, the intricately draped chains like a web holding each golden piece around her woven hair. If it wasn't the weight of her adornments that distracted her, it was the pins that held them through her braids. Every pin touched her scalp like an unwavering pest.

How her mother did this for decades was baffling. That woman was irritated at the slightest noise. Yet she had always held her composure, and spoke so expertly that her adornments never clattered together.

Zalette was told the adornments of a queen is the weight of responsibility and a reminder of the burden of this position. A physical reminder of the burden was not necessary, in her mind. Bastillos was crumbling from the inside out.

Senator Hureis, an older man who shaved his head clean, but sported a thick, white beard adorned with metal beads, had the floor as he spoke of his son's report from Nabannon.

"The orcs of Usun'Drovad have been in talks with Nabannon's court," Hureis said. "It is unclear the subjects of their talks as my son was not invited to their meetings. He has been asked to make arrangements to return home or face imprisonment. I ask that we send word to Nabannon without delay to inform them of his departure. I do not believe we should risk him remaining."

Behind the senate within the darkness of the rising steps were a select group of scholars and diplomats invited to sit in on the closed session. The scholars quickly scrawled notes and accounts of the session, their hands fervently writing shorthand with wrapped graphite. The diplomats leaned in towards one another as they whispered.

Sitting beside her, facing the senate, were the remaining representatives of Edros. The elvish druid, Xurshai, wore his traditional woven garb made from stripping fibers from a plant stalk that gave the garment an earthy, almost fruity scent. His long, black hair was braided down his back, his beard close to his jawline with a short forward braid at the chin. Ambassador Nin of Krei was beside him, narrow eyes intent on the session, jaw tight. She looked resplendent in traditional Krei fashion in deep, vibrant hues of cyans and purples with delicate embroidery along the cuffs of her sleeves and pointed shoulders.

The representative of the Edrosi Coalition of Trade, Elanath, was younger than anticipated, her inexperience evident in her wide, overwhelmed expression. Her concern was evident, vibrant blue eyes unblinking and a firm grip on her armrests. The Edrosi Coalition of Trade was an independent organization that swore no allegiance to any one monarchy to remain neutral in times of war, but war would not make business easy.

Beside her was the ambassador hailing from Dradmida. He was the most stoic out of the lot, and middle aged. He wore flowing material draped over his shoulders with loose pants, his dark skin striking against the bright colors.

"If I may, Senator Hureis, provide a counter," Senator Frenau said as she rose from her seat. She always had the appearance of looking down at others from her sharp nose, eyes heavy lidded. Senator Hureis bowed his head to show he conceded to her proposition to speak.

"If tensions are rising in Nabannon, we need someone to advocate for Bastillos and remain the voice of the Queen," she continued. "If Ambassador Hureis extracts himself from Nabannon, it will be far more difficult to reason with them without immanent violence. I assume the same is of Ithrad."

She turned to look at the other senators for Ithrad's report, to which Senator Nuros stood and bowed her head. "Indeed, Ambassador Gein's last missive spoke of orc collusion. Messengers are being turned away at the border, so we have not heard from him since."

Nuros returned to her seat, and the floor fell pensive. Senator Frenau gave Hureis a worried look, and his face creased. He turned to Zalette to address her directly.

"My Queen," he said, and stepped closer to her perch. "Given the reports of border engagement and our neighbors' disinterest in negotiations against aggression, I would request that we at least ask for our ambassadors' return from both Nabannon and Ithrad before escalation."

"We need to think of the people, Hureis," Senator Frenau reminded. "Our ambassadors will be safe—"

"And what if my son returns to me as a headless messenger?" Hureis hissed through his teeth. He closed the distance between him and Frenau with seething anger, and she returned his emotional outburst with calm neutrality.

"I understand your fears," Zalette said before Frenau could speak. Hureis, embarrassed by his display, shirked away from his colleague with an apologetic bow of his head. Attention turned to the queen, and she fought to keep her head still as she spoke.

"I do not wish to see our representatives harmed, and I do not believe our neighbors to be so barbarous as to send such grotesque messages," Zalette continued. "Edros is advanced. We are known to the world as the Country of Commerce. We did not become this through violence. We achieved it through communication. Through talking and understanding each other, and somewhere along the way we forgot ourselves. We. Bastillos.

"They may be bolstering their borders, but consider it may be out of fear than out of want for violence. Bastillos has the largest army in Edros, no thanks to our own unfortunate history of control. By our poor attempts to handle our own infighting, we have created an image that does not speak well to a want for friendly negotiations. We cannot fault Edros for anticipating the worst when we have given our worst.

"Send a messenger to the borders requesting the allowance of diplomats for negotiations to enter their lands or speak to a representative of their choosing at a location they desire. In the meantime, I want you to choose two diplomats best suited for these negotiations upon approval. We will provide our own escort and allow them to determine the number allowed. It has been well over a century since all of Edros has faced a war. I do not anticipate any of us are eager to break that achievement."

Zalette fell quiet, her stomach churning as she held back anxious tremors. While she kept her head still, she watched the senate quietly ruminate, their exchanges of glances telling. They were hesitant and reluctant as they bowed to their young queen.

This would be her first command that would place their fates in the balance. The last queen to hold such weight was her mother, and it ended with a civil war and her heart pierced through with a vengeance. The death toll of that war was two hundred eighty-two.

The history books state the last Edrosi war resulted in thousands of deaths, and many more presumed, but not counted. It was considered one of the bloodiest and ruthless wars that required outside intervention from the dragon riders to the east. Did they still exist?

Decisions based on unknowns would not serve her people well. To prevent this war, a compromise would need to be determined, but in order to determine a compromise, a reason had to be located. They needed to actually listen to their neighbors.

"I will ask Nemmay of House Vertagn to come forward and present the plans for our new trade routes," Zalette said, and the two standing senators deeply bowed, and returned to their seats. A proposal for reopening trade routes would aid in the diplomats' negotiations. The line of diplomats sat with wide eyes as the head of the Guild of Architects took the floor.

Two of them would be given a burden heavier than her crown, and it seemed they understood what was to come.

1
YSELLA

Chaos resounded from outside her travel carriage as steel clashed and commands called through the cold grey air. Ysella Ronasin pinned herself to the plush seat upholstered in green velvet, her heart slamming against her throat. The sounds beyond her closed door coiled to shrieks of pain and frenzied fear. She shut her eyes tightly to will away the growing nightmare.

It had been three days since Ysella of House Ronasin left the comfort of the cavern city of Lumin. She was chosen among the slew of diplomats for a deeply important mission, and to that, she had ventured with an air of overconfidence and a condescending superiority.

This, of course, was very little difference to her usual behavior, and for the first time in her twenty-four years of life it actually seemed relevant to her circumstances. There had been no ceremony to her appointment, but Ysella believed wholeheartedly that she was chosen for the task on her merit, and no one was going to tell her otherwise.

Over the last month, Ysella had studied the notes regarding the growing escalation along their borders. Nabannon, head of the west and an ally with the Orcish Nations of Usun'Drovad, was rumored to be plotting for war. All points led to the tunnel collapse in Bastillos years prior, though the Head of Commerce and the representative for the Edrosi Coalition of Trade gave evidence the overly stringent laws limiting orcish trade were to blame.

The two were entwined. The orcs had been smuggling Bastillosi slaves from Lumin for decades, and the tunnel collapse had only exposed their operation to authorities. Action had to be taken.

Bastillos was the center of trade in Edros. The best routes flowed through their network of caverns, and even if a merchant braved their surface valleys, they would still be met with checkpoints and tariffs. Reports did show Bastillos had become more severe regarding imports and exports, heavily documenting and searching through wares that caused delays in entry and exits.

These precautions were made in an effort to control Bastillos after the civil war. They were still recovering. They were weak to this threat of attack, and it placed a heavy burden on the diplomats they chose.

Ysella had been assigned to Nabannon while diplomacy in Ithrad was awarded to her colleague, Rotheel of House Degent. Two young, upcoming diplomats of Bastillos assigned to an esteemed mission that would prevent a war. Their households would be elevated.

She had been admiring the royal seal on the letter to Nabannon's monarch when her carriage came to a quick halt. Her guards shouted, voices hitching as something struck them to silence.

Her carriage was designed for lengthy travel with spacious room to lounge upon plush cushions and a supply of food to enjoy at her leisure. The windows, open to allow airflow, were partially covered by gold colored drapes. Sunlight was so bright to a Bastillosi. She strained against the light as she peered out to the chaos.

Blood sprayed against the carriage, splattering against the curtains, and she shirked away with a yelp that merged with the pained outcry of one of the guards. Another agonizing cry gurgled with the slick sound of a blade pulling through flesh. Instinctively, she brought a hand to her chest, palm resting comfortingly against a ruby amulet that sat neatly in the hollow of her throat. Her gold adornments rattled as she frantically curled into the darkest corner of her carriage to catch her breath.

An attack? She was assured the guards were a formality, their duties intended to handle the exchange along the border or provide protection from wild predators. Risking another glance, she slowly crept back to the window. The clash of steel sounded as though it were on the other side of her carriage.

The terrain here was rocky and partially wooded, the land undulating with grassy knolls dusted with spots of snow that glittered among stony crags. The sky was swathed in pale emptiness, the shrouded sun casting striated shadows between dark grey and white clouds. A crisp cold brushed against her cheeks with a heady scent of pine, and she realized a silence had settled outside.

Stomach twisting, chest tightening, Ysella found she could not move. Her eyes fixated on the splatter of blood that stained the fibers of the golden drapes and dripped to a pool on the lip of the window. Looking down at the road, a ribbon of red lead to the body of a guard, eyes wide open in horror, an arrow lodged in his wind pipe.

The crunch of rocks beneath sturdy boots alerted her to eminent danger that screamed for her to act. The sound of an unfamiliar voice, harsh and commanding, roused her from her fawning.

"Open the door."

Her hand shot out and grasped the handle to the carriage door in desperation to keep it closed. "I…" Her voice cracked in her throat, and she was embarrassed to find she was already crying. "I am Ysella of House Ronasin, an ambassador of Bastillos on a diplomatic mission of great importance! You will leave immediately or face the consequences!"

"I know who you are."

The voice sounded exasperated, almost inconvenienced. Whoever the man was, he was no longer being contested by her militant escorts and did not sound concerned. The sound of a sword returning to its scabbard hissed mutedly through the thick iron plated carriage.

"Don't make this difficult on yourself," the man continued. "Either you come out of your own volition peaceably or I smoke you out. I've got plenty of bodies to burn, and being inside a heated metal box as you choke on smoke is a terrible way to die."

Bodies...

The weight of the word struck like a hammer to the gut, Ysella's counter points effectively rendered useless. She was alone and unarmed, and up against someone who had killed her only protection without a whisper of mercy. She didn't know the guards well, but there was no part of her, even from a strategic angle, that had wanted them to come to harm. Not for her sake, not for anything. Now they were dead and she was on her own.

"Fine," Ysella replied after a moment. "Step back from the door, please." Blinking, swallowing hard, she straightened up in her seat and pushed back her shoulders. If she was going to be taken, so be it. She would maintain her dignity, all the same. The door swung open with a metallic groan.

She wore her best for the journey: a full black velvet dress bedecked with purple and red gemstones, and a cloak with a warm fur collar. A gold circlet crowned her head, fitted with jewels, a similar light blue to complement her eyes, which fixated on a singular, rugged looking man.

Rugged was a nicer word used when speaking of the citizens of the Grey Hinterlands. They did not keep up with the latest fashion, often wearing layers of animal furs that made them look twice their size.

The man outside her carriage was the epitome of the Grey Hinterlands. He wore a thick cloak draped in the pelt of a wolf on his shoulders. At his back was a quiver of arrows and a bow, and to his side a sword where his gloved hand calmly rested. Black, curly hair rustled in the cold breeze collecting snow that gently fell from the grey above. He sported a short beard along his jaw, dark eyes intensely focused on his prize.

"You're making a horrible mistake," she continued, and though her jaw quivered and she could taste the salt of tears on her lips, there was a practiced strength to her voice, a sense that while she was afraid, she would not give that fear an easy course to traverse.

One man. A single man bested four soldiers of Bastillos whose blood splattered his cheek. The thought scared her more than if he had been part of a group. No sweat glistened his brow from the skirmish. No remorse behind his eyes for the unspeakable carnage at his feet. He stood there, waiting while she anticipated a request for her fine adornments or pristinely cut gemstones.

There came no request for her valuables. He was not there for the riches wealth provided. He was there for her.

Not an ounce of the deep anxiety she felt showed in her steely eyes as she met the gaze of the stranger. "This will be considered an act of war. When the queen hears of this, you'll be sorry."

"I don't rightly care," he stated flatly, and then approached Ysella, forcibly taking her by the arm to pull her closer. She struggled against him, but his grip was unyielding, tight enough to bruise. "The politics of it all are none of my business. There's a bounty on your head and I intend to fetch it."

From his belt chimed the recognizable clink of chain link in iron, but the shackle he produced was larger than a wrist manacle and linked to nothing more than a handle. It was a slaver's link; a device designed to lock around the neck to prevent clever escape. It was usually paired with wrist restraints.

Holding the device up into view, he watched Ysella carefully. Her teeth chewed the inner corner of her cheek, but she would not give him the satisfaction of more tears.

"You pull anything or even sneeze out of turn as I put this on you, you die," he said. "Understand?"

Staring up at the man, Ysella bit harder until a coppery taste touched the back of her throat, and then gulped down a gob of nerves. She hadn't expected her threats to work - not really, but there had been some hope that perhaps he was a highwayman looking for a quick robbery. He wasn't a common thief, and she wasn't going to get anywhere with a title and weighted pretense.

A bounty. That was it, then.

For a moment she considered negotiations or offering him the sum and more for her safety, but there was no doubt the price was impressive if he dared to come alone. Her family had wealth, but the war had deeply affected their coffers.

The man rattled the shackle again, impatience sharp in the motion. Her eyes widened as she took a step back, shaking her head, her hand instinctively rising to her throat. Of all her features, her neck, long and slender, was easily the one most befitting of her vanity.

His threat, however, was anything but hollow, and with a sniff, her hand dropped to her side, her eyes narrowed. "You won't get away with this."

Unlatching the shackle, he fixed it around her throat and secured it with the pin and lock, the mechanism twisting in some way she couldn't see. "Actually, I will," he stated matter-of-factly. She flinched as his gloved hands pushed the heft of the metal up to allow his fingers to unfasten her necklace. It was a duty done with a gentle nature, yet only through fulfilling a task. He collected the necklace and grabbed her hand to force her to take it.

"I'm sure, given your profession, you're aware of the laws of the Grey," he said, and then held up the chains that connected to her collar. Ysella knew each laerd of the Grey Hinterlands had their own set of laws, some of which were consistent, but all of which were hardly regulated. The Grey Hinterlands were somewhat of a joke among scholars in Bastillos. A land of chaos and greed pretended to have regulations and rulers just to feel as though they had weight in Edros. The truth was the land here was too perilous to traverse, the soil rocky and difficult to till. Only the unsavory would desire to live in such a place.

"We don't like trouble unless there's worth in it," the bounty hunter continued. "Now, you could very well get me in trouble with the law of any laerd, and I don't blame you for trying. But with this on your neck, all you're going to do is paint a target on your head. Everyone knows what this means. So you can choose to get rid of me and lose the best protection you've got, or you can accept I'm your best option of getting across the Grey alive. Bear in mind your head is sufficient."

He pointed to the guards further out from the carriage, their bodies still heaps on the frosted earth. "I'm no stranger to combat," he continued. "But I'd like a smooth ride."

Walking over to the horses, he yanked the chain to Ysella's collar, urging her to follow while establishing the status quo. Keeping one hand on the end of the chain, he freed the horses with the other, picking two for their ride.

She stared at him with a cold bite akin to the metal around her neck, defiance overruling her obvious fear. Tears were held at bay by sheer will, her body giving an involuntary jolt as he neared.

As he spoke, it occurred to her just how hopeless things appeared, because while she did know the laws in each laerd's land, she knew very little else about the way the world functioned. Studying that which pertained to her occupation took precedence. So little of her studies focused on anything more than eloquent prose to spin a thought or still an argument. Was it possible that no one would help her out of pure fear of the implications a simple collar gave? She was a diplomat. Her dress was elegant and of status. Surely, that had some bearing.

The dirt road was wet with partially melted ice and snow, darkened with blood, littered with bodies. For a moment, her eyes closed in a vain attempt to scrub the sight from her memory. Her voice cracked on a wave of emotion. "They had families. So do I. Remember that... Because I'm sure it seems like the money is worth it, but time breeds regret quite efficiently, no matter how much coin you possess."

Straightening, eyes snapping open again, she turned and moved toward the horses. It wouldn't do. None of it. She needed to do something before the option was removed from her entirely. Once upon the horses, he had the power. A fall from a horse with the collar on her neck would undoubtedly be her end. If she was going to act, it had to be fast.

"The chain's long enough for two," he assured as he kneeled and cupped his hands together for her to use to mount. The horse, having been pulling a carriage, had no saddle or reins to grasp.

Ysella turned as if to acquiesce, then with as much force as she could muster, she kicked out, aiming the heel of her dainty shoe to the bridge of his nose.

It might have been a clever move, but the impact caused his arms to straighten, and then he purposefully jerked back with the chain to take her feet off balance. Ysella went down hard, barely catching herself as she hit the ground, the sound she made somewhere between a strangled cry and a cough. Her eyes teared, fingers gripping the stony earth, and when he pulled against the chain a second time, she was jolted upright a little too swiftly, tearing the hem of her dress with her feet.

Pulling off a glove, he swiped his thumb beneath his nose, then tested the bridge with his fingertips. She hadn't drawn blood, and it wasn't certain if the nose was even broken by her effort. With barely a grimace, he yanked the chain closer to him, and glared down at the noble Bastillosi woman.

"You can walk, then," he growled, and pushed her away from him, pulling on his glove and then hoisting himself onto the bare backed horse.

"Treading close to being more trouble than you're worth," he warned as he nudged the horse forward.

If it weren't for the pain surging through her skull, her back, and her neck, she might have scoffed. She wasn't surprised... not that he was angry, but the notion of making her walk seemed like it would have been the initial plan. Regardless, the realization of her coming travels sunk her spirits deeply, her mind fully aware of the nice dress shoes she wore adorned with intricate beading. She opened her mouth to protest, and then shut it once more.

More trouble than she was worth. What was that sum? Any amount was enough to drive her stomach to her knees. He would kill her, she had no doubt, and that was enough to effectively silence her.

2
ILAI

The locals called it the Grey. Edros called it the Grey Hinterlands, and it had always been the land of the free people. There were no kings in the Grey, only Laerds who govern their own lands separate from one another. Their trade agreements, alliances, armies, and watchers were their own, and that is the way it has been. It was believed this caused lawlessness, as once one walked out of one laerd's land, they entered into a new set of laws.

The watchers were intended to be the enforcers of each Laerd's Laws between borders, but they could be bought for the right amount of metal. That was where the appeal of bounty hunters prevailed. When the law failed, a Lander found other means.

A bounty hunter was apathetic, requiring only details of the acquisition that would measure the metal reward. Whatever the reason for this diplomat's capture, Ilai did not care. The posting defined her as a diplomat of Bastillos headed for Nabannon. The award was twenty heads of gold; a significant sum.

It was also a ridiculous sum. In the three days it took for this moment, Ilai measured the worth, reading over the ink again and again in case he had missed a tell. A client wouldn't list an unreasonable sum unless it was legitimate and desperate, or it was a trap. He still had time to consider. Nearly an entire Season, in fact.

The chain drew taut with clinking links as Ilai pulled the diplomat forward. Twenty gold heads would not make this trek an easy task, and he gripped the leather around the handle tightly. Looking down at her stumbling across the unforgiving terrain was amusing. Having a horse required sticking to the roads for more even footing, and yet the woman still found the loose pebbles every other step.

A dull pain pulsed through his nose, radiating from the spot where her foot had struck. He gingerly tested the tenderness with his gloved fingers. She had been clever, applying a fair amount of force, but it didn't feel broken.

The diplomat kept pace with the horse, eyes fit to burst into tears as she set her scowl forward. She looked up at him, eyes narrowing as they met. "Who placed the bounty?" she demanded, almost as if she was owed a repsonse. She would not be the first bounty to demand answers, yet it seemed more amusing coming from a woman so beautifully clad and donned with fine jewelry.

"You are concerned about things that do not matter," he stated pointedly.

"They matter to me," she muttered, her fierce eyes unwavering. She looked like a woman who had never been denied a request. Bastillosi nobles were known among Landers as the oppressors who lived lavishly and thoughtlessly. The people they once commanded often fled to the Grey for sanctuary and freedom. He could see in her why they would leave. Even with a shackle around her neck, she thought she held authority.

The horse's mane was gathered in his hand in a tuft of white, his body comfortable in its stride.

"You tell me, then," Ilai posed. "Who would want a diplomat of Bastillos?"

She carried the fabric of her dress in hand as she cautiously walked in beaded slippers caked with mud from the frosted road. "I'd say there are many people on that list," she stated. "If you care so little, and I'm likely dead regardless, why not just say it? What does it benefit you to leave me in the dark?"

Details were unnecessary and frivolous, but no posting stated the client's name as a means of protection. There was always a drop off location, or a code name, but never their true identity. It wasn't important for a bounty hunter to know, but he could hazard a guess with this one.

"There's a tree line on the border of Edros and the Allied Kingdoms called the Twisted Woods," he said. "It travels right next to the northernmost Laerd's Land. There's a tower called Ethyrnon, named by the elves that built it. It's said those woods are corrupted by foul magic. The creatures within are more deadly and aggressive because of a curse, and rumor has it there are people who live in there, too. People who have lost their minds."

He glanced down to her, the chain clattering as her foot scuffed against a wagon groove in the dirt road. Her focus had turned towards her journey, eyes studying the road ahead for the next rock that would cross her path. She seemed determined not to trip, and perhaps the demanding task was what quieted his captive. She hadn't barked at him for nearly a minute.

But only for a minute.

"And why keep me alive?" Her voice cut through the quiet between them without any signs of fear. "Why bother? Or do you find pleasure in prolonged torment?"

This would be a long journey, and a small laugh escaped him at his fate. She was grating and testing his resolve through her insistence. The metal was good, though. It was more than enough to pull through the torment of a woman's questions, if it were real.

There was still the matter of the bounty's legitimacy. Her incessant talking would cut into his needed contemplation. Without an answer to satisfy her, she continued to prod.

"No doubt you do," she continued. "Cowardly scoundrels enjoy that sort of thing, don't they?"

Desperation manifested in each acquisition differently, but in ways he could follow. She was attempting to find his mental weaknesses, to chisel away his apathy and gain the upper hand. Anger was an easy emotion to manipulate. Men grow irrational when rage is stoked, and mistakes are made with ease.

Ilai was a patient man. Anger did not come easily.

"I think it is you who is tormenting yourself," he countered calmly, a hint of amusement on the edge of his lips. "I offered you a ride on this horse. You could have had that luxury. You should thank me for the lack of haste, diplomat. How nice am I to keep the horse slow for your little feet to keep pace within the length of that chain."

Looking down at his captive, Ilai was met with a pretty scowl and heated determination in her eyes. If she were a Lander, he might have feared that look. There was intent there and a keen glisten of someone who would not lay down and die.

"You are worth more alive." He met her stare with a cold, even gaze. "I only need to get you to the border while you still have breath. Nothing more."

There was honesty in the statement. The posting did request her alive to garner the full amount, though it did say a modest fraction was allowed with proof of death. It was in his best interest to keep her alive and able to walk on her own, regardless. The last thing he cared to do was drag a half-dead body across the expanse of jutting rocks and hidden ridges.

It was still no easy task at such a slow pace. The horse had been acquired to ease the journey and quicken the time, but with her punishment came delay. "This is going to be a long crossing," he advised. "Things are different out here in the Grey. Just because I've succeeded in your capture does not mean the attempts are over. The bounties were posted in almost every Laerd's Land. I can at least guarantee I will protect you as long as you do not try to kill me."

"Ha!" Her mocking laugh expelled venomously. "Yes, a true gentleman! I'm sorry to have offended your noble sensitivities! Why, I probably should thank you for the collar as well! No? What a lovely fashion statement."

He would have laughed were she not his acquisition. She was annoying, his patience tested with every syllable uttered. It was logical to accept his protection. He was a bounty hunter, yes, but he was also her best chance at surviving the Grey. If she tried anything stupid, she could get them both killed.

"If you think the pace makes any difference, you're an idiot as well," she continued. "But then I'd wager you've never been on this end of one of these miserable contraptions, have you?"

Few Landers never had the displeasure of cold metal against the skin. The damned things were adopted from Bastillosi refugees long ago, the chains first repurposed by watchers and eventually those in the line of nefarious work. Ilai could still remember how his neck burned and how the cold permeated his body.

"You're despicable."

Her voice was neither soft nor meek, each syllable sharpened with resolve like a blade striking toward his defenses. He pushed away the annoyance, more at her insistence on speaking than at the words themselves, which carried no real weight.

Rocky terrain merged with tall grass as they turned down a lesser path, though not for any benefit of his captive. It would be an unfortunate thing for a horse to break its leg. Most travelers stuck to the roads as the wagons tended to push the rocks further into the mud. With gentle nudges he guided the horse steadily through the grass, twisting and turning to avoid certain obstacles. There was flatter and more forgiving land ahead.

"It's a war they want," the diplomat said. He nearly groaned at the return of her voice. He wasn't sure if she was talking to him, but he listened regardless to pass the time. "I'm sure of it. But I'm sure you don't care. You can take your money and run for the hills, ignorant to the thousands of lives you've ruined. You really don't care, do you? What happens..." Her voice trailed off only momentarily, and he did not answer.

"You're perfectly content with whatever happens to me, so long as you get paid. And what makes you so sure you'll receive it? They might just as soon kill you for knowing too much. I hope they do. And I hope they chain you up and drag you around by the neck first. Maybe they'll be nice about it."

"I've considered it," he admitted, and hummed thoughtfully. "Hmm, so you think I know too much, thereby sealing my fate in death within the exchange."

It wasn't far-fetched. He had thought so himself, but it was amusing to gauge her thoughts. "Do you like imagining my death? Do you think of it in detail or is it just a fleeting feeling born from your situation?"

"Like it?"

She nearly stumbled over a pile of loose rocks hidden within tall grass, her balance teetering as she fought to remain upright. "No, I don't like imagining it. But there's nothing fleeting about it, that much I can assure you. You seem the sort who imagines, with great effect, that he has everything figured out, but I do hope there is some bit of logic in that head of yours. Though, I suspect it's foolish to expect you to rely on reason or sound judgment."

Her words made little sense to Ilai, given he was a man of logic. She was naive of the ways of the Grey, even more so of his profession, so it could be excused. His attempts to understand her reasoning knit his brow, and he chose instead to focus on what he did understand: the journey ahead.

The small path through the tall grass opened back to another worn road, this one a bit narrower than the last. They would soon cross into Laerd Grath's territory that led into the Scar. A trip to a settlement would be inconvenient for miles.

"I have done nothing to you. Nothing." She interrupted his thoughts again, though she was starting to sound more like a normal captive. Her voice wavered. "Yet you would turn me over to these men without a second thought. For a fistful of coins... You are doomed, whether by this endeavor or another. So what do you want? I am a negotiator, after all. Surely there's something I can offer you that will secure to me whatever false loyalty you've promised elsewhere."

"There is something you can do," he responded, and looked down to her. "You can tone it down a bit. The desperation is noted. Cutting me down with words trying to claw for a bit of compassion somewhere in the belief that all people are inherently good. Not that I condemn that sort of thing. It is alright to be optimistic and fantastical. But as you said, I am despicable. I think I have everything figured out! Reason and sound judgment are not part of my character, and I'm doomed!"

He waved his free hand through the air, fingers wiggling for a mystical effect as he touched on all her points as he smiled. "Not everyone is inherently good, Diplomat. How many slaves did you own back in Bastillos? How many of those working in poor conditions did you turn a blind eye to? Or were you not even aware of how inhumane and tyrannical it all is? How does that collar feel again? Piss off. You're just as bad as the rest of us if you can get your bejeweled head out of your ass."

Turning to look at her briefly, he added, "And it's metal, not coin. We don't smelt the precious metal into little chips like you cave dwellers. Fingers, fists, arms, heads. That's what determines the worth."

A jagged lonely mountain jutted high into the sky out ahead known as the Skyblade. The formation looked unnatural, but it was ancient and pierced the grey veil like a sword through the sky. Their path would not lead them to the monument, but it would watch their descent above trees and hills. Ilai knew from its proximity that it would be a day's pass along the Skyblade's craggy foothills, and three more to the edge of the Scar.

"So that's it then?" she asked. "Because my family had people working for us... I deserve this? Inhumane and tyrannical? Try being a little less ironic while leading me to uncertain fate chained about like a dog, would you? I'm not attempting to appeal to any sense of compassion, because I don't imagine you actually possess any. You are despicable, I stand by it. You are an abhorrent, self-centered bastard. And that is what I'm appealing to."

She drew her cloak around her, and even from his saddle he could see the faint traces of fear in the way her eyes stared ahead. He knew not to allow himself to become complacent in such a stare. Her fire would burn hot again, close to when she felt the most threatened. Women were never to be underestimated, even when they looked as frail as she.

"I will ask again," she continued, "and please, this time, spare me the lecture on my failing to make nice with my captor. If I thought you wanted false compliments, I would have started there. I want to know what you really want. Money? Jewels? You name it, and I will see to it that you get it, provided you stop immediately and release me."

"You're very linear," he stated. The pace never ceased, and the trek continued on up gentle slopes and down rockier paths. The horse seemed comfortable with his guidance, which had him wonder if the caves of Bastillos were perilous. As silence grew, he contemplated allowing the conversation to end. While it was good practice to have his thumb on his acquisition's disposition, she could become a liability with how much she talked. His gaze kept to the road with disinterest, though he knew she would not let this be the last of it.

"I'm taking you to the border," he stated firmly. "Whatever you think of me is what it is. Regardless, I am taking you to the Twisted Woods, and there's nothing you can do to change that. Nothing. You will need to come to terms with that."

Glancing down to her briefly, he hoped it would provide the acquisition clarity. He needed her to relinquish the fight and lose that determination still lighting her eyes. His words could have the opposite effect, but one that would have to fester. It was different with each mind, and she did not seem to be the type to lose hope. He'd need to keep one eye open at night.

"You assume much, which I suppose you have to in your line of work," he continued. The light within her did not dim as she marched down the road, her chin upturned. "But have you ever considered you were wrong? Do you think your initial thought is always right? I fancy you ignorant. Does that mean it is true? Of course, you will say no. Most people don't realize their own flaws just as they don't realize the flaws of the world."

She would at least pause in her own ranting if he spoke. She listened with practiced patience, her brow furrowing as he watched her carefully dissect each word.

Decidedly, he continued before she could interject. "I'm not excusing myself or denying I'm despicable or whatever term you wish to affix to my character. I know what I'm doing. I know that collar is irritating and will bruise your skin and hurt your bone. I know you have nothing to offer that will stop it from happening. You can argue that is an assumption, but see, you assume so much about me it's clear you'll have nothing to barter with."

Silence between them grew from seconds to moments as the road winded into a sparse wood of varied trees. Victory came in the solemn fall of her shoulders, her mouth closing and clenching tightly.

3
YSELLA

Ysella's expression faltered as she looked away from her captor, a sharp inhale shuddering through the cracks of her emotional barrier. Coming to terms with the inevitable was always difficult, but never more so than when one was facing mortality. She didn't want to die, and whatever he said, she had no assumptions that there was any other fate for her but death. Even if it wasn't immediate, it would come.

The tears stung, and she squeezed her eyes shut against them. "I never got to say goodbye. It's odd, the things you think of when you're going to die. I was so excited to be chosen for this mission. I never stopped to say goodbye. You think you'll see them again, your family. You think... you think nothing could possibly go wrong." Exhaling a scoff, she willed her eyes open. "The worst part is, if I never return, they'll probably just be disappointed that I didn't complete my mission."

They had dined and entertained a few senators in the weeks leading up to her assignment. Her mother's brow had been creased with stress each time, worried they might ask into the shame that cast a shadow on House Ronasin. It hadn't been nearly long enough since the rebellion for people to forget what had transpired in their household that day.

The bounty hunter scrutinized her from atop his horse as if to read her story upon her forehead like a book. "We're all given a life we didn't rightly choose. Well, for a start. Everything after we learn is our choice. Everything the two of us did led to this moment," he said. "But you're not dead yet. And you don't know if you're going to die. I don't even know if you're going to die. Haven't given me a reason yet, anyway."

Ysella cast him a glare sidelong, drying her eyes with her sleeves. He might have been handsome in other circumstances. A bruise bloomed from where she had kicked him near the nose stippling purple and brown across the bridge. Even from her height next to the horse, she knew the foreign stench did not belong to the mare. In High Lumin, baths were a customary formality. Out in the Grey Hinterlands, it seemed, they were few and far between. He smelled of dirt and leather; an earthy musk muted by the cold. But beneath the start of a beard was a sturdy line to his jaw, and his brown eyes were clear and deep. A scar lightly etched the skin, dissecting his left brow and embossed his upper cheek.

"Why do you care what I think about you?" she asked. "What difference would it make if I was understanding or compliant? You said I was wrong about something. What was it? Doesn't make sense to keep it to yourself if I'll never see you again after all this. So what was it?"

A smile broke from his stony expression, almost amused. "Nothing specific," he answered. "I was just being general.

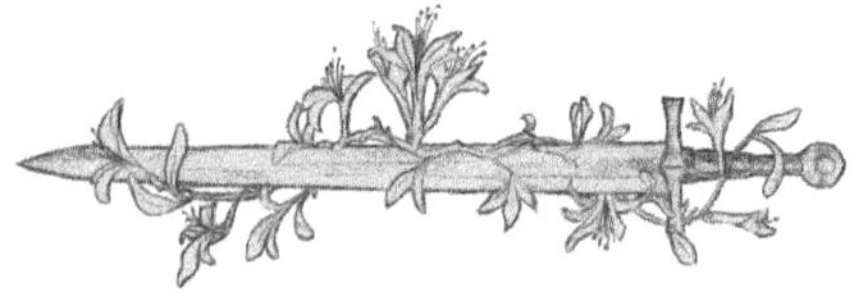

They traveled through the windy plains, the biting chill a reminder Spring had not yet arrived. Soon the fields would be lush with bright lupine and thyme. Thick-coated sheep would venture out to graze on thick clumps of crimson sorrel, mountain-hare hiding in the clustered vines of berry brambles and willow shrubs. The sun peaked and then descended by the time the bounty hunter found a place to make camp. It was a patch of woods composed mostly of pine that provided enough of a wall against the wind and a good sight of their surroundings.

She fell silent during the long trek, either out of resignation, or because for the first time in a long time he had given her something to think about. She hated him for it, perhaps more than she hated him for his treatment of her in the first place. She hated that he could compel her to consider anything. His words lingered, refusing to leave her mind, churning her peace. Everything she had done led her to this moment. But it also occurred to her that she was able to get him to talk, even if it was just to belittle her. Perhaps there was hope she could still escape her fate.

She winced as he dismounted, and putting a hand to the collar, she touched the space between the metal and her neck delicately. The skin felt raw, and there was no doubt some bruising. It would get worse before it got better, but if she could convince him that it wasn't necessary, no, she would convince him it wasn't necessary. And when he did give in and release her, she would run. Whatever it took.

"We need firewood," he said, interrupting her thoughts. "You're going to either follow along or help me gather. Are you going to give me any trouble?"

As he approached, she dropped her hands to her side, determined that he would not see the pain she was in. "I won't try to kick you in the face again, if that's what you're asking." The thought of gathering wood hardly appealed to her. It was a menial task her servants were responsible for back home. They purchased the wood from the merchants and brought them to the kitchens where the fire would not stink the halls.

She looked down at the once-elegant dress, the hem a mess of frayed edges and tears, the velvet fabric marred by mud. Some of the beaded designs had come loose, the beads now long gone from a portion of the skirt. There was even a hole at her side where the threads had unraveled, likely due to stepping on the skirt. Her fur-lined cloak was heavy with mud that slapped against her calves.

And her shoes! They were completely ruined by the dirt, the beading around the edges lost. Her hand idly reached for her necklace, tucked carefully into a pocket at her side, and found its presence comforting. At least one thing had survived the journey intact.

"What do I need to do?" she asked hesitantly.

Her captor stared at her sternly, gauging if she was making a false promise. She certainly would have liked to kick the man again, but it had caused her considerably more damage last time than it had to him. She was unsure if he would kill her if she tried a second time.

The chain was still gripped firmly in his hand, pulling her along through the sweet smelling pines, her feet hitching on mats of dark green and greyish moss as she pulled her skirts away from her ankles. He picked up a stick the length of his forearm and showed it to her. "Look for sticks like this," he instructed, and then handed it over to her. "It should feel like that. Breakable, but with some give. Go ahead and break it in half. We want that kind of wood. You can get thinner sticks if you'd like. You don't need to worry about anything thicker."

They continued through the woods and gathered varied sticks at the bounty hunter's command. They were dirty and left smudges up and down her arms. By the time they had gathered enough, she had broken three nails and scraped the fragile skin of her palms raw and red. The distinct impression her captor was enjoying himself made it all considerably worse.

He pulled her through the process of gathering sticks three times taking a different route each time. Eventually, they gathered enough wood to stoke a modest fire for the night. It was tedious work, and exhausting, but Ysella realized the exertion had kept her warm enough to pull back her cloak.

"Let me know if you start to sweat," he said. "Take some fabric off your dress there and stuff it between your neck and that collar. It'll relieve the pain and keep the metal from freezing you to death. I hear it's a peaceful way to die, if you'd rather not ruin your dress further. Like going to sleep."

Brushing her hands off on her skirts, she looked at him as if he'd asked her to jump directly into the fire. "This is my best dress! I would sooner—"

Her words halted in her throat, realization settling like a heavy blanket. Freezing to death might have been a better way to die than the unknown that awaited her, but it was still unappealing.

Her dress was fairly ruined, as much as she hated to admit.

Bending, she tore a scrap from where the hem had separated, folding it around her neck like a scarf, then tucking it into the gap under the collar. The relief was near immediate.

"You could just take it off, you know," she remarked coolly, motioning to her collar, "since you're so concerned. It's not as if I'll get very far, as it is."

The hunter carefully placed wood on the growing fire, the heat steadily growing in a small radius.

"We'll never have that kind of trust," he stated plainly. "We can't. What this is, what's happening between us means we can't. I know your word is worth shit because you're a desperate woman thinking she is going to die. And you've got a lot of opinions about me. Do you really find me that much of an idiot, or do you think I carry some sort of compassion towards your situation?"

He piled the surplus sticks within arms reach to feed the fire through the night. "I've got cured meats," he continued. "If you want something more, we'll have to go hunting in the morning. I've got water and some u'gul, if you're inclined to the warmth of alcohol."

Desperate frustration welled deep within her in a sickening pit. The way he spoke, and perhaps more so her own inability to argue them, diluted the hope that once filled her mind. She was accustomed to getting what she wanted, and when that task became impossible, it wasn't a feeling she cared for.

She sank down to the dirt, fingers adjusting the fabric under the collar, grimacing as she felt along the sore spots. Her captor still held the end of the chain connected to the iron collar as he one-armed every task. He sectioned out sticks, leaning them against the tree. Idly, she considered giving it a tug to see how lax he may be, but she followed the possible paths in her mind. It had too many potential outcomes against her favor.

A part of her, that stubborn part that had gotten her into trouble all too often, considered declining the offer for food entirely. The choice would have a momentary triumph that would lead to her detriment as the days drew longer. She couldn't chance becoming any weaker than she already felt, and as long as there was a chance to escape, she needed to do what she could to preserve her strength.

"Water is fine. I've had u'gul during a trade summit. It's atrocious. What are you building?"

The arrows in his quiver clattered as he unclasped and removed it from his side, resting it against a tree. He slipped his hand behind his cloak and produced a canteen. The hunter tossed it in Ysella's direction without a word in warning and seamlessly continued with his work on the lean-to. There wasn't much keeping the sticks together other than the force between two trees and the earth he used to keep them in place.

"It's a shelter," he finally explained. "Something temporary for the night so we don't freeze to death. This temperature might be tolerable during the day, but at night it can feel like the dead of Winter."

His gloved hand patted the lean-to appreciatively. "It's no cave, but it helps. You will want it. Trust me on that. It'll catch some of the heat from the fire while we sleep. I hear you mountain folk don't like fire."

She took the canteen, taking a draw of the cool water that tasted slightly earthy. The canteen had a leather strap, and she tested the weight of it, considering what sort of weapon it could make. He was strong and no doubt faster than he looked, but if she could get behind him...

Frowning, she put the canteen to her lips once again. It was too risky. If she tried to use the strap as a garrote, he would overpower her in seconds. The only avenue was to club him with the canteen's sturdy hide. She'd need to hit his head just right to disorient him at the very least, though there was little chance she'd get to him fast enough to align the strike.

"Bastillos is warm enough without fire pits. So too, I imagine, was the inn I was meant to be staying at tonight." She tossed the canteen back to her captor. It skid across the dirt and tapped his boot, but he did not flinch. "How did you learn to do that? The shelter."

"I learned it from the same woman who taught me how to hunt," he answered, plucking the canteen from the ground with his free hand.

"The woman?" Ysella asked. It was strange to think a woman would volunteer for this lifestyle and take to such primitive tasks. It was strange to think he traveled with a woman to any capacity, and she wondered if it was a mother figure. Only a mother would care for the likes of such a man, she supposed.

"I see only one shelter," she remarked. "Where will your little hovel be?"

A faint grin pulled, masked by the canteen he brought to his lips. His eyes drifted past her, the smile fading. Following his gaze, Ysella caught sight of something lingering at a distance in the treeline, dark gray and hunched like the dogs in Low Lumin.

"I know you won't like it much, but we're sharing the hovel."

The distant creature must not have posed a threat by the way he brushed off its menacing presence. To her, it looked predatory even on its own.

The shelter was small, and while it looked sturdy, it did not afford much room for movement or comfort between the two. Especially with his bulk. It would be a tight fit, and one typically reserved for more familiar company. Even when she was younger, she had occasionally shared a bed with her sister, Odessa. It had been a large mattress they both fit on comfortably. This was the closest she'd ever sleep next to another.

"Don't like it, then you can freeze to death," he continued. "This isn't about anything but survival. I'm not looking for a romp, but I can understand you might be uncomfortable—"

"You must be joking!" She half-yelped, her cheeks paling in the firelight. One solid glance from her captor told her otherwise. "You're not joking."

He moved closer and settled by the fire, pushing his cloak aside to reveal his sword. His gaze fixated on the spot where the strange beast still lingered, and she wondered then if it was a threat he was gauging.

It was a similarly pensive look she'd seen on the senate floor. Senators would watch each other as they spoke, analyzing every motion or demeanor shift. Could they be swayed? Could they find the weakness, not just in their argument, but in their mind? What sort of threat was across from them draped in fine robes?

The bounty hunter carried that same assessment in his stalwart eyes as he scanned through the tree line. Ysella's posture stiffened at the exposed weapon, the outrage over shared accommodations fading into growing anxiety. It was a day of firsts for the noble. Her first venture outside of the kingdom, her first diplomatic mission, her first time being kidnapped, her first time sharing such a small space with a man.

Her throat tightened, and her fingers brushed the collar.

If he truly wanted to, he could easily take advantage of her, and for the first time since exiting the carriage earlier that day, Ysella wasn't half as afraid of death as she was of living.

She shifted, and her vision drifted, catching movement at a distance. The creature had come closer, soft paws making nary a sound through the underbrush. Its silhouette was massive and towered almost as tall as a human. With a gasp, she edged instinctively closer to the bounty hunter, fear of her abductor momentarily outweighed by fear of the unknown. "That beast. What is it? Is it dangerous?"

The beast fixed its yellow gaze on the pair, body still in a moment of study. Its short ears twitched, and it looked to its right and turned away, disappearing through the bushes.

"You mountain dwellers need to get out more," the bounty hunter said, amusement perched on his lips. She became suddenly aware of her proximity to the man, the scent of musk and earth muted by the cold air. His body radiated warmth, and as much as she desired to distance herself from her captor, she found herself frozen in place.

"It's called a worg," he explained, his breath rustling her curls with how close she leaned in towards him. "They'll feed on the likes of us if they feel they can take us. Intelligent creatures. That was either a scout or a loner. Let's hope it was the latter."

Ysella stared at the dark woods where the beast had once stood, her hands wringing together. She had no delusions about her upbringing. Most of the nobles who dwelt within Bastillos were, at best, sheltered creatures with little to no notions of the outside world. They surfaced to gaze at flowers or glow their skin in the sunlight. They were happy that way.

Troubles were trivial matters for those who rarely faced them. Ysella was not naive enough to ignore how that made them look. They looked weak and ill fit for the world, and were it not for the vast army the kingdom held and their impenetrable caverns underground, they would not appear to be much of a threat.

Perhaps they were being tested.

As a diplomat, she studied the dangers, at least where man was concerned. Beasts of the wild could not be reasoned with words and gifts. They were primitive and therefore were of little use to her studies, strategically or otherwise. It occurred to her that perhaps this had been foolhardy, but she had never anticipated being kidnapped and forced into such conditions.

The threat of an ambush was never on her mind. Queen Zalette had used sound logic when she spoke to her and Rotheel. Their neighbors were afraid, but had not yet acted in violence, and that was a good sign. They had agreed to accept the diplomats. It hardly made sense for them to sabotage the effort. Her guards had been a formality.

Was Rotheel suffering her same fate? She imagined he had reached a cozy inn for the night and was settling down with a glass of wine and a book. He always read recorded histories saying they were the best way to learn from our past mistakes and prevent its repetition. He had suggested at one point that they travel some of the distance together, but Ysella had been determined, prideful, even in her solitude. Rotheel was a good man, but one who, by nature, often underestimated her capabilities. She wondered now if she might have been mistaken in her decision to go alone.

"I had no need to read about worgs," she said with a frown. "I don't suspect they were meant to be in attendance at the senate." She was slightly shrewd in tone, but there was still a considerable quiver to the current, and after a few seconds, her eyes snapped back to watch the path.

"Wh..." Clearing her throat, she straightened and tried to muster resolve. "What happens if it wasn't a loner?"

The hunter pulled a folded cloth from a side pouch on his quiver containing a stack of cured meat strips. By Bastillosi standards, the cloth was remarkably plain. It was blue and worn, its edges frayed as if torn from a larger piece. There wasn't even a pattern or accent coloring.

"They're typically part of a bigger group," the hunter explained. He held out a piece of cured meat for her to take. "The group is called a pack, and a pack of worgs is more difficult to handle. They're smart creatures. It's what makes them so dangerous."

She stiffly drew her cloak around her, sitting herself upright while taking the offered meat. It wasn't what she was accustomed to, her teeth pulling the tough strip apart. She hadn't eaten since earlier that day, her stomach ultimately winning over whatever reservations she might have had about the unusual meal. She mulled the little bite over for a moment andd decided it was passable. It wasn't as leathery as it looked, and it was at least seasoned.

"I think they understand what a weapon is," he added. "They seem to lose interest if they know you're armed. But if they don't see you as a threat, they'll pursue you as prey. Their bite is powerful and can snap through bone if they can get well enough around you. They should probably teach anyone who travels outside the mountains about these things."

"People, I find, are inherently more dangerous than animals," Ysella remarked, "and seeing how that's usually the sort I deal with in my profession, I wasn't inclined to study anything else. And we don't exactly get a great deal of wildlife beneath the ground, so there's not much point in teaching about it down there."

He shrugged indifferently. "In that case, do you have any regrets?"

"Regrets?" She eyed him incredulously.

"Well, your willful ignorance could be your doom. If you're going to die by a worg tonight, best not to have any regrets on the mind."

The corner of her lip twitched in a bemused smirk. "Being kidnapped comes to mind. It wasn't exactly part of the itinerary."

"Your whole life, and this is your only regret?" he asked, amused.

"I could have more regrets without a weapon," she added with a slight shrug.

He huffed a chuckle in response. "I'll keep you from the worgs if it comes to that. No need to arm yourself. Especially after sharing such regrets."

The dark curls of his hair rested in a dirty mess on his head, and his facial scruff looked like he hadn't shaved or even attempted to make himself presentable in days. She was once again drawn to look at his profile, strangely shadowed by the firelight, and the silvery scar that created a divot in his cheek. She opened her mouth to ask about it when he interjected.

"We have a custom here in the Grey," he said. "We respect our kin through their shared stories. There's a place called The Cave where we go to leave memorials of those who have passed. Air out our regrets. Remember their lives. Hundreds of hears of this tradition kept within a cave. It's on our way. You'll be one of the few outsiders to see it, you know. I've got a piece I need to drop off and pay my respects."

There was a moment, just a moment, where indignation and fury mingled, twisting his offer into something insulting. A memorial was something treasured. Something sacred, and in that flickering moment, she wondered how someone in his position could place such worth in anything. But then, like a spark, fanned quickly to flame, she recalled what he had said. How little she really understood about the world from a personal level. For all she knew, it was their most sacred rite. And to show it to her. Even if it was just a means of showing off, it had to mean something.

That, and the longer their journey, the better chance she had of escaping.

"I would like that, yes," she said, and stared into the mesmerizing fire. How would she be remembered when she passed? Would they don the red veils and sing her into memory? Would they even know she was gone? "Have you a proper name? If we're to be traveling a great distance, it won't do to call you any of the things I've fashioned in my mind."

"Ilai," he answered, though gave no last name. She knew the people of the Grey Hinterlands had similar customs to most of Edros with regard to naming conventions. Family names were important and defined one's status and were passed down maternally. The only societies in Edros that were paternally focused were Dradmida and the Laerds of the Grey Hinterlands.

"And what would you have called me otherwise?" he asked curiously. "I can only imagine the possibilities."

Ysella's lip twitched upwards ever so slightly, almost unconsciously, as she steepled her hands in her lap. "Most are not for polite company. Though... Hm. Worg, perhaps? It seems appropriate, after all."

4

ILAI

org. A name fit for a survivor. Ilai felt it was an appropriate nickname, though perhaps a bit too garish for his liking.

The faint smile of amusement faded from the diplomat, and she looked at him quizzically. "I suppose you know my name. I'm a little curious what else you know. I don't imagine it's much. You don't strike me as the sort who enjoys getting to know those you're condemning to death."

More words meant to jab, yet it felt more like a tap from a stick.

"There's no joy in it," Ilai stated honestly. "It is what we hunters do. It would be easier to just ignore you or shut you up. I suppose that's why hunters of the Grey talk to the acquisitions. It maintains a sense of humanity to some degree. You are a person, as am I, as is everyone. Make no mistake, we aren't friends, and you will continue to hate me. And I will continue to carry out the job. At some point, you'll retaliate, and I may just have to kill you sooner than later."

He listened to them all, as he was taught. The job was not an easy one. The Grey needed bounty hunters to do the dirty work the watchers and Laerds wouldn't or couldn't do. Life had never been kind to him, and he was stronger for it in the end. Not weak like his captive who grew up lavish and without want. She likely never knew what it felt like to starve.

Stoking the fire, he watched the flames stir, embers kicking into the sky in orange streaks. "I know it's good money," he said, and raised the chain up into view. It clinked and glittered from the firelight. "Every life has a worth. I know you're a diplomat and you've got a high price on your head."

Ysella scoffed. "Is that supposed to bring me comfort? To know I've got value?" She turned away from him as though his presence was an affront. "I don't care if the money is good. What you do? It's wrong. And someday you'll atone for it. Maybe not while I'm alive, but there will be a day. Don't mistake conversation for a show of humanity. I think Worg was a far more appropriate name for you, now that I think about it."

Her ignorance was astounding. She liked to talk, yet she did not like to listen. She lectured on compassion yet displayed none in herself, not that he wished it. She was a conundrum, and still possibly a liability. Ilai looked out at the darkness beyond the surrounding trees.

From his peripheral, she tugged at the metal collar. "We'd best sleep," she said. "You'll want to be done with me as quickly as possible. More lucrative if your turnaround is swift, yes?"

Amusement struck him, and he watched her move in familiar patterns. The collar was taking its toll, the weight pressing uncomfortably on her frame. "I'll not be sleeping just yet, but you can have a go."

"Then I'll stay awake as well, if it's all the same," she stated.

He stifled a groan with a grunt.

Her stubbornness to keep control of her life was commendable. He would have done the same and foregone sleep until his captor had done so. Most of his acquisitions lacked such common sense.

Her lips softened and pulled to a frown, hands dropping to her lap as she drifted in thought. "I've a sister," she said. "Odessa. She's nineteen, head full of clouds. I suppose in a way we all are underground, dreaming about the world above. What it's like. What the people are like. She has all these fanciful notions of traveling. Finding herself in other cultures. In other people. It's sad to think how disappointed she would be with reality."

He could scarcely prevent his eyes from rolling. The diplomat was on another mission to manipulate him, it seemed. He had to remind himself he was supposed to listen and remember the stories of his acquisitions. She looked at him pointedly and caught his surly gaze.

"You may not enjoy it, Worg, but you can be very certain I'm going to tell you every aspect of my life that I can until it's over. Because I want you to remember me. I won't be another sum of metal you collect so you can be on your way. You will feel it this time."

She did not know their ways. She did not care to know his ways. They were dismissed and remade into her own liking. He listened in the ways of the Landers despite his profession. Every life held a story to tell, and it was the responsibility of the living to carry on the legacy of the dead.

Not every story was entertaining or interesting, but he was taught to listen, and more importantly, remember. He hated that part.

His profession as a bounty hunter hardened his heart from the diplomat's tactics. Each life held a story, yes, but some lives came with a nice payout that would buy him food and shelter and mend his weapons and replenish his arrows. Most bounties deserved their fate.

"Go on, then," he prompted, and took a swig of u'gul. Its potency bit with a smooth floral taste, the liquid warming the body as it flowed through him. The orcish spirit had a kick that was like a spice coating the back of the throat, becoming more pleasant with each sip. "Tell me about your sister. Or any other siblings."

"It's just the two of us," she replied. She seemed willing to carry on without further remark towards his character. "My parents were focused people. They never wanted a big family. I had thought differently for a time. But as it was, I took to the political life. I thought there would be time. I guess I was wrong. Odessa will change the world, though. I know it. She's got a heart too big for the rest of us. I can't imagine why, but she looks up to me." Frowning, her gaze shifted, meeting the fire, "It won't sit well with her, my being gone."

Pulling her cloak tighter around her frame, she glanced up to him again. "Do you have a family, Ilai?"

"I do not," he answered simply, almost too dismissively.

The temperature dropped as the sun set lower in the sky casting an array of golds and oranges among the clouds. "What were you sent out to do?" he asked. "With such a large buyout you must be important."

A pause came with contemplation dancing across her eyes as she fixated on the firelight. She had been eager to speak of personal things, but her livelihood caused hesitancy. The only benefit he could garner from such information would be the negotiation of the bounty's price, and even then he wasn't sure he'd risk losing twenty heads of gold with poor negotiations.

"I was headed to Nabannon," she finally said, "to discuss terms of peace. Rotheel to Ithrad. There... there have been threats made. Threats of war. A war that Bastillos cannot win in its current state. We may very well have been the last efforts to stop it."

The kingdoms of Edros often forgot the inhabitants of the Grey Hinterlands. They were hardly a threat, and hardly of interest given the land they claimed. Would war even affect them? Perhaps only in food. The Laerds that controlled the border lands would have to decide amongst themselves who they allied with to ensure supplies make it into the Grey. He only knew Bastillos was an important center in Edros.

"There have been whispers of a war in the lower Laerd's Lands," he said. "Most of the Grey relies on trade for proper food. Orcs used to travel through the Scar to get to Bastillos, and with that came many valuable merchants. Not so much anymore. It's said it's to do with Bastillos turning strict after the civil war, or to do with orc fares being of high cost. Nabannon has a large orc populace as well. I think whole settlements, if the traveler's word is true. Restricting their trade means restricting Nabannon's trade by association."

"I don't suppose it matters much," she responded thoughtfully. The diplomat held her gaze to the fire with a recognizable focus. Flames held a hypnotic quality, causing a fixation on its dance without thought. She was plotting her path with the pieces laid out before her. "They'll see mine and Rotheel's abductions as an act of aggression. I wouldn't doubt for one moment that's entirely why there was a bounty put on us in the first place. Bastillos will never side with the orcs now. Not if they think their diplomats were taken under hostile circumstances. You played right into the hands of whoever orchestrated this plot."

The speculation was not to Ilai's liking. Speculation could be a useful tool to solve problems, but in this instance it felt more like manipulation once again. He pushed back his annoyance to preserve his patience. The orcs were a keen people who would at least keep trade open between their immediate borders. They would also not be so quick to violence and war.

"You think you'll escape it?" she asked as she brushed her fingers across the collar at her throat. "The Hinterlands? You think you'll be able to avoid the war? It will spread like wildfire, and it will destroy everything in its path."

It was almost amusing how predictable she was. The diplomat still attempted to strike at his heart to make it bleed for a cause that was not his. The Landers were a strong people, and even with a famine they would find ways to persevere. The land forced them to learn where others lived in comfort. Laerd Valarad in Grey Point had a solid trade agreement with the orcs of Maldrad'and. He could settle there with his twenty heads of gold to wait out the tensions. Even then, there were more options for survival than she seemed to understand.

"Maybe that is why I see foreigners fleeing for the Allied Kingdoms," he said thoughtfully. "The Twisted Woods and the mountains are enough of a barrier to keep that wildfire from spreading too far. The orcs are in good standing with the Allied Kingdoms, so they'd likely push the front more towards the Glassy Sea. The Grey has a good chance at keeping out of any battles. There's no land for a proper skirmish."

"Do you know what the most valuable commodity is in war times, Ilai?" she asked rhetorically. "Men. Soldiers. The advantage of a battle almost always goes to those with more forces. And those men need to come from somewhere. Even if there's no required service. Even if your people manage to escape it, the armies aren't likely to stay away forever. They'll need weapons and tools and food. Where do you imagine they'll get those supplies? The materials?"

The way she tried to snake to a point elicited a chuckle from Ilai. For someone of high status and education, she knew very little of Bastillos's neighboring territories, by his account. At least, she knew very little of the Grey.

"It'd be a desperate day if the west came looking for aid from the Grey." His head shook slightly, an amused smile still evident as he threw another log on the fire. Embers flew up into the smoke from its heft like shards of light that fizzled out into the growing dark.

"The orcish relations in the northern territories are strong," he continued. "Their tactics are intelligent and formidable enough to cause significant pause towards waging war against even their allies. We're taught about the territory wars our ancestors fought. Survival turned aggression, and they were the only ones smart enough to learn our language only to find out we were out on our asses.

"Your queen has been unfair to them, if the rumors are true. They're only allowed in Bastillos if they submit their carts and wagons to heavy searches and incredible fees. Smuggling accusations, was it? I think that's what I heard. Allegations of smuggling slaves, and they roused the lower people towards fighting for their freedom. Rumors of supplied weapons they should have never held."

They were truly only rumors for Ilai, and ones he'd only noted in passing through settlements. Orcs had notoriously been liberators of such oppression across the continent. If the rumors were indeed true, Bastillos was their final effort to rid the lands of it.

Ysella frowned as she glanced to him. "They're very serious allegations. People died, and while we don't have any proof it was them, they may have interfered and caused violence where none was needed. I fear the same is happening again. We're attempting to stop a violent war from happening and with no ambassadors to speak for Bastillos there's little hope to stave it off."

"Attempting to stop a war that could have been avoided entirely had your queen thought about it a little," he added flatly. "Maybe you can convince your paying captor to help you save Edros after I've got my metal."

"She's a child!" Her voice carried in the stillness of night with its pointed inflection. "One who inherited an impossible situation. What more can be expected? At least she is trying."

The fire held the only color in the pallor of the coming night and the only warmth around them. Behind where the cold brushed the crown of Ilai's head, bristling the thick black curls, a worg howled somewhere within the woods. He turned his ear to it, gauging the distance. It wasn't close enough to be a threat, but it was watching them.

She turned to the direction of the howling and swallowed hard. "And don't be stupid. You know as well as I do, Ilai, they'll kill me. If they wanted to stop a war they wouldn't have put a bounty on my head to begin with. They'll probably kill you, too, to keep their money."

"You might be right," he responded thoughtfully. That was a common risk, and one he felt confident to combat. It wouldn't be his first encounter with a client attempting to swindle. He'd never encountered those who wielded magic, but he felt confident nonetheless.

"I would say it's just hunters like me, but in reality, everyone in the Grey are used to the possibility of being crossed. We fight to take it. I'm a cunning hunter with a good shot and a long and heavy sword."

"Cunning. That's one word for it." A small frown pulled her lips. "I don't see what good it does me if they betray you. You're no more trustworthy. I think I may sleep after all."

He would gain no benefit by killing her, apart from the quiet. The diplomat could not seem to grasp their dynamic. He shrugged indifferently as he felt the need to educate slipping towards apathy. Some people did not wish to understand things, and in this instance, he did not wish to understand her thought process.

The chains clinked as she shook her head and turned for the hovel. She paused, suddenly rigid, but as she relaxed, she did not look back towards him. "I'm told there is a special darkness after death for men who take advantage of unwitting women," she stated. "Goodnight, Ilai."

His lips upturned in disgust at the insinuation. He was not without morals, though how was she to know? A foreign woman in an unforgiving land held captive by a man she hardly knew. He looked down at the links he held and pushed back the creeping sense of humanity. He had a job to do. He set out to do it.

Now he was far more reluctant to sleep. The cold air still played at his ears and head, and he lifted his hood up against it. The still and silent night was his comfort and peaceful communion with the world. When the wind blew through the barren trees, he listened to the fluted tune that brushed through the bark. When the fire popped and sparked embers that lifted into the night, he watched the orange sprites dance through the smoke. His lungs breathed in the biting air, accepting Winter for what it was as he carefully positioned himself in the small shelter.

She poisoned the practicality of survival between the both of them. It was the remark that infiltrated his mind and made him feel just like the people he ran from years ago. Frost collected on the links between him and his captive where the heat could not deter the cold.

Ilai stoked the fire, ensuring the heat would collect in the makeshift shelter for the night. He laid himself cautiously beside the woman, arms wrapped around his own midsection as he situated himself close enough to share warmth beneath his cloak with a respectful distance. Her body tensed at his proximity and he frowned. She was clearly awake despite his efforts, and he held his breath in fear of more pointed chiding.

He was a hunter collecting a human being for heads of gold. There is no justification for his actions being honorable or good or right, and he knew this. He did not need a Bastillosi noble berating him for a life he already understood.

Between each other and the fire, they would find enough warmth for a few hours' rest.

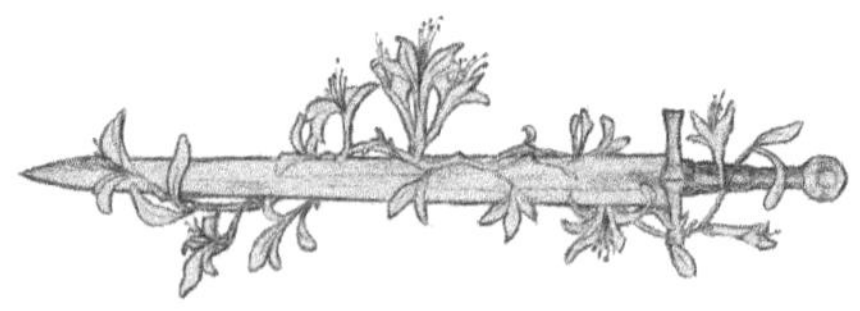

It was an instinctive feeling that bolted Ilai from his sleep. Light sleeping was common practice among Landers, particularly with those in unsavory professions. From what he could see, there was nothing in the waning dark, not even the fire now that it had dimmed to smoke and embers. That did not mean they were in the clear, and just as Ilai began to cautiously exit the lean to, he heard the deep, gravelly rumble of a worg's growl.

The beast stood as tall as an ox, its thick hackles raised and its wide snout curled to show its sharp set of teeth. Brown fur was dappled with grey and black stripes along its back with a thicker mane along its spine that stood up like spikes.

Ilai halted his movements and looked to the ground where his sword and bow lay and calculated his moves against the predictions of the large worg. Was it just the one? He scanned their immediate surroundings as best he could and caught glimmers of watchful eyes and movements of silhouettes. This was no lone worg.

"Diplomat," he whispered, "don't make any sudden movements. Not yet. See if you can bring your hand to my sword just at your back. When I say, hold it by the scabbard towards me as quick as you can. Are you good with a bow?"

The diplomat didn't acknowledge his words at first. He could see her hand slowly move towards his sword, her body closing in on itself as the morning chill blanketed her without the heat of fire or the added warmth from under his cloak.

He knew there was a decision to be made by his captive. She could wield his sword and stick him in the back while his attention was on the ground where the worg stood. This course would leave her to fend the beasts on her own, and he hoped she would have better instincts.

"I've never used a weapon." Her voice was quiet, trepidation lacing her words with a quiver. It would have been more ideal for her to have some knowledge with a weapon. The nobles of Bastillos must not be required to learn.

"Stay in the lean to, then," he whispered back and slowly leaned towards her, hand open to receive the sword. The nearest worg growled more fervently at his action, a foot pressing forward in threat that gave him pause. "Keep yourself away from them. I'm not going to hold onto the chain. If you run, you die. Understand? One... two... GO!"

The hilt of his sword hit his palm just as the worgs launched at the pair with hungry, gnashing teeth. He dodged, the sword coming free of its scabbard in a song that collided with a yelp from one of the beasts. The blade released from its flesh to swing towards the next preventing its advance, its body colliding with the makeshift shelter in the momentum.

"Ilai!"

Her voice struck like the song of a blade through the air as another large beast launched itself towards Ilai. Their size called for precise blows to either cripple or kill, their bulk and quick thinking requiring deft dodges and fast action.

He heard the clink of the chain behind him in a struggle, Ysella grunting against a force that was, at least, not pained by the pressure of a worg's maw.

The chiming metal distracted the other worgs. They gave pause at the sight beyond Ilai's field of view, and as he swung out against one of the beasts, he caught a glimpse of two worgs nipping towards Ysella's feet with a feigned a charge. She yelped at their advances, shuffling back as far as her chain would allow. It had snagged on the root of a sapling, clanking and pulling taut as she shied away from the threat.

Ilai turned, mind sharp towards the chaos as his blade sliced through a worg's jugular. It fell heavily to the dirt with a gargle, and the other worgs shifted their interests to keep distance between their prey. Jaws snapped at his legs causing him to shuffle back and reassess his advance. His longsword spun in a dance over his head cutting through the jaw of one and the leg of another, the blade driving their cluster to part.

The diplomat, unable to pull the chain free from the wooden vice, scrambled towards the displaced fire, the beasts growling at her in warning, gnashing in a threat. Her eyes glistened with fear as she pulled a burning stick from the dying fire, wielding it with both her hands like a club, wildly swinging it towards the surrounding worgs. She stepped back with uneven footing and stumbled leaving an opening towards the chain, but as Ilai reached for the links, one of the worgs snapped towards his hand. In a swift motion, he swung his blade across its head and neck, teeth sinking through fabric and flesh like hot spikes.

Grunting against the pain searing through his left shoulder, his fingers managed to pull the link free, and he punched the snout of the beast with the pommel of his sword. It yelped, but the act only inspired the beast's jaw to clench down more with pressure against his clavicle and rend its prey with a thrash of its head. Skin and muscle ripped with each jarring toss, and the world blurred and turned to white.

Two worgs joined to win him as their meal. One tugged at his boot, the teeth burrowing in the sole and grazing his foot while the other clasped the other end of his cloak and tugged until the fibers started to rip. He was pulled three directions with the one at his shoulder causing lapses in consciousness. In a flash of light, Ilai swore for a moment he was in the dredges of death's hallucinations. The sharpness of the air, the smell of fire, and the weight of living righted his senses.

Dressed beautifully in black velvet that glittered like twinkling stars, Ysella swung at the beasts with nothing but a smoldering stick and determination in her eyes. Fire blazed from its end in growling streaks of orange with her forceful swings. The elegant dress had ripped and torn from the worgs' attacks, yet still created a striking silhouette of a different sort of warrior. Her hair had fallen from its adornments and cascaded in ribbons of golden brown. A worg yelped with the impact of her blow, embers sparking from the collision that gave the pack pause. They barked and gnashed their teeth.

"Your bow!" she called to him. "It's to your left!"

Ilai kicked the worg at his feet squarely in the eye, and as it relinquished his boot, he removed his dagger from his belt and slammed the blade into the head of the one at his cloak. With his body free, he scrambled towards his bow and pulled an arrow that had scattered on the ground. The force it took to pull back the arrow caused pain to shoot through him, and it loosed prematurely as he cried out from the sudden pain lancing through his arm. To their fortune, the arrow lodged itself within a worg's skull.

Torchlight from Ysella's stick illuminated the wooded area and the pile of bodies slain. The worgs assessed their fallen and the ones that still remained and stepped away with warning growls. This was not their fight despite Ilai's waning strength. To them, they did not seem to see it wane fast enough to continue their play, and they retreated further into the woods. A final howl settled the morning with uneasy finality.

5
YSELLA

It was still in the darker hour of twilight just before dawn lined the horizon in its golden band. Winter carried a quietness to the night, and it made the pounding of the heart striking in the ears. Long after they had disappeared into the forest, Ysella clutched the burning branch, half afraid the worgs might change their minds, half afraid they'd woken worse things in the night. The horse was gone. She was not sure if it survived, though the lack of its body was encouraging. Only when he spoke did she look to Ilai, and her breath escaped in a vapor as the branch dropped into the fire.

"You ever look at the stars and wonder what's up there making that light?" Ilai's voice speared through the silence, drawing Ysella's eyes away from the treeline. He lay on his back still, his eyes looking up through the thick canopy to the dappled sky overhead. His jaw was tense, brows furrowed tightly in focus, but darkness shrouded most of his form.

Slowly, her eyes trailed upward. "When I was a child, I imagined the sky was just another cave and they were mirrorlight of a brilliant expanse beyond. That there was a surface above the surface." Through the system of mirrors that provided Bastillos its daylight, there were some privileged enough to see the reflection of the stars. She had that privilege in the drawing room where the skylights were closest to the surface. She was entranced by them, daydreaming about the wonder and possibilities. She didn't think that way anymore. "Are you hurt?"

She moved, not at all oblivious to the throbbing pain in her leg where a worg had struck through her skin, and sank down beside the bounty hunter with an edge of uncertainty. It wasn't as though she should be genuinely concerned for him. She had, after all, entertained the thought of ending him herself not too long ago, but it was a distraction. One she desperately needed.

There were smatterings of blood across his dark leathers and fur linings. His cloak still rested where they had once slept, now in a heap under the wooden rubble remains of his lean to. It left the man more exposed to the elements than would be comfortable, his torn pants and shirt from the fight visible beneath the heavier gear.

"I met a Maldviri once," he continued, apparently choosing to ignore her question, "The desert people. They have this legend about a well of stars. Or maybe it's The Well of Stars. They believe when you die you become part of it all. That your soul, after good deeds and morality, transcends to become the stars. I think it's some sort of map of the afterlife that surrounds us. It's a bit confusing, but I'm somewhat fond of their version of life after death."

He grunted in his efforts to rise upright and collect his weapons. "Not that I believe I would become a star," he added with a small chuckle. "As I'm sure you can gather, I've not been an example for good and moral. But it's still nice to think about souls becoming stars. When the moon hides its face we can still find our way with the stars. Unbiased. Damn souls."

He stretched out his right arm, and from the grimace she could tell he had pushed his body past its limits. "Are you hurt?" he asked, rolling the shoulder over in assessment as he stooped down to retrieve his cloak and the end of her chain. He was favoring his left arm; the arm the worg had grappled.

She studied him as he plucked the chain's handle from the rubble. Still a captive, of course. She hadn't expected that much to change, but somehow, it was still a touch disappointing, "One of them scratched my leg, but I don't think it's bad."

"Let me see it," he commanded as he looked her over. "Far too well dressed for the woods."

"I was dressed for a diplomatic summit," She muttered, her expression weary. She nevertheless lifted the hem of her dress to her knee, hissing as the cold air struck the scratched skin along her calf. Four striated gashes ran in a sweeping arch from below her kneecap to above her ankle, deep, though not so that it would prove life threatening. She had hardly noticed in the midst of their struggle, but the throbbing pain resonated now, in full.

His inspection was at a polite distance, eyes narrowing in thought as he assessed the wounds. "Can you walk on it?" he asked. "If you'll allow me, I can clean it up. As you can see, however, there's no horse for you to ride this time. So I'll need to know if you can make the journey at any length."

"It'll hold." She remarked, with almost a defensive air. He'd already warned her he wouldn't keep her alive if she proved to be a difficulty, and in truth it hurt, but not enough to affect her pace. "A bandage should do fine." Something to keep the cold from irritating the skin. She thought it would be a relief, the cold, but it stung and caused an ache she did not like.

He held out the cloak for her to take and used his foot to drag his pack to her side. "Put this around you," he said. "And keep your skirts up so I don't have to push around it."

Ilai kept a distant air as he removed a fresh roll of bandages from the small pack he had removed from his belt. He was careful, purposeful in his actions as he cleaned and wrapped the wound, his hands rough and calloused, but surprisingly gentle. Blood took to the fibers from the angry red lines as he secured the bandage with a slight tightness.

She watched him while he worked, flinching only slightly, focusing as little as possible on the pain. It was an unusual position, feeling indebted to a man who, for all he'd done to help her, was still effectively sending her to her death. Unusual and frustrating.

"Thank you," She murmured, "for... for the bandage. And for..." Protecting his merchandise? "Well. You know."

"Let's move out, then," he said, and collected his belongings.

Rising, she lowered her skirts again, her eyes following him, a brow lifting as she caught sight of the dampness seeping through the torn leathers at his back, "You're bleeding, Ilai."

"It's worg blood," he said dismissively. "We'll wash when we find a suitable place. Put the cloak on and let's go." His hand raised the chain, and he nodded towards the break in the trees that would lead to another field.

A brow lifted in doubt, but she shook her head and shrugged indifferently as she followed after him. Ysella prided herself, perhaps a bit too much sometimes, on being a rather intelligent woman, and it was plain enough to see that he was injured. If the man wanted to die, what was it to her? She'd get away, at least, and wouldn't need to do her conscience harm in the meantime.

As she pressed her foot into the ground, she was surprised to find it hurt less than she'd expected. His bandaging, at least, would hold out, even if it would more than likely scar her once pristine skin.

The morning barely warmed as the sun remained behind a steady stream of clouds. Blue veins of sky momentarily peeked out from between them, sunlight spreading its rays in brief bands of light across the woodland. The trees were dense among uneven terrain, and at one point they narrowly missed a shallow ravine leading to a creek.

In the distance, she could hear voices echoing through the trees, one of them laughing. They sounded gruff, but celebratory, and she looked out into the woods for signs of other life. It was time to put his threats to the test.

The bounty hunter pulled her away from the voices, but it was an effort in vain. A man ran up a ravine into view, limp rabbit in hand as he caught sight of the pair. He was tall, lanky, and had a head of brown hair that stuck out in all directions. A taller, stalkier man pulled himself up next to him carrying a large amount of game slung over his shoulder by ropes.

"Hey, you!" the lanky man called. "Bounty hunter!"

Ilai groaned and turned to face the men. "What do you want?"

The two strangers eyed Ysella hungrily, though not in a way that felt untoward. She could see in their eyes she was an object, yes, but their roving eyes were assessing her price.

"You two look a little rough," the lanky man stated. "Need some assistance with your acquisition?"

"I'm handling it," Ilai assured.

"With one arm down?" The taller man pointed towards Ilai's left arm.

By the looks of it, Ysella surmised she would not fair better with these two. Part of her felt oddly safer with Ilai.

"We've got food." The lanky man held up his fresh kill. They had far too many for just the two of them. "I'm sure we can come to a good arrangement. She looks like she'll bring in enough to split."

"Back off," Ilai warned, partially unsheathing his sword. The two men held up their hands in surrender.

"No need to get hasty," the lanky man said, and turned his body away, nodding down through the woods in the opposite direction. "We'll be on our way."

Ilai stood silently, hand on the hilt of his sword, eyes glaring in a threat as he watched the men walk away until they were completely out of view. Even then, he watched for a moment longer, and then turned back the way they were traveling.

For a time, she traveled in silence, pulling her own cloak tighter around her to keep out the chill. Eventually, her eyes drifted over to him, and despite what she told herself, concern bled into her voice as she caught a glimpse of a pained grimace across his rugged features. "Are you alright?"

"Yes," he said, and huffed a laugh as he motioned out to the rolling hills and barren trees. There was no longer a sight of another living thing as far as they could see. She could hear the rustle of wildlife foraging the icy earth, but could not find its origin. "Would it be nice if I died? Out here in the Hinterlands, you might get lucky."

Frowning, Ysella stopped, her eyes narrowing. "Do you honestly think I would ask if I were hoping for that, Ilai? Tell me. How do you think I would last out here, on my own? If you die, so do I and while my conscience would not mourn you for too long, I don't intend to give up that easily. Now. Stop being stupid and rest a moment. I'm not a physician, but I know a thing or two about how to dress a wound, and we'll both fare better if you aren't bleeding to death along the way."

He didn't stop, however, and yanked the chain as it ran taut. She yelped as she was forced forward, stumbling, her eyes scrunched to a glare. "You're getting worked up over nothing," he said. "You know what we could use? Or I could, anyway. There's a waypoint down the ways a bit that might have some better food than I could trap. Do you like orcish cuisine?"

Straightening herself, all concern for the man faded. "You're an idiot if you think that's nothing." But it was all she would say on the matter. He could die, for all she cared. She would find a way to survive on her own. At this point it seemed she had no choice. His pride would force her into survival alone.

"Aren't they cannibals?" she asked, a brow lifting somewhat in alarm.

She remembered seeing the diplomat for Usun'Drovad. Ambassador Manak. He was an odd marriage of intimidating and elegant, his protruding jaw tusks adorned with gifted rings and gems that jingled as he spoke. He had a thick head of hair he braided down his back, and elegant robes with beautifully stitched embroidery. Manak was fascinating, but she never spoke to him. She never had the time to fully mingle with the ambassadors unless they wished it.

It was rumored they had been smuggling their people out, not in an effort to liberate them, but as food, and the misunderstanding was what caused the riot.

"A campfire story, nothing more," he answered. "They definitely know how to roast and season every type of food you can think of. Some of the best sauces I've ever tasted. You feast as good as kings."

Ilai looked back at Ysella. "That is as long as a famine does not take hold. No famine in the area that I know of. At least, not yet. Trade does affect that somewhat, you know."

She looked away. "Well then, I guess it's an unfortunate thing that I won't be able to make my meeting and repair the trade issues, isn't it? Let's go. If you pass out from blood loss, I'm not dragging you along. I hope you know that."

He laughed with genuine amusement and turned his attention back to the path he set. There were no roads or walkways worn in sight, but he seemed to know where they were headed. Hours passed in their journey off the beaten paths, further into woodland with trees of grey bark densely gathered along the rolling, uneven earth. Ilai continued his pretense for a good while, but eventually, his feet began to drag more, his shoulders hunched and despite her earlier irritation, Ysella's burgeoning concern outshone her attempts at indifference. As she was about to suggest they stop, he noted that they were close to the waypoint. His pace quickened as they descended down a hill and around a bend to the entrance of a cave marked off by wooden planks set up as a door.

She was only halfway down the hill after him when he stopped her, with a hand up. Looking past him, she frowned at the sight of the door. The interior was aglow inside the cavern, and conversations could be heard echoing from within, but the tension in Ilai's posture was unmistakable.

"Keep walk—"

"Lucky stars." A deep voice cut through, and Ysella felt the chain tighten in Ilai's grasp. It was the larger man from further in the forest, the game he had over his shoulders now gone and replaced with a strap of leather holding a sword to his back. Now that he was close, she could see he was a head taller than Ilai, which was considerably tall to her standards.

The large man unsheathed his sword, Ilai doing the same as he placed himself between the stranger and Ysella. "Didn't think you'd bring her to our doorstep," the large man said. "Hey, pretty lady, where's this hunter taking you?"

Straightening, Ysella stepped back as far as her binds would allow, her eyes flickering between him and his sword. There was something to be said for known danger, versus the unknown, yet if there was any chance at all...

"The Twisted Woods."

Ilai shifted, chain held in his left hand with his sword in his right, raised as a barrier and a threat.

"That so?" The large man slowly brought both hands to the hilt of his sword to bear the weight.

"We can split the earnings," Ilai said, though did not back down from his stance. "She's a handful. I wouldn't mind the help."

The stranger rumbled a laugh that held no friendly notions to it and nodded towards the cave entrance. "You'll be headed in there," he said.

From her spot on the hill, she could see Ilai's shoulders sag with a sigh, his head bobbing in a nod. Slowly, he turned sparing a glance over to Ysella as he gestured for her to follow him. He walked towards the cave's entrance, the stranger following behind them a few paces back.

Ilai leaned in towards her, his voice dropping to a whisper. "Can you run on that leg?"

A brow lifting, Ysella glanced to Ilai. It wasn't the question she had expected, really, and for what it was worth, she had assumed, apparently incorrectly, that he'd fully intended to go through with his suggestion to the stranger. She had no real delusions that he was at all interested in protecting her, so much as he was in protecting his bounty, but she wasn't going to argue the despicable nature of his plot when things could, and probably would be, considerably worse if they stayed.

Slowly, inconspicuously as possible, she nodded.

"When I say go, you run," he whispered again almost at an inaudible level. "Run until you can't breathe. Ready? Go!"

Ysella didn't hesitate. She ran. Despite the pain in her leg, the pain in her neck, she ran and she didn't look back, not for anything, not until her lungs truly did burn, making even a simple inhale nearly impossible. The forest floor had little brush, the earth loosing as the snow and ice melted where the intermittent sun could warm through the pines. The slopes were uneven, ravines hidden even with the stalwart trees carving clear paths.

Their escape gave the stranger pause enough to give them a good head start. No doubt they were being pursued, for she could hear shouts from the man behind them. But she didn't dare take the time to look behind her.

Without warning, Ysella jolted to a painful stop, a cry escaping her as Ilai crashed face-first into the dirt behind her. More pursuers had joined the burly man charging up the hill. Looking up, Ilai met her panicked gaze and swiftly released her chain to grab his bow, sitting up to nock an arrow.

"Keep running!" he called out to her.

And she should have. She should have kept running, and never looked back, not once. And in truth, she thought about it, even made it a few steps until the weight of what she was doing became too heavy. He was a scoundrel. A man who killed for profit, whether or not his acquisition was deserving of such a fate. And he had been cold and cruel and given her little reason not to leave him behind to die.

Yet she had known from the moment he fell that while he might be all these things, she was not. It was the same feeling which had driven her attempts to look after his wounds, and it was going to get her killed.

He cried out in pain as he attempted to pull back the string to his bow. He could barely make it bend, and the arrow fell from his fingers.

With a growl of frustration, she ran back to his side with a shake of her head. "I'm not leaving you. They're still a ways off. Get up. I can help you."

The bow fell from his grasp with a wince and Ilai reached for his sword with a shaky hand. She could hear their pursuers closing in. A snarl escaped him, and he pushed himself up, shoving her away from him. "Key is in the quiver," he said to her. "Take it and go! These are caravaners, Ysella."

"Stop telling me what to do!" Ysella barked back, and reaching out, she plucked up the bow from where it had fallen. She had no real knowledge of firing one, beyond what she had seen and those few lessons she had taken at her father's insistence, but there was a certain mastery to her stubborn nature, and desperation and adrenaline were two of life's most efficient teachers.

Plucking an arrow from his quiver, she nocked it against the wood and yanked back. It was tighter than she remembered, requiring strength her arm screamed against. Pain radiated against her chest and shoulders, but nevertheless, she pointed her arrow to the men rushing up the hill. A downward slope made for a much easier target, but she was no skilled marksman, and not even instinct could make one of her. With a sharp exhalation, she released and let the arrow fly.

Somewhere in the arrow's trajectory, it occurred to her that if it did indeed strike true, she would have taken a life. Murdered a man. The horror of that thought brought her heart to her stomach, but there was little time to dwell. Reaching into the quiver again, she grabbed a second arrow, and though her shoulder ached from drawing a bow much too large and taut for her frame, she yanked back and released it down the hill.

The second arrow lodged itself successfully within one of the men's shoulders sending him rolling backwards down the hill. They wouldn't give her time to nock a third arrow as the rest closed the distance with swords drawn and pointed at their throats. Ilai swung out with his sword, the blow easily parried from his position on the ground.

"You," the stranger from earlier hissed, addressing Ysella. "You gonna cause us trouble?"

Dropping the bow and shaking her head, she looked to the larger man, her hands raised in front of her. "No. No trouble."

There was a short distance between the entrance of the cave and the den. It was a rather large cavern for the Grey Hinterlands, but nothing by comparison to the grand system of caverns in the mountains of Bastillos. Wooden shanties were built in tiers along the far wall for business and privacy, four covered wagons lining the path through in a neat row. There was a cluster of horses tended by a few men grooming their velvet coats and a bridge over a freshwater pond that led to a cooking fire. It was there a man sat, gaze intent on the contents within a pot that carried a sweet aroma.

"What have we here?" he asked, stroking his salt-and-peppered beard as he looked up at Ysella. He did a double take of her, brows furrowing as his fingers reached into a jacket pocket for a pair of spectacles that looked far too dainty for the gruff man's features. He was a tall man, his thick hair receding around the temples where grey wove through black. A worg's pelt was draped over his shoulders, the brown mane framing angular features and a thick neck. His broad physique nearly spanned twice her own.

"Another bounty?" he asked, his spectacled eyes noting the collar around her neck. One of the men nodded, and the bearded man huffed a laugh. His accent was thicker than Ilai's with less of a melody and a longer drawl. "Bless the Stars of Elssar. You're in luck, little lady. What's your name?"

"Doesn't seem terribly lucky on my end," she remarked, trying to meet the man's spectacled gaze with one that belied the tremors of fear running through her.

"You get to live," the man said matter-of-factly, hands outward for emphasis as he stood and approached her. His glasses were tucked away into his pocket with a swift and practiced motion. "And you want to live, am I right?"

"Yes," She released a breath, nodding. "Yes, I do."

A smile spread across his face, wrinkling the dirtied skin and revealing a set of graying teeth. "That's good to hear," he said, and meandered back to the cooking fire. "Are you willing to do anything to stay alive?"

Blinking, she hesitated, her expression falling to a wary frown. "Wh... what do you mean?"

"It's a simple question," he said as he sat on the stool next to the fire. "How badly do you want to stay alive?"

"If it's a simple question, why won't you answer me? No one asks a question like that in a simple situation." She swallowed hard, trying to ignore the look the man gave her. "I want to live. Of course I do, but I won't hurt anyone to save myself."

The man's head nodded in thought, fingers scratching just below the line of his beard as he reflected momentarily on her words. "You a virgin?"

Her breath caught and for a moment her jaw clenched tighter, voice losing its grit. "Yes."

A final nod rose and fell, and the man swiped his hand through the air. "Go fetch the key to the lady's collar," he said to the man on her right. He promptly released Ysella's arm and headed out of the cavern. It was in that moment she realized they had not brought Ilai with them, and for a second she found herself wondering if he had survived, wondering whether or not she cared to know.

"I'm Regan," the bearded man said, and motioned her over to sit with him by the fire. "And what's your name?"

"My name is Ysella." Apprehensively, she sank down, knotting her hands together in her lap. "Why did you ask that question?"

"I like to get to know people," he answered, and stirred the contents in the pot once again. It carried the sweet aroma of chocolate. "Now, Ysella, I noticed how you're ringing those dainty little hands of yours. I'm guessing you're a little nervous and got some questions of your own? Would you like some hot chocolate?"

"That isn't the sort of question one is generally asked when getting to know someone else. You asked for a reason, and I want to know what that reason is." She pressed her palms flat against her skirt, wiping away the sweat as she shook her head. "And no thank you."

"Ah." His head nodded, and he picked up a tin cup. "Buran, you want some?" As Regan held up the cup, the other lackey nodded, and the man happily ladled the hot chocolate for his comrade. "It's a delicacy and a rare import to make it so far from Bastillos. I think it comes all the way from Yethi. The import of such goods has to go to great lengths. Buran knows how to enjoy himself in our circumstances."

"Indeed, sir," Buran said as he took the cup in hand, grinning, holding it out in thanks as he turned away from the cooking fire. Regan's attention turned back to Ysella, and he smiled.

"I'm trying to figure out how best to use you, Ysella," he said. "Make you sellable. Otherwise my guess is you'd rather die, and I'll just save myself the hassle. Now, you've got a half decent shot with a bow, but you don't want to kill anyone to keep your life. Sex is another option. Especially with a pretty face like yours."

"Sellable..." The words felt flat, without inflection, and Ysella glanced to the fire as she shook her head, heat behind her eyes threatening to spill down her cheeks. "You could let me go. My father, he'd reward you, I'm sure. Please. I... I just want to go home."

Regan poured himself a cup from the contents of the pot, setting the pot to the side as he watched Ysella keenly, a flicker of amusement in his indifferent eyes. He smiled approvingly at his drink, nodding to himself in a thought as he spoke to Ysella once again.

"If your father has the mind to come here and buy you, then you get to go home," he said. "I can't let you go, though. Otherwise, I've got to kill you. See it now? You either want to live, or you want to die. And there's no guarantee someone else won't pay for you before Papa gets here. You got any other skills, darling, or is this what we're left with?"

"I'm a diplomat, Regan," she said simply, sitting up. "I'm paid to deliver secrets of utmost importance between crucial heads of state. I'm sure I don't need to explain the benefits here?"

The stool he sat upon creaked with the shift of his weight as he mulled over the prospects of the skill. Further down into the cave, a cry of pain echoed. No one seemed to pay it any mind. "How am I supposed to sell a betrayer?" he asked.

Other men filed back into the cave, one of them handing over a key to Regan. "The hunter?" Regan asked as he handed the key to Ysella. His eyes were still trained on his men, trusting the woman would take the key on her own with the presentation. She wondered what sort of weapon it might make, but quickly gave up the idea at the sight of his companions and the swords at their sides.

"Eh, he might be useful if he doesn't die," one of them said. "You know how hunters are. No guarantees he won't try and break out."

"Get Seir to bring him in here," he commanded, and with a nod they headed for the entrance.

It shouldn't have given her any sense of hope, yet somehow, in spite of herself, Ysella breathed out a sigh of relief upon hearing Ilai was alive. Certain was always better than uncertain, and he, at least, had never asked after the nature of her innocence.

Looking to Regan, she shook her head as she palmed the key held out to her. "You sell me as an informant. People will pay a lot for that sort of information. And I can't imagine your clientele are particularly concerned regarding the morality of the purchases. They're buying people, after all."

Sitting back on his stool, Regan took another sip from his battered tin cup. Dirt lined his fingernails. He wore two steel rings on the hand holding his drink, both rings connected by a long spiked plate. "Mm, well, you got me there," he said with a chuckle, "but informants are risky as slaves. They always want to go off on their own and run away, which once I pocket my money I don't give a damn. You understand I got to find a dumbass and convince him to buy you as an informant? There might be one in Nabannon. Eh. Got any other skills?"

"Extreme patience," she muttered as she pushed the key into the lock and turned, the mechanism clacking on release. With a breath and a wince, she pulled the collar away, but there was no true relief in the feeling. How long would it even last? Freedom.

Looking up, she met the man's gaze again. "I'll be honest with you, Regan, as you've been honest with me. I intend to escape, regardless of what you sell me as. So you might as well make it up to suit whatever will give you the greatest payout." Running a hand across her neck, flinching at the raw skin there, she looked tentatively to the man. "The hunter. You ought to see to it he survives. He's an ass, but he's gifted. You'll get your money's worth with him."

6

ILAI

Pain created a blur of grey and green and muted sounds of shouts Ilai couldn't quite discern. Two strong men picked him up by both arms, agony searing through him once again as the worg's bite pulled from its healing. The men dropped him and argued, one of them kicking him in his gut and shouting something in his face that launched spittle to his cheek.

"Go fetch the sled," one of them said. He was an athletic looking man with the sides of his head shaved to show off an old tattoo that depicted stylized worg heads.

"He isn't worth the labor, Cammon," the other murmured. There was a pause, and the two watched Ilai for a moment as he regained his bearings. The one named Cammon pushed at Ilai's shoulder causing another groan. Ilai had nearly pushed himself to a stand had the effort not skewed the world in a dizzying whirl.

The two men laughed as he collapsed back into the dirt. Based on what he could feel, the pain only radiated from his arm, but it lingered and throbbed with the

65

onset of fever on his sweaty brow. They had likely taken Ysella by now. Ilai knew that was no place for her to end up regardless of the bounty.

In their brief debate, the two caravaners did not see the resolve harden Ilai's gaze, nor the leverage he positioned with his leg. He charged forward and rammed his good shoulder into the unnamed caravaner who fell heavily to the ground. Cammon laughed until Ilai pinned the man down and rammed his fist against his cheek.

The first punch slammed his head back, eyes in shock as the impact vibrated up Ilai's good arm. He struck a second time and felt his knuckles collide with the hard bone of his nose with a crack. The third blow barely grazed the man's cheek as he was pulled harshly by the collar of his cloak.

"You little shit!" the caravaner spat as he checked his broken nose for bleeding. A bit of red streaked down his mustache.

Cammon slammed his boot into Ilai's gut, and as Ilai doubled over the other caravaner reached under his cloak and clenched his fingers hard around the wound. Blood and flayed skin squelched under the fabric by his angered grasp. Ilai's vision turned white and blurry once again, his ears ringing with the searing pain. "You do that again and I'll kill you," he growled.

The man's fist collided with his cheek, and the world once again spun. A gloved hand pulled him up from the cold earth by his hair.

"You walk or you die," Cammon warned. They hoisted Ilai up to his feet forcibly, the movement agitating his wound further. He didn't recognize them personally, but knew their type. Caravaners acted the same towards everyone that wasn't their own, yet all still had to prove their usefulness to the caravan or find themselves at the pointed end of a knife.

They took turns pushing him forward when his pace would slow. There were a few wagons parked along the main road that consisted of housing or metal cages, and two covered in canvas towards the end. Their stock looked empty based on what Ilai could see.

One of the wagons was opened on one side and within sat an older man with a wooden leg just below the knee. Several caravaners stood about his desk in conversation, their eyes turning to look as Cammon shoved Ilai to the stairs.

Between the man's fingers were several leaves of parchment, all containing job postings torn from bounty boards. He carefully looked through each and sorted them into piles.

"Seir," Cammon said as they approached. The man at the desk barely acknowledged the greeting as he searched through the loose papers.

"Twisted Woods..." He repeated the words as he skimmed the lines of printed text, eventually falling on Ysella's post. He pulled the parchment out from the other piles and tapped it for the other two. "That's the one. Is that the hunter or another bounty?"

"Just the hunter," Cammon said as he plucked the bounty posting from the desk and read it over. His eyes widened as they rested upon the large sum. "That can't be true. Twenty?"

"Take it to Regan and see what he thinks," Seir said and waved them away from his wagon.

"Regan wants you to give—"

The caravaner's voice was cut off by a simple glare from the man. He didn't look like their leader, but the authority he exuded among them suggested he was second in command. Given his wooden leg, Ilai could surmise that he was cunning enough to compensate for any perceived weakness.

"Does he got a key?" another caravaner asked Cammon. Ilai's pockets and pouches were searched. They shoved him at uncomfortable angles to find the key to Ysella's collar, and once produced one of the men rushed off ahead.

Ilai felt a wave of nausea fight his senses, and he clenched his jaw tight. He was right back where he swore he would never be, and his body was in poor condition to fight back.

Worse yet, the diplomat worth twenty gold heads was now their prisoner. The churning in his stomach worsened, sweat beading on his brow. She talked too much. It would do her no service here where patience was scarce.

Cammon and the other caravaner pushed Ilai towards the entrance of a cave walled off by well-cut wooden slats and a proper hinged door. They nodded at the two men guarding the entrance and forced Ilai further down into the cave illuminated only by the light ahead.

Waypoints were common throughout the Grey. They were often a sort of shack or abandoned building close to a road where business could be conducted or stores could be placed to make room for better goods. This particular cave made for a convenient waypoint where buildings were few and far between. It was close enough to the road to be convenient.

Deeper within the cave was lit with everglow. The rune-etched crystals were rare in these lands, and they seemed to be temporarily placed around the interior camp by ropes or placed in unlit pyres. Ilai was forced to his knees before their leader, and he felt his entire body collapse. His weakness fueled a fear he desperately fought back. Strength was valued among caravaners. It displayed usefulness.

One of the men pulled Ilai's head up by his hair, and he could do nothing against the discomfort. His weapons were confiscated, the supplies along his belt pilfered. He spared a glance to Ysella noting her collar had been removed, and then to the leader of the caravan who appraised the hunter thoughtfully.

"She's a hefty bounty, Regan," Cammon informed, and handed over the bounty posting. "Seir pulled this from the pile. It's more than what we could sell her for, that's for sure."

Regan stood and set his cup on his stool, fingers brushing through the tip of his beard. "Is it legitimate?"

"Got a hunter interested," Cammon pointed out.

Regan lowered himself slowly to eye level with Ilai who steadied his own gaze in return. Caravan leaders gained their position through cunning and strength, and it showed in his weathered features and piercing gaze. His jaw sported a deep scar that struck down his neck and split his groomed beard. His bulky frame was hidden underneath warm layers, and he brushed his hand across his mustache thoughtfully as he studied Ilai.

"Hunters are always thorough," Regan remarked. He held up her posting to Ilai and pointed towards the words inked crisply in black. "Ethyrnon Tower. Does Laerd Valarad own it, or is it occupied by someone else?"

A lack of answer would garner a swift beating and a slow death unless they forced his compliance. He was better off answering. "Rumors suggest Shadow

Casters. The sum suggests an organization. The bounty suggests it's more than what it seems. They will want her alive."

Knowing flared in Regan's eyes as he pulled back from Ilai, a brow raised with growing interest. He scratched under his chin as he stood, contemplation churning.

"Someone wants Edros to go to war," Regan stated thoughtfully. "I don't think it's Shadow Casters, given the woman's profession. Why would they have interest in Edros? The orcs, however... We could ask them on the road north."

The other men remained quiet while their leader thought out loud. Whether they could comprehend or not, to interrupt their leader would be insubordination. Ilai was no caravaner. Not anymore. His defiance to their ways brought words to his lips.

"There is another diplomat from Bastillos with a similar posting," he informed. Cammon pulled his head back and placed a small blade to his neck in response to his defiance.

"Is that so?" Regan sat back down on his stool, blade still at Ilai's throat, and eyed Ysella over in another thought. Turning back to Cammon, he shook his head, and the blade fell from his neck. "Tell Seir we're heading north. The lady is not to be touched other than to put her in The Box. Any bruises and I'll have your head, understand? Keep her skin smooth just in case we can make a better profit in the long run at a brothel. If you feel the need to beat something, use him. Take them away."

"You're making a mistake, Regan," the diplomat warned, her voice unwavering. "It won't be favorable."

She knew nothing of caravaners or the dangers of being their captive, but she was brave nonetheless. She was likely unaware of her defiance towards their ways, but she was protected. And in a way, so was he. The only way he would receive a beating is if he goaded them on, but he would not be killed, at least not yet.

The worg had assured a weakness before these men, and he felt the start of a fever. It was likely he would die along the road. Being faced with his mortality felt strange and yet distant. He accepted death, while also in denial of its close embrace.

"You'll get no trouble," she assured the men as they guided her out of the cave by her arms. "Let's go."

The men chuckled at her command, and even Regan broke a smile, his head shaking. He gave Ilai a warning look that needed no words. He was to choose his path: live or die. He might even seek to recruit him if he could force submission. It was a position he could play to his favor if need be.

As sunlight broke among the trees and rolling hills outside the cave, the other caravaners loitered around the wagons preparing food or sparring for sport. Women of a caravan were protected from a man's hunger, but had to prove themselves more openly in displays of combat. It garnered reverence and fear among the men knowing these women would cleave them in two should they fall out of line.

The diplomat would be protected by the same laws, though without the gained respect. She was goods to be sold, and those were best unspoiled. They threw her into the cart comprised of thick iron bars inside and sturdy wood planks along its exterior that blocked out most of the sunlight. Ilai was thrown in with more force, his body slamming into the wood floor. One of the caravaners pulled himself up by a bar and used his momentum to kick Ilai further into the Box. They laughed as they closed the door, a lock clicking as light was nearly snuffed out.

A grunt escaped Ilai as he situated himself to sit upright. "The stars favors us," he said sarcastically. "We've run into a caravan."

His shoulder felt aflame, yet carried the prickle like being stabbed repeatedly with shards of ice. He tested his hand's grip and the movement of his arm. Pain coursed from his shoulder to his fingertips and radiated up into his skull, his hand shaking with the attempt, but he kept such weakness muted and fought back any vocalization that would give it away.

"I'm beginning to think you've been poorly misinformed of what is favorable, Ilai," she spoke as she shifted across the cage. He could barely discern her features through the light filtering through small slat above.

"Seems we're going to need to work together to get out of here," she said as she sat next to him against the bars. "How are you? I might be able to convince them to bring supplies to patch you up. But you'll need to be on your best behavior. Think you can manage?"

She was genuine in her offer. He could see it in her naive eyes. How could he explain he would be dead by their hands if they had to ask for aid? Worse yet, he couldn't help but wonder if the diplomat was devising a plan to negotiate her release. Generosity like hers always came with a price. A life for a life, in this exchange. He could not place himself in debt with an acquisition.

"I can manage," he assured. He would have to find a way and hope the chilled sweats were only due to exertion rather than a worsening fever. "I'll be alright. The beast bit me, but a day or two of rest to heal will do it some good. How is your leg?"

Her head canted as she saw through his diversion. "Oh, you can't really be that stupid, Ilai." She said his name a lot. He surmised it was a way to garner his trust to further manipulate his feelings as if the repetition could bridge tensions. "You've lost a lot of blood, but that's not the concern here. Do you understand how dangerous an infection is?"

He knew. He was aware of his predicament, but he did not wish to jump to conclusions while in a caravan's Box. It was more dangerous to appear useless than it was to weather a fever. Her ignorance was frustrating.

"And believe me," she continued, "I don't like you. Not in the slightest." He huffed a laugh despite her words. "But I am not cruel enough to suffer even you to that fate. Especially since I'm not likely to get out of this without you."

He met her gaze, her soft blue eyes glistening with severity. For a moment, Ilai felt a sense of trust and hope that was unbecoming of a hunter with his acquisition. Her machinations were clever as she searched for his weakness. Perhaps it was the fever.

"Now, where's the worst of it?" She wasn't going to give up easily, and he wasn't sure he had enough strength to continue just as stubbornly. His heartbeat pulsed in a radiating ache he knew would strike like lightning through his body if he moved. He just needed a day, maybe two to recover.

"My shoulder," he admitted quietly. She leaned towards him and pulled back his cloak. The fibers of the fabric pulled at his skin where the blood had hardened.

Fresh blood caught the dim light of the day from the window above, and she bit the edge of her lip in contemplation.

Did she truly believe she needed him to get out of this predicament? She was disheveled and dirty, but her eyes still carried the light of determination needed to survive, albeit without the knowledge of how to do so in the Grey.

"What's the difference between me and them?" he asked. "We're all going to the same place, you know."

"You may be a scoundrel, Ilai, but you made your intentions clear from the start," she said. She didn't look at him when she answered, her eyes straining in the dark as she looked for signs of inflammation. "I abhor men who would make the pretense of friendship when their motives are less than honorable. That man's first question to me was on the matter of my chastity."

He recalled a time years ago, a chain around his neck. A woman's soft sobs and pleas for release were the sounds he heard each night in an attempt to sleep. Caravaners were cruel with their intent, and they weaponized humanity to hook their prey.

The diplomat met his gaze, and he pushed away the fear he felt for her future. They would not beat her to submission. Her resolve would free her from their confines. Her strength was a hidden secret that did not manifest in muscles or physical prowess.

"I don't imagine I need to explain to you why that makes you the lesser of two evils," she stated, and he felt the sting of her words for the first time. Caravaners were evil despite their contributions to the economy in the Grey. She defined his work so closely to them, but he had always separated himself from caravans. Now he questioned his own logic. With all his other hunts and all the pleading acquisitions, he never once cared for such a jab at his character. He surmised his fever was to blame.

Leaning forward was a strain as the pain connected with the muscles on his back. He grunted, his flesh threatening to pull apart further, and the fabric of his shirt irritated the wound. Outside a few men spoke to each other, their words muffled by the walls that separated them.

"Caravaners are unforgiving towards their captive women," Ilai explained. "They're protected from abuse that would harm their outward appearance, and that is all. If you are considered weak in their eyes, there is only one use for you. Your leg. How bad is it?"

She reached down towards her foot and gingerly shifted the fabric away as best she could. Even through the bandage, jagged red tears streaked her lightly tanned skin. It was deep towards one end, but it was closed and situated in a location that would not be agitated by movements.

"It needs to be cleaned again," she surmised calmly in her own assessment, "and dressed properly. It'll scar, that's certain."

An amused smile formed at her mild concern towards a scar. He wondered if this was her first and tried to remember his own first. His more apparent scar struck from his forehead to his cheek and narrowly missed his eye. Others, like the one he most recently received, were tucked away under layers and out of sight of curious eyes.

"I may be dragging you to your death by a chain," Ilai said, "but if you can believe it... I can't let the caravaners take you." A genuine sentiment, but one he hoped would not be misconstrued. "Don't think too much on it."

The echo of memories forced themselves to the forefront of his mind and threatened to build the foundations of empathy and compassion. Ilai reminded himself of his purpose as a hunter. He was required to be detached.

Twenty gold heads, he reminded himself.

"I do believe you," she responded thoughtfully. He almost wanted to rescind his words and reignite the baseline disgust of him once again.

She stood, and he envied how easy the effort was for her despite her own wound. She favored her injured leg, yet would not let it slow her purpose. It was a commendable perseverance she held, and one that brought deep shame churning in his stomach. He was becoming weak of mind and weak of body, and he couldn't determine the logical path.

"Hello? Someone there?" She stood on the tips of her toes, her elegant shoes caked in mud as she called out of the small slat for a window. Ilai felt his stomach lurch in a moment of panic. He did not wish for the caravaners to perceive his weakness so soon.

The voices around them carried on, tones echoing down the chamber of the cave. The Box shook and clattered as it was secured to a hitch, horses snorting and scuffing as they were guided into place. The diplomat's call was ignored. Ilai calmed at their captors' lack of interest, their voices only to offer commands or banter amongst themselves.

"Ah, don't bother," Ilai said dismissively, and rested back on the metal bars. It felt cold against his wounds and helped numb the pain after the initial pressure. "We'll just need to think more quickly on our escape. Caravans travel the main roads from town to town. It's a long, slow ride to the Twisted Woods. We have time to think. To plan. Just sit back, and try not to be too annoying."

Her lips twisted and pulled downward as she sank down beside him. "I am not annoying." She spared a glance to his shoulder. "You just don't like me because I remind you of what you are."

A worg. A survivor, vicious and cunning with wit as sharp as his teeth. A beast. A monster...

He huffed a laugh, brow furrowing at her remark. "I know what I am," he stated plainly despite the cut of her intellect. "You're only stating the obvious, and that is what can get a bit annoying."

The Box lurched forward as the Caravan started its journey north. His shoulder hit the bars uncomfortably in the sudden movement, and he winced uncontrollably.

"And you can just accept it?" she asked, a brow lifted. Her voice held no accusatory tone. Only curiosity. "You're perfectly fine with the man you are? Never wanted to be anything more? Anything better?"

Sunlight pierced into the dark enclosure as the canopy of barren trees thinned. He could see more of the diplomat with the brightness of the midday sun, and she held his gaze with wise observation that steeled his features.

"Everyone lives with the life they're given," he answered. "We all learn to make the best of what we have. We all have variations on what brings peace or content or sadness or joy. Are you perfectly content with the woman you are?"

Throwing such a question was designed to deflect and throw her manipulation tactics right back to her. While the life of a diplomat was nowhere close to the atrocities he had committed in his life, he knew one thing was certain for every person: no one was ever satisfied with the life they were given.

7
YSELLA

The cart rolled onward. Ysella took a breath and leaned back against the bars. The wood slats clattered along the cart's frame in a constant jarring cadence. For a moment, she genuinely considered Ilai's question, searching inward for an answer she was fairly certain she already knew. "Not perfectly, no. But I think I'm a decent person. At least I tried to be. I give the most in what I do." Staring ahead, she frowned gingerly. "Would I have chosen the same path if I thought I could go elsewhere? Perhaps not, but I suppose it doesn't matter much, now. What about you? Would you pick another life if you could? Who would you be?"

He hummed in thought for a moment. In the darkness of the caravan, Ysella studied him, noting for perhaps the first time the subtle depth in his dark eyes. "Perhaps the queen of Bastillos," he said with a chuckle. "Lavish life she lives. Practically dictates the livelihood of Edros. Imagine me in those fancy robes. Then again, in that life I would be a pretty woman of Bastillos. Wouldn't look as silly."

Despite her better efforts, Ysella laughed and for a moment, only a moment, the anxiety in her ebbed away and felt every bit the young, vulnerable woman she was. "Be fair. It's not all lavish. It's a hard life in its own right, for someone so young. Though you are already awfully pretty. The robes might suit you."

"It's the hair," he said as he ruffled a hand through the mess of dark curls. "Frames my face and gives me that bit of intrigue women always have. Hmm, if I were the queen of Bastillos my robes would be blue like the night. But with those little gems like on your dress. Am I doing this right?"

Another soft chuckle escaped and Ysella shook her head. "I'm not sure 'right' is the word for it, but you are putting a terrible lot of thought into it and I suppose that's admirable."

"What about you, then? What sort of life would you pick if you could?" he asked.

The smile faded at his question and pausing, she turned her gaze forward.

"I don't know. I suppose I never really thought about it much. I was always just prepared for this role. I imagine it might be interesting to…" Swallowing, she folded her knees up to her chest, chin resting against them. She'd never spoken it out loud, not even to Odessa. It had always been a private thought, and one she'd never even hoped to encourage outside of her fantasies. Still, they were likely dead, and he had asked. "I'd like to be a physician. Our world has so much harm in it. It needs healers."

"People in Bastillos need good physicians, from what I've heard," he said. "I suppose the caves can only be so good for so long. Would you help the poor get well, too? That uprising still stings a few of your kind. Surprised they could manage it."

"For someone so obsessed with earning his bit of metal, Ilai, you're ironically concerned for the poor." Looking at him again, she frowned. It was hard to believe the Low Rebellion was only a few years ago. In that time, she decided to learn the ways of mending and medicines to aid the injured. The healers of High Lumin were assigned to the more delicate cases or sequestered for protection. "Yes. I would help them. I would help anyone who needed it. Apathy solves nothing. Violence solves nothing. It didn't make the poor any less poor, it didn't open the eyes of the rich to see their own folly. It didn't stop you and I from ending up in this cage." Turning her eyes away, she blinked, gaze distant. "I wounded a man for absolutely no reason. We didn't even get away."

A smile broke on his lips briefly at her comments, a small laugh escaping through his nose in almost a sigh. "That injury could be enough to stop them from using you before they sell you," he said. "Women who do that aren't easy prey. They snag the weak ones. But your stunt with the bow affords you some breadth. And I would say that violent uprising from your slaves granted them freedom to now fight for better pay. Ah, hm, let me count on my fingers, here, I must be mistaken. You said violence solves nothing yet I count two examples where it has."

A brow lifted and for a second, the corner of her lip twitched, her head shaking. "We can argue semantics all day, Ilai. But in the end, the violence never had to occur had High Lumen opened the doors for a true conversation with the lower class. I could have talked my way out of that situation, but instead, I panicked and chose a crude and uncivilized method. I now have blood on my hands because of that decision."

A sigh escaped, and her eyes drifted to the cage door. "Maybe it was better, because of what you said they would have done otherwise, but I lost something, either way. And the slaves? Maybe they're free, but they're also on their own, and people hate them for it. It's not right, no, but it's society. And people on their own struggle significantly more than those under protection. It's all well and good to look at the bigger picture, but under the surface there are nuances that make all the difference and reacting violently. It almost never ends well for everyone."

Looking over to him again, she smiled faintly, apprehensively. "You and I are a perfect example of a situation that has no predictable outcome. I could have left you. I should have, all things considered. But I didn't, and I still don't entirely understand why, but I do know that things would not look the way they do now, had I made another choice. We have a chance. Not much of one, but a chance to get out of this. But that might mean using an approach you're not entirely accustomed to. I need to know if you're capable of looking beyond your own instincts."

"I can't guarantee that," he answered plainly. "We need to get out of here. If you have a plan, I'm willing to hear it. But if it's shit, I won't do it."

"Interestingly enough. You might like it, as it has at least the illusion of what you're accustomed to. They need me in good condition in case this goes poorly. And they've no real notion that you and I are even willing to work together. In fact, I rather encouraged them to sell you, too. Sorry, but I figured it was the best way to implore them to keep you alive. At any rate, when those doors open, you need to pretend that you're willing to kill me. I know it will be difficult, considering how close we've become." She smirked. "But they don't want damaged goods. Not when they aren't even sure the bounty on my head requires me to be alive and well. It's my thoughts given the way Regan was so concerned about bruising that they won't risk hurting me to get to you, and if we can get out of the cage, we can make another run for it."

"I go to kill you," Ilai said thoughtfully, "and then what? They'll pull us apart and get you to safety and wait to see how badly you're bruised. You've got the chance to run. Who's to say I won't get skewered for my efforts in the ruse? Doesn't seem at all in my favor."

"You're a powerful man, Ilai. Do you think they'd risk trying to get me away from you by force? Regan might be a disgusting opportunistic pig, but he seems smart. Frighteningly smart. If he wants me in one piece, he won't hurt you. Just be convincing enough, and they'll let us walk out of here if only so they can come after us in the open."

"You'll have to be between them and me," he said. "They'll put a sword in my gut to make me stop. I'll have to use you as a shield. Are you willing to do that?"

She gave a nod of mild confidence. "I am. I trust you." And she was surprised, a little, to find she meant it. Perhaps she would never fully trust him or his intentions to the degree she might someone met under better circumstances, but a man in a desperate situation wasn't likely to betray his best shot at survival. "Though if you get me killed, I will haunt you until the end of your days."

His eyes narrowed somewhat at the mention of trust and he seemed to study her for a long moment, no doubt trying to gauge the genuineness of her words.

"The stars shine in my favor, then," he said with a huff of a laugh. "There's no such thing as ghosts."

"Tell that to the people in Low Lumin. There's a ghost story for every shrouded corner or deep tunnel through those caverns. My sister was partial to one regarding something in a light tunnel that bit the head off of anyone who came near it."

"That doesn't sound like much of a ghost to me."

Pushing himself upright, his legs bearing the brunt of the work, he slid up the wall to bring himself to a stand. His eyes trailed up to the slats in the Box's walls, falling distant as he looked out at the sky overhead. "I've run from a caravan once before," he said. "It won't be easy." He looked over to Ysella with a fixed, sober expression. "You'll need to be more selfish. When we make a run for it you can't be as stupid this time. You run this time, or your next capture won't end well. If I fall behind, that is my own failure. Do you understand? I'll leave you behind just as quick, if knowing that will make a difference."

For a moment, she was quiet as she considered his words. She wanted to say it was an easy decision - but she had thought that earlier, and still had chosen to stay and fight. Maybe because in reality the idea of leaving a man to his death was a lot more difficult than in theory. She wanted to believe that she could look at all he'd done, all that he deserved and forgo her emotions, but her empathy had tripped her up once. What was to say it wouldn't happen a second time?

"Don't worry about that," she said. "We'll have to get out, first, and that will take enough of our concentration. We can worry about the rest, later."

The caravan traveled the uneven roads of the Grey Hinterlands, through creaking barren woods and bright open skies that threatened overcast as the day drew on. The Box was cold as it swallowed in the air of Winter; a numbing, unforgiving cold that seeped deep to the bone. There would be little comfort for a rest, and the hours of travel drew further in the mind. Ilai didn't complain about the pain of his wound at this point, but Ysella imagined he could barely feel much without occasionally walking about the small enclosure to keep up circulation and warmth in his body. Ysella was encouraged to do the same, but found her legs quaking too much to give it decent effort. It was a solid plan, as much as could be made, but it was not foolproof. If anything went wrong, what awaited either one of them would not be pleasant, and there was little comfort found in the frigid darkness of their cell.

Their stop came among a clouded, dimming sky. The Box shook at the halt, horses huffing in relief as men called out commands for their night's stay. It was nearly time. Ilai looked over at Ysella with severity, rolling his injured shoulder slowly and fighting a grimace that tightened his jawline. "As soon as you find an opening, you run," he whispered. "Are you ready?"

Throughout the journey, Ysella had remained largely silent, but internally, war had waged. She had fought, violently with her mind, trying her best to convince herself that the plan would work - that it was the only plan they had. In truth, it was the thought of being sold, of being traded for vile acts that drove her to such determination, but it was a thought that needed to stick, and so she had forced herself to dwell, to imagine the atrocities that could befall her, should they fail.

Failure, as it was, was not an option. Not ever. So she nodded firmly, her expression a mask of that same blazed resolution.

"I'm ready."

Balling his fingers to a fist, he rammed them against the iron doors to cause a loud bang that pulled a yelp from the diplomat. Calls of curiosity billowed outside and footsteps pounded towards their cage. With a calm nod, Ilai reached for Ysella's throat. "Better than banging you up," he whispered, a smirk etching on his features briefly. His grip on her neck was loose, yet convincing in its curve as the hand enveloped her skin in a black leather glove. "Put your hands around my fingers and act like you're struggling to breathe. I'll push us both out when the time comes."

For a moment, fear flashed through Ysella's eyes, real and genuine fear, as his fingers closed around her throat. It hurt, even without the employment of his strength, the gentle bruising left from the collar all too fresh, all too new. Flinching, she curved her fingers around his as instructed, and a part of her wondered if he had practice at this ruse, for he seemed to know all too well just what strangling a person ought to look like. And yet there was a shockingly gentle nature to the approach that unnerved her in a different way.

He turned her back to his chest and his arm curved around her, his fingers maintaining their pressure against her neck. She could feel his heart beating against her back. It seemed calm, particularly against her own, which beat like thunder against his ribs. The acrid smell of sweat, dried blood, and dirt burned her nostrils.

Desperate to take her mind off the concerns roiling in her head, she met his gaze with a sharp-eyed focus. "If we survive this, you may want to consider a bath." Then, gripping her fingers tighter around his, with just enough force to give the impression she was fighting back, she inhaled, holding her breath as much as she dared.

"You don't smell like flowers either," he muttered. There came a clatter against the door as the caravaners approached and unclasped the lock. As the doors swung open, the steel of their swords caught what little light there was left in the dusk hours, and Ilai roughly swung Ysella around to place her between him and the caravaners.

"He's at her throat!"

"Pull them apart!"

"Get an angle on him!"

They tried to flank Ysella, coming at Ilai with their blades as best they could. It was a haphazard dance they performed, Ilai maneuvering her by her neck with a loose grip while desperately trying not to catch a blade in his ribs or legs or skewer her in the process. The wagon was tight, however, and the movements of the men stilted and awkward. As an opening appeared, with one final thrust forward, he managed to split the assailants, pushing her through the group and in the clear to run. He wouldn't be able to make it out without a fight, but he gave her the briefest look in urgency as he brought the heel of his boot to the chest of one of the men.

She should have run.

She should have turned and run and never looked back. But infuriatingly, for the second time that day, Ysella found herself frozen by indecision. He'd gotten her out. It hadn't been the plan, but he'd done it anyway, and while altering the plan made her just angry enough to leave him behind, the part of her that knew right from wrong was all too aware she'd never intended to follow his orders. They were in this together, now, whether they liked it or not, and she could not abandon him any more than he'd let her take a shortsword to the chest for him.

Spinning back to the wagons and swearing an oath that was both unladylike and undiplomatic, she swung her arm into the cage and praying it didn't lose her a hand, grabbed the ankle of the closest man, yanking as hard as she dared, to drag him off balance. Mid-step on the other foot and with nothing to catch himself on, he toppled into the side of the wagon, cracking his head on the heavy iron bars and falling into a heap on his side.

With one down, Ilai lurched on another, rolling outside and out into the open. Other caravaners began to stir, noticing the fray and garnering more unwanted interest. As they took leave of the campfire and raced towards the Box, Ilai kicked off the man atop him and rolled upright, grasping Ysella by the wrist and pulling her free from the caravan door.

"Keep running!" he yelled to her, dragging her forward towards the distant treeline.

She needn't be told twice. Why she had stayed in the first place, even she could not fully understand - but her compassion could get her killed. As her feet hit the ground, Ysella matched his pace effortlessly. She wasn't accustomed to running - particularly as fast, or out of such abject necessity, and her lungs tightened, her chest burning but she pushed herself further, faster, praying silently that they would give up. That they would realize their quarry wasn't worth the struggle and let her and Ilai go.

A few arrows flew past until they ran out of range, leaving only those on foot to contend with. Ilai didn't look back, but he released Ysella's arm in favor of providing them better momentum in the ensuing chase. Pain rippled across his face and he kept his left arm closer to his body. Behind them, she could hear calls and shouts from the caravaners as they pursued in the hunt for their goods. The hope they'd be too much of a hassle to deal with was dwindling, and when Ilai looked over at Ysella with concern, she matched his expression.

"They're not woodsmen! We need to reach the forest! Stay with me!" he called out to her. A sudden volley of arrows flew past, some dangerously close and Ysella looked up to see that the archers had repositioned themselves closer to the tree line. Heart racing, she trailed after Ilai's concentrated movements. With every step, she waited for one to burrow, to find purchase in her back, in her legs, but their aim never married true and the woods came closer and closer as she pushed herself with every ounce of strength she possessed. If they could just reach the edge. If they could just make it, and use the trees as cover.

"Ilai! The archers!"

Ilai cursed through gritted teeth, and reaching back, grabbed Ysella's hand, pressing forward at a faster pace. An arrow flew past him, ripping through the fabric of his pants and narrowly missing his flesh. He shifted to the left swiftly and Ysella found herself nearly tumbling down a steep embankment, held up only by his relentless grip on her hand. A stream wound the length of the horizon, surrounded by heavy, dark stones and boulders, thick, hooded pines and towering firs. Behind, their pursuers could be heard making swift work of the path they'd left. Ilai released her hand and took a few steps forward into an open grove, the groundwork covered in fallen pine needles. Looking around for their next route, he turned to Ysella.

"Keep—"

Ilia's voice was cut off by a sharp crack and the sudden shift of earth beneath their feet as the world fell out from beneath them. Ysella could barely manage a scream as the pull of gravity sent the pair in a free fall through the gaping mouth of a cavern hole, splashing into a frigid pool below.

8

ILAI

ater swirled around him, the murky palette lit with a disorienting glow. Ilai couldn't feel which way was up, and the pain from his gnarled wound clouded his momentary judgment. Fatigue and blood loss compounded his struggle to the surface, and just as his lungs threatened to take in water, he breached and took in air.

The diplomat stood at the edge of the pool with worry painted on her features. She was soaked, water dripping from her hair and tattered dress that plastered to her small frame. Light refracted from clusters of crystals that caught the sunlight from the opening above and the disturbed pool below, blooming, bathing the cavern in a misty luminescence.

Ilai kicked with every ounce of energy he had left, his good arm propelling him to the water's edge. He pulled himself onto the rocky bank and felt the desire to rip his arm clean from its socket with how it throbbed.

Judging by the placement of the hole, Ilai guessed they had fallen farther than two stacked houses. The simple kind, of course. The ones with barely a loft and built to withstand snow. It was possibly enough of a height to cause the caravaners hesitation in jumping in after them. There was no indication they even knew they had fallen into a system of caves.

His dark curls clung to his face, and he pushed the locks from his eyes. "Perhaps you are bad fortune," he said jokingly, his exhausted voice echoing through the hollow spaces with the lapping of disturbed water. "At least, that is what I should believe. Are you superstitious, Diplomat?"

A frown diminished the fear she once displayed, and she dropped to her knees beside him, her head shaking. "I'm not," she responded, "but it's less than what you deserve for kidnapping me in the first place. Maybe the cosmos simply knew how badly you needed a bath."

He could see the edge of her lip twitch with amusement at her own jest. It was distracting and calming, and as he laughed he felt the pang of pain at his back. His predicament was a growing annoyance, but at least the cold water served to cool his feverish body.

"Come on. We need to see where we've ended up." She extended her arm to him, and he suppressed a scoff at her gesture. The woman would never be strong enough to pull his bulk dry. He now carried the weight of a soaked cloak in addition, but he grabbed her arm to stabilize his own effort to push himself up to a stand. The cold water had numbed his shoulder, but the effort struck him like a lance.

The cave spun, his knees shaking under the weight and his loss of blood. There was no deity or religion he turned to, yet in this moment he begged Elssar for mercy and strength to prevent a debt to his captive.

"With any luck we might find some of your kind down here," he said. "Bastillosi refugees escaping your noble tyranny often found places like these more comfortable than surface homes. Most laerds offer them protection if they swear their loyalty before Elssar. Others just leave them be as long as they find a way to contribute to their society."

She ignored his attempt at a distraction from his state. He was sure he held an even tone, but it was likely his near lack of balance that betrayed him. "It's getting worse, isn't it?" she asked. "Your arm. Will you please... Please just let me see if I can do something about it."

He wondered if his lack of faith in anything but himself caused some deity or god to worsen his plight. Perhaps Elssar was real and this was his penance for his rejection of beliefs. He turned from a life of piety the orphanage demanded in favor of this life.

He was faced with choosing logic or ego. His survival was of the utmost importance yet it would come with the price of a debt he was sure would contradict his current course and cost him those twenty heads of gold.

"Not quite sure what you can do for me now," he said as he sat upon a smoother jut of a natural pillar. With one arm he managed to unclasp his cloak, and it fell in a heavy heap at his back. His leather jerkin was mangled and shredded to pieces and stained even darker by his blood. He shrugged it from his shoulder and lifted his shirt from his body to reveal the nasty wound.

The gnarled shoulder hardly held a resemblance of a bite where the teeth shredded his skin and muscle. Parts of exposed flesh were puckered and red with a tinge of yellow that collected in deeper sections.

"They've got my damned sword," he realized. "And my bow." Those weapons had traveled far with him over the course of his time as a bounty hunter. His mind lingered on the memories of their acquisition and the woman who taught him how to survive. The trip to the Cave seemed almost shameful, now. His tribute was gone.

The diplomat leaned in closer to him, her wet hair revealing soft curls of her own. Her fingertips barely glanced over his skin around the wound and felt like fire. He didn't realize she was talking, but saw her lips move in a completed sentence.

"You've some discoloration," she said. "I can't tell if it's bruising or an infection or both. There are herbs that might help... probably could dig some up in the woods above. I can wait 'til nightfall and see what I can find, but we can't wait much longer."

Rising, she moved to the edge of the pool and bent down, her hands pulling at the waterlogged edge of her skirt. It was frayed along the hem, worn from the distressing travel and ripped from the worgs. She pulled until a strip of the cloth came away and dipped the piece into the water.

She returned to his side kneeling to his left pressing the cloth against the wound. Gingerly, she worked against the grit and dirt that further irritated the marred and exposed flesh. The pressure caused pain that danced like stars in his vision. Was that the god, Elssar, warning him of his coming place among the stars? Religion had such strange manifestations.

No. Even the text held similar requirements as the practitioners of Inner Light. One must be good to return to the cosmos. He wasn't sure he wanted that as an afterlife. He wasn't sure he wanted the black nothingness either. The diplomat was a powerful weapon against his carefully placed walls that deterred all his prior introspection. Her eyes revealed truths in mere glances, and he couldn't look her way out of fear of his soul becoming further exposed.

The bruises around her neck painted a splotchy collar on her sun-kissed skin. Wet rivulets of brown curls barely covered the affront as she leaned towards his shoulder. She was close. He wanted to push her away, and in his lethargic attempt, she moved his hand out of her field of vision with a careful swipe.

"Shouldn't have let it go this long..." Ysella's voice brought him back to the present, his brow furrowing in confusion as he watched her work. The pain seared with every brush of her cloth, and he clenched his jaw tightly. His body tensed.

"I didn't anticipate a caravan taking over the waypoint," he admitted. "Caravans are filled with the most ruthless in the Grey. They work in trade and are reliable for goods throughout the Laerds' Lands. Watchmen allow them into settlements as long as they obey the laws while inside. When you're far from any settlement, you're on your own. The watchmen are rarely out to find the trouble."

Squeezing out the cloth of ruddy blood and dirt, she surveyed the wound again. "Not much more I can do until I can get those herbs. You should rest. Let it breathe."

Standing, she set her hands on her hips and glanced upwards to the hole they had fallen through. It was as wide as the pool below, but far out of reach in any convenient way. "How do you suppose we get back out?"

There was a chance the portion of the cavern that was darkest led to a system of tunnels where at least one would lead to the surface. "If you're lucky you can find a way to walk out," he answered. "If you're not lucky, you climb."

His eyes scanned over the lip of the hole. There was a sturdy vertical wall of rock that jutted down into the pool with a brim about the width of a wagon. The rest of the cave belled out to impossible angles.

"Do the noble people of Bastillos learn to climb as well, or is it just a skill of the peasants?" His question was more born of curiosity than a jab at her higher status, but a playful air helped mask the severity of his situation. Any distraction was welcome.

Ysella narrowed her eyes as she looked back towards him, her hands reaching for the ties on her bodice. Her determination was readily on her features, yet he could not place her course of action as she unraveled the ribbon until it was completely removed from each eyelet.

He was no fool. This was not an attempt to undress down to her chemise in any provocative way. Her expression of determination was to the contrary, eyes glancing up to the wall of stone that led back up to the lip of the hole above. Her wet gown fell around her feet heavily. She was disrobing to remove added weight for her climb.

A playful smirk spread across his features. "Try not to fall," he added.

She did not offer a response at first, her gaze studying the juts and crags along the rock face with an expert eye. "I'll have you know, I could make it to the top of our family's cavern outskirts in less than ten minutes' time." Her delicate fingers reached out for a handhold just along the nearest edge, her foot wedging into a space just above the pool. She was lithe and appeared weak, but he could see the muscles in her arm flex as she pulled her weight skillfully.

The rumors of the mountain people must be true: they were all skilled climbers. "By all means, then," he said with a motion to the hole above. "I'll be counting down."

She mocked him with a dry expression, white teeth bared for emphasis. He couldn't have known how much time passed for her to reach the surface. His consciousness was slipping, and time was not all accounted for.

Her voice echoed and blurred from above, and he may have watched her silhouette move out of view. He was not sure. He found himself staring at the water and watched the ripples slowly still themselves from their disturbance.

Something in him felt immanent, and he felt as though he would die if he remained idle. Standing came with a light head that struggled to keep upright. He clutched the pillar for support and peeled off his damp leather gloves once he regained enough balance. His fingers were cold and had pruned from the contained moisture.

A fire was needed if they wanted a higher chance to survive the night. They were soaked to the bone from that drop, and they would surely freeze to death once the temperature dropped further.

There was plenty of waterlogged debris scattered along the pool's embankment. Ilai traveled further into the darker portion of the small open cavern for dryer spaces. Brush and small trees had taken root where the sunlight could reach, and he pulled from their dead for firewood. There were some vines that reached up and out of the lip of the hole that would help as kindling.

With every task he would find himself glancing up towards the mouth of the cave opening up to the cloudy blue sky. The sticks were piled away from the pool and wet soil. Ilai found only a few items were not pilfered from his person, one of them being his tinderbox. Caravans had better means of starting a fire, and they must have plenty of it.

He struck a spark to his modest pile, smoke curling as embers grew to flames. It was a decent location for respite. Orange fire danced higher as the wood burned. Ilai watched to see how quickly the flames broke down each stick, covering its shell in black and coating it in light. With one arm he lethargically hung his cloak and clothes near the fire's warmth.

If he were to die that night, there was no one to carry on his memory, nor the memories he held of Shera. Landers carried on in memories and tales, but there wasn't a single Lander who truly knew his story. He was just a hunter. Just another vagabond slowly plucking the filth from the Grey. He would die and the Grey would forget him.

9
YSELLA

"Try not to fall."

His comment awarded him a wry look, but it held an air of amusement as she continued her climb. She was quick, as promised, though it was decidedly more difficult in the darker space, even with the light of the crystals surrounding them. Still, she made it roughly three quarters of the way up, and then, it was a matter of more carefully planned positioning of her hands and feet. The wound on her leg stung, the wrapping damp and chilled. It could not have been more than seven or eight minutes until her hands grazed the grassy undergrowth of the forest floor.

Looking back, she called down to him as quietly as she could, "I think they're gone. I'm going up to get the herbs." Then hefting herself over the edge, she disappeared beyond the rim of the hole.

It was still quite cold, particularly in so thin a fabric, and the overcast beyond the barren canopy did not help to stave off Winter. Now dampened from the cave water, she had a small time frame to gather the herbs and return lest a relentless chill set deep in her bones a fire could not alleviate.

The woods were quiet, but in the distance she could hear a man call out in the direction headed back towards the road. No one could be seen, however, and perhaps that was a good thing.

She didn't linger. While silence could indicate she was alone, it could also have been a ploy, and if she were grabbed without Ilai around, she would not escape again. Moving swiftly, she kept her eyes down, searching through the foliage for anything familiar.

During the war, she had spent time with a healer who had a library of herbology texts Ysella read through. There were books regarding medicinal herbs only found on the surface with illustrations and common locations that aided in her search. The encroaching darkness overhead rushed her hunt, and she nearly missed a patch of hanabran's lace in the rush. It's blooms were good for pain when made into a tincture, and its smell was calming.

Graciously, she found a clump of calendula not far from their cavern entrance, which carried anti-inflammatory properties. Dropping to her knees, she pulled it out by the root. A second clump was discovered a little further down the path and she took this as well. Shivering, she rose and moving swiftly, she retraced her steps back to the hole.

At the mouth of the cave, she paused. She was free. She could simply turn away. Run. She was clear of the collar, and as far as she knew, their captors had given up their search. Ilai would be too weak to climb the wall, and if she dropped the flowers down to him, he could apply a poultice and with fresh water nearby, he might be well enough to carry on in a few days. Her conscience would be unburdened.

She should have left, but instead of dropping the clumps down into the hole, she stuffed them in her bodice and descended back into the cave. Her hands stung from the cold, but she had eventually made it safely back to the cavern floor.

In her time away, Ilai did not sit idly by. A modest fire crackled in front of him where he added brush and vines collected from the cavern walls. He had completely stripped himself of his leathers, shirt and boots, the garments laid out on the ground to dry.

Removing the flowers from her bodice, she dropped to her knees by Ilai, plucking the bright orange blooms from their greenery. "No sign of our Caravan friends. I could hear them near the road, for a time, then nothing. I think they've moved on."

"If not, we have an advantage down here," he said. "We're not much in the way of climbers around here. They'd have to jump. I didn't go too far, but I'm not sure what else is down through here."

He looked Ysella over, brow furrowing in a thought. "I'll be honest," he said, "I didn't expect you to come back."

She worked without meeting his gaze, tearing a few more strips of cloth from her discarded dress. Her hands smashed the flowers, mixing it with drips of water to slowly form a paste. "I didn't expect to come back." She finally spared a glance up towards him. He was still watching her, and she quickly looked back to his angry wound.

"You are a lot of things, Ilai, but you are also the best chance I have to survive out here. I'm no monster. You would not have made the climb in your condition, and maybe you could survive for a few days, but eventually, you would die. So maybe in a way that makes me your best chance to survive, as well."

With a quivering hand, she swiped her finger through the yellow-orange paste, then turned her attention to the wound, gently pressing it into the bite marks where the pallid flesh appeared the worst. "This should work to stave off a worse infection and bring down some swelling. But you will need to rest."

Grimacing, he seemed to fight at a flinch as she worked the paste into his wounds. It would undoubtedly be more difficult to combat the pain now that the inflammation had caused the flesh to become a bit tender. She could make the tincture with the hanabran's lace now that a fire was going.

"Rest?" Ilai repeated. "We need food. Everything I had is gone. I'll need to hunt or both of us are going to be stuck in here without enough strength to get out."

"Ilai, please. That's ridiculous, and you know it. Even if you were able to, you said you didn't know the first thing about climbing. And in your condition you'd be bested by a field mouse." Wiping the excess poultice from her fingers, she took another strip of cloth, gingerly winding it around his shoulder and across his chest, looping it again until it was tight enough to tie in place. Beyond the gnarled flesh on his shoulder she saw a map of his life in scars. Lines crossed on his side, his back, his chest. Marks like stars burst where he might have been struck by arrows. The dangers of his profession lingered in healed wounds. The silvery line running down his cheek was more apparent at such closeness. It was clean, as if a blade had made the mark.

"You can tell me what to look for, and I'll find us food."

He raised his arm to allow her more room to work in wrapping his wound, but the range was limited, the muscles tightening from the strain. A wince escaped through his teeth he quickly covered with a chuckle. "Ah, we'll forego the hunting, then," he said. "Unless you want to strangle a rabbit to its death. Gathering and foraging might be better."

He brought his arm down after the makeshift bandage was secured, and nodded slightly in thanks. Falling quiet, Ysella found herself wondering what he was thinking. It must have been strange to be in a position where he wasn't in control. Perhaps there was fear there, though none showed in his features. As much as she said she couldn't survive without him, maybe in a way, he realized needed her too, now.

"Thank you," he finally murmured. "Are you only familiar with medicinal herbology? The base knowledge will still help."

"I can cook with them, too." She said, not without a touch of pride. Her smile was soft, guarded, but genuine. "I did gloss over the chapter on poisons, but I know what to avoid. I've got some hanabran's lace. If we can find a way to boil water, I can give you something to stave off the pain."

Pulling back from him, she studied her work, satisfied that it would hold, "Now then. You sit tight. I'll see what I can find up there." It had gotten cooler, and with her cloak still damp, she would need to go without. It did not escape her attention that she would need to exercise caution, and haste.

Taking a steadying breath, she grabbed one last strip of cloth, thicker than the others, and slinging it over her shoulder, she moved to the edge of the pool again and began the climb.

The change in temperature was far colder now on the surface. The fire Ilai had prepared allowed heat to collect in the small cave, but little smoke was able to flow from the opening, so they might remain undiscovered, at least. Surrounding the lip of the cave and all throughout the woods were the thick of hinterbrush pines and gray stocks of the barren trees silently jutting towards the still cold air. There were no calls like before. No caravaners in sight searching for lost goods. It felt almost too quiet in the stillness and calm.

Anxiety collecting like water in a bucket, Ysella moved from the cavern hole along the route she had traveled earlier. She had seen a few stone mushrooms and edible moss, and what might have been a clump of hen of the wood. It wasn't ideal, and without butter and stock, it would be a little like eating dirt from the path, but it was food, and that was something. She wasn't keen on laboring long, as it was, the cold bit into her bones, her teeth chattering as she struggled to concentrate on the task. She worked as quickly as her numb joints would allow, collecting enough to make a satisfying, if not earthy meal. By the time she returned to the entrance of the cave, light stole through the canopy as the moon glowed overhead, painting the forest in a broad brush of ethereal gray.

The sound of steel clattering against stone echoed up from within the cave and at the mouth, Ysella froze in surprise. Below, she could see Ilai was caught in a fight, and even from so far above she could tell it would not end well for the bounty hunter.

A caravaner slashed at Ilai's middle with a short sword, a knife held in his other hand. Ilai leapt backwards, skidding on the smooth slate, teeth gritting against pain as he held his left arm close to his body. He reached for the blade that was no longer at his side, cursing under his breath and dodging another swipe that ruffled the curls atop his head.

The hunter growled and hurled himself forward, ramming his good shoulder into the chest of the caravaner just as his sword began its descent. A cry caught in Ysella's throat as the pair crashed into the dark pool below.

From her vantage point, she could see a second man sneaking through the darkness of the deeper cave, his weapon catching a glint of firelight.

Without thinking, Ysella dropped her foraged bounty and bent, hands searching the brush until they connected with what she sought. Grabbing a fist-sized stone, she stood and hurled it down through the opening, striking the man's temple. He went down hard, and Ysella did not allow herself the consideration of what it meant. Propelled by the fear within her, she leapt over the edge and jumped towards the pool.

Icy water struck her form, constricting her every move, her senses screaming. Every move felt like she were swimming through shards of glass. Kicking her legs, she surfaced with a gasp, only to find a pair of arms at her shoulders, roping around her, fist grabbing her hair, yanking her back under with a strangled cry of panic.

The second assailant. She had not seen him resurface, but he clung to her, dragging her through the water and holding her under. Her arms flailed, her fingers clawing, feet kicking out until she slipped from his grip with enough time to breech the surface and gulp in a desperate breath.

Her head was pulled back under by her hair, senses plunging as heavy hands tangled in her curls. She tried to pry herself away and kick at her assailant, but her exertion caused her lungs to scream. Fingers raked against the skin she could contact, the feeling numbing in the cold, and she took in water.

Somewhere in the terror and waning hope, she heard another splash and a release of tension in her hair. Her imprisonment took its toll, searing her vision red at the edges.

Only it wasn't just her vision. The water itself had turned red, her mind not yet understanding what she saw as her body surfaced by the grace of cradling arms.

Sputtering, water spilled from her lips from her lung's rejection. Ilai swam her through the swirl of bloody water, her arms clinging to neck with desperation.

Defying his injury, Ilai hefted them both over the lip and onto the rocky surface of the cave and Ysella lay there still, unmoving for several seconds.

"Hey, look at me. Ysella. Look at me." A hand lifted to her cheek, cold and calloused, but gentle as Ilai guided her eyes to his. "You're safe. We need to leave," he said softly. "Are you fit to travel?"

Sucking in breath, Ysella looked to him, nodding. There would be more. There had to be, and neither of them were in any state to fight. "Let's go," she answered, teeth chattering.

Helping her to her feet he gestured to the edge of the water where a blood-slicked blade had been tossed. On the surface she could just make out the sturdy bulk of a figure, floating face down in the dark waters.

"Grab the sword," he commanded, and walked over to the second heap of a man lying next to the fire. With his fingers, he checked for breath from the man's nose, then stripped him to his undergarments.

"Get undressed," he continued, "you'll freeze to death in that."

With a shaking hand, she reached for the sword, tearing her eyes away from the still form in the pool. As Ilai began to work at the buttons of the second man, she straightened. She couldn't look at the body, but it haunted her, the mass gently floating in a swirl of his own blood.

"Did I... is... is he dead?" she whispered.

Pulling the shirt over the man's head, the hunter didn't look her way, mind focused on survival. "Does it matter?" he asked, holding out the shirt for her to take. "You need to put on dry clothes."

The man he stripped was dead, head bobbing as Ilai pulled off his boots. His eyes were lifeless and stared up into the nothingness of the cave rock illuminated by firelight. Orange danced across the lifeless features of the caravaner, shadows hollowing out his sockets in momentary flickers.

Hot tears brought warmth to her cheeks as she meekly responded. "Yes, Ilai. It matters. Please just... just tell me."

10
ILAI

"We kill to survive, Ilai. Remember how this feels."

The dagger was slick with red in Ilai's shaking hand and matched the blooming throat of a caravaner at his feet. Angered eyes softened as a last breath gurgled through the blood, and Shera clasped his hand around the dagger's hilt tightly before he could relinquish the foul blade. It felt heavy in his hand and radiated malice.

It was only one body in the masses that littered the road. The older woman turned his head so that their eyes met, her brow furrowed with severity and concern as she watched him process what he had done; what they had done. His heart pounded in his chest.

"Take in a deep breath," she advised. "In through the nose. Slowly. And release through the mouth."

He followed her instructions, his body calming. "Why must I remember how this feels?" he asked.

"We cannot forget the weight of a life. If you are going to survive out here, this will not be your last kill."

Ysella's eyes were haunted and glazed with a remembrance he knew all too well. Two dead bodies sullied the cave where they had intended to utilize as shelter from the cold night. They would invite unwanted pests.

Ilai reflected on his own experiences and felt a cold wall envelop him, shards of pain striking at his shoulder. He had been a complacent idiot allowing his thoughts to linger on his mortality. Had he been more present he would have seen the men approach. He nearly lost his life to a blade rather than sickness.

The man was limp in his hands, blood caking his temple. Removing his shirt revealed a battered body that twisted unnaturally. He was dead. Ilai could tell, but it seemed as though Ysella did not know what death looked like.

Approaching her calmly, Ilai handed over the dryer clothes. The man she struck had only partially fallen into the pool dampening the lower section of his pants.

"It does not matter," he stated softly. "You cannot dwell on things like this. Out here is about your own survival. You do what you have to."

Comfort was absent, his words unsatisfying as she stared at the offered clothes. "It won't be a pretty fit, but it will keep you from freezing," he said.

She moved instinctively, her expression showing her partial return from her thoughts as she reached for the shirt. "Turn around," she said quietly.

With a nod he turned and kneeled back down where the man laid and unbuckled his boots and trousers. "The pants definitely won't fit you, but we can hold them up with the belt and make another hole if we have to. Don't forget to take off your stockings and let your feet dry."

He rifled through the pockets and pouches and tossed them back without looking. He had a tin of leaves that smelled good for tea, and a few pieces of copper knuckles on him.

"How are you feeling?" he asked as he picked up his own drying clothes. They were still damp in a few places, but dry enough to suffice for a trip elsewhere.

"I don't know how to feel," she admitted. He could hear the jingling of the belt buckle behind him. "Frightened, I suppose… Cold."

The jingling continued, and he saw the belt held out to his periphery. "It'll need another hole," she informed.

He took the belt in hand without a glance towards her, and he held the length in front of him to see where to create the new hole. "When you were top side, did you see any worn paths or another place we could use as shelter?" With a steady push, the peg of the buckle pierced through the worn leather. "We may still have some time to look. I'm not entirely sure where we are exactly, but we are either close to the Wayward, or too far to bother. If there's a path, it could be the former."

Holding the belt back out for Ysella, he surveyed the cavern again, noting the darker portion where it opened to a smaller tunnel.

"There were a few paths," Ysella noted as she took the belt, "but I didn't see how far they went. I suppose this will do."

Ilai handed over the man's cloak and noted its weight to the left. From within its pocket was a metal flask that had a small amount remaining.

"Ilai," she continued with a little more hesitancy. "You can't climb. How are we going to get out?"

He held out the flask to her and shook it, the liquid sloshing within. "Do you want any before I down it?"

She took the coat instead with a quick snatch. "That is your plan? Getting drunk and scaling thirty feet to the top? You realize, of course, that is completely ridiculous? What about the caves? Do they go any deeper?"

He laughed and unscrewed the cap, taking a sip of the awful contents. It was a crude spirit with no quality in taste, and burned harder than U'gul. Grimacing, he downed the remainder quickly. It would surely dull his pain enough for him to be unburdened. "Yes. That is the plan. They came through those tunnels. It's just a matter of determining where."

Stooping down, he retrieved his shirt and slipped it back on, adorning his leathers once again. "Don't forget the sword," he reminded, and rung out the water from his cloak and rolled it over.

Her hands wrapped around the sword's hilt as she lifted the weight with all her strength and held it out to him. "Ilai," she said hesitantly. He watched her look from the sword to the man that lay in a heap on the rocks. She held the blade as though it were cutting through her.

He rose and carefully took the sword from her hands, her eyes fixating on the pool where the more obvious dead floated at its surface, red wreathing his form like woven ribbons. Her grasp was weak, and he returned the blade to its pilfered holster.

"Thank you," she said. "You saved my life."

She subverted his expectations once again. Ilai gathered the remnants of her black velvet dress and wrapped it in his cloak, his gaze diverting away from the woman who threatened his resolve. The contents of the flask had made his body feel light and the pain in his arm subsided. Even when sober, he knew their dynamic had changed, and that frustrated him.

"We should not linger," he said, dismissing the thanks. She had saved his own life, too, but admitting it out loud would be a weakness he couldn't afford. Already his mind was toying with the edge of guilt.

He did not wish to dwell on this fact. He did not want to admit that he had failed on the best job he could have found. The payout was so significant, and he was letting it fall through his fingertips through her good nature.

Setting off through the tunnels, Ilai tried his best to track the route the caravaners had used to gain entry. It was disappointing to leave behind such a perfect shelter. Before the dead bodies, it had a pool of fresh water and a solid enclosure that contained the heat from the fire. As soon as they left the enclosure it felt like he walked through a wall of ice.

Smaller crystals lined the tunnel walls intermittently, refracting what little light filtered through. The path wound and sloped upwards until it narrowed and fanned back out into another cavern space just a bit wider than the last. Dim moonlight filtered through the gray clouds and gently poured into the space from an opening just above a steep incline.

"Looks like a better way out," he said, and motioned upward. "Ladies first?"

She glanced to the opening with a small, faint smile. "You might still want to go ahead of me. It's steep, and if you slip, I can..." Looking him over, she blinked, then laughed softly. "Well, I guess I won't be able to catch you, but I can try."

Cradling the rolled-up garments under his injured arm, Ilai cautiously tested the slope with a firm grip to a jutting rock, his boots secure against the stone. It was a careful sort of climb, and luckily one at an angle that did not feel too straining.

Or perhaps the alcohol was at work. He felt like he could move at the shoulder a bit more with only the slightest hint of pressure, but he held enough of a mind not to test the theory in full. In the last stretch, he threw the garments out onto the woodland floor and used both arms to hoist himself out of the cave, still favoring his left side. His theory proved incorrect as pain coursed through his arm and down his back. Ilai quickly pulled himself inward as soon as he surfaced and turned back towards the opening.

"Come on, then," he called down, holding out his right hand towards her in encouragement. His shoulder was throbbing and annoying at this point. "I'll help you in the last bit."

Ysella followed his moves carefully, her feet working against the path he had made ahead of her. Only at the top did she reach for the offered hand. They weren't necessarily out of danger. The men from the caravan had come from somewhere, and there was a chance there might be more.

"How's your shoulder?" she asked. "Alright to keep going?"

Ilai could feel the burning fatigue of his muscles and an ache that threatened his range of motion. All the events they suffered had caused neglect that would take at least a full day to recover. He could barely push himself up from the ground as his affliction protested in the exertion.

"I might have had a bit too much," he said to excuse his struggle, and then feigned a grin to match. He was barely tipsy from what little drink was in that flask. "I can keep going. The question is: can you keep up?"

Ysella held out her small, dirtied hand towards him. The events had disheveled her further, griming her up to look like a vagabond, perhaps even a Lander. There was dirt caught in the beds of her nails and the caravaner's attire were like filthy pieces of cloth draped over her frame.

"You are a ridiculous man, Ilai," she said. Her words were far more educated than a Lander's, and her tone smoother and inviting. She looked at him expectantly, her hand beckoning for his. "And you're roughly the size of a bear. I cannot carry you. And we'll freeze to death out here if you pass out."

It was curious after her statement towards his stature, and he canted his head with a grin. "You mean to keep me stable?" He playfully pushed her hand away with a sigh. "I won't pass out from drinking. I did not have enough for that. Come now. Show me where you found a good path."

He didn't like the way her body recoiled as he rejected her gesture. "We'll need to backtrack a little, but it's this way," she said as she motioned around a bend. "Have you any idea where we are? Or where the nearest town might be?"

Thick overcast veiled the evening light completely, but there was still enough to see. The constant cloud coverage was what gave the land its name, and all that was missing was a bit of rain or snow. Ilai couldn't fully gauge the hour, but there was a spot within the clouds that seemed a bit brighter suggesting a thin swath of coverage.

"I can take a guess," he admitted. "I feel we're close to the Wayward. It's an inn along one of the main roads. There may be a road sign nearby if we can make it to a road. How far back is the path?"

"Not far," she advised, her eyes searching their surroundings as she recalled her steps. "Maybe a few minutes' walk."

She looked back down the mouth of the cavern they crawled from, her eyes roving over the lip that looked like a yawning creature melting into a grey-green sea. As her head turned, her feet carried her through the memory of her once-trodden path that narrowed through brambles and widened into clearings where the trail was nearly lost or obscured by overgrowth and tree roots. There was a point where the path looked to completely end, but she found it again a few paces beyond an overturned tree.

Ilai was able to keep pace with her recounted steps. Her tempo was purposeful as she guided them northeastward. She seemed to have a keen memory given how foreign the lands looked at night.

His wound angrily reprimanded him with radiating, annoying pain, and he held his arm close to his body, his thoughts consumed with the management of its pain. Each minute, the air chilled further, and they had only their exertion to thank for warmth.

An hour's walk eventually led to a common road. Shallow grooves worn in by passing carts upon the narrow dirt road showed recent travel, likely by merchants or traders given the lack of multiple tracks. Markers would be common along a road such as this, and Ilai took the lead.

"How are you faring?" he asked without slowing. He felt as though he could collapse if he paused for even a moment. Nausea threatened his insides and caused his entire body to shake.

"I'm alright," she responded, her arms clinging to her slight form. She was limping again, her leg wound likely aching with the cold. "And your shoulder?"

"It's still attached," he responded lightly, hoping his air would cull further concern. It took a few minutes to find the first sign posted between a split in the road. Posts were maintained by knowledgeable travelers, often caravaners, resulting in boards that varied in shape and legibility. For the most part, they were engraved and spelled correctly.

The post displayed several names nailed to the sturdy wood that stood a good foot above his height. Two names down from the top was the name "The Wayward" in red with yellow paint in the engraved letters. The side to his right was cut to a point to indicate direction.

"There," he said as he pointed to the sign. "It's down this road. They'll have food and hopefully a bed available. It's a frequented establishment as it's right where roads converge."

Despite all his focus on each step, he could sense his body's decline and subsequent shut down. He couldn't determine how far the journey would be. His thoughts were on how his knees shook and gave with his weight, and he had to fight against his body's want for collapse. This was a danger born of stupidity, and yet he could not bear to reveal it to his captive.

He felt cold and hot and all his mind could think about was rest. Every bed of moss or nook between tree roots looked opportune. His eyes felt as heavy as his body, and the world pulled him downward.

But it was a gentle touch that prevented his full descent, his mind honing in on the strange sturdiness it provided. "Lean on me if you must," Ysella offered softly. "We'll get there."

Reluctantly, he accepted the aid. The burden of his actions led him to this failure. His weak body could barely attempt to pull himself up to a better posture or prevent his boots from skidding along the dirt road. His gait shuffled, and with each hitch he contemplated his moves and how he could have fought better against the worgs, or at least anticipated their attack.

Each step grew more laborious as his strength waned rapidly. The only sensation that reached him was her hand gripping his right tricep, while the rest of his body was consumed by ache and longing.

A nice bed would do wonders, plush and warm. He could skip the meal, for now, as the nausea did not greet a hungered mind favorably. The comforts of safety and the assurance of good medicine was just ahead.

His vision was clipped with brief moments of recollection. The road led towards a large establishment three stories high and built wide with river stone and thick wood. A stable housed a few horses and a couple of carriages, and he could smell the familiar scents of bread and hay.

"Ask for Sabin," he said wearily, his body fully giving out just as the roads converged. He couldn't recall how he reached the door or how he was able to cross the threshold, and he barely registered the arm around his back.

It was quiet inside with a few patrons in clusters around the large hearth. A fire gently crackled in the fireplace where a lady stoked the embers and placed another log upon the grate. Her identity was difficult to discern in his state, but he felt his lips move and the woman's attention turn to look at Ysella first. It looked like Ryla, the matron of the establishment.

Ryla rushed past them, and Ilai felt the cold stone floor press against his cheek. He was still conscious, and the pressure his weight placed on his shoulder shocked him to clarity long enough to hear the voice of the Wayward's owner, Rusty.

"Drag him this way," Rusty said with his familiar tone of disappointment. He felt the man's thick hand reach under his torso. "Is he still awake?"

"I can make it," Ilai muttered, but the man pointedly laughed.

"Suit yerself," he said, and released his steadying hold. "You two get robbed? I don't want any trouble here."

Fire shot through Ilai's elbow and down his back, blurring his vision with a white veil as he fought for his balance. Within his mind, he heard a familiar voice chiding him for his stupid state.

"I thought I taught you better," the memory echoed in his mind.

He couldn't remember certain features anymore. Her face was vague with dark eyes he couldn't quite shape. There were folds from aging that laid close to her lashes when her brow furrowed, and the lines between her brows lingered. She had thin lips. He could remember that, yet he forgot where the faint scar dipped the ridge of her lower lip.

Time caused memories to fade without warning, and in what felt like his final hours, he did not wish to face the end with poor recollection of the one person that mattered to him.

"Worgs." Ysella's voice was sharp against his thoughts as she tried to cull Rusty's concerns. "No trouble."

Ilai managed to steady himself on his own, just as he promised. A sturdy wooden wall supported his weight as they waited for the Wayward's owner to unlock a door.

"Don't suppose you got any silver knuckles on you?" Rusty asked, and opened the door for the pair.

"Where's Sabin?" Ilai asked, and the older man rolled his eyes as he turned away. The hunter flashed a playful smirk towards Ysella who looked less than amused as they entered their room.

His hands gingerly lowered himself onto the nearest bed still in fear of the nausea and feverish aches. "That was Rusty," he explained. "He owns the Wayward. Go and eat. I'll be in here."

He could finally allow himself to let go and rest. Sabin would come into the room at any moment to tend to the likely infection festering in his shoulder. Resting back against the head board, he worked at releasing the tension in his joints, but his upper body would not relent.

Confidence waned, marred by the pain that coiled his body tight. His mind reminisced on all the relationships he kept at a distance. Sabin knew of him only because of Shera, and any respect likely died with her. The healer would possibly be as exasperated as Rusty, his concerns towards what conflict may be in Ilai's wake rather than the state of his life.

"I'll wait here," Ysella said. "We don't seem to fare well separated."

He desired her to leave to spare him the embarrassment of his declining state. Heaviness drew his lids downward, and his fever threatened to shake his entire body. His death would lack interest or glory or anything worth a tale in the candlelight of the Caves. Ysella would be the only one to recant his tale, and it would likely not be favorable.

Her words were easily imagined by the hunter. "Cruel as a worg," he imagined she would say. "A man lacking compassion or empathy. He died because he was arrogant and overconfident in himself."

Unworthy of pilgrimage or tribute. He did not yet deserve a candle for his name.

Twenty heads of gold. The diplomat's bounty would have provided him enough to become a laerd himself. He could have bought land and lived out the rest of his days content and in solitude. Every job he took only gave enough to scrape by with what little skills he carried.

Ilai turned his head to look at his acquisitions. That was what she was despite her noble efforts. Their agreement would not serve her if he were dying.

"Tell Sabin what you are," he said. "He can get you home safe."

11
YSELLA

Shifting, Ysella moved closer with a twinge of hesitation, settling down on the edge of his bed. "I could have left a hundred times, Ilai. I still don't know why I haven't. Not having answers is bothersome. These people, the ones who placed the bounty on me, they're after something. Something more than just my soul, and whatever they want, they won't stop if I go home. I need you, Ilai. I need your help." A thought drifted her attention, one that had been gnawing at her since their escape from the wagon. He deserved little concerning compassion, having been the source of her present struggles, yet her conscience wouldn't rest easy.

"If I'm honest, I don't particularly enjoy the idea of leaving, and wondering if... if you made it through."

As he attempted to respond, a man entered the room clad in simple robes carrying a basket of supplies. He was slender, with dark burnished skin, golden in the candlelight. His hair was cropped short, a close beard rounding out his narrowed features. The robes draped on his form were elegant in their simplicity, made with a breathable fabric and layered for the colder weather. The cloth sash around his waist was a dusky blue and held by a thick brown belt with loops potentially to house a scabbard. When he looked at her, he flashed a warm smile. "When I was told you were back and in bad shape with a woman," he said, giving Ilai a pat on his uninjured shoulder, "I was hoping it meant you'd retired, settled down, and gotten fat."

"Just dying, Sabin," Ilai joked and laid back on the mattress with a grimace.

Pulling up a chair, Sabin motioned for Ysella to sit. He was an older man with more greys in his hair than wrinkles on his features. The golden brightness in his eyes refracted light like polished gold. "Take a seat," he said. "My name is Sabin Akav. Is there a name I may call you by?"

Sabin was a Maldviri practitioner of the magic known as Inner Light. They were an uncommon people in Edros, usually passing through on holy missions. From what she had read in her studies, Maldvir was a large country with the most concentrated human population in the world. Their lands were so varied they were self-sustaining for centuries. It was a strange, beautiful land, with traditions and customs even she didn't fully understand.

Shifting from the edge of the bed, Ysella moved to the chair, not fully realizing how uncomfortable she was until she leaned against its sturdy back. She had been too long without food, without fresh water, without sleep.

"Ysella of House Ronasin," she answered, pinching the bridge of her nose. "His shoulder. That's the worst of it. We were attacked by worgs. I think it was last night? Perhaps two nights ago? I can't recall."

Sabin's rummaged through his basket for a leather roll tied neatly and tooled with angular patterns. "Laura?" Sabin called out towards the hall, and in moments a young girl appeared dutifully in the doorway. "Would you please fetch these two a plate of food? I believe your mother has some left over."

"Yes, sir!" the girl said with enthusiasm, and rushed down the hall.

"Ysella," Sabin repeated thoughtfully. "Bastillos defines its feminine names with repeated consonants."

"An astute observation," Ysella remarked. "You must be well traveled. I'm afraid I don't know the naming conventions of Maldvir."

"Well traveled? No." Sabin chuckled and motioned for Ilai to sit upright. "It's a pleasure to meet you, Ysella. Ilai, are you able to take off your shirt?"

Reluctantly, Ilai pushed himself up from the bedding and gingerly removed his torn leather jerkin and shirt. The wound on his shoulder was aggravated, the makeshift bandages of Ysella's torn dress now sticky with his blood. Sabin peeled the bandages back with a pair of metal sticks joined with a hinge. Ysella recognized it as forceps commonly used by healers.

The dim light of the cave had shielded her from the severity of Ilai's wound. Within the bright light of the lanterns in the room, she could see the shreds of skin and the deep, red lines where the jaw had secured its hold. Calendula paste crusted the edges and over the more shallow portions of the wound. There were clear signs of infection in its infancy within the deeper crevices.

"Ah! Calendula?" Sabin said as he uncorked a potent bottle of alcohol. "Are you a healer, then? It looks like Ilai is indebted to you."

It was an odd thing to acknowledge - such a debt. Sabin was ignorant to their former dynamic. Ilai was her captor, and it was a very strange act to save him. Her intent was never to gain leverage or debt, and she didn't believe his heart could be humbled, even if that had been her goal. She had saved his life because it was the right thing to do, but she didn't expect Ilai to honor that account.

"Don't tell him that," she murmured instead.

Sabin soaked a cloth with alcohol, wiping the blood away and cleaning the deeper punctures on Ilai's back and shoulder as he spoke. "So you're from Bastillos. What brings you to the Grey Hinterlands?"

He handed over a different bottle for Ilai to drink from. Ilai remained quiet, head hanging low with dark curls flowing over his face. His muscles were tense, perhaps anticipating the sting of Sabin's work so he wouldn't flinch. His only movements were to take an occasional sip of the spirit.

"I'm a diplomat," she answered. "Ilai was escorting me when we were attacked. It's been an interesting few days."

She was unsure why she lied for the hunter. Maybe it was out of pity, or perhaps she feared that Sabin might not heal him if he knew what Ilai was. Did he already know? They have a history, after all. Either way, the words came out without thought, and it left her avoiding the Maldviri's gaze.

Sabin's brow creased, though he did not make any comment. Concentration honed his attention as he prodded Ilai's shoulder eliciting a grimace from the hunter. "The state of Edros is not much of a concern to the residents of the Grey," Sabin said as he soaked a needle and thread in the alcohol. "But they're all a prideful people that don't like to admit they rely on the trade to and from Bastillos. The upper Laerds Lands have some trade agreements with the orcish settlements or Ithrad. The majority of the lands, however, need Bastillos."

She expected a scoff from the hunter. His argument from the start had been that his people were removed from this conflict. In all her studies, she knew the Grey Hinterlands was framed by land just as unforgiving as the one they occupied, and relied heavily on trade. All their laerds had their own trade agreements, which all included Bastillos.

"When is your anticipated arrival?" Sabin asked Ysella. "Perhaps I can arrange a courier to send word of a delay for you."

"Tonight, I believe." Ysella cast her eyes to the window where the darkness of night presented a blackened void. What day was it? "The meeting isn't going to happen, though. My colleague is likely in the same predicament I'm in, and if neither of us show up, well, let's just say that we needed to be there."

The repercussions of her absence swallowed her as if the darkness outside could suck her consciousness straight through the glass. She hoped Rotheel at least made it, despite his bounty.

"Will he be alright?" Ysella asked as she nodded to Ilai.

Ilai's head lowered, bottle resting on his knee as he lolled in place. "He'll be fine, I think," Sabin said, and placed a hand on Ilai's good shoulder. "Turn around. I need to stitch the back."

As Ilai complied, Sabin helped situate the hunter to face the wall. The Maldviri eyed Ysella with a knowing look. "I know what he is," he said, and leaned over to begin suturing the worst of the wound. Some of the flesh was too far gone, and he removed it carefully with a clean pair of scissors. "And the bruising on your neck is telling, Ysella. I will liberate you, if you ask it of me. Your subterfuge would require permission, despite my knowing."

While she did not know the nature of his relationship with Ilai, she felt relief her instincts were correct in its assumption, especially given the owners of the Wayward were not overly fond of him. Had she not defied her gut instinct with a lie, she might have felt a little triumphant in her skills of deduction. Embarrassment flushed her cheeks, a light grimace pulling at her lips, fingers brushing against her bruised throat.

"There are worse things than worgs in this world, sir," Ysella finally answered. "If you know what he is, then you might be able to ascertain why I may not wish to be liberated. He may be dangerous, but he is also the only chance I have to get to the people who may have forced Edros to war. If I were liberated, I would have to take that journey on my own. That bounty will still exist, and from what I understand it's quite significant. More will come looking for me, and I don't imagine I can work my way into their debts quite so effectively."

Sabin did not retort or argue, nor did he provide any thoughts to her logic. The rhythm of his sewing maintained, head canting as he followed the jagged lines of the torn flesh.

Laura returned to the room with a tray of food and a sheepish smile, head inclining towards Ysella as she set down the tray on the end table between the beds.

"Thank you, Laura," Sabin said without looking up from his work. "And tell your parents I will handle the cost."

"Yes, sir!" Laura exited, glancing sidelong to Ilai as she passed.

"There are worse things here than worgs," Sabin eventually agreed. "It's why I've dedicated myself to the Wayward. They're the only stop for miles around here, and along a common road frequented by caravaners and merchants and Laerd Trevan's watchers. I have connections - good connections - that can see you homebound. You must forgive my insistence. It is part of my oaths."

Ilai's posture slumped and lethargically leaned forward. Ysella couldn't tell if he was still conscious, but she grabbed the bottle of spirit so it would not spill on the linens. Sabin tied off the final suture and cut the string, the closed wounds painting a clear picture of the worg's jaws.

The final task was to dress the wound, and Sabin had a pile of fresh bandages rolled in a satchel. She was reminded of the soiled bandage around her leg, its fabric heavy and annoying.

"I can't go home," Ysella admitted, and leaned down, pulling up the too-large trouser leg to remove the wrapping from her own wound. The lines were irritated, the moisture preventing the wounds to close.

"You're injured as well?" Sabin asked, and quickly finished wrapping Ilai's wound. He guided the hunter's head to the pillow. "You should have said something. Let me look at it."

Ysella turned in her seat and held the trouser up to her knees. It would have been unbecoming if she were in a dress. The pants made her feel more modest in the act of exposing her skin.

Sabin's hand gently guided her leg to turn to the light, and he cleaned the wound with a fresh cloth and alcohol. She sucked in a wince and fought the urge to recoil from the sting.

"Why can't you go home?" he asked.

"If I return now, I will be an outcast," she explained. "This journey was meant to prevent a war and if I've failed. I will be a catalyst in something that Bastillos cannot hope to win."

Ysella's breath wavered in an exhale, hesitation pausing her words. "Six years ago, there was a rebellion in Bastillos. Are you familiar with it?"

"I am," Sabin said. He applied a paste to her cuts and wrapped the leg.

"They came in through my family's home," Ysella explained. "The war... it was everywhere, but it was not in Lumin until the end. They came in from our mirrorlight tunnels. They chose our house because of its location close to one of the gates, and because we had less staff. The queen died that night."

"It would have happened regardless," Sabin countered.

"My point is, this is just the same," she continued. "My family faced shame for years. My parents nearly run from their jobs. I cannot return home knowing I have started a war that will surely collapse Edros's economy. I cannot return home empty handed. I need to know who placed this bounty and why, or I have nothing."

Securing the bandage, Sabin rose and threw a thick blanket over Ilai. "You do not believe your family would be grateful for your return?" he asked as he sat on the bedside.

Lowering her pant leg, Ysella sat back in her seat heavily. "My sister, Odessa. She looks up to me, at least before her thoughts rise to the clouds."

"Then you have *something*," Sabin offered, but quickly continued to avoid retort. "Your conviction is admirable, and I will not get in its way. I urge you to remember your sister as you brave the dangers of the Grey. There is no shame in living."

Shifting, she leaned to collect one of the bowls the young girl had dropped off. While she was starving, and the smell alone was enough to set her stomach growling, her appetite had waned with the honesty of her words. She hadn't allowed herself to consider it, but now that she had said it aloud, it resonated loud and clear within her.

"Thank you, for your kindness, Sabin of House Akav."

The man chuckled. "That is generous of you to address me so, but Maldvir does not have houses like Bastillos. We are all given family names passed down from our fathers. No one is without a last name."

"My apologies," Ysella said, but Sabin waved a dismissive hand.

"Maldvir is a long way from Edros. I can't expect our ways to be known around here, especially since my people have been notoriously reclusive."

"What brought you to Edros?" she asked.

"Are you familiar at all with the religious aspects of Inner Light?" he asked, and she shook her head. "We gain our connection to this magic through good deeds. Through moral rights and ethical practices. It's a delicate thing, as it is in our nature to individualize morals, and so our journey is constantly understanding what is truly good to bring out our Inner Light.

"Our antithesis is Shadow, and we have been at war with it since the beginning. It is part of the reason why we are so contained within our lands, but some of us are called to aid elsewhere. It is our belief that our Inner Light is connected to a guidance system that leads us to where we need to go. I hopped on a boat with nothing but an inkling and set sail first to Thallas and found myself journeying up and through the Twisted Woods and back down through the Grey Hinterlands."

"And you stopped here."

"It seemed right," he said. "It felt like I needed to stay here. I haven't been pulled anywhere else since."

"Do you have family back home that would miss you, too?" Ysella asked, and he smiled.

"Indeed," he said, "and we write to each other as much as we can."

Smiling gingerly, she picked at the meal in her lap, forcing herself to take a bite. Ilai was certainly asleep now, and looking at him, she was struck by how ordinary he seemed - just a man, caught in the confines of a cold and heartless wilderness. He did not seem to have someone to miss him. "It's little wonder the way they turn out."

"We're all a product of our upbringing," Sabin said solemnly. "Landers are as cold as Winter's bite, and harsh to outsiders because they've learned what it takes to survive out here. It took me a year to get Laura to smile, and I've got some very good jokes to tell. But it eventually happened with some persistence and nurturing. Do you think Bastillos could warm the Grey Hinterlands to change and fully integrate into Edros, or do you think they will resist it forever?"

"I honestly don't know." She studied the hunter, eyes trailing the bandaged shoulder, then shifting to each of the scars carved along his back like a twisted map of his own fraught history. "If you had asked me even a day or so ago, I might have thought no. But I'm starting to see that people have the capacity for change, even when you don't think it possible. All I know is if it comes to war, Bastillos is going to need all the help we can get."

"There's a darkness that looms over Bastillos," Sabin warned. "I can sense it all the way out here when I meditate. I know the whole of Edros is a little more lenient towards Shadow Magic and its use, but I would still advise you to be cautious. It is a magic known to corrupt. Has there been a rise in such magic in Bastillos?"

Frowning, she returned to picking at her plate, taking another reluctant bite between thoughts. Shadow Magic was used during the civil war on both sides, but not to any concerning degree. In the entirety of the war, she could only recall witnessing or hearing of it twice.

"There were some that used it during the war," she answered. "There's been no rise."

He frowned. "Strange. If that is the case, then, they are operating in secret, and have yet to reveal themselves. Bastillos may face more danger from within. I'll send word to my brother. He's been traveling through Krei when last he wrote. I'll ask him to check in on your people."

"That is kind of you," Ysella said. "You've done so much already. Is there anything I can do for you?"

"Rest," he said. "Wash your leg in the morning and let it air so it can close. You should be right as rain within a week."

Boisterous chatter filled the main hall of the Wayward, breaking the quiet with a lively energy that felt out of place after the previous calm. Sabin stood to close the door, eyeing the newcomers outside their room curiously. "Watchers," he informed, and looked back over to Ysella. "Is there anything you wish to know? They're good for gossip. Constantly hearing rumors in their line of work."

"They'll rob you blind if they pick up on your curiosities," Ilai murmured from his pillow, stirring and shifted his position to better look at the two. "They're a gambling sort."

"Could you see if they've heard anything about Rotheel of House Degent?" she asked, ignoring Ilai's warning. "He apparently has a bounty on his head as well, but I don't know if anything has happened to him."

"Get some rest. Both of you." Sabin inclined his head and took his leave, shutting the door behind him.

With Sabin gone, Ilai rolled over lethargically. "So, what now?" he asked as he pushed himself up to a sit. "You can't go home, or so you said. What are you going to do now?"

"So you were listening?" Ysella set the half-eaten bowl aside and leaned forward, voice quiet. "We're going to figure out who wants this war in Edros and why." She braced herself for an argument, her mind sharpening to steel in preparation of her counter.

He wearily rested against the wall and their eyes met without a challenge. Nothing was said between them despite his contemplative look. It could have also been judgement.

"That is," Ysella continued, "if you're willing to help me. I can't do it alone, Ilai. You know I can't."

"The caravan stole my weapons," he said. "I've only got one good arm, and we've no metal to even purchase a little knife. I think I managed to pilfer a few copper knuckles. Enough for a drink and maybe some food. I don't see how I can help you. I need to find work, and you need to go home. Bastillos can better help you."

Each word pulled Ysella's lips downward in disappointment. He was giving up, but she would not. "Then we find work! We do what we need to instead of giving up! When you were listening in, did you hear the part where I can't go back home? Why I can't? And I won't! I'll send a courier to my family and ask for gold if need be. They'll gladly give it for this cause—"

"Don't!" Ilai sat forward in a rush, eyes open and alert. "Don't do that."

"Why, because I'd actually be doing something?"

"No. Couriers are intercepted all the time here. Some even accept metal for the exchange of information," Ilai explained. "They'll still deliver the messages, but it will paint a target on the Wayward. Besides, I need a weapon now, not after. If you're hiring me to act as protection, I need the tools to do so. I can't be of much help to you until I line my pockets or steal a sword."

"Then what good are you?" Rising swiftly from the chair, running her fingers through her hair in utter frustration, Ysella stormed from the room. Raucous banter filled the tavern, more lively with the presence of the watchers. Three of them sat at a table across from Sabin who looked to be in the midst of an animated story. They all seemed to enjoy the tale, so transfixed on the Maldviri and his words they hardly noticed Ysella enter.

"What'd you do with the rodent?" one of the watchers asked.

"I'd've skinned it and made a hat," another said.

"I'd say he's our most regular patron!" Sabin laughed as he swooped out his arms, his eye caught the Ysella questioningly.

Ysella hesitated in the alley between tables, the harshness of her own words settling like a heavy pit in her stomach. The three watchers turned their attention towards her, curious as to why their own conversation had lulled.

"Come and sit with us," Sabin offered, and motioned to the empty chair next to him. She willed her feet to move and steeled her mind from the intimidating stares of the rough looking men across from her.

"Apologies for my intrusion, gentlemen," she said, and they chuckled lightly.

"Gentleman," one of the watchers repeated.

"I like her," another said.

"Watcher Foer, Bane, and Kavan," Sabin introduced. Foer had a broad chin and greasy hair as he removed his brimmed watcher hat and set it on the bench beside him. Bane was the thinner of the three, and also appeared to be the shortest with Kavan being taller and barrel chested.

Ilai's warnings ran through her brain, halting her introduction to form a lie. "Tarrah. A pleasure to meet you. Please forgive my impatience, but do you have any news at all regarding the Bastillosi diplomat?"

Foer scratched the stubble on his chin and leaned forward, his voice hushed. "We were just telling Sabin here about it. You'd need to be more specific on which one, though. There are two bounties out for two different Bastillosi diplomats. We've heard some things flitting about. Their journeys aren't going too well."

"Rotheel of House Degent," she said. "I'm specifically looking for information about him."

Bane held out his hand, palm upward on the table, eyes watching Ysella expectantly. "How much you can offer determines how much we can offer."

She had wished Ilai and Sabin's warnings were untrue; that they were just trying to scare or intimidate her into avoiding a source of information. All three watchers scrutinized Ysella with each passing second she didn't produce a piece of metal.

Scoundrels.

"I... I don't have anything of value," Ysella admitted. Even Ilai said he had nothing but a few copper knuckles. Would that even be enough? Down the hall, the door to their room was open, and Ilai darkened its frame as he shuffled out into the tavern light. He wore his dirty, bloody shirt, the tears around his shoulder allowing the bandages to peek through.

Sabin leaned forward to intervene the watchers' exploitation. "Tarrah, perhaps you could offer them an exchange of information. She's been traveling for some time, now, and may perhaps know something suitable to your interests."

The watchers nodded, agreeing to the terms. Bane retracted his hand. "Tell us why you're so interested in Rotheel of House Degent," he said. Kavan smirked and crossed his powerful arms over his chest.

"He's a friend of mine," Ysella admitted, though faltered in hesitation. She could continue with her lies, but she was unsure, now, if it would be a hindrance. "My name is not Tarrah. It's Ysella of House Ronasin. I am the other diplomat."

"No kidding," Kavan said as he leaned back in his seat, bushy brows lifting with interest. "You're quite a ways from your own path. Shouldn't you be in Nabannon?"

She could see Sabin's arms tense and jaw tighten, but there was only a hint of concern on his face. He did not intervene despite the internal conflict, his attention pulling to a passing form.

Ilai carried two mugs in one hand as he passed, and she caught his eyes with a curious look.

"Be careful with your intake," Sabin suggested to Ilai. "And try not to carry anything too heavy."

"It's just wine," Ilai assured as he raised the mugs in his right hand. "Though you're welcome to carry it for me if you must."

Ilai leaned over the table between two of the watchers to set down the mugs, and while Sabin laughed off the gesture, the other men were not as impressed.

"Do you mind?" the Foer asked in irritation, fingers tightening around his own tankard.

"Of course," Ilai said. With his injured arm, he reached for one of the mugs with a wince while the other slipped downward into Bane's jacket pocket. He palmed a something in his hands as he straightened. "I'll leave you to it."

"Well," Ysella started, her eyes watching Ilai leave for their room. "I was supposed to be in Nabannon, yes. I was delayed by a caravan interested in my bounty. That man-" She pointed down the hall to her room. "-helped me escape."

"Was he the cause of those bruises?" Kavan asked, nodding to her neck.

"No." The lie felt helpful this time, at least. The watchers seemed less interested in Ilai, and the trio looked between them in silent deliberation.

"I'd say that's a sufficient trade," Kavan said, and the other two nodded in agreement.

"Please understand," Sabin cut in, "that this diplomat is under my care, as well as her appointed bodyguard. You be sure to include that should you sell this information."

"Sure," Foer said. Ysella felt nausea spin her insides. She had just given away her location to other hunters; to anyone looking for her high reward.

"Last we heard, the other diplomat was picked up as well," Bane said. "Headed east across Laerd Fathgar's land towards the Scar. Alive."

Relief flooded her senses, tension releasing with a heavy, thankful sigh. "Thank Elssar, this is good news. Thank you. And thank you, Sabin, for your hospitality. I don't imagine we would have survived much longer if we had not been so close by."

Rising from her seat, she inclined respectfully to the men at the table, and excused herself to her room, taking her mug of wine with her to celebrate.

12
ILAI

Maldviri of Inner Light never held grudges or counted favors, their kindness irritating to Ilai's conscience. Sabin was a good man, his intellect allowing him to navigate the harshness of the Grey without finding himself dead in a ravine. Ilai had never witnessed the man use his magic. Apparently its use was also sacred. If he ever had to defend himself, it would be with his hands, avoiding lethal blows unless absolutely necessary.

The signs of his good soul were evident in the golden light of his eyes that glistened like disks of metal, his skin flecked with the same warmth and light. He was a stark contrast to Ilai; to most of the Grey. His vibrancy was to his very core, and perhaps the only sunny disposition in all the Laerds' Lands.

Rusty always believed Ilai took advantage of Sabin's nature, and if he were honest with himself, it was likely true. Sabin was a convenient means of survival. If he needed anything, the Maldviri would give it, though it would come with some lesson or thought to provoke introspection. While Sabin did not agree with Ilai's choice in profession, he'd never tell him to stop. They believed in free will.

Ilai's shoulder was stiff and throbbed a constant reminder of his actions. The worg attack could have happened any night regardless of bounty, but he happened to find himself a woman just as kind as Sabin to use all the same. He held little regard to others. Survival had been everything his entire life. Selfishness was how one survived, and how everyone operated in the Grey.

Everyone but Sabin and Ysella, it seemed.

Ysella's words drove through him like a hot knife to his heart. "Then what good are you?" she asked. She struck through his well-crafted veil and frayed the threads of his composure, storming from the room in a fury that lashed his heart in her wake.

Useless. Worg.

The door remained open with the inviting banter of patrons. Ysella headed towards a table with three watchers entertained by what appeared to be a grandiose tale from Sabin.

Ilai knew the layout of the Wayward, and he looked to his window just at the end of his bed. He could leave and be rid of these burdens and find another job in the next town. Ysella could ask for Sabin's aid and he'd gladly give it. The man was more equipped for such a venture, if he'd ever leave the Wayward.

He caught Sabin's gaze, golden eyes inquisitive as a frustrated Ysella lowered herself in the seat next to him. Ilai shook his head in quiet answer and grabbed his shirt.

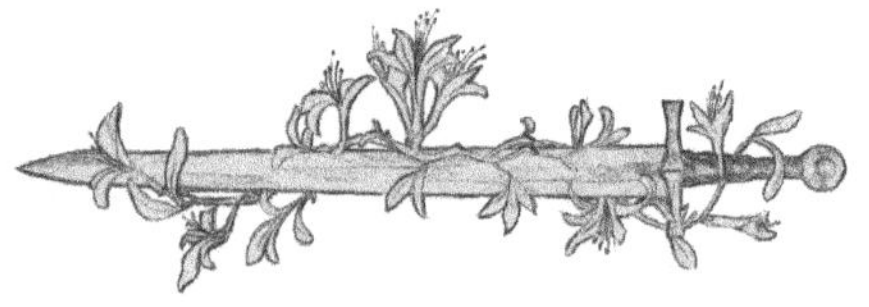

"You run if it means your life," a familiar voice echoed in his memories. *"You don't if it means a friend's."*

"What if it means we both die?" he asked in a snarky challenge. The logic made no sense to his young mind, especially when he hadn't known a friend who would do the same. But her eyes held his with severity that challenged his playfulness and subdued the competition.

"Do you not have confidence in my teachings?" she countered calmly. He shook his head sheepishly, but with rebellion. "Heed my lessons and you will be able to defend yourself and those you care about. How do you think I have lived this long?"

"But you've been alone."

The regret in his words was as immediate as the hurt that crossed her features as she turned towards the firelight. Her braided hair faced him with ribbons of grey woven through dark strands.

"I'm sorry—"

"I will forgive your ignorant words this once, Ilai." Her voice was calm and even, her back still facing him, and he dared not to look at her. "When we met I was alone because I was captured, just like you. I hope one day you will find someone to care about. I don't want you to become complacent in your solitude. That is what makes criminals and caravaners. But not us."

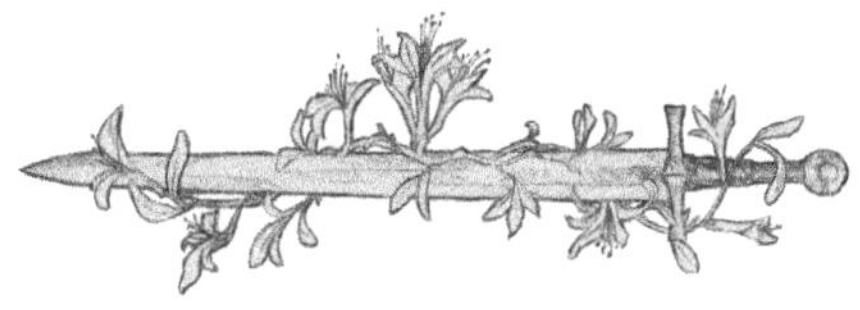

Rusty handed Ilai two mugs of wine with a cautious glance. "You sure you got it?"

Ilai hooked his fingers between the handles of both mugs, holding them up with his good arm. "It's why I asked for mugs."

"Don't start anything."

"I don't plan to," Ilai assured.

"You never plan to, but the last time you were here we ended up with two broken tables and food all over the floor. Potatoes were mashed between the wood slats."

"I promise," he said as he turned from the bar.

The three watchers had their backs to the bar, but he could tell by their silhouette they were larger folk, save for one. Watchers tended to be a combination of muscles, intelligence, and cunning, all of which made for too great of a power dynamic between them and the Landers. Ysella's frown was mirrored by Sabin as they conversed quietly with the imposing trio.

It didn't seem like she was getting the information she wanted, but perhaps he could make the endeavor worth their time.

"Be careful with your intake." Sabin's warning was met with a wry smile. "And try not to carry anything too heavy."

Ilai lifted the mugs in his right hand in a display of his dexterity. "It's just wine, though you're welcome to carry it for me if you must."

There was enough of a gap between two of the watchers to lean through and set the mugs in front of Sabin, the man laughing.

"Do you mind?" The watcher with the broad chin looked at Ilai incredulously, his body leaning back while he motioned towards the table to insinuate their ongoing business. The other two shook their heads, one waving his hand through the air as if shooing a fly from his face.

"Of course." Ilai reached back out for one of the mugs with his left arm, the stiffness protesting at the weight of the drink. "I'll leave you to it."

In one fluid motion, he slipped his right hand into the smaller watcher's pocket, fingers brushing against the cinched brim of a weighted pouch. With practiced ease, he loosened the opening just enough to slip in two fingers, rake out a few metal knuckles, and let them fall into his own pocket.

Glancing to Ysella, he offered a small nod that could have been mistaken as a farewell. He did not linger to gauge her understanding, and retreated to his room, setting his mug on the nightstand.

The pilfered metal were silver pieces the average size of a man's knuckle. Knuckles and fingers were the most common for people to carry on their person.

Anything larger and a smith is commissioned to mold the metal into the sizes most easy to carry.

Silver knuckles were good, and far better than the copper he'd lifted from the caravaner's body earlier that day.

Ysella entered, and he motioned for her to close the door. "I got four silver knuckles. Not enough to buy a weapon. We'd need a whole fist worth of silver for that. But it'll buy us food and lodging along the road. Did you learn anything useful?"

Ysella lowered herself on the bed across from his, fingers grazing over the molded metal pieces. They weren't impressive coins stamped with designs like most Edrosi currency, and they certainly weren't polished.

"Rotheel is alive," she said with a soft smile, and tentatively drank from her mug. It was a dry red wine, and she fought a grimace. "He was last seen in Laerd Fathgar's lands headed east."

"I only had the copper," Ilai explained.

"What?"

"The wine."

Ysella looked down at her mug, and then set it on the nightstand. "Oh, it's fine."

"Doesn't look like it." Ilai took a sip from his own mug. He wasn't overly fond of wine as he could never find one that tasted right. This one was just the same as all the others, its tang coating his throat and lingering with an odd aftertaste.

"It's just dry. It's fine, just not what I would get," Ysella explained, and huffed a small laugh. "Not to your taste either, it seems."

"They all taste the same to me," he admitted. "So the other diplomat is alive? You're sure?"

"He was, at least, when the watchers heard of it," she continued. "North of here. Headed east."

North of the Wayward was a vast part of the Grey Hinterlands that opened up into the Scar. Due to the canyon's reach across the land, it was unlikely whoever had Rotheel would go around. The trek down the cliff's side would certainly slow them down, but there were many paths.

"They'll take him to the Twisted Woods, right? Where you were taking me?"

"I would assume," he answered thoughtfully. Her posting merged with his in Ilai's memory. They were strikingly similar with the only divergence being an illustration of their likeness.

Ysella retreated into her mind, her small hands retrieving the mug just to have something to hold. The contents barely sloshed as she turned it with her fingers idly.

Ilai stuffed the metal knuckles back into his pocket. "If what they say is true, it's the only logical destination to the east."

"Have you any thoughts to who might have him?" she asked. "What is the likelihood that... that we might reach him before he is handed over at the tower?"

Ysella was a kind soul, as made evident by her inability to leave Ilai for her own well-being, but her heart was pulled differently when it came to Rotheel. This was no mere colleague. He could sense a closer bond within her determination.

"It's difficult to say," he answered truthfully. "We potentially have the ability to intercept them, but without knowing exactly where they are or how they're traveling, I can only guess. Are we changing our focus, then, and going after him instead?"

"Not entirely, no," she said. "I think we're capable of doing both. Rotheel is an important man. To Bastillos..."

She trailed off into the recesses of her mind, eyes glazed with thoughts she didn't share. Determination brimmed her features, pushing her brows closer together. Rotheel was a lucky man.

"Rescuing him would be in your favor as well," she added, and while she appealed to the nature in which he presented, he felt the heat of offense at his core. "You will be owed a debt two-fold. I'm sure that's better than any amount our bounties combined could award you."

And while offense was taken, there was a great appeal to those prospects. He always carried doubt there would be even one head of gold awaiting him at Ethyrnon Tower, but he had a feeling that Ysella would pay out. Another kind soul, too soft to pull from a promise.

"Traveling blindly in hopes of crossing paths won't do us much good," he said. "Our route could take us to a merge, but I can't guarantee it. We'll have to ask around as we get closer to the area. At the very least, we can confront whoever's at the end of the line. If your diplomat friend is at all as clever as you, he'd know how to get this far without his hunter killing him."

"There's a certain appeal to confronting whoever is responsible for the bounty," Ysella admitted, and removed her mug from her fidgeting hands. "I've been wanting to do so since the start. Why have you changed your mind?"

He drank from his mug to delay his response, his palette met with an affront more bitter than having to face his truths. "If it is as you promise, and your family will pay more handsomely than your bounty, then it's just the better job."

"There's no loyalty when it comes to bounty hunting?" Ysella asked. Her tone did not suggest judgement.

"The loyalty comes in metal," he explained. "Those who post a bounty must understand this. They have to anticipate any buyouts and get ahead of it, or we'll turn for the highest pay. It's just the nature of things. There are a few out there who stay loyal. But we never take the acquisition's offer."

"Isn't that what you're doing now?"

Right. She was his acquisition…

"This is different." Ilai waved a dismissive hand, and she chuckled.

Her soft laughter was soothing like creek water trickling through stone. It was cool and gentle and carried its own tune that called to his parched heart.

Drinking the awful wine was all he could do to drown the wind chimes of her merriment.

"Did Sabin suspect anything?" he asked, biting back the aftertaste of his drink.

Her smile faded. "Suspect what?"

"The theft," he reminded. "Men of Inner Light are men of morals. Stealing goes against that, and I imagine if he suspects it, he'll have me pay them back."

"I got the impression Sabin was not fond of watchers," Ysella said.

"He'd still have me pay them back," Ilai assured. "Sabin doesn't like much in the Grey, but that doesn't stop him from his moral highness."

"He seems to like *you*," she offered with a shrug.

"He's like that with everyone," he dismissed.

"I imagine he does not approve of what you do," she continued, "but it doesn't seem personal. How long have you known him?"

Counting the years were of little import to Ilai. He concerned himself with the Seasons, as they determined the harshness of the Grey, but he could only guess at how much time had passed since he met Sabin. He was not even sure of his own age.

"Long enough, I suppose," Ilai answered. "He used to disapprove of our profession until he realized the bounty hunters were doing a better job than the watchers at keeping criminals off the streets. Watchers are the lawmen of the laerds, but they're just as bad at perpetuating crime, and Sabin loves to uphold the law."

"Our?"

"Hmm?" Ilai looked at Ysella questioningly.

"You said 'he used to disapprove of *our* profession.'"

An innocent inquiry, but one Ilai quickly dismissed. "Did you tell those watchers who you are?"

She frowned at his deflection. "I had to," she admitted. "I think they already suspected. I don't imagine they would have given me the information had I not confirmed their suspicions. I had to take the risk, but Sabin said we're under his protection."

Groaning, Ilai took her mug of wine and knocked back a swig. She still did not understand her value, or perhaps she had forgotten why she was in this situation entirely. The watchers would surely carry her identity as a prized piece of information.

"We'll just be more cautious," he said. "Word doesn't travel fast out of the Wayward until people carry on their way. We've got time before rumors of your location spreads."

His mind counted the days it would take in their journey without hindrance. There were three main roads: two that curved around the Scar, and one that went through it. There were many settlements above and below, but the Cave was within the canyon close to its bottlenecked center.

His offering to Shera had been stolen by the caravaners. It was a pointless route stop now, but if they had a chance of intercepting whomever had Rotheel, they'd still need to travel that way. The village of Halvish would be a good stop in the Scar.

"Are you opposed to taking up work?" he asked. "We'll need to both pull our weight for metal. Posting boards in most towns, and not every town has a need for violence."

"I'm not opposed, no," she answered, and seemed more keen to the idea than he anticipated. "What sorts of other work is posted? I won't do anything unscrupulous."

Nobles and their big words. Unscrupulous. What does that even mean?

"Sometimes it's mucking stalls or washing bedding for an inn," he answered, hoping that wasn't whatever that word meant. "Nothing too laborious for a diplomat, and nothing like what I'll end up doing."

"I'm not perfectly useless," she muttered. "Just because I've never done it doesn't mean I can't."

Never done it? Ilai shouldn't have been shocked, but he was ignorant to Bastillos and their ways. He'd heard of laerds punishing their children with such labor as a means to humble their ego or provide a life lesson. Even with the too-large clothing swallowing her small frame, it was evident the only weight she ever lifted was herself.

"What exactly is your kind of work?" she asked. "That is, when you're not abducting diplomats."

Her ignorance to his line of work held a charm, especially when mingled with her pointed attitude. He could almost mistake it as playful despite the underlying truth. Under better circumstances, he could have enjoyed meeting her. Their dynamic now was irreparable, and this was no light banter.

It was, admittedly, disappointing.

"Odd jobs," he answered plainly. "Often more violent. They pay nicely, and I can do them. Sometimes it's handling a pack of worgs to protect livestock, and sometimes it's kidnapping a diplomat. The places that support a hunter's work either have a local contractor or a job board and we take our pick. Are you saying you'd rather do my work than something more... of your capability?"

Imagining Ysella trotting along on a dangerous bounty left Ilai hopeful she'd express disinterest in his work. Could she even hold a sword with those thin arms? While he wasn't the sole reason for her survival thus far, he knew the risks of working with someone who was not his equal or better in a fight.

He had been her once. Weak of body, strong of mind, and a burden to survival.

"I'm not kidnapping anyone," she murmured, and he huffed a small laugh. Acquisitions like hers were uncommon, and would most certainly call for a detour he did not wish to take.

The hour drew further into night, the day taking its toll heavily on Ysella's features. Her shoulders were slumped, head barely held upwards while she attempted to engage in conversation. Her words were coming out in murmurs, soft and slurred.

"We shouldn't linger," she said as she rose from her bedside. Ilai clasped his hand around her wrist to halt her from moving to the door. A sharp inhalation pulled through her nose and caused him to recoil, as did she.

"We should rest," he urged. She placed a hand to her chest to still her nerves, fingers coiling around the silver chain behind the wide collar of her shirt.

"What if the watchers figure out you're the cause of their lightened purse?" Ysella countered. "I don't think even I can talk our way out of that mess."

"Ysella, we need to rest," he reminded. "We can leave in the morning."

This was their last chance for days to sleep on a comfortable mattress, and he was still feverish from his wound. It would need to be checked before they left on their excursion through bitter cold and rough terrain. Her soft blue eyes fell on his shoulder, the shirt mangled and stained as a reminder of what presided beneath. He wasn't manipulating her kindness, was he?

"You won't leave without me?"

A strange concern given all she had gone through in the last two days. Ilai was still just a stranger, and had told her on multiple occasions to run when survival required running. He had even said he would do it without a second thought.

By this point he was sure the promised bounty was a ploy. It was too good to be true, and he had every right to abandon the acquisition in favor of his life. There was always a chance it was real. A very small chance.

His only guaranteed payout now was to ensure she made it home safely where her noble coffers could spill. She did not seem to grasp the nature of his business.

"Why would you think I would leave without you?" he genuinely asked.

"I don't know. I thought I would have left without you a hundred times by now. Yet, here I am." She returned to her bedside, hands smoothing down the trousers to her knees. "I suppose I'm not sure what to expect anymore."

She removed her shoes, hands massaging the aches and assessing the blisters and irritation, eyes heavy and threatening to close. "Good night, Ilai."

Lowering herself to her pillow, she pulled the blankets up to her shoulders, eyes closed in relief. Ilai snuffed their lamps, plunging the room in darkness with only a sliver of light cutting through from under the door jam.

He rested back on his own mattress, eyes staring up at the wooden slats in the ceiling. His throbbing arm was a reminder of a debt he should have never incurred, and perhaps it was the catalyst for accepting an acquisition's counter-offer. She could have left him to die, and she should have.

Yet she did not, and through her compassion he was able to live and work another day. Even without the promise of pay, there was a part of him that felt some deep need to honor this second chance towards her efforts.

He would not find rest easily, and gave up his attempts to sleep soundly by the early morning sun. He slipped from the room following the scents of cooked meat and earthy spice.

13
WRAITH

They called him Wraith, for that is what he was: an evil wight born from malice and magic. He never corrected the name as his true name had become irrelevant. Wraith was the last of his kind, spared for the purpose of the Tenebris. They thought they owned him. He let them believe it was so. There were mutual benefits that came with his cooperation and their illusion of control.

He traveled the Grey Hinterlands in search for his prey at the behest of his employers. These lands were rife with miscreants and vagabonds; lost souls running from turmoil in search for peace.

Turmoil was decadent.

His appearance garnered questioning stares, and he met their stares with his glowing eyes marked by the Sight of Souls. Their souls danced in their bodies like white wisps undulating through their silhouettes, pulsing with a growing fear of what his presence defined.

Two men stood from the fireside at Wraith's approach, one cautiously leaning towards his sword while the other kept his hand firmly around a chain. Behind the pair was another soul hunched next to the fire, engulfed in the expanse of blackness bathing the forest behind them.

"Best move on, stranger," the one reaching for his weapon warned. "It's two against one."

From his back, a wicked blade dimly gleamed in the moonlight, and Wraith felt its magnetism. It hungered as much as he. Jagged runes were etched into the steel spanning its length and carried down through the hilt where, at its pommel, a crystal was contained. The crystal held similar runes connected around its facets and glistened with violet strands of magic.

The two men stiffened with resolve, postures straightening at the clear message from the man with the glowing eyes. Wraith pulled back the hood of his cloak revealing long brown hair framing an angular face pulled by a grin. They did not see his magic coalesce in the night, the dark tendrils snaking through the air, connecting to their dancing shadows. He could sense their heartbeats quicken as the ethereal links pulled taut between the trio.

Fear lingered sweetly in the air, but it was not potent enough for a feast. His free hand rested on the pommel of his longsword. Wraith continued his approach, each step calm and direct. They were predictable in their reactions, pleasing him with the song of steel.

The man who offered warning pulled his sword from its scabbard, swiping it through the air with a melodious clang as Wraith met the blade with his own. They clashed in frenzied attacks, Wraith's longsword swallowing the firelight like a line of pure darkness, extending the distance effortlessly as the blade spun through the night air. His prey faltered in a parry, and the wicked sword sliced deeply into the man's arm.

Blood spilled and pooled unnaturally along the steel, pulled by the foreign runes etched along its length, and then the blood disappeared into them as if sucked through the metal.

There it was: the rushing heartbeat and the clouded thoughts that spiraled with alarm. He could feel the effects of the men's anxiety through their ethereal connection. Their swords clashed as he played with his prey, whittling away the warning man's resolve. Wraith could see the man's need to fight switch to survival, the man's eyes focused too intently on the dark sword. His footing faltered as he backed into a root hidden beneath leaves and dirt and snow.

The other man, seeing the odds turn against his companion, relinquished the chain in favor of his bow. He knocked the arrow and pulled back the string just in time to see Wraith's blade imbed into his companion's chest. With a muted crack, the man's body was pulled from view in an instant, a white light siphoning down the blade into the crystal at the pommel.

The remaining man called a name, voice laden in shock and fear as he let loose his arrow. The arrow grazed Wraith's shoulder, the force pushing him towards the tree. It was a terrible shot that only served to draw blood, and as Wraith turned he could sense the man's terror spike. He abandoned his bow and ran, arrows clattering around their campsite.

Wraith smiled brightly for the hunt.

He allowed the man a few precious seconds of hope that would sweeten the fright through his veins. Frantic calls echoed into the dark woods, but Wraith could sense him through the ethereal link. Even more, he could still see his white soul in stark contrast to the night.

Drawing in the essence of Shadow, the firelight dimmed, and his form whisked into the darkness. Fluttering like a streak of ink through water, he charged towards his prey at considerable speeds, weaving through the trees. The man yelped as Wraith manifested corporeal and grasped his arms, his cry cut short as sharp fangs pierced into the flesh of his neck.

Hot blood oozed against Wraith's tongue as he lapped at the life force. All the fear and pain coiled through the liquid laced with flashes of thoughts and memories. Through the ethereal tether, Wraith ensured his prey remembered terror in his final moments.

Simpletons clung tightly to the threads of life even as they frayed and unraveled. Wraith could taste memories firing through the dwindling mind as it fought against its end. He did not mind. It gave him more time to savor the drink of life and the rush of energy through his system.

He felt the third ethereal tether pull. "You will stop," Wraith commanded, his mouth wreathed in blood. He turned his head to look at the final prey run.

The runner was their acquisition, his chains rattling with his hurried steps. Wraith sighed and set his feast down onto the bed of dried leaves. A waste of final moments, but his true target was attempting an escape. It was quaint, and he allowed distance for the thrill of the chase.

Rasps of air sucked through the acquisition's throat as he rushed into the darkness. Wraith stepped lightly and paused, head tilting back as his final prey slipped into bouts of fear. Raising a hand, he clenched his fingers tightly, and the acquisition screamed in the distance.

"I commanded you to stop." Wraith walked calmly toward the billowy white soul of his target, guided by their ethereal link. Shadow magic flowed through the connection, filling his mind and amplifying the sweet taste of fear. He didn't need to venture far into the woods to find his prey, trapped in a mental snare, body lifted a few inches off the ground.

The tense body radiated despair, eyes rolled back into his skull as his mouth hung agape. Wraith's hand slowly lowered the man to his feet, the acquisition's mind shrouded by magic pumping visions of agony into his psyche. He so wished to taste his blood in that moment. Oh, the things he would feel with such a drink.

But he released the anguish and caught the acquisition by the throat with his hand, glowing eyes glaring as he bared his teeth. "You will listen to me now."

He knew the acquisition was called Rotheel of House Degent and was an important diplomat from Bastillos. His employers desired him alive to pick through that mind of his. As Rotheel nodded in compliance, Wraith grinned, his hand flowing down his manacled neck to the chain.

The ethereal tether remained. It was far more effective than iron.

"Do you feel that deep inside your soul?" Wraith asked rhetorically. "There's something there that connects us. Should you step out of line, I will ensure your regrets haunt you."

A mouse knew when to freeze, to play dead, to fight back. Rotheel was less than a mouse, his dark eyes fixated on Wraith as his body tensed and writhed with inner turmoil. Wraith could feel the instinctual scream to run coursing through Rotheel's mind, and the folly of desire to fight. Impotent. Cowardace.

The acquisition's thoughts drifted to family, to warmth and comfort, and Wraith dismembered each with a channeled despair.

"Whatever your employer is paying you, I can pay double," Rotheel assured. Wraith licked the remnants of blood across his lips, a small smile gracing the edges as he pulled the chain. Air from the diplomat's throat caught in a croak as he lurched forward, feet shuffling through the light dusting of snow.

"My payment is in your torment," Wraith informed. Through their magical link, Wraith felt Rotheel's fear and weariness, but determination still remained. It was a delicate dance to remove determination. Too much despair could bolster the courage to counter.

They passed his most recent delicacy, the lifeless eyes staring up into the dark of night, blood staining his cloak. Frost had collected around the tears that fell from his dull eyes. The memory of his sweet taste was water through his mind, cooling at first, but fleeting and slipping from recollection.

It would be nearly a fortnight of travel across the Grey Hinterlands, perhaps more if the Great Scar gave them trouble. Roads were carved down the cliffs leading into the valley, but they were perilous, especially when traveling with one dressed in fancy shoes meant for interiors. The diplomat could serve to sate his hunger during their journey, but at the cost of delay.

Inconvenient.

The horror that struck his nerves passed through the diplomat, honing to what felt like calculations through the ethereal link. Wraith observed the diplomat's machinations, and it plucked at his hunger. He licked the edge of his lip, tasting the iron tang of his former feast, and steeled his patience for his next meal.

A luxury came with Wraith's power. While Rotheel's steps grew sluggish by the hour, Wraith did not slow his pace. Sleep was not required for one such as he.

All he needed was a feast of blood to coat his throat and bathe his psyche in glorious, concentrated emotions. Even a taste could sustain him for a day, but Wraith could not restrain himself against the decadent font.

His acquisition would become burdensome if he did not find a place for the mortal to rest. Wraith was not allowed to devour this one.

Wind brushed through the barren trees as he journeyed against the flow, cloak pulled over his form tightly as he crested a hill that led further into the woodland. Light from the moon refracted off the snow and brightened the night. They could see through the woods as clear as day.

"We will make camp soon," he informed. "If you run, I will know."

"I understand." Rotheel's voice was resolute, but his soul radiated hopelessness. "I also understand you need me alive. Otherwise I would be like my previous captors."

Wraith grinned, but did not look back at the clever diplomat. Their connection fed him with Rotheel's slow ascent towards bravery.

"Would you like to make a proposition?" Wraith asked.

"More an inquiry," Rotheel said. "You... Back there you were..."

Their boots crunched through the snow, down a gentle slope leading to a small ravine carved by a frozen creek. As they stepped over the ice, Wraith looked back at Rotheel. The hesitancy was amusing, and he could sense his unease and confusion.

Rotheel's eyes darted from the ice to Wraith as his concentration split to avoid slipping. "You were drinking his blood, were you not?"

"Yes," Wraith answered.

"I've read the Maldviri text of the Blood Mage uprising," he said. "It spoke of Blood Mages who learned the ways of Shadow and became... Well, the text called them abominations. I have no other word to describe it."

"Wraiths."

"Is that what you call yourself?" Rotheel asked.

"Is this your inquiry?" he countered.

"Well, no, I suppose it is more of a precursor question before I ask the true question," the diplomat clarified. "That is, if you're willing to answer more than one question."

"It is what I am called," Wraith stated, and Rotheel scrunched his nose. His confusion was more evident through the ethereal tether than his contorted face. Once his features smoothed, he regained a more composed demeanor.

"It spoke of the wraiths feeding off of blood," Rotheel continued. "I can't live off of blood."

"I am aware," Wraith said. "You will be fed. And you will find rest."

"I am at your mercy, I know, but my last captors had me walk all day," he said. Their path continued forward into the night, the tree line thinning to a slope covered perfectly in untouched white that led down to a dense collection of pines whose bows hung low. Wraith led him through the pine fronds where the ground around the tree trunk was dry. It smelled of sap and pine and the faintest tinge of rot somewhere in the earth.

"Sit," Wraith commanded. The chains chimed as Rotheel took a seat upon the dirt with an aching grunt. Given his young and fair appearance, it was likely the man had never exerted himself so demandingly. There was hardly a muscle to move his bones.

Reaching under his cloak, Wraith opened one of the pouches closest to his hunting knife and pulled out a pack of dried meats, tossing it to the diplomat. Rotheel caught the bundle in his hands and unfolded the cloth, revealing the hardened slices.

"What is it they want with me?" he asked as he nibbled at an end, attempting to hide his hunger in slow bites. Wraith offered him his skein of fresh water, hesitation halting Rotheel's chewing entirely.

"They want you alive," Wraith answered simply, and grinned. "You seem hesitant."

"You told me your payment is in my torment, yet you tend to my needs," he said, and took the skein in his free hand. "It's a strange practice."

The muscles in Wraith's cheeks pulled back, the containment of his revelry abandoned as his sharp teeth were made bare. Rotheel squirmed, writhing like a worm as Wraith lowered himself to level with his eyes. At such a closeness, he could practically hear his prey's heartbeat quicken, the pulse coursing through the wisp of his soul completely veiling the diplomat's features. The cadence of life flickered with familiarity in ethereal veins of violet webbing through the white that flowed like gossamer in a breeze.

"How interesting," Wraith mused. Rotheel's lips parted in an attempt at further inquiry, halted abruptly as Wraith's hands snapped to the diplomat's temples. It made a potent connection when channeling Shadow so close to the mind.

Magic thrummed between them, swallowing them in the abyss of Darkness as their minds connected.

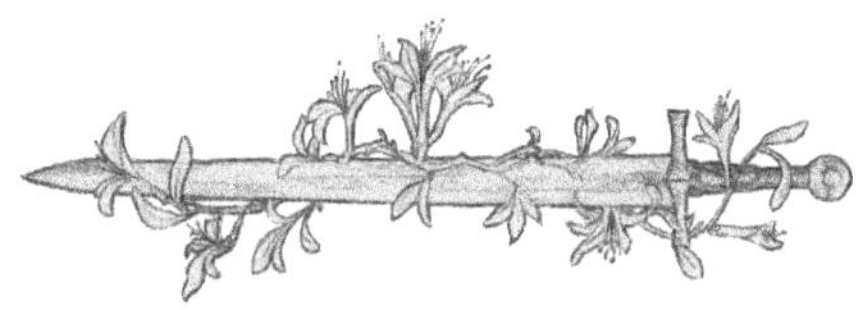

Before House Degent made its name in the caverns of Bastillos, Rotheel's ancestors hailed from the shores of Krei. His family touted this fact, attributing their heritage to their naturally darker skin and high cheekbones. The Degent name carried not only the prestige of generational nobility and wealth, but also the striking genetics that made Rotheel the most advantageous match in all of High Lumin.

The estate of House Degent presided near Lumin's highest point known as the Precipice. Being the estate closest to the palace, its view overlooked a majority of the city's cascade.

Within the open halls of House Degent, a party took place in Rotheel's honor. He had passed his examinations, elevating his status from scholar to diplomat, and while he was proud of himself, he wished for a moment of peace.

Dressed in fine garments of Krei and Bastillosi fusion, Rotheel looked and felt sharp, his hair perfectly coifed and curled. He wasn't fond of the pointed shoulders and how they bunched up as he leaned. Daylight beamed through the mirrorlight tunnels surrounding the Precipice and pooled into the dark below where fires glittered like stars in Low Lumin.

Rotheel could feel a lingering presence in the dark below. It vibrated with energy he could not fully fathom, but he could sense it, almost reach out to it as if it were a tangible thing. Curiously, he held out his hand towards Low Lumin, his finger tracing a beam of light through the air until it disappeared into the expanse below. The indescribable energy flowed through him like a splash of water, and then it was gone.

"Hiding from your own celebration, brother?" Ardante of House Degent walked out onto the balcony with a knowing grin and the faintest hint of longing. He'd married into a higher status, his wife being the cousin to the queen and due with their second child. He was a handsomer man by Bastillosi standards with a sharper jawline and darker skin.

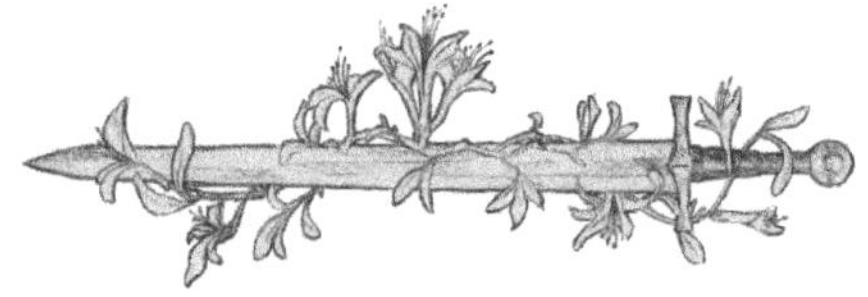

Sentimental. Endearing. Boring.

Wraith groaned as the two men embraced within Rotheel's memory. He was an observer through his magic, only able to watch scenes unfold as the prey recalled experiences on his command. It was akin to reading a book, the memories its pages as he carefully flipped through each one within the spell.

Perhaps his mental invasion had been too precise in its inquiry. It showed the exact moment when Rotheel had noticed the beauty of Darkness and the power he had yet to tap.

But the shimmer of Shadow was only vague upon the diplomat's soul. Did he have potential? Did he taste the magic and laid himself bare before Darkness?

Wraith pulled himself further through Rotheel's history in search for the answer, Shadow Magic swirling and turning the pages of his mind until the familiar vibration of relevancy surged through their link and pulled him into the void.

"Did you read the journal?" Elanath asked as she leaned onto the table, supple breasts pressed against the painted wood. Her blonde hair cascaded down in straight lines like mirrorlight brushing against the surface. Papers were neatly stacked in piles according to their subject alongside a few books to his left. One was open before him as his point of study, the subject regarding the trade agreements throughout Edros.

Admittedly, his eyes wondered from the page, lingering upon the line of her breasts that plunged within a steep neckline. It was fashionable in western Edros, its design becoming the new wave in Bastillos. He liked that she was ahead of the other women in Bastillos. It elevated her beauty.

As he trailed his eyes up her chest, he caught sight of her knowing smirk, the expression widening has he met her stunning, otherworldly blue eyes glistening in the mirrorlight overhead. They looked as bright as the elvish crystals used for everglow, yet as deep as sapphires plunged in dark waters.

"Oh, tell me you did," she added, and he leaned into her tantalizing neck, savoring her intoxicating scent of sweet flowers and spiced fruits as he pressed his lips to her soft skin. She exhaled a breathy moan, head pulling back further to allow his ascent to her jaw.

"I did," he said, though he wished for the conversation to end. His lips trailed to hers.

"And?" she asked between kisses. Rotheel stood from his seat, hand following the length of her leg from under her skirts. She hooked her leg around his torso to close the distance between them.

He smiled and answered, "You're right. That's exactly what I feel."

What Rotheel had intended to be a session of study turned into another hour of distractions and intimacy, all of which Wraith skimmed through to the aftermath where the two, naked and bathed in mirrorlight, continued their prior conversation.

"Shadow Magic seems more inherent than we think," Elanath said. Rotheel trailed an index finger up her arm generating gooseflesh and an airy giggle. "Am I boring you?"

"Not at all," he said. She swatted his hand playfully.

"You know what I mean."

He met her incredibly blue eyes, unable to hold back a smile. Had he believed in Elssar, he'd swear the god had blessed him. Maybe some higher entity glimpsed his dreams and ensured their lives would cross paths.

"You're not boring at all, Ella," he assured, and tried his best not to admire the curves of her body. "Inherent Shadow Magic is an interesting thought. The elves say it's unnatural."

"That is because they believe you have to be born spouting their limited forms," she countered.

"Their Shadow Casters lose their inherent magic over time and die. I see why they believe that." While he was taught to find a logical path through emotions, Rotheel sensed his shared observation soured the mood. Her smile faltered, and she hid her dwindling mood by lying on her back.

"You've been talking to Xurshai," she mused, but her tone had lost its mirth.

He shrugged. "I have to talk to Xurshai. It's my job."

"Do you only talk to me because it's your job, diplomat?" She seemed to carry a playful air, brow quirked and eyes focused.

"I talk to you because I fear if I do not, I'll wake from this dream." He kissed her exposed shoulder. "I talk to you because I enjoy your candor. Your voice is the lullaby that sings me to dream." He kissed the crest of her collar bone, and she chuckled, guiding his head to look her in the eyes without diversion.

"You're distracting me, Rotheel."

"Is that so terrible a thing?"

Brushing her fingers through the curls at his temple, she sighed. "I think it's a shame we aren't allowed to fully learn Shadow. To explore its potential. Even in Edros it's regulated." Following the curve of his ear, she trailed her nail down through the stubble to his jawline.

"It's to protect Shadow Casters from dying, Ella. They all agree to it," Rotheel assured.

A worse observation to share. Elanath sighed and pulled herself from the bed, wrapping her body in her undergarments. He could still see the silhouette of her body under the sheer fabric as she fluttered over to his table. Her hand plucked the journal from its place.

It was a simple looking thing written with a very old form of handwriting he could barely read. Yet as he deciphered the old text on each page, he felt a connection to something grow linked to a dark haunt of his mind. The Darkness was tangible. It was an energy he could feel and harness. But to what end? Shadow Magic had power, but that power was used by Low Lumin to win the Bastillosi conflict five years prior.

Rotheel's mood soured. He dressed himself well enough, his curls in disarray as he crossed the room to join her. Her delicate fingers held the leather bound journal, eyes roving between the old writing and his notes.

"This is incredible, Rothy. How did you figure out so much so quickly?"

"It's just patterns." Rotheel shrugged. The scratchy handwriting presented the brunt of the challenge, but once he found similarities in the glyphic text, he could break the code.

Elanath combed her fingers through his curls, pride radiating and reigniting his desires. Her smile was beautiful, and he liked that she was smiling at him.

"Did you feel anything when you figured out this much?" she asked.

The question felt invasive, and for a moment Rotheel closed himself off from their connection.

"What's the matter?" She kissed his cheek, his jaw, his neck. Any hesitancy melted away, and was replaced with desire.

Despite Rotheel's lack of answer, Wraith knew Rotheel could tap into Darkness on a deeper level. He had read a passage regarding its connection to the mind. Shadow Magic was mind magic.

Just as Wraith was inclined to end the spell, he felt an inkling of a thought forming in Rotheel's memory that would halt their second intercourse.

"Do you know anything about the Tenebris?" he asked.

Elanath pulled back, confusion contorting her perfect features. "What?"

"I overheard someone in the Academy years ago say they were a secret organization of people who perfected Shadow Magic," Rotheel explained.

"Not very secret if they're known by outsiders," Elanath said playfully, and kissed down his collarbone.

"Well, if they're real, maybe they'd want to know about this," Rotheel said. "Maybe they could tell us more. Teach us."

She drew back again, curiosity pulling a groomed brow to an arch. "You really want to learn Shadow?"

Rotheel stumbled through an answer, uncertain of his own feelings. His ambition desired elevation, but his heart feared its potential. All he could muster was a shrug.

"I can look into the legend. See if there's some validity," Elanath offered. "But if nothing comes of it, we can always teach ourselves."

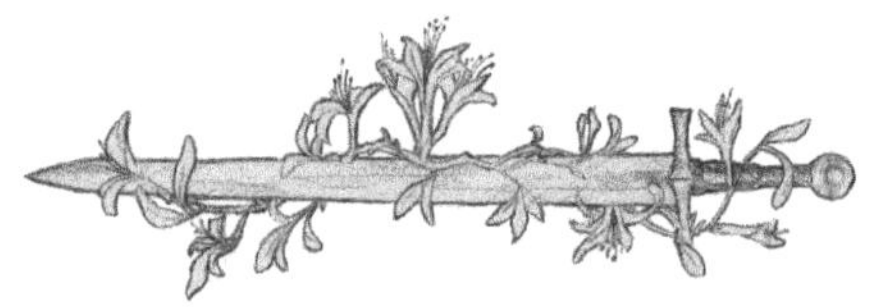

Laughter escaped Wraith as he severed the spell, his hands releasing its hold on his head. Rotheel crumbled into the frosted forest bed, eyes wide in shock, body limp and unmoving.

How amusing.

Sitting back against the tree, Wraith reveled in the shared memory as the diplomat gripped his chest as if he had been stabbed.

"What did you just do?" he asked, and coiled into a fetal position.

"It seems you already know," Wraith answered.

"I felt like I was burning from the inside out," Rotheel noted. Forcing himself out of his stupor, he pushed himself upright. "I felt like I was dying and reliving my past. But it all seems like a distant dream now. Did you take from me?"

Interesting. He knew a spell already, but that spell was a closed practice.

"No, the memories I saw are still there," Wraith assured. "So you know you can take with Shadow, then?"

"I have heard of it," Rotheel admitted. "But you... You're different. You weren't just in my mind."

Wraith studied the silvery-white soul shimmering in the diplomat's silhouette as flecks of violet energy twinkled like the night. He looked less fearful of him now. Instead of fright, curiosity bloomed. Wraith did not like that. A line was being crossed too quickly.

"I am a wraith," he reminded, his mirth retreating. "I am more than just Shadow and Blood. I am the power they fear."

"Yet you are a bounty hunter?" Rotheel countered. Wraith smirked.

"Yet I am a bounty hunter," he repeated. Correcting the man was of little import. He liked when his prey thought he was common. It allowed for a rise of hope and the thrill of a chase.

14
YSELLA

Ysella stirred to a sense of unfamiliarity. There were no cold stone walls or dim morning mirrorlight. There was no comforting smells of minerals in the air. It was all wood and the scent of candle wax and straw stuffed mattresses.

The blurriness of sleep veiled her consciousness as she regained her bearings and swallowed dryly. There was dirt under her fingernails, and she was wearing clothes too large for her frame. Her body hurt in unfamiliar ways, not only from the myriad bruises and cuts, but a deeper ache in her muscles and joints.

And then she remembered she was a bounty hunter's acquisition.

She shot upright. The bed across from her was empty, the blankets disturbed and pillow creased where a head once lay. Rolling her fingers through her hair, she pushed herself to her feet and felt the exposed mattress for the warmth of its former occupant.

It was cold, but so too was the room. She shivered and winced at the twinge behind her temple as the last vestiges of sleep were ushered away.

The morning was quiet, save for a conversation down the hall where patrons could gather and eat. She eased open the door only a fraction and found Ilai remained. He sat next to Sabin, the Maldviri securing fresh bandages around Ilai's shoulder. They spoke quietly, Ilai keeping his left arm guarded to his body.

She'd never seen muscles quite like his, though she assumed soldiers would have a similar physique. Definition etched each muscle in his good arm; an arm built from wielding large swords and lifting heavy things. She shuddered to think of what heavy things a bounty hunter would carry, and she shut the door quietly.

Crossing the room, she plucked the small pitcher sitting on the bureau and poured the fresh water into the washing basin. A mirror, blistered and puckered across the glass, revealed her skewed reflection. Ysella grimaced at the state of her appearance, her mess of mahogany curls in disarray with dead leaves and twigs as adornments.

Dark, mottled bruises dappled her neck where the collar had pressed into her throat. Scratches hatched her cheeks from tree branches and dirt lingered on her skin in splotches.

Dirt swirled in the water as she scrubbed the grime from her skin. The cold water soothed her bruises as she carefully dabbed a wet cloth against her neck. Only a few days ago she bathed in warm milk and lemon verbena, her hair treated with her mother's luxurious oils that made her curls vibrant and smell of mountain honeysuckle.

The remnants of her gown was tangled in a heap next to Ilai's cloak, the imported fabric frayed and shredded where the worgs had attacked. That dress cost a small fortune, the merchants of the fabric alone requiring recommendation from trusted clients.

Her necklace was tucked within her cloak, the chain catching the morning light from the window. Ysella pulled the necklace from its hiding, unclamping the delicate links and securing it to her neck. The heavy beads were cool against her throat, the red gem at the center a welcome weight. Her fingers curled around the pendant, eyes stinging with tears she swiftly blinked away.

With or without Ilai, she would find her answers. She would bring those answers back to Bastillos and they would see what she went through. They would see what she endured for them and they would accept her back with loving arms.

Wiping her cheeks dry, she turned and slipped out of the room in search of her once captor. Ilai had donned a new shirt slightly large for his frame. The sleeves were cuffed, yet still threatened to slip down to his thumbs. He was in the process of rolling them up as Ysella approached. Sabin smiled at her warmly, beckoning her to join them at the table.

The patrons from the previous night were nowhere to be seen. Either they had moved on with their travels, or they were still asleep. The quiet morning was only interrupted by the occasional sounds of crackling fire, sizzling pans, and quiet conversation from the kitchen.

"The yield from the chickens has been favorable," Sabin informed. "We're being treated to quiche this morning. Ah, and by the smell of it, sausage. I have some fresh clothes for you, by the way."

Sabin scooped a stack of folded clothes from the bench and held them out to Ysella, who graciously cradled them in her arms as she sat. They looked smaller than what she wore, at least.

"Hopefully they fit," Ilai said.

"They keep a bin of clothes patrons leave behind," Sabin explained. "You'd be surprised how often people come in looking like the two of you in need of a change of clothes."

"Thank you," Ysella said.

"Did you sleep well?" Sabin asked.

"As well as possible." Ysella nodded towards Ilai's shoulder. "How is it?"

"Stiff, but manageable," he answered. "We should determine our course of action before we leave the Wayward, though."

"We?" Ysella straightened, a look of surprise flashing across her features in disbelief. "So you'll help?"

"We'll travel by foot until we can get some metal," Ilai continued, "and we need weapons. We should head north through the Scar to Halvish. It's not the most direct route to Ethyrnon, but it'll take us through more forgiving lands."

Ryla brought plates of quiche and sausage to the table, filling glasses with fresh water. Ysella tamed her hunger, eating at a polite pace despite her stomach's protests.

"I'm afraid I don't know much of the layout of the Grey Hinterlands," Ysella admitted. "I've read documents notating Laerds' Lands and their jurisdictions. Halvish is under… Laerd Davargan. He owns lands both in and out of the Scar and believes in the Nine Patrons. They're closed off to other religions as well as outsiders."

"They teach you well in Bastillos," Sabin remarked.

"They're reasonably wary of outsiders, but not closed off," Ilai clarified. "It's preferred you swear to Laerd Davargan before doing business, but they won't turn you away as long as you don't cause trouble."

Sabin's jaw was clenched despite preparing a bite of sausage from his plate. It was the familiar look of someone holding back an opinion, and she caught his gaze with a knowing look. He smiled and shook his head.

"I'll retrieve some medicinal supplies for the two of you," Sabin said. "Ilai has a habit of running out and spending his metal elsewhere."

"U'gul is just as good of a medicine as any," Ilai jokingly retorted.

"For a Lander, your survival instincts leave much to be desired. You're going to need it, Ilai." Sabin cocked a challenging brow, and Ilai sighed.

"Thank you," he said almost sheepishly.

Brightly smiling, Sabin rose. "Good man. I'll be right back. I don't want to forget."

The large interior of the Wayward was warm from the large fire crackling in the long hearth at the end of the room. Despite this, the Maldviri drew his robes closer to his frame as he walked toward the staircase on the other side of the hall.

"Sabin wants me to convince you to go home," Ilai said quietly.

"He must know it's not a matter of my safety anymore," she said.

"I *know*," he said. "I explained how stubborn you are."

"Stubborn? This isn't a petty thing, Ilai."

"I know." He held out a hand to remind her to keep quiet. They were still the only ones in the large dining hall, but Laura cast a wary glance their way as she cleaned the tables. "Sabin is torn. He's got a big heart. I think you need to talk to him."

"Alright, but we need to leave sooner than later," Ysella said. "I don't want to put Sabin or the Wayward in any danger."

"I'll gather our things," Ilai said as he stood, and popped his last bite of quiche in his mouth. "What little we have, anyway."

Ysella watched the hunter leave, grateful he left the door to the room open as he packed. Her anxiety fluttered in her stomach, and as Sabin returned, she mustered a smile.

"Everything alright?" Sabin asked. He set a leather pouch down on the table and unfurled it to show the supplies secured between straps. Tin cylinders carried powders and balms, glass bottles filled with dried herbs and tinctures, and there was a selection of metal utensils and needles and spools of thread.

"Everything is fine," Ysella assured. "We're just preparing to leave. But, Sabin, this is generous." Her fingers brushed over the containers. There were labels pasted on each, the handwriting elegant and in Edrosi common.

"It's my traveling set," he said. "I have a larger supply up in my room, but I don't have much of a need to carry my medicine with me these days. Unless..."

"Unless what?" Ysella smirked at his attempt at a segue, and he bashfully laughed at his lack of nuance.

"Ilai said you were stubborn," he said. "But I wanted to offer my services instead."

"You're welcome to join us," Ysella offered, but he shook his head.

"I would go in your stead, Ysella. And Ilai would take you home."

Ysella reached over and clasped her hand around his, giving it a squeeze. "I am going regardless of who journeys with me. I *must* go."

Solemnly, Sabin nodded his head and squeezed her hand in return. "I understand."

"You can still help me by staying here. When all this is done, it would be nice to know where I can safely go," Ysella said. "You said there's darkness in Bastillos. Can you send your brother to check and make sure all is well there?"

"I will send a letter as soon as possible," he assured, and tapped a pouch that clinked with metal. "It's a few silver knuckles in there and some iron fingers. Most of my metal goes right into supplies for the Wayward, but this is from my reserves. And before you protest, I still have some left. I will need it for that letter."

"I don't know how to repay your kindness, Sabin," Ysella said.

"Survive."

It was a gentle request, but one laden with severity. Sabin's smile hid his disappointment and concern, and her own smile was apologetic. "I wouldn't be able to do it without Ilai."

"Bounty hunters of the Grey Hinterlands are known for their selfishness and lack of concern for others," Sabin warned. "I've known Ilai for a long time. He's hardened over the years. There may be a sliver of his soul you could appeal to, but I worry he could lose himself. Don't get yourself tangled in a man who loses himself, Ysella."

It could have been an attempt to deter her journey, but Sabin's worry was palpable. "Is Ilai dangerous?"

"No, I don't think so," Sabin said, and glanced over to the door to their room. "He is still there. But promise me if you see he's lost, you'll escape and contact me before continuing."

Rising from her seat, Ysella collected the medicine pouch, a faint smile pulling her lips. She rested a hand on the Maldviri's forearm briefly. "You needn't tell me twice, Sabin. I trust it won't be easy. Not for either of us. Who knows what we may learn if we stick through this together."

"I pray for your safe journey," he said, giving her hand a pat.

"Thank you for your aid," she said. "We would not have gotten very far at all without you. I look forward to seeing you again."

Golden sun rays splayed through scattered clouds as Ysella trekked through the woods alongside Ilai. The air was a brisk bite nipping at her nose and cheeks, frost glassing the earth in a thin layer of ice.

They walked for days with minimal signs of civilization, albeit brief. They passed a merchant headed west who gave a nod to the pair as he passed. Ilai glanced over his shoulder as the cart carried on and caught a glimpse of Ysella's wary look. He lofted a questioning brow, and she quickly turned her attention elsewhere.

Sabin's warning about Ilai weighed her mind. She was traveling with a stranger, betting her life on the unspoken promise of his aid. What if it was a ploy to make it easier to hand her over to whatever waited for her at Ethyrnon Tower?

She had missed another chance to escape.

The hilly woods opened to a clearing of grass with the faintest line defining their path. Ilai stooped downward and plucked a fallen branch, gauging its length and breaking off the end so that it was about the span of his forearm.

"You should learn how to hold your own," he said, beckoning her over to him. "A knife is a good size to start out with. It doesn't require a lot of your own arm strength just to wield it. What matters is where you pierce or slice."

He demonstrated a few quick motions with the stick, and then held the end of it towards Ysella. "If you have an opening, here is a decent spot," he said pointing to her stomach. He lifted the stick, jabbing it towards her heart. "The heart would be the goal, but the bone right here can get in the way if you're not careful. If you can get at their back, you go for these spots."

He stepped around behind her and pressed a hand to the base of her neck, then the small of her back. Ysella shivered at the touch and the thought of the act, and spun to face him. He held out the stick for her to take. "An actual blade will feel differently in the hand."

Slowly, she curled her fingers around the dead wood, her palm brushing off the last remnants of its bark. She imagined the stick as a knife and frowned with disdain. All her life she'd been raised to seek out peace, to negotiate and compromise with knowledge and compassion. Holding a weapon, even if in concept, felt unnatural. She didn't want to take a life even at the cost of her own.

But the thought passed, and her mind wandered to the memory of the man in the woods wounded by the arrow she let loose, to the man in the cavern who she ended with violent means. The bed of red she laid him to rest upon burned through her like embers to parchment. Ilai had never confirmed if the man was dead, but a part of her suspected this was an odd kindness on his part.

Survival, it seemed, called for an absence of one's conscience. She may not want to take a life, but she could not die for lack of trying. Ysella gripped the stick readily and repeated Ilai's movements.

"So here... and here?" She gestured to his stomach, then his heart.

He tapped his finger to his chest. "Only here if you're certain you can generate enough force to get through the bone."

He guided her grip, changing her hold on the stick knife where the length pointed down her arm. Their hands were covered by soft leather gloves, but he was still gentle and without force. "Use both hands if you have to, but this grip will give you more power at that angle."

"Will it get stuck?" she asked.

"It could," he advised. "If that happens, you run."

Ilai picked up another stick, this one slightly longer, and he held it like a sword. "If they're armed, you should run, but if you have no choice, you fight with what you've got."

With a downward motion he demonstrated a move and halted. "Do you see the places exposed now that the blade is down? Flank opposite of the sword and cut the arms or stab the stomach. Then run. Go on and try it."

He went through the motion again, slower this time to give Ysella the chance to strike. Eyes squeezing shut, she jabbed her improvised weapon forward, stepping into the motion with little aim in mind. Easily, Ilai moved to the side and tapped her torso with his stick.

"Eyes open," he said. She expected him to laugh at her, but the air of concern in his voice was alarming. "You need to be aware of your surroundings, otherwise you could hurt yourself in the process. Let's try that again. This time, watch what you're doing."

"Right. Sorry." Slightly flushed, Ysella stepped back and waited as Ilai readied himself. This time, when he swept downward, Yeslla drove the stick inward, eyes opened, managing to scrape along the inner edge of his underarm. It wouldn't kill anyone, and it was doubtful it would even maim, but she'd struck.

On her third effort, the stick dropped, and uttering a rather unladylike oath, Ysella bent to retrieve it. On her fourth attempt, she forgot, again, to keep her eyes open.

It was by her seventh try that she managed a successful strike, this time driving the stick into Ilai's abdomen with a frustrated grunt. When she made purchase, she gave a small yelp of surprise, squelched by her hands as she covered her mouth. "I'm sorry! Are you alright?"

Doubled over momentarily, Ilai chuckled. "I'm alright," he assured as he stood upright. "You did well. Hopefully you'll never have to use it."

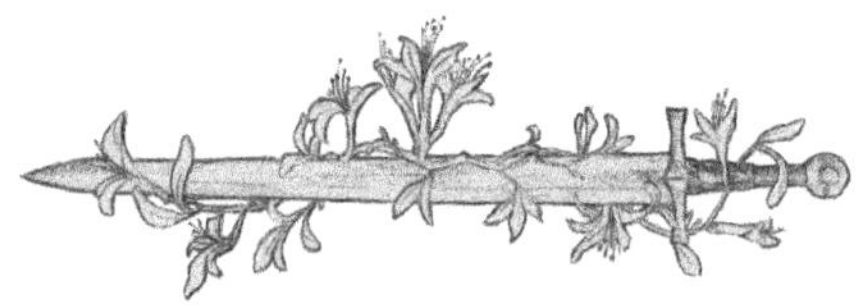

Days passed, and their journey led up a tree covered slope that broke out from a smooth rock face that looked to have split long ago. The rolling hills and litters of moss covered stones revealed the land's strife in its rubble. It was an unforgiving land to outsiders, but Ilai's steps were calculative and sure. The trail eventually rolled through a small and shallow creek framed by barren trees desperately awaiting the gracious rains of Spring.

Ilai halted a moment to fill his canteen. "How is your leg?"

She had nearly forgotten her own wounds, mistaking the pain for an annoying itch that occasionally picked her brain. Her new clothes fit well enough, the pants holding better to her waist with less irritation to her legs as she moved. The scratches were nothing more than a fleeting annoyance now.

Her confusion shifted as she realized this was the first time Ilai had inquired into her well-being. She stooped down, following his lead as she filled her own canteen.

"I hardly even remembered," she admitted. "I suppose that's a good thing. Though, I've also never been partially mauled by worgs, so I'm not entirely certain what it should feel like. How is your shoulder?"

He rose with a hesitant air, almost apprehensive in response. "It's stiff, but in a few days I'll be perfect."

The cool water rushed over her fingers as it filled the canteen, the chill biting until her fingers felt completely numb. She stood, and he shifted uncomfortably, eyes scanning over the tall embankment.

"Is something out there?" she asked as she secured the cap.

"No." Confusion furrowed his brow, and he motioned to her with his head. "How's your neck?"

Absently, her hand rose to her bruised throat. "Sore. But healing."

There was something different about the way he asked, as though it had slipped from his lips unbidden. Twice now, he'd inquired after her, and each time she had the impression it was genuine concern. Studying his features, he couldn't look at her for long, and in his eyes she almost thought she could see the signs of regret.

"Ilai?"

"Hmm?"

She held up her canteen. "I'm done."

He curtly nodded and continued down the path, the high bank of the creek eventually leveling enough for their crossing.

"How many times have you done this before?" Ysella asked.

"Done what?"

"These bounties." Her tone was soft and devoid of accusations, curiosity devoting her words as she fought the odd dichotomy.

"Human acquisitions?" He held out his good arm for her to use, hoisting her up over a ravine. Even with one arm, his strength did not waver, and she gasped at the sudden rush upward. He pulled himself up by a sturdy tree branch and continued through the open woods. There was little brush between the trees, which were mostly pine, their tall trunks reaching for the clouded skies with their tufted fronds.

"I've been at this for some time," Ilai said. "Does it matter how many times I've done it? Does more than once make you think of me differently?"

Her fingers curled around the back of her neck, rubbing out the chill. "I just wonder if you know. If you've counted them. And I suppose I want to know how it doesn't get to you. You're hardly as ruthless as I thought. They were people, after all. Has it ever bothered you?"

"The life I live is one that requires you to look at people differently." His voice carried an odd strain, as if he battled with the words as he spoke. "You don't view people as people, if that makes any sense. Their begging is the same as a barking dog that just won't shut up."

He fell quiet, the trail leading out to a wider path through the trees. She couldn't help but wonder if even in his silence, he said more than he meant to.

"And your thoughts now?" he asked, looking back to her over his shoulder.

"I don't believe you." There was no direction for the words, as though they were little more than a commentary on the weather. In contemplation, she too fell quiet, the rattling canopy and crisp crunch of dead foliage the only sounds for minutes.

When she spoke again, it held a note of what dared to sound like sympathy. "I think that's what you want to feel because it's easier. I don't believe a man who keeps a practitioner of Inner Light for a friend, who did not hesitate to face worgs and frozen water and those monsters in the caravan to save his acquisition would or could lack the conscience to feel every single burdensome weight of those you hunted. I believe you think it's necessary to detach yourself. I believe what you do could be necessary out here. But I don't think that you are capable of forgetting them."

A half smile briefly graced his features, marred by possible pity or sorrow. "I suppose it's difficult to explain," he said. "It's not that we can't recognize that the acquisition is a person with thoughts and ideas and family. We do respect that part of their life. But in order to get through it we can't think of them with compassion. And we don't think of them after we get our metal. They have a bounty on their heads for a reason, and that reason is none of my concern.

"Sabin is friends with everyone he meets. It's an exploit for people like me. I know compassionate people struggle to say no, and they feel compelled to do what they think is right. Sometimes that's a free meal. Sometimes it's medicine. Out here, though, compassion will get you killed. The only reason why Sabin survives is because he has magic."

Frowning, Ysella mulled over his line of logic, studying him curiously. Sometimes people said things, but did not feel them, and she could see cracks forming in his visage. He carried himself differently now. Hesitant, his eyes looking everywhere but to her; his acquisition.

Yet, when she was simply a hefty sum of gold, he held a confidence to his answers and met her gaze defiantly. Their dynamic was something different now, something more complicated, and it had changed something within him.

"No. I don't believe that, either. I think a part of you has convinced yourself it's true," she said, "but Sabin is a wise man. He would not suffer ill intent. There is a shrewdness he hides, but I could see it last night with those watchers. He might do for them what he did for you. It doesn't seem in his nature to let anyone die, but for whatever reason, he sees something in you that you cannot. Maybe he cares for you."

"All the easier to exploit the man," Ilai countered.

"I think you regard him as more than just a passing kindness to exploit," she said. "I think you're afraid of it. Compassion. I think to put value on something, to give it a meaning, invites attachment. You don't like it, being attached to anything, do you?"

All the hesitancy hardened into a barrier, his jaw clenching. His voice was calm, indifferent, but she could see the irritation etched on his stony features. "You play a clever game, but you already have my aid. You don't need to manipulate my feelings. The pay is enough."

"What makes you think I'm playing a game?" she asked. She wanted to reach out, to stop him and force him to have this conversation face to face, but she didn't and Ilai pressed slightly ahead of her.

"I'll admit," she continued, "at the start I was certainly trying to manipulate you. I won't apologize for it. I was being held against my wishes, chained and battered about. I would have done nearly anything to escape. But I've hardly the need for such posturing now."

He continued without interjection or contradiction. She could almost mistake it as being defiantly ignored, but she saw the faint shake of his head in a thought.

"The truth?" she continued, hoping to break down his walls. "For being a diplomat, I've seen very little of the world. I confess, this culture, the ways of your people, the hardness of it all, the coldness, I struggle to understand it. Then I remember I—"

She hesitated, recalling the body lying on the cave floor, unmoving, unflinching, even as Ilai stole his clothes from his back. The head lolled as Ilai pushed him about, eyes lifeless, limp in the way he rolled partway in the water. She knew even then, and knew with certainty now. Ilai never confirmed if it was her fault. He avoided answering that question entirely.

"I killed a man," she said, her voice breaking. "I did it without a thought in order to save you and myself. I cannot help but wonder where that thread unravels. It matters. How does one stop feeling? Or can you even feel? I'm far from perfect, but I happen to like who I am. I can sense pieces of me unraveling, the threads of myself fraying the longer I'm out here. I think that scares me more than anything else we've faced."

Ilai scoffed, a brow lofting as he watched her curiously. "You killed no one."

"He was dead, Ilai." Her tone was even, but there were threads of confusion behind the words, as she tried to understand his contradiction, "I may not have know it then, but I know it now."

"And what do you know, other than he is dead?" Ilai pulled a drink from his canteen and corked it. "He is dead. You are not. That is a good thing."

"I took a life. Even if it wasn't a good one, I did that." Her arms coming around herself, she shivered at the thoughts that traced through her mind, the memories that she had refused to see until now; how the rock struck, how he crumpled and never moved again, "I killed someone."

"You may have thrown that rock," Ilai said, securing the canteen to a holster on his back, "but I was the one to break his neck. A good strike to the head only causes a headache in the end. Now finish up. We should keep moving."

"You—" Blinking, Ysella met him with a stare, and while her words trailed off, her mind did not relent. He had been dead the moment the rock struck. In her heart, she'd known it then, and she certainly understood as much now. But why then did he feel the need to fabricate another scenario? Did he truly believe he was responsible? Or was he attempting to bring her comfort? She had never known him to concern himself much with her emotional well-being in the past, so what had changed?

"Right. Moving. Lead on, then."

The sun crested somewhere behind the clouds, the light dimming to show the coming evening. Ilai was pensive following her thoughts, his internal battle keeping them at a brisk pace until he finally stopped among a cluster of trees.

"This looks like a good place to camp for the night," he said.

The location was ideal with a bit of a clearing to rest upon moss and the sound of a creek close by. Without waiting for her to answer, he turned away to collect wood for the fire.

Momentary defeat pulled her shoulders downward, and she set about making whatever comfort the small area would allow. She had wished Ilai would at least retort or share his own thoughts, opening himself back up to conversation or debate.

The thickened evergreen canopy overhead was heavy with dark, stringy coats. The air was sweet, pungent sap almost certainly promising king boletus and hedgehog mushrooms nearby. After brushing the ground free of fallen needles, making space for them to lay their heads for the night, she set out to look for the edible fungus. She found a few suitable selections not too far away with a satisfyingly bountiful currant bush. Collecting a cloak full of mushrooms and berries, she returned to their campsite to prepare a meager meal.

160

15

ILAI

Ysella carved through his psyche with skillful points, making Ilai question how he truly felt about his profession and acquisitions. Not every job was a person, but he had only just realized he'd never counted. As much as he was taught to respect the individual, he couldn't remember their names or how many times he'd taken an acquisition to a drop off or facilitator.

She was unusually quiet as they sat by the fire, day dimming quickly to night. Each intake of a breath, he braced for another speech that never came. He rationed out their food with Ysella's foraging included and set two tin cups by the fire.

"How far have we to go?" she finally asked. He poured water into the cups and felt the stitches in his arm pull at his skin.

"We'll get to Halvish before sundown if we get an early start," he answered.

"Good," she said. "I hadn't realized how long it would take for us to reach a settlement out here."

"I've been avoiding most of them," he admitted, and pushed the cups closer to the base of the fire with a stick.

"But we need the metal," she reminded. "You need a proper blade. And it probably wouldn't hurt if I had something to protect myself with as well. In case we're separated again, of course."

Her insistence on a blade was concerning. An acquisition needed to be un-armed, unless the bounty hunter wished for a swift end while he slept. He had taught her how to use one, and he wondered if he should regret that decision. She seemed so reluctant.

Perhaps his lesson had sparked a new interest in the diplomat. He recalled the first time he held a blade and how he was taught to use it for defense. The little knife stuck into a bail of hay covered in thick fabric that had a satisfying rip.

Ysella tossed a stick into the flames and stared disquieted. She had managed to tame her brown hair, the waves pulled back with a chord and made to cascade down her back freely. The shirt and pants draped over her frame were worn and practical. Her nail beds had been cleaned of dirt in the last creek they passed, and her cheeks were devoid of grime. They were by no means clean, but she looked a bit more comfortable.

She looked so different now. In their first encounter, she had been a visage of opulence, her dress pristine and beautiful. Her silhouette was complemented by fabric like the night's sky draped with starlight, her head crowned in Bastillosi ornaments.

The visage had been tarnished over time, worn by the demands of the Grey. As she stared into the flickering fire, he saw her eyes were losing their luster.

It was still there, faintly glowing like a dying ember. Her determination was slowly diminishing as weariness or uncertainty took its hold. A familiar haunt veiled her eyes, and he reeled for the turning point that dared to snuff out her light.

"Thank you," she said, "for the lesson. I feel better knowing I won't die without some effort."

A dry smile pulled her lips, but barely reached her eyes. "So long as I remember not to shut my eyes," she added, the fire casting deep shadows across her noble features. Ilai tested the water in the cups with his finger, judging the heat and pulling them away to steep some tea.

"You don't have to continue this journey," he offered. "You can stay in Halvish and trust I will go the rest of the way. You could catch a merchant for a ride back to the Wayward or back home. Nothing says you have to risk your life."

"And be denied your delightful company?" she teased, but then her smile faded, eyes drifting back to the fire to stare in a momentary trance. "I've failed my diplomatic mission, Ilai. I've failed my home, my family. All that's left is for me to either abandon everything I've ever known, or find a way to prove that it was designed to fail."

He saw his own failings in the exposed portions of her neck, the bruising nearly healed and yellow, yet unmistakable. Just by the collar's removal, he'd failed his own mission. It was not removed by his hand, but without it, she was human like him; a person, not an asset.

"I would have no life if I went back," Ysella continued. She fidgeted with the hem of her cloak idly. "I know it's foolish, but I need to do this if for no other reason than to discover why someone wants a war in Edros. My home is not much to those on the outside, but it is everything to me. I need it safe."

Despite their vast differences, they were alike in ways he had once refused to acknowledge. She was headstrong, willing to put her life on the line to get a job done, just like Ilai. His homeland meant everything to him as well. The differences were evident, and it had closed him to the parallels. She was beautiful in contrast to his rough Lander presence, but she had exposed his core through her own and the flaws irritated his psyche.

Ilai's hand hovered at the diplomat's back, lingering in hesitancy as he fought to offer her comfort. It's what Shera would do, he told himself. Ysella's head tilted upward to look at the fire, and he recoiled as if her hair were the flames themselves.

"Can't have you getting killed when I still require metal," he said, playing off his foolishness with a light air.

"At my count, I do believe I've kept you alive a fair share of times," she countered with a small smile. "And I'll have you know I'm quite skilled with a knife."

"If you can keep your eyes open," he teased.

A fleeting chuckle escaped her, the smile fading into the night and merging with the shadows hollowing her face. The weight of the world pressed on her mind, consuming it, alongside a familial longing he wished he did not understand.

They retired for the night, and he waited for her to situate herself on the bed of moss, removing his cloak and laying himself respectfully beside her to share warmth. She pulled the fur pelt up to her neck, the furs framing her jaw as she closed her eyes. Her body had not tensed in his close proximity. Perhaps she found some form of comfort and trust in him through his promise of aid.

What a mess he'd dragged himself into. He found himself indebted to his acquisition and thus lost the job for another concept of a payout. The unspoken rule was broken, and Ilai was now the idiot. It was not an ideal dynamic for the bounty hunter, even knowing the payout at Ethyrnon was likely a ruse.

His shoulder was not so much of a burden anymore. He couldn't put his full weight against it, but his range of motion was improving. Sleep came more easily for the hunter as his wound healed. In the night he dreamed of fragmented golds, rocky terrain slipping into deep woods, and a sky of sunshine. The Elssar religion believed dreams had meaning and told of deep desires or premonitions. Ilai could barely remember the dream once he woke.

Waking was frequent that night. Every time he stirred, he'd feel a spike of alertness, as if something was watching them in the distance. Ysella tossed on occasion, but otherwise remained at rest. He left her within the comfort of his cloak while he stoked the fire and searched the dark surroundings.

Embers carried upward as he fed the flames with fresh wood. There was no breeze to flurry the dancing lights diminishing into the night sky. There was also nothing in their surroundings but trees and brush and dancing shadows from the firelight. Ilai returned to his portion of the moss and carefully brought the warm cloak over his form.

The fire cast enough light for him to faintly discern Ysella's features. She hadn't moved apart from the occasional twitch or the tilting of her head to bury her nose under the cloak. He knew in that moment he cared for someone other than himself, and he wished it were not so.

16
SABIN

The clouds parted for a rare day of sunshine outside the Wayward. Sabin was quick to enjoy these moments as they typically did not last more than a few hours. The weather churned in the Grey Hinterlands from the mountains and the rivers, and it was constantly cold even with the sunlight.

Sabin ventured out into the surrounding woods for foraging, sun rays streaking through the trees. He knew an excellent route to collect the best mushrooms and winterroots. Laura liked to accompany him when he foraged, calling it an adventure. She'd never known much of the Grey outside of her family's tavern and inn, at least not personally.

They carried baskets she wove from wicker, his donned with a gold ribbon to match his eyes. Hers had red only because it was her favorite color. Red was the color of the wildflowers that grew in the field a few minutes' walk from the Wayward. She would have to wait for Spring to see them again.

Snow still clustered in the shadows of the woodland, but where it had melted away Sabin could see the sprigs of wintersprout growing on the sun-drenched base of the trees. It was best to get the root before the vine grew tall enough to cling to the bark, not that the aged root was bad. It was more bitter than he preferred. Winterroots had an earthy taste with a hint of peppery spice when brewed, and he liked to add the zest of citrus when the fruits circulated the Grey.

There were a few flowers that complimented the root well. Sabin watched as Laura collected a few yellow primrose in her basket. She was a child no more than twelve, and at that age she teetered between childish play and thoughtful growth.

"Father says I'll inherit the Wayward," she said as she brushed her gloved hand through the leaves. "Mother says I will only if I don't want to do anything else."

"Is there anything else you'd like to do?" Sabin asked. He dug around a wintersprout with his bare hands, careful not to snap the root too soon. He liked to feel where the root splayed in the dirt.

"Oh, no, I don't think so," she answered. Her little shoulders shrugged beneath her furs with a slight hesitation. Her uncertainty was born from ignorance of the world, her curiosity begging for a second guess.

"All the stories you've heard from patrons never excited you?"

Her eyes lit up as she smiled, her childlike wonder returning. "They do! But it's like bedtime stories. They exist only through the imagination, really. I don't know if I have the interest to go out into the world. It seems dangerous."

"Dangerous, indeed," Sabin agreed. "Did I tell you of my adventure through the Twisted Woods?"

"More than twice, now," she replied with a chuckle, and he grimaced.

"Age is catching up to me, it seems," he said.

"Do you miss traveling?" She climbed up the side of a short ravine where the roots of trees were exposed like a spider's web down to the bank of a small creek. Sabin continued down the creek and watched her shadow dance across the water.

"In Maldvir, we have a saying that goes: 'We travel until we rest,'" he said. "There is a journey in every encounter, every conversation. I cannot miss traveling if I am still on the journey."

Laura scoffed, eyes rolling as she swung off a tree over the small ravine, landing back on the tall embankment. "You know that is not what I mean. You have stayed at the Wayward ever since I can remember. Well, I do remember when you came."

"You were a tiny thing," Sabin recalled fondly. He remembered when his own daughter, Naniv, had been that young. She had the brightest smile and the most beautiful voice. That age was so fleeting. It seemed only yesterday when Laura was a little thing. Soon, she would be just like Naniv with her own family and life and strong will. He would one day return to see his grandchildren again, Light willing.

"Maybe one day I'll see Maldvir," Laura said thoughtfully as she pulled a winterroot from the soft earth. "It's hard to imagine sand dunes or sun columns catching the light for the night. That's such an odd thing."

"No more strange than everglow," Sabin countered. "It's technology of the same vein. The elves carve arcane runes into those special crystals that help it retain its luminosity. Just as the sun columns are carved with runes of Inner Light."

"We hardly get everglow," Laura said as she hopped down to the creek, her boots splashing just at its edge. "The caravaners and watchers always keep it for themselves. Are the sun columns made of crystal?"

"They're made of stone and metal," he said.

His heart lurched with a sudden unease, and he searched their surroundings for a disturbance. A hawk called overhead where it perched in the trees, its head tilting as it surveyed the woodland below. Squirrels foraged through the leaves as their little bodies rustled through the brush. A light wind blew gently through, carrying the fresh scent of pine.

Nothing was out of place, but he felt an odd need to turn back to the Wayward. Following his instincts, he calmly walked out from the ravine with Laura close behind. She was oblivious to his concerns as she carried on with her thoughts.

"Perhaps my parents will let me see the world before they retire," she said. "I would very much like to visit you in Maldvir. I suspect at some point you will go back."

"I will when the time is right." The cold air sharpened his focus with every inhalation, his senses detecting a familiar blanket lingering in the aether. Pulling in his Inner Light, the energy flowed through his center, calming his nerves as it honed in on the burden of a threat emanating from the Wayward.

"How do you know when the time is right to go anywhere?" she asked. Her eyes cast upward and looked beyond the trees. "Looks like more clouds are coming in. I bet the wind will start up in an hour or two."

"It's good we're headed home, then," he said. "You have a good eye."

"Is that how you knew to go back home?"

A distant scream echoed through the woods, causing the young girl to freeze, halting the crunch of leaves beneath her boots. Sabin did the same. Hopefully, it was just a bird. But no other sound followed, and neither of them could bring themselves to move.

"Sabin?" she whispered.

Darkness welled through the aether, the light of the sun dimming with the shift in energy. Another wail carried with agony, and Laura became a meek child once again, her eyes welling with fearful tears. She shook where she stood, and as Sabin stepped to her, she clung to his coat.

"What is that?" she asked quietly. Sabin's heart raced with urgency, but he steeled himself as he knelt to her eye level and held her at her shoulders.

"Laura, I need you to be focused," he said calmly. She shook her head as if anticipating his next words.

"Don't leave me," she pleaded through sobs. Sabin's resolve shattered at her fear, and he embraced her tightly. Screams merged with unholy whispers seeping through the foul energy.

"I need to make sure everyone is alright," Sabin explained as he pulled back from their embrace. She covered her face with her hands and stifled her sobs in an attempt to keep them quiet.

"I don't want to be out here alone," she said. "I don't want to go there either."

"I don't want either of those things for you, too, but we need to think with logic now," he said. "Go back to the ravine and hide within the roots. Watch the sun for mid-day. If I'm not back by then, you go to the stables and you get a horse and you head east on the main road until you find people. Do you understand?"

She nodded her head meekly, and he gave her his basket. "Keep it safe in the meantime," he said. She was reluctant to move, but she took his basket in hand and rushed towards the creek.

Standing, Sabin took in a deep breath, his eyes watching the young girl disappear from view down the embankment. He turned his attention to the dark presence. Something in the energy snaked out in search for prey and recoiled at his presence. Sabin stepped closer and closer.

Help me!

The cry pierced through his mind in a voice he did not recognize. Sabin's pace quickened, the back of the Wayward filtering into view through the parting trees. The horses in the stable whinnied and chuffed with unease as Sabin rushed through the back door and up the stairs.

Blood coated the floorboards and dripped down to the lower level, the pool collecting around a heap of bodies strewn between overturned tables and chairs. Rusty's lifeless eyes stared up at Sabin from his disembodied head that rested within the pool. Sick sucking pulled his attention to a man bathed in red, his body hunched over the owner's wife, Ryla. Her skin was pallid, blood soaking her bodice where the man had latched his maw.

The darkness swirled around the stranger, his glowing white eyes looking up towards Sabin with curiosity. His lips parted from Rylan's neck with disgust at Sabin's presence, blood pouring from his mouth as he grimaced.

"One of you," he said, and licked his lips. "I thought I felt the bite of the Light."

He relinquished his hold on Ryla, and she fell heavily to the floor. The other bodies looked as though they had been torn limb from limb, their flesh mangled from an incredible force. The stranger grinned as he noticed Sabin's attention.

"I didn't want their souls," he said, as if it would mean anything to Sabin. He'd never met a practitioner of Shadow with such power. This was beyond what he had to combat in Maldvir.

"If you know what I am, then you know what I must do," Sabin warned. "Do you wish to relay any last words or forgo your remembrance?"

The stranger groaned and pulled a longsword from his back that swallowed light, the steel most of his height and etched in runes he didn't recognize. "Yes," the stranger said. "I'm looking for a diplomat traveling with a bounty hunter. You see, I have the other one and I'd like to complete the set."

The stranger pressed against a portion of his cross guard, and a mechanism released the crystal from the sword's pommel. He held it aloft to reveal its rune-etched facets and a subtle white glow. A presence within stirred. Placing the crystal into a pouch along his belt, the stranger watched Sabin cautiously.

Fear trickled through his mind, and he fought against the font. Ysella and Ilai were in danger, and should he fail in this encounter he would have no way to warn them.

The stranger breathed deeply as if a pleasing scent lingered in the air. All Sabin could smell was death.

"What a glorious scent," the stranger said, and readied his stance with his blade held in both hands. "I doubt you will taste as sweet. You will let me pass or I will extinguish your Light."

Swiftly, Sabin called upon the Inner Light, the energy welling inside him in an instant. He slammed his hands together, brilliance illuminating the room in a white flash. The stranger hissed in pain, body manifesting into darkness until it were nothing but a streak of black rushing through the dining hall. In an instant, the stranger closed the distance, manifesting into his corporeal form with his blade at the ready. The longsword sung as it swept through the air, the momentum flying towards Sabin's neck.

Sabin channeled the Light within him, and time slowed to a creep. The blade's song was low and slow, like a dirge slicing through thick air, and Sabin easily dodged its swipe long before time snapped to its normal pace.

Darkness swelled deep within the stranger's core, his angered expression fueling the power behind each strike of his sword. Sabin dodged, each flash of Light a passive attempt to wait until his assailant was too tired to continue his onslaught.

He sensed an affront to his soul as something dark latched onto his mind, burrowing its way through his resolve. With a roll of his hand, a beam of brilliant light seared through the dark spell like flame to kindle. The stranger did not tire, and the irritation in their battle served to fuel his resilience. Sabin realized he would have to choose between his oaths and taking a life.

Every life mattered. He was no Judicator called by the Light to exact harsh punishment upon the wicked. He was just a Luminary. A healer. A protector. He had never taken a life, and he had never regretted it.

Sabin collided with the stranger, his hesitation causing the blade to slice through his robes near his leg. They tumbled down the stairs, and amid the clatter, the stranger vanished into an inky cloud, flowing down to the landing with his blade drawn and ready. Sabin slowed his advance with another spell and rolled to the left, infusing his fist with magical energy. The impact to the stranger's side burst with Light and singed through the fabric of his jerkin.

At such close quarters, the stranger dropped his sword, plunging his hands towards Sabin's throat. It was dark in the lower tavern. None of the candles had been lit, nor had they started a fire in the hearth. Sabin's Inner Light felt the shift in the darkness pulling towards the stranger. It churned by his command, ethereal tendrils snaking out towards Sabin's limbs, coiling around him with a sizzling contact.

Darkness was a choking force that sought to rid the world of Light, corrupting the soul over time. It could not touch Sabin like it could others, but it still tried. First, it started with worry, plucking at his concern for the Wayward and for Laura. Just a fraction of such a hold could spiral a weaker mind, and he fought against the torrent.

Eyes closed, Sabin took a calming breath. Unlike his adversary, he did not need the physical manifestation of his magic to find the Light. It was always within him. Inner Light empowered Sabin, granting him strength more powerful than any other strand in the aether. His skin burst with brilliance and the tendrils disintegrated.

The stranger shielded his eyes from the Light. While he was vulnerable, Sabin charged, his magic surging from his fingers as he rammed them into the stranger's jugular. The stranger coughed and spun his hands about in a spell's call. Shadow swirled, inundating Sabin's mind with the weight of his fears.

Poor Laura, out in the cold, afraid for her life and orphaned by the hands of an abomination. Ysella and Ilai journeying through the wilderness with a looming threat waiting at the end of the road.

A soft glimmer of life radiated from Ryla's Light above. Sabin clung to the hope of that Light, honing his resolve and pushing away the anxious feelings. Darkness would not prevail.

Pulling his leg upward, the stranger kicked Sabin away, diving to the ground to retrieve his sword once distance was drawn. Sabin centered his Inner Light, utilizing the hope from Ryla, and channeled his magic through him that focused to a brilliant beam.

Light clashed in the dark, the wicked stranger careening with a cry of pain. In a whisk of darkness, the stranger dissipated into a streak of black, crashing through the nearest window into the cold air. The roof of the stable clattered as the darkened streak passed in a rush.

The darkness receded.

Sabin quickly concentrated his Inner Light, heightening his senses in anticipation of the stranger's return. But with each passing second, he knew he would not, and rushed back up the stairs to the main floor of the Wayward. His boots slipped through the thick puddle of blood wreathing the pile of limbs.

Ryla's life was dangling by a fraying thread. The vein in her neck had been punctured, a stream of red oozing with each beat of her heart. Sabin held his hand against the flood.

"Where's Laura," she whispered.

"She's safe," Sabin assured.

"Rusty?"

Sabin shook his head mournfully, golden eyes mirroring her pain as they welled with tears. The Light left her eyes as tears wet her cheeks in her final moment, and Sabin allowed his to fall in her name.

"Find peace among the stars, soul of Light," he prayed.

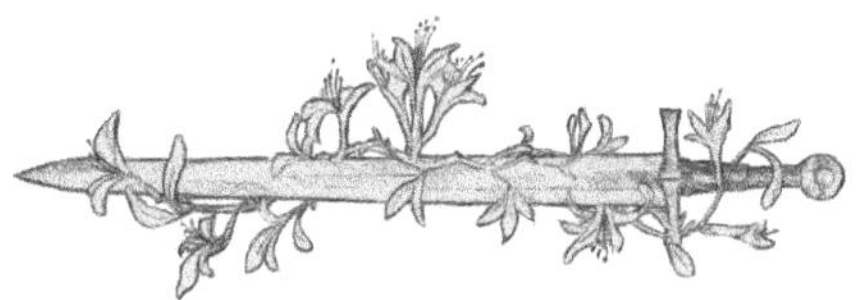

The bodies were placed away from the carnage and cleaned in preparation for the pyre. Sabin removed them from their blood, mopping the pools as clean as he could to make the Wayward momentarily presentable in preparation for Laura's return. Sabin stepped out into the cold, his brow glistening with sweat and his robes stained with blood. Laura stood at the door to the stable, her puffy red eyes widening at the sight of the Maldviri.

Her mouth parted to speak, but all she could manage was a sob as she rushed to him in a tight embrace. "I was so scared!" she managed to say through heaving breaths.

"Are you hurt?" Sabin asked as he crouched down to her level. She shook her head in answer, unable to form her words.

"Mama?"

Sabin fought against the tears and held the sides of her face gently as he shook his head. She cried harder and collapsed to the ground to wail through her feelings. Her arms wrapped around herself until Sabin sat on the dirt road with her. As he cradled her shaking form, she clung to his dirty robes and stained them with tears until she had nothing left to cry. Even then, Sabin did not dare move until the girl was ready to face the next step of her sorrowful journey.

"Maybe they're alive," she said.

"They are gone, child," he said. Her sobbing returned, denial begging for relief. He rocked her weeping form like he had done with Naniv after a nightmare. He held her like the people of Maldvir who lost their loved ones to Shadow Casters. It was a terrible loss. Darkness carried evil and frightening things, some which grew into a difficult reality.

Laura wouldn't leave his side once reunited, even after being told of what she would face should she follow him through the threshold of the Wayward. The little girl couldn't stand the thought of being alone again despite the absence of threat. He asked her to close her eyes as he guided her inside, and he advised her to stay behind the bar as he cleaned the remaining blood from the floorboards.

A few broken chairs and tables were set aside in a pile for the pyre. He kept Laura occupied by stacking the wood in the clearing just off the road. Every so often, she'd glance back at the large window that looked into the front, checking to see if Sabin was still there. Each time, he would wave to her, smiling despite the hurt in his heart.

The bodies were wrapped in sheets he sewed shut with twine, trying as best as he could to place the right limbs with the right bodies. They resembled their former silhouettes as he placed each one on the long pyre. Laura helped him situate the broken tables to create an even surface for them to lay.

Night surrounded them, punctuated by the torch Laura held aloft, face hardened with the numbness of sorrow.

"We live on so that they live on," she said. "That's the way of the Grey."

All childlike wonder vanished from the little girl standing next to him, replaced by a hollow voice too severe for a girl her age. Sabin placed a hand on her shoulder for comfort.

"Your mother made some of the best meals I've ever tasted," he said, a solemn smile gracing his features for a fraction of a moment. "She was so kind to everyone. So inspiring."

"My father put his soul into the Wayward," she said. "His pride shows in every stone and table and hearth. He would have wanted his patrons to have a proper funeral, but I did not know them."

"We can keep their names and belongings for when someone may come around looking for them," Sabin suggested. Laura nodded meekly, her lips pulling downward as she fought against her grief.

"I don't know what to do," she admitted.

The fire grew tall and hot and crackled in the darkness of night. They were the Light now. Their bodies were wreathed in flame that consumed the fibers of the linens.

"We will continue your father's business," Sabin said, and looked down to meet her hardened gaze. "You are your parents' greatest pride and their deepest love. Honor that love however you see fit. I will care for you with the same grace."

Her head nodded with a solemn acceptance and returned pensive, hypnotized by the hot flames. Sabin stood with her for as long as she wished the funeral to commence. As the heat of the fire stung his eyes, he wondered where the stranger had run to. He was in search of Ysella.

May such evil never find them.

17
YSELLA

The chill of morning greeted them with the soft white of snowfall filtering through the pine and grey barren trees. A delicate layer of frost kissed the ground, flecks of snow spiraling down from overhead alighting on Ysella's tresses. Ilai gathered what little they carried and snuffed the fire with a scrape of his boot through the dirt.

"That may be the first time I've slept well enough to call it sleep in days," she said.

Ilai tested his range of motion with a slow roll of his shoulder. His injury seemed to be healing well.

"It will likely be colder today," he advised, pacing their trek at a brisk walk. "We'll need to keep moving to keep warm."

The air barely held a breeze allowing the snow to fall in gentle lines. White blanketed the soft hills hiding the loose rocks and uneven paths through the woodland. Ilai's familiarity was handy navigating the hidden paths. She followed his boot prints through the snow, yet despite this, she still stumbled through the dirt. Exhaustion set in by mid-day, but she hadn't the courage to ask for a break.

Ilai paused as they broke through the tree line to a spectacular view. Towering cliff sides narrowed close together within the valley of the Scar the length of several miles. Two figures were carved into each cliff face spanning their heights. They were dressed in robes, one carrying a sword and the other a shield, their free hands held to their hearts.

"They represent the simple folk being our own appointed protectors," Ilai said as he pointed to the stone reliefs. "They've been here so long no one knows who carved them. Some say it was a gift from the elves when we were given the land. Others say it was made by the first Landers who came together to build the symbols from their own hands."

Awestruck, Ysella was transfixed on the two figures. She'd seen many relief sculptures in Bastillos, some towering behind the Precipice barely visible behind the palace. Seeing one span the entirety of a cliff's face, heads scraping the clouds, was far more wondrous.

"You can travel the entire world and still find things that make you feel as though you've never crossed your own threshold," she said, stepping out into the clearing. "They're magnificent."

"Swords and shields are often used as important titles in human societies," Ilai said. "They are the closest people to whoever rules the land. But in the Grey, we have laerds who work together to rule."

"You know politics," she mused. "Do laerds have appointed swords and shields?"

"No," he said, and nodded back to the statues. "They're the only ones in these lands, and no single laerd can lay claim to them."

He led them down a small hill, across a creek, and through the woods where the path wound through dense trees. It was well-worn, and he halted in front of a tall, nondescript stone. Looking upwards through the canopy, Ysella could see the tall eastern cliffs jutting out into the sky.

"Do you remember when I told you of The Cave?" Ilai asked.

"Where you go to honor your dead," Ysella answered.

"Each Laerd's Land has one," Ilai explained. "They're all called The Cave. We cremate our dead and scatter the ashes, unless the Lander was devout to Elssar. I am unfamiliar with that ritual, but here they're placed on a pyre where they died, but they're commemorated in The Cave that has already been a part of their history. We write their names among their kin and leave objects that once belonged to them. And we bring a candle to light each visit."

Peeling back the brush, Ilai revealed a narrow fissure in the rock that curved inward. He motioned for her to follow, turning sideways to enter. It was a tight fit, but once inside, the cave opened up to a space only partially illuminated by daylight through the slit. Ilai picked up a torch from a pile and wrapped a cloth around its end. Once lit, more of the wide space was revealed.

The space appeared to have once been a naturally large, oblong cave, its walls now chiseled and smoothed and opened up to other similar adjoining rooms. At chest height, a strip was carved into the rock where candle wax stuck to the surface at varying heights. There were a few candles still lit, hinting to a recent pilgrimage.

Placed along the stony floor, leaning against the carved walls, were folded clothes, fur pelts, weapons, and even a few paintings. Along the walls, names were carefully carved into columns and lines, all in different handwritings.

"Why do people leave these items here?" Ysella asked. "Wouldn't you worry of theft?"

"It's believed the items left as tribute to their memories will leave a curse when stolen from The Cave," he explained. "The spirit of the one it belongs to will haunt the thief to their death unless the item is returned."

"And if it is never returned?" she asked.

"I'm not sure," he admitted. "It's up to the Lander what they believe. I don't believe in curses, myself, but the superstitious would find a way to calm the spirit. There are some Landers who make a living off of appeasement of the dead. We call them Revenants."

They journeyed further into The Cave, halting in front of a section with several names written stacked on top of each other. At their feet was a broken bow, a wooden bowl, and dried flowers. He held out the torch for Ysella to take. "It's customary, when guests are present, for the host to speak of the people we knew," he stated, and pointed to the column of names. "We speak on each one in their history."

Reverence was a comforting blanket, the memorial a show of humanity. Memories lived on in every mind, and shared stories would commemorate them for generations. "When you spoke of this place before, you said you needed to bring something here."

"It was taken," he answered, and pulled a small candle from his larger pouch. The wick had been lit once before, the wax frozen in a weep. Ilai held the wick to the torch's flame, and then melted the base of the stick, placing it on the collection of wax in the relief.

The candlelight flickered, and then evened to an orange line pointing up to the names above.

"We try to carve the names in a line with the people they knew," Ilai explained, and pointed towards the first name. "Hulgar. He died well before I was born, but he was a man with many tales. He tamed a wyvern named Stoke, and because of it no one would cross him. Except for one man, Egult, who found Hulgar a threat and rallied his own militia just to take down Hulgar and Stoke. This was against the wishes of the laerds, and he ultimately failed. Hulgar rode Stoke through the small army and cut them down with one swoop of his sword."

He motioned to the next name above. "Baile married Hulgar sometime after that battle. She was known as the Ghost of the Scar. There were few who knew it was her. She often saved settlements throughout the Scar from giant spiders, bandits, wyverns, and worgs. Some instances were not her, but her infamy carried out the tale. She could walk through the woods as silent as the still of Winter, moving through brush and trees without disturbing them. Posting boards would specifically request the Ghost's aid, and within days it would be done."

Ilai looked over the final name, hesitant in reverence. "Shera was their daughter and a hunter. She taught me everything I know. She had once been captured by a caravan, and with all the skills her parents taught her, she freed herself and slaughtered almost every one of them single handedly. Being a captive, they rob you of your weapons. She had to fight and kill for one, utilizing whatever she could find to gain the upper hand. And when she did, she freed the caravan's stock and guided the carts to the nearest settlement, giving away the supplies for free. The bow was hers."

The bow was broken as if snapped in two by force, the string holding the two wooden pieces together futilely. "What happened to her bow?" Ysella asked.

Remnants of a memory glossed Ilai's dark eyes, curls falling over his face as he looked at the splintered weapon. "It was broken in her final fight," he answered.

Slowly, Ysella stretched out a hand, hovering it over his shoulder until she let it settle. "You cared for her."

"She gave me guidance. Taught me how to survive," he explained. "The Cave isn't for me to speak on how I feel. It's to know the stories tied to these names."

He pulled the glove from his hand and let the pads of his fingers brush over Shera's name. "She didn't die in that fight. Despite her bow breaking, she won and walked away with her life. She's one of the fortunate ones to die in a warm bed with the comfort of strong walls around her. She had a good meal. There was no suffering. She did not wake in the morning.

"Most of the names you see here died in battle or of sickness or some sort of long suffering, because that is the way of things in the Grey. I think Shera might have liked the thrill of dying in a final fight."

He took a step back from the wall. "We leave the candle to burn until the wick is spent. It's a way to let others know they are remembered. It shows their presence lingers even after we're gone, like the candle."

"It's poetic," Ysella said.

"Does Bastillos have ways to honor the dead?" he asked.

"We lay our dead to rest in tombs," Ysella explained. "Most of the ceremonies are small, family and the like, unless they're someone important. We remove our adornments and instead we don sheer red veils that completely cover us. Laments are sung, passed down generations. We leave things in their tombs. Memories like these. Small tokens to carry them to the next life."

"Red veils," Ilai said thoughtfully.

"They're quite striking," she said, "and beautiful in its sadness. When you're in the crypts with those veils, you stand out among the dark stone. I've not been to many ceremonies. The last one I attended was held all throughout Lumin after the rebel war. We lined the streets in our veils. We looked like the very veins of the city was alive as we mourned. And we mourned not just those that died in the war, but our decisions that led to it."

She read the names carved into the stone by the candlelight. They did not have bombastic symbolism or incredible ceremonies in the Grey Hinterlands, but the intimacy was endearing. Despite never knowing those people, she felt connected to them through Ilai's recount.

"Thank you for bringing me here, Ilai."

He replaced his glove and pat the stone in quiet farewell. Snuffing the torch in a pool of water near the entrance, he discarded the stick on their way out. Their journey through the Scar continued in silence. Ysella expected some form of sorrow or semblance of grief from their pilgrimage, but he carried on, his former apprehension dissipated.

Their path led them close to the eastern figure carved into the cliff, the relief of the sword's point grounded at its base above the tree line. Snow collected on its feet and danced about in softly falling clumps.

"There's a folktale about how the Scar came to be," Ilai said, cutting through the silence. "The elves have a story about this incredible sundering that split the earth into the lands we know. That's how the mountains were formed. The orcs say the Scar defies logic. It is a canyon that stretches from the base of the mountains of Bastillos to the highest peak in the Muldras Range. It travels from southwest to northeast without regard to the formations understood by the Sundering."

"It doesn't seem natural, does it." Ysella looked behind them, the trees obscuring most of the path they had traveled. She could barely make out the edges of the cliffs around them. "I believe there are great things in this world we will never fully understand. Great and terrible things. Magic and otherwise. Whatever caused the Scar, I find myself glad it doesn't appear to be around any longer. What is the folktale?"

The eastern protector stood stalwart, its eyes so far up the facade seemed to bend. Its left hand crossed over its chest for the hand to hold against its heart. The sword was held with its point to the earth gripped tightly in its right hand. The feet were bare, and she could see goats climbing up on its base to reach a cluster of bushes.

"The story," Ilai continued, "goes a little like this: Once there was an elf, powerful in his Earth Magic, who fell in love with an orc. The orc was not impressed with the elf's magic, but said that if he could perform a spell no one had done before, she would marry him. The elf scoured all of Estyr for a spectacular spell, but nothing seemed to woo her.

"He said he would find a way to fly and catch a cloud, and he did so. She received the cloud and placed it with another given to her by an engineer who had already shared the skies. He said he would bend precious metals to make the finest and most unique jewelry, and he did so. She accepted the jewelry, wearing it alongside other, more spectacular pieces crafted by the finest jewelers of her kind. But there was one spell he knew even the most ingenious engineer would never be able to master.

"For an entire Season he pulled the highest peak in Bastillos across the lands and placed it among the Muldras Range with incredible force willed by his magic. She received it, and they married, for he was the one who would move mountains for love."

The Scar felt different with the folktale. She had assumed it was made from something dark or unfortunate with a tragic end, but instead she was met with romanticism. It moved her, her eyes misting as she thought on it. "That's our most powerful magic, is it not?" she mused.

"What is?" he asked.

She smiled fondly. "Love. It has begun wars and ended them. Saved lives and cost them. It's transformed nations and kingdoms and thrones. So small and overlooked, yet unconquerable. It's the one thing they could never teach us, in all my years as a scholar. Yet at its core, love is diplomacy's greatest weakness and its greatest strength."

"I would think it was hate that drives wars and conflicts," Ilai countered. "I would think fear is the reason for diplomacy."

"Ah, it would seem that way, wouldn't it?" She chuckled and carefully shuffled down a steeper slope in the path. He took her hand in his to steady her descent, and just as she thought she reached level ground, a root took hold of her foot.

Toppling forward, the earth careened quickly, halted by a powerful grasp at her waist. Ilai hoisted her up to her feet deftly, and her breath caught in a gasp.

"Careful there," he advised, amusement perched on his lips. "Seems your head is clouded."

Heat flushed her cheeks, and she curled a stray lock of hair behind her ear. "Thank you."

He motioned forward with a swoop of his arm, and continued their journey. "I think it's certainly an ideal way of thinking love is the power, but it's not logical."

"Certainly, some wars begun with hate, but you might be surprised to find how many battles were fought in pursuit of, or in the absence of love," she countered.

"Is the absence of love not hate?"

"I would say it's apathy," she answered. "Apathy does not require hate, but it does require one to forego love. There are some in Bastillos who believe the rebellion began when a woman's lover was killed by the nobleman who owned him. The incident with the orcs sparked their action, but love sparked the idea for opposition. Even if that story is untrue, it's undeniable Beyah's love for her people formed the Low Rebellion. She was their leader, and they followed her into battle for a reason. Love is one of the few universal things people will fight for.

"Take your story, for instance. The elf could have accepted defeat and moved on. He's an elf who will live long after an orc, but love empowered him to do what others would think impossible or impractical. There are many things that drive us, but what other motivation is there that is so worth the effort?"

"I could think of a few," Ilai countered playfully. "Let's see... metal is a powerful motivator. Survival. Food. Ah! Food is a good one."

Ysella laughed. "It should be proof enough that love is power when such a story is told in the Greylands, where by your own claim, compassion is a luxury few can afford."

His smile was bright, the mirth unmistakable and infectious. "It's just the Grey," he informed, chuckling. "The shortened form. You'll expose yourself as an outsider if you call it something like the Greylands."

"But I am an outsider," she mused. "Though, I am fairly certain that would not be the thing that gives me away. More likely, it'll be the lack of weapons, or my ignorance in hunting."

"There are plenty of Landers who don't carry weapons,"he said. "You could look the part."

"Bastillos feels like such a different world now that I've traveled through the Grey Hinterlands," she said, and then corrected her wording. "The Grey."

His grin returned. "You're already getting the hang of it."

"Even if I had to stay here, I'm not sure I could ever fit in," she admitted. "Though, I do appreciate the practicality of trousers."

"Skirts are easier to make," Ilai said. "Our ancestors wore skirts and draped fabrics over their bodies without any sort of tailoring. They were just as skilled. I'm more partial to the protection of trousers, though. Easier to ride a horse, and no updraft."

"Dresses aren't the most comfortable things I've worn," Ysella said. "Skirts, perhaps. But there is a lot of fabric and a lot of pinning and preening and hemming."

Their journey continued, and for the first time Ilai engaged in the banter for longer than a moment. Occasionally, he'd pause to assess their path, attention momentarily drawn in thought when the trail drew worn and overgrown. Once their course was determined, he'd continue the conversation.

This was the man she knew was hidden under the severity and cold logic. It gave her some comfort to know not all his humanity was lost. The sliver Sabin had worried about was still present, still living under all his mental fortifications. She wondered what fractured the mask and what allowed him to feel again. Perhaps it was Shera who reminded him of his soul.

18
ILAI

The snow stopped falling by the afternoon, though the clouds still did not part for the sun to warm the Grey Hinterlands. Ilai drew his cloak around him and felt the absence of his sword by his side. His footsteps grew urgent as the vacancy propelled him northward towards the cliff face where a streak of a waterfall glimmered like a line pulled from the sky to divide the rock face.

Ilai pointed towards the white needle of water. "Halvish is just there."

Within the hour, they reached the small town of clustered buildings built with thickly thatched roofs. The roads climbed steadily uphill that was muddy and wet from compacted and melted snow. Smoke billowed from every chimney to keep the cold at bay. A wooden board built sturdily before a large tavern and inn was used for job postings, the papers nailed and shelter provided by a sloped roof.

The sign for the inn swung with a creak as a gust of wind flew down the hill in a whistle. It displayed the head of a boar with its mouth open and tusks outward with the name "The Boar's Bite" written in Edrosi common. Further down the road among the murmurs of distant conversations was the clanging sound of a blacksmith's hammer.

As Ilai approached the board, he scanned for work that was worth his time. The postings were sparse, mostly filled with notices or odd jobs around the town. While the work wasn't beneath him, he couldn't shake his reluctance to consider them. There was a posting for a kitchen hand and another for a farm hand, both offering pay that would require long-term commitment to justify. Next to them, a request for medicinal herbs was pinned beside a job regarding a giant spider problem. There was a facilitator in town by the name of Branvas, his card tucked within the board's frame. He'd likely be in The Boar's Bite to facilitate payment for the job with the spider.

Heat from within the tavern rolled across his face as a patron exited with an uneven gait. She shut the door behind her and eyed Ilai with scrutiny, her gaze flickering to Ysella as she passed.

To those unfamiliar with Landers and their nuances, they might find Ilai to be common in appearance. Landers were more keen to the sight of a bounty hunter. They came with scars far deeper than typical, their faces cold and stony like a statue chiseled without emotion. Despite the lack of apparent weapon or noticeable build under his cloak, his physique and stature denoted far more than survival at stake.

He moved a gloved hand to the post describing the issue with a giant spider nest nearby. The spider was eating the local livestock, the webbing littering the neighboring forest that deterred hunting and a supply route.

"This pays well," he remarked, his finger tapping against the proposed payment. Landers often took currency from neighboring kingdoms and smelted them into pieces known by their sizes. This also meant the sizes could vary from piece to piece. "Twenty gold fingers. If all goes well you may not have to take on any work. Unless you desire to do any of these other postings."

Ysella answered dryly, "Oh, I don't know, giant spiders sound quite thrilling." She roved over the board, reading every paper completely.

A particular posting halted her movement, her breath catching in a small gasp. Eventually, she willed her gloved hand to brush along an accurate drawing of her features captured in dark ink, her bounty listed in bold letters.

Twenty gold heads. He'd have enough metal to settle his affairs and purchase a plot of land somewhere remote. It was once his motivation. Even just the potential for one gold head in the end was worth while.

The bounty soured in his mind, churned by the fear in her eyes.

"Well, you weren't lying about the price," she stated, and sucked in a sharp breath as if the paper had sliced through her skin. Her hand slowly returned to her side, eyes lingering on the posting as she drew her cloak around her. Rotheel's was pinned beside hers, the same promised price, both entries wanted alive. She stared at his likeness sketched on the parchment.

Ilai realized the accuracy of Ysella's depiction. She was drawn just as clearly as she was standing next to him. The client knew them.

"If these are still up, does that mean there will be others looking for me?" Ysella pulled away from the board, voice quiet. "Are we safe here?"

No place was safe for Ysella in the Grey. He'd known that from the start, yet he felt his thoughts stir with trepidation born from the soft tone of her voice. She hid her fear well, her voice collected behind a focused visage. Perhaps that was the mask of a diplomat.

Ilai ripped her bounty from the nail that held it, swiftly pulling Rotheel's in the process. "Possibly," he answered, and stuffed the papers into a pouch along his belt. He could at least deter Halvish from their pursuit.

The hill town of Halvish was built of stoic stone and wood facades and sloped rooftops made for heavy snows. Most of the people were indoors away from the cold, but even through glass windows Ilai could see the occasional glances their way. Travelers and outsiders weren't uncommon in the Grey, but a scarred, gruff looking man with a proper looking woman beside him was enough to question.

Time and survival had loosened her hair, allowing it to fall in dark rivulets around her shoulders, soft waves cascading down her cloak. Her face remained unblemished, flushed with the chill of the air. But even amidst the chaos of their travels, she hadn't acquired the grime and weariness of a Lander and it gave her away.

She'd need to roll in the mud with the pigs and break her back with labor to look less noble. She carried herself too proper and had healthy gums between her teeth that gleamed as brilliant as the marble stones from the Muldras Mountains.

With a frustrated growl, he turned from her. "We'll need to stick together. And perhaps find something to cover your face as well when we get the fingers. How do you feel about spiders?"

She shot him an incredulous look. "Please say you jest." He dared to meet her gaze, face pulled to a stony calm to test her mettle. Bastillos likely had its fair share of giant spiders crawling around their mountain tunnels, but he had reasonable doubt she'd ever had the displeasure.

Given her wanted status, she'd have to brave the job with him instead of working in town on her own. It was not ideal, but it would ensure her protection. Even then, there was no guarantee someone wouldn't try to fight for the acquisition. They could take advantage of his attention when fighting the spider or intercept them on their way back to town to take both evidence of the spider's end and acquire Ysella in one swoop.

"If I die by a giant spider," she said, cutting through his thoughts, "I can promise you I will not be happy. I'll haunt you, and you'll have to hire a Revenant to appease my soul."

He scoffed in amusement. Revenants were a farce. They preyed on the grieving and cared little of the hurt they caused. "I would not be happy either," he said. "I can't imagine you'd be a good haunt."

She brushed past his lighthearted attempt with determination. "How much is a sword?"

Their pilfered metal was meager, even with the amount Sabin provided in Ysella's travel supplies. It wasn't enough to purchase weapons for the both of them. He would have to haggle considerably, which would risk offense.

Behind him, the clanging hammer honed his thoughts, and he motioned for Ysella to follow him up the hill toward the blacksmith. "The cost of a sword is dependent on the blacksmith. But with what we have, I don't think we'll get more than one."

"If I am to fight a giant spider—"

"You'll not be fighting the spider," he interjected, swiping his hand through the air to dismiss the thought.

Ysella's brow furrowed, nose upturned defiantly. "I'll not just stand about and watch."

"You will have to," Ilai countered, and looked up to the cloudy sky. The day was young as the covered sun crested over the eastern cliff face. "We haven't the metal for two swords, Ysella."

Her hands reached under her cloak to the nape of her neck, and with a soft click of a latch, she collected a golden chain and produced a pendant of a deep red gem framed in a gold setting. "I imagine this will do. It's useless to me otherwise."

The cut stone glinted, refracting the dim sunlight that dared to peek through the clouds. It was impressive the caravaners hadn't swiped the necklace from her long ago. Ysella had cleverly hidden it, secreting it away for so long he was sure of its sentiment. She cradled the necklace in her hands, the act defying her play at apathy. The metal alone would pay for a second blade, and the gemstone would provide enough for a homestead or horses or attire made by a laerd's clothier.

"Do you understand how currency is made here?" he asked. "That metal will be melted down and poured into forms. It looks enough for a gold finger. Understand once you trade it, you'll never get it back."

She rotated the pendant in her palm, thumb brushing against the cut facets. It looked like a red star bursting into a thousand glittering pieces, taking in light and swallowing darkness. It looked like a part of her soul was contained within the stone. She was recalling memories in the touch. Whatever roved through her mind in that moment, she did not share. Instead, she steeled her expression to stoicism.

"I don't believe I have the luxury of sentiment right now," she said. "We need those weapons."

Her stubbornness was frustrating. Only he needed a weapon. She did not, yet she was willing to sacrifice something of personal value to get it, accepting the loss with grace before the piece could be taken from her hands.

"A gold finger isn't much," he said dismissively, and lifted the pendant to feign scrutiny. "A stone like that would be worthless in trade around here."

He placed the pendant back to her hands and continued up the hill towards the smithy. Ilai knew the sting of sentimental loss. The absence of his sword, *her* sword, was evident. It was its own wound gnawing at his side, far more potent than a worg's bite.

19
YSELLA

Ysella's necklace weighed heavier with the rejection. It was worth an incredible sum in Bastillos, even moreso in her heart. She could still remember the moment her mother had given it to her.

It was the eve of her first diplomatic mission, and her nerves waved through her in intermittent tremors. She'd spent the entire evening pacing the open halls of her estate, up the stairs to the roof, and back down to the lower quarters. Her mother finally called her into the drawing room, hands outstretched with a small wooden box and a grin. The box was tied with a golden bow and a sprig of mountain honeysuckle.

"What's this?" Ysella asked, approaching apprehensively.

"Can a mother not dote on her daughter?" Her mother, Dalliah, stepped forward and practically shoved the box into her hands. Ysella pulled the bow loose, setting the flowers down on the table to open the box freely. The garnet stone caught the light from the chandelier, the gold and pearl chains cascading in a delicate pattern. It had a sturdy modern clasp, not ribbon, making the piece all the more fetching.

Her mother clasped it around her throat and turned her to the mirror over the mantel piece. She smiled brightly and brushed her fingers through Ysella's curls.

"My darling, if you cannot win them with words," she said, "which I'm sure you shall, but if you cannot, you'll win them with your beauty."

The piece was stunning. Ysella drifted her fingers over the beads plunging to the pendant. "Mama," she said breathlessly, and turned to face Dalliah. "It's beautiful. You know Father would not be pleased if I went through all my courses and studies just to use something as fleeting as a pretty face to garner diplomatic solutions."

Dalliah held her by her shoulders, an airy laugh escaping her. "Your father is not easily pleased by much. But I have never been more proud of you, Ysella."

It was the first time her mother had uttered those words, and the first time Ysella felt a modicum of closeness to one of her parents. The necklace was only a trinket; a gift she was fond of wearing. It was beautiful, yes, and quite expensive, but the memory it held was more important to her. That moment meant every-thing. In that moment, it felt like her mother loved her.

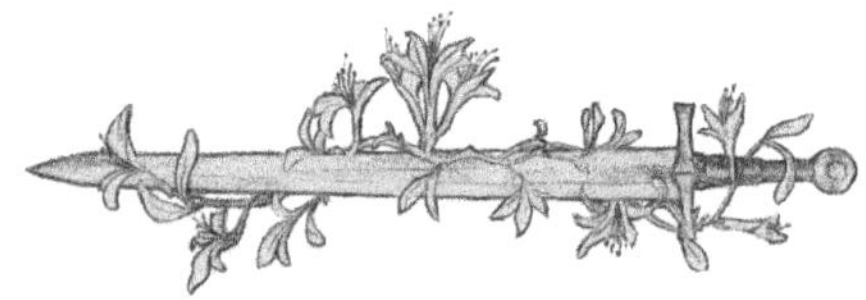

Ysella had no retort for Ilai's rejection. While she did not fully understand how currency worked in the Grey Hinterlands, she knew the look Ilai pretended he did not show. He understood the value to her. She placed the necklace back around her neck and hid it under her clothes once again.

Had she not sat in the front rows of a play to see a true actor play their part flawlessly, had she not sat within senate debates for days watching their careful machinations, Ysella would have taken Ilai's dismissal at face value. She stood a few paces away from him as he spoke to the blacksmith to gauge prices. Around the blacksmith's neck was the symbol of the Patron of Oaths; a shield with a sword set upon it, and a hand placed at the center.

It wasn't uncommon for worshipers of the Nine Patrons to tribute to one specific Patron, but she found it interesting a blacksmith would tribute to Oaths. The Patron of Oaths was of unending loyalty to either something specific, or a moral way of life. It was the Patron they called upon for handfasting, the births of their children, and bending the knee to a monarch or leader. She would have thought a blacksmith would have been tribute to the Patron of War or Death as it would generate the demands for his skills.

Then again, the infighting in the Grey Hinterlands was minimal the last one hundred years. According to Ilai, they did not care about wars outside of their own lands.

Turning from the blacksmith with a wave, he approached Ysella. "How much did Sabin give you?"

"Well, I was thinking," Ysella said. "I saw a posting for a need for medicinal herbs. That could fetch us more metal."

"Any knuckle counts," he said. "Where are they needed?"

"The local healer," she said, attempting to recall the name listed on the posting. "The name starts with an A. Astrid, I believe. Astrid Cohl."

"We'll need to find the healer's hut, then," Ilai said, and looked up the road following the sloped rooftops. Without a sign to catch their attention at this level, he resorted to asking the locals for her location. They all pointed up the hill around a bend.

"Oh, Astrid?" A squat looking man said, eyeing Ysella too curiously for her liking. "Her hut's just that way. Take the right and you'll see it in the clearing. You can't miss it. Laerd Davargan gave her a nice plot of land to grow some herbs, but Winter has been harsh this year."

Ilai thanked the man and held a hand to her back to gently push her forward. The healer's hut was less a hut to Ysella's definition, and more of a hall. It showed the laerd of Halvish felt the business was important.

They stood under an arched awning, the request for herbs nailed to the door where Ilai knocked. A young blonde woman adorned with crow feathers and wolf furs answered the door, blue eyes glancing between the pair as she pulled the door open fully.

"Are either of you injured or sick?" she asked.

"No, we're here regarding your need for herbs," Ilai answered. They stepped over the threshold into a large hall with rows of beds partitioned by wooden privacy folds. It was empty, save for a woman resting soundly in a bed at the far end, a damp cloth to her forehead.

Ysella untied the medicine pouch from her belt and held it up into view. "I have a few herbs and tinctures."

"Ah, indeed, this way." Astrid motioned for them to follow her to the corner of the hall filled with shelves lined with bottles and a counter she used to craft her medicines. A wood stove hummed with a fire, a kettle resting upon it, and to its left a grand fireplace that crackled with freshly lit flames. She gave Ilai a wary glance as Ysella unfurled the pouch, the containers gently clinking.

"They're all labeled correctly," Ysella advised. The healer turned the bottles and tins to read each label, plucking up a few bottles with loose, dried leaves. "I've been out of a few particular remedies in need of these. And antivenoms. You wouldn't happen to have anything of the sort?"

"If we have any antivenoms, we may need it," Ilai advised Ysella. "We're ridding Halvish of the giant spider in the cliffs."

"Is that so?" Astrid studied Ilai with a hardened look, her voice lowering to Ysella as she pointed towards a few bottles, pretending as though that were her subject of conversation. "Two men have died trying to rid us of that spider. Three injured. They took the last of my antivenom. I would advise against it."

"I've seen that man take down very capable men all on his own," Ysella whispered back. "He's even more impressive than he looks. We'll be fine."

"Are you his bait?"

"What?" Ysella glanced to Ilai at her outburst. He looked at her questioningly, and she shook her head to appease his concerns, her voice lowering to Astrid again. "No, he would not use me as bait."

"Are you certain?" Astrid's concern was warming, and for the woman's sake, Ysella did fully weigh her certainty. Ilai's entire demeanor had shifted in the weeks of travel to Halvish where he seemed more in tune with that sliver of a good left within him. He treated her differently and never gave a reminder to their distant dynamic.

"I am certain," Ysella answered. "Could you make more antivenom if we brought back the spider's sac?"

"I'll pay a good price for whatever you can bring of the sort," Astrid said. "I'll pay a gold fist for a sac. And for these three bottles, I'll pay two silver fingers for each."

Ysella looked to Ilai for approval, but Astrid cut in. "I'll not be haggled by the likes of a bounty hunter."

"I wasn't going to haggle," Ilai said pointedly.

Astrid pulled a pouch from her side, fingers fishing through its clanking contents, her attention turning back to Ysella. "I've also got better suited clothes for your figure, if you wish. And some ribbon for your hair." Leaning in towards Ysella, she dropped her voice to a whisper. "And a way out."

"I would not begrudge a change of clothes," Ysella said quietly. "I don't quite follow, though. A way out?"

"She means away from me," Ilai clarified, annoyance evident in the set of his jaw. Despite their lowered voice and the distance he held, their quiet conversation had been heard. Astrid straightened, placing the silver fingers in Ysella's hand.

"You'll have all of Halvish at your throat if you kill me," Astrid warned, and turned to Ysella. "I now realize why you strike me as odd. I recognize you from your wanted listing. You can stay with me, under my protection. This building is a sanctuary for all, and my protection is the laerd's protection."

"No," Ysella answered, with a carefully arranged smile. "No, it's not like that, at all. He's helping me."

"Use logic, healer," Ilai said. "I would kill you and be gone before your laerd found your rotting corpse. There'd be nothing pointing to me."

"Ilai." Ysella eyed him incredulously. He was *not* helping.

The healer scowled, eyes falling on the remnants of discoloration lingering around Ysella's neck. "The offer still stands. And if you return from the spider's den with a venom sac, come back to me. I'll pay the gold fist."

Astrid crossed the room, opening the door leading to her private living quarters. "I'll fetch you some clothes. Free of charge. And if you'd like a bath, I can warm the water."

Shocked by the gesture and lured by the comforting thought of clean skin and warm water, Ysella was nearly too dazed to speak. "That would be lovely, thank you."

Astrid smiled, casting another warning glance to Ilai as she disappeared into her quarters. Ysella stepped up to him, handing over the silver fingers. "You could try to be more diplomatic. Is this enough?"

"Should be," he said as he thumbed through the metal. "I'm not one for appeasing constitutions like hers. I'll head to the blacksmith while you take a bath."

"I can trust her?" Ysella asked.

"She seems to have your best interest at heart," he surmised. "I don't think she'll force you to do anything you don't want to. Healers don't have that kind of want."

Ysella breathed heavily in relief, all the more excited to bathe and wear something more her size. "She knows of my wanted status. She will not give me away?"

"I sense she wants to protect you from your acquisition," he said.

Hesitantly, she fidgeted with the hem of her shirt sleeve. "And you'll return?"

"I will return," he promised. He was genuine, and his voice was soft and devoid of irritation from her insistence.

"Why does she not like you?" Ysella asked. "I know Davargan's lands are wary to outsiders, but I did not think that would extend to bounty hunters. You are a Lander, after all. And I thought bounty hunters helped more than watchers."

"I represent the failings of these lands," Ilai explained. "If people died trying to handle a problem here with the spiders, and I come in and handle it, that's a mark of their failings. Same with the acquisition of unsavory people. Davargan doesn't like those failings so exposed, and thus, his people have adopted such an outlook."

"You speak ill of Davargan's people again, I'll not allow you back into my hall." Astrid returned from her quarters, folded clothes in hand and a scowl on her face.

Pocketing the silver fingers, Ilai bowed his head curtly. "I'll come back when I'm done."

Uncertainty crept through her as Ilai made for the door. Weeks ago, Ysella might have done anything to be freed of the man, or at least she believed she would have. Even prior to the Wayward she made excuses born from her conscience.

Doubt grew in her mind. He had promised his return, but he had said many times he would leave if it suited him. It's been weeks, and they traveled so far, but Astrid had promised her protection. Would that be enough to sway his promises?

What frustrated her most of all was a lingering notion of melancholy. She would miss him.

"Be safe," she called to him. The door hesitated in its closing, and while she could not see him beyond the wood, she imagined he gave a nod as he closed the door behind him.

Astrid guided Ysella into her quarters and tested the heat of the water in the bath, stoking the wood under the metal base of the tub resting on a stone floor sloped to a drain. The tub was made of wood held together by metal rings like a barrel.

On a small table was a pot of tea and a tray of rosemary shortbread. "Help yourself," Astrid said. "I have a patent that needs tending. I'll be just out in the hall. The water is warm."

She set the folded clothes on a chair next to the bath and situated the wooden partition to shield her from the windows and entrances. "Soaps and oils are on the tray next to the bath. Use what you like."

Once left in the eerie quiet of solitude, Ysella sat on a stool to unlace her boots, occasional paranoia stealing her attention. She'd pause long enough to study the sounds beyond the crackle of fire or soft conversation out in the hall or the sounds of the surrounding town life.

Undressing and sinking down into the blessedly agreeable water, Ysella took careful appraisal of the myriad of scratches, bruises and marks marring her once pristine skin. The scratches on her legs were practically healed, the remnants of scabs a shallow line curving the width of her calf.

Whatever came of this trek she would, in many ways, be forever changed, yet not all of the scars could be seen. The Grey Hinterlands had transformed her. She had changed; she'd become braver, perhaps. Wiser in some ways. Calculating, and maybe even a little cruel.

Astrid's soaps smelled of rose and honey and nourished her Winter dry skin. She lay in the bath until her fingers and toes pruned, and by the time she climbed free, steam rose from her skin.

The clothing Astrid had given her fit well. The dark colored trousers actually fit the hips of her frame and tapered to the heel to allow the tall boots to cover the calf for more protection. A long, pale linen shirt cinched at the neck and cuffs, and a fawn-colored jerkin was fitted with a wide leather belt. A blue wool scarf was the only striking color.

She pulled her damp curls back into the ribbon, settling the scarf carefully around her throat. Astrid was in the healer's hall boiling a pot of water when Ysella emerged.

Clearing her throat, she announced her presence. "Thank you for the bath. And the clothes. I feel much better. It was Astrid, yes?"

"Aye," the healer said.

"I'm Ysella. I know you probably already know that from the..." Her voice trailed off, eyes catching the shift from the patient in the bed down at the end of the hall. "We were not properly introduced."

"It's a pleasure to meet you, Ysella," Astrid said, inclining her head.

"May I ask you something?" Ysella asked.

"What can I do for you?"

"This may seem impertinent to ask, but how can Landers tell when someone is a bounty hunter?" Ysella asked. "People seem to judge Ilai based on appearance. They know what he is just by looking at him but to me he just seems like any other."

"It's difficult to explain," Astrid admitted. "It's not just the way they look. It's how they act. How they interact with others. We aren't people to them. We're just things that exist around them. They're colder than Winter's bite and you can tell just by looking at them they'll snap you in two."

"They're all that way?"

Astrid nodded. "Your bruises also tell a tale. I know what those are. And I can see how you two interact. He didn't bother to have you cover them up because he's not ashamed of them. People like us, like you and me, will cover them up to protect you."

Ysella situated the scarf around her neck absently. "I just had no way of covering it myself. It's no fault of his."

The healer studied Ysella as though she were an open book, a brow lofted. "Even if you've hired him for protection, don't forget there's a bounty on your head. That sum is a ridiculous weight, but there are hunters who will chance it. If he's led someone to the slaughter before, he'll do it again. Don't think for a second you're any different than the rest of them."

"A few weeks ago, I might agree with you," Ysella admitted. "Something's changed in him. I'm not sure what or why. He was injured, near death, and we were captured by caravaners. He couldn't make it, and he just let me go."

"You didn't run?" Astrid asked.

"I couldn't," Ysella admitted, shrugging. "Together, we managed to escape, and ever since he's been different."

"Either it's an act or he feels indebted to you," Astrid warned. "If it is the latter, pray to Oaths he's a man to honor the life debt. But if it's the former, you'd best find a way to gain the upper hand. They can play a long game of wits."

A knock on the door interrupted their conversation, and Astrid was diligent to answer. Her demeanor shifted when Ilai darkened the door frame, but she remained cordial, allowing him inside.

20
ILAI

Ilai exited the healer's hall, his chest stiff and unyielding with a sense of odd unease. He had enough metal to buy himself a few weapons, and he no longer had the diplomat at his hip.

He could be rid of her with good conscience. With the aid of the healer, she could potentially petition Laerd Davargan for proper protection and aid to see her plot through, especially with the promise of Bastillosi gold.

Drawing his earthen cloak around him, fur pelt bristling in a breeze, he stepped back to the road and down the hill to the blacksmith with the silver fingers tight in hand.

The family of smiths carried on their tasks as Ilai approached, the father nodding to him in greeting. The mother and son were crafting horseshoes, the son setting a completed shoe to the side.

"You've returned," the son said. He was no more than the age of twenty, his soot covered brow sweaty and without blemish. "I assume you've got the metal?"

"Everything as discussed," Ilai assured. The son motioned for Ilai to follow him inside a long building made mostly of stone. The interior was cool and dry with blades hung on racks lining the walls.

"A sword and a knife, correct?" the young blacksmith asked.

"Aye." Ilai set the fistful of silver fingers down on the top of a table, and the son wiped his hands of soot, counting the pieces with his eyes. The smith pushed two of the silver fingers back to him and collected the rest in his hand. Ilai plucked the remaining metal swiftly.

Two swords were pulled from a rack, both short with sleek and simple cross guards. Adornments weren't necessary to get the job done. He tested the weight and balance of the swords while the blacksmith searched for a few knives. Pulling the sword to his left hand elicited a grunt, the weight pulling at his still-healing wound.

"We've got a selection of knives, depending on what you want," the young blacksmith said as he set the blades on the counter. They varied in size, the longest of which was half the length of his forearm. "Is it for the woman I saw you with earlier?"

"Aye, something modest will do her well," Ilai said, and tapped the counter next to a knife with a blade the length of her small hands. It was sharp on one side.

"I recognize her from the listing," the smith remarked. Ilai paused, contemplating his next move. He remembered the pendant of Oaths hanging on his father's neck. None hung from the son's, but that did not mean he was not tribute to the Patron. In what way did their oaths sway?

The young blacksmith threw his hands up. "It's just odd you'd arm an acquisition."

"I have my reasons."

Ilai stared at the man in pointed warning, gauging his mettle and disposition. He had a strong build from his years handling heavy weapons and hammering metals daily. Fighting him would likely mean fighting his parents, who had the same builds. It'd be a tough fight, and one he did not wish to do.

The young smith nodded, and slid the knife towards Ilai. "A pleasure doing business."

Ilai took the knife and its sheath without another word. It seemed the blacksmith's oaths would not cross his own. Yet something in him felt alert and skeptical, scrutinizing all intent regardless of custom.

"You look... clean," Ilai said as he handed Ysella the knife. She had donned a fresh set of clothing that complimented her lithe frame. Her hair had been pulled back and tied with a ribbon, a blue scarf draped along her neck matching her eyes.

A coy smile graced her lips as she appraised his less clean appearance. "When one is offered a bath, one should accept it readily." Her fingers tapped against the hard leather sheath resting against her palm, head canting. "A philosophy you might be prudent to adapt."

Truth be told, Ilai had desired a bath of his own. Baths weren't typically offered to the likes of him, though he was often removed from civilization for weeks, even months at a time. Given their coming task, he knew a bath would be wasted metal. He could take one on his return.

Ysella pulled the knife free and eyed the blade. It was simple and clean with a fine wooden handle. Sheathing it again, she nodded approvingly. "Thank you. It's better than a stick, at least. What did you get?"

Pulling back his cloak revealed the simple short sword at his hip. "Enough to get through the task," he said. Astrid remained close, ear to their conversation while she feigned her idle tasks.

Ilai lowered his voice to a whisper. "You will be safe here while I handle the spider."

"You're not getting rid of me that easily," she whispered back playfully.

"It's not a matter of being rid of you, Ysella, it's about being safe."

She dismissed his concern with pursed lips and determination set on her brow. "You'd best be careful, Ilai. I'm starting to think you're concerned about my well-being."

"I think it'd be practical for you to stay here," he said. The healer's hall was warm. Too warm for him in his cloak and fur pelt. "You're inexperienced. I won't force you to stay here."

"As much as I feel safe at the moment," she said, "I would feel safer if we stayed together."

The heat was unbearable, and Ilai swung open the sturdy door, exiting into the welcoming chill outside. The cold air washed over his brow, steadily cooling his core as he stood under the awning.

Autonomy was more valuable in the Grey than any metal. All Landers were born from some sort of oppression, whether personally lived or lived by their ancestors. Despite what she once saw in him, he could not dictate her life any longer. He had to trust she would make the best decisions for herself, and trust that it would not get him killed.

She was not his acquisition anymore. Telling her what to do or where to go was no longer an option, and he no longer carried the desire.

By midday the clouds had thickened, and snow fell in sparse clusters that dappled the rocks and grass. Muddy roads formed thin layers of ice that crunched beneath Ilai's weight as they walked the path towards the looming cliff face.

"Have you done this before?" Ysella asked. "Fought this sort of thing?"

Snow dusted the protruding rocks on the cliff wall in a cascade of white. The sloped ground below leading towards the tree line was already blanketed in a thin layer of stringy white too odd to be snow. The white clung to the cliffs in an odd patterns and caught the clouded light in diagonals.

Thick strands of webbing pulled like banners between the cliff side and the ground and led to a cave about the height of ten average people. The webs funneled densely into the cave.

"I have," Ilai said, "though I've not had to handle one so high up." The height of the nest loomed taller than he'd like, especially given the state of his arm. The wound ached in anticipation, and he tested his range of motion with a slow rotation. Most of it had closed considerably, the aching more due to stiffness than angry muscles.

He approached the base of the cliff about twenty paces from the rock. Most of the base was left untouched by the webbing allowing for a sure start, but a quarter of the route up was obscured. He contemplated his approach with the curve of the rock, eyes noting potential footholds.

"You're going to climb?" Ysella asked, her tone skeptical. He clenched his left fist and felt the tension pull through his arm as he flexed under his cloak. "Ilai. Be reasonable."

He scoffed, turning to find her incredulous. She did not know his pain. It had been weeks, the stitches ready to be cut. It was only a matter of regaining his lost strength.

"We lure it out then," he suggested, eyes scanning their surroundings for their next step. Giant spiders were carnivores, hunting deer and any lone strays, including humans. Their webs stretched down to the cluster of pines, casting a shadow over the woods. It had likely already eaten most of the larger game in the surrounding area, which led it to hunt the livestock nearby.

Ilai studied the silvery strands as thick as ropes, woven sturdier than any substance known to man. Cutting through it wasn't impossible, but it was difficult. Melting the webbing would be easier, its sticky coating a quick tinder.

"Start looking for sticks," Ilai said. "We're going to build a fire."

Ysella did not move at first as she studied the rock face leading up to the webbed tunnel. "And then what?"

"Spiders are soft beasts," he explained. "Once we get it out of its hiding hole, we go for the legs and immobilize it."

They piled a modest collection of wood under one of the slightly translucent threads clinging to a jutting rock at the base of the slope. The thread was as thick as the width of his arm and looked like the sinew of a skinned beast. Sparks flew from his flint rock and ignited the kindling, and he carefully coaxed the flames to catch the sticks. Smoke rose first, teasing their efforts until the orange fire danced to life.

As the flames rose higher, they touched the strand of web clinging to the nearest rock. It unfurled with embers and melted as a small flame trailed up its span. Ilai added sprigs of pine needles to created a thicker, more pungent smoke that rose up to the hole in the cliff. He took a few paces back, standing next to Ysella as he watched the fire take its course.

Ilai brought his newly acquired sword in hand, the weight foreign but suitable. It was a balanced blade, and felt right enough.

Smoke thickly trailed in a slanted line within the westward breeze, carrying it into the spider's nest. Two long, bone-like legs emerged, followed by another set, and then another in quick succession. The ends were pronged with edged scopulae that scraped against the stone as it rushed from the affronting smoke. The cephalothorax was grey, furry, oblong, and only slightly smaller than its bulbous abdomen.

Chelicerae as large as his torso chattered, the pedipalps protruding from its front twitching as the creature skittered east across the cliff face and paused, extending outward in observation of the fire. Its body turned with quick jolts and rushed down the cliff headed straight toward them.

"Ilai!" Ysella's voice wavered, and he heard her shuffling behind him. Instinctively, Ilai held out his off hand and placed himself between the creature and Ysella, fixing his attention forward.

The spider towered over him, the muted sunlight darkening further by its presence as it lunged with incredible quickness. Its fangs snapped as it missed

Ilai. He swooped out with his sword to deter its advance towards Ysella, and as it recoiled he sliced across its closest leg.

The free legs pounded the ground in retaliation, and it turned to find its primary aggressor. Through the chaotic clattering, Ilai rushed towards Ysella who had pulled herself tightly inward, the knife gone from her grasp. Frustration overwhelmed him, fear rising to take the reins as he pulled the diplomat out of the way just as the spider regrouped, slamming its two front legs frantically where she once cowered.

"Stay close to the fire!" he commanded, and turned back towards the beast just as it lunged for his side in a shriek. Ilai spun, swiping at its flank and garnering the full attention of its eight black eyes the size of his fists. The spider, despite its size, was agile and quick to keep him out of its blind spot under its belly. Ilai worked swiftly, finding an opening to lunge forward, skidding through the dirt on his knees as he drove his sword through the lower belly of its cephalothorax.

Recoiling with a screech, it lowered the full weight of its body in a thrash, Ilai narrowly missing its flaying.

Skittering up the slope, it nearly looked as though it would retreat, but the smoke lingering above them caused the creature to pause. It halted, indecision placing its stance between fight or flight, chelicerae jittering. In a fraction of a second, it hunched, ready to pounce, when orange light danced close by, heat fanning his cheek with the rush of Ysella's form.

Fire in hand from a crudely fashioned torch, she rammed the flaming stick into one of its eyes. Fire streaked through the air, the roar of flames merging with a shrill shriek as the giant spider stumbled further back. The flames caught its fur on the side of its head, wreathing its flank with heat.

Ilai jumped towards the creature's bulk, piercing through the frontal cephalothorax. He managed to back away just as it slumped to a lifeless heap to the cold ground, a final gurgle escaping its form.

"Sharp thinking," Ilai said as he wiped the viscera from his sword. Her valiant effort did not diminish the frustrations born from her initial fear. It complicated the fight, causing him to divide his attention between protection and attack.

This was exactly why he did not want her to come, and she should have known better.

He scanned the tree line and up to the cliff face for signs of movement. While he was sure by now it had only been the one spider, he needed to distract his mind and find a center of calm.

She was no Lander. She was no woman raised with a blade in hand. Ysella could not be faulted for not truly knowing how she would react when faced with new danger.

"Are you injured?" Ilai turned to Ysella as soon as he felt some of his tension relieved.

Ysella inhaled sharply, face hidden behind her shaking hands. "I'm not supposed to be here," she said through heaves. All manner of frustration dissipated, and he quickly returned his sword to its scabbard, approaching her apprehensively. Her cloak shielded much of her form where there were no immediate signs of physical injury, but he feared her ailment was deeper.

The way she shook. The way her body begged for air and heaved into sobs. She was in some sort of shock.

His hands gently tapped against her wrists, fingers slipping around them carefully to coax her hands from her face. She jumped, startled by his touch.

"Look at me." He spoke calmly, and her eyes met his. "You need to face your reality. You are here. We are alive. The spider is dead. It's time for us to return to Halvish to collect our reward."

"Reality?" Her voice shuddered from her lips, eyes wide and welled with tears. "The reality is I should be home! I should not be here! You brought me here! And you really don't care, do you? You've taken everything! Changed everything! I can't ever get it back. Who I was is gone!"

Her words struck his heart like thousands of thin blades pulled into a gripping vice. Each syllable was a knife stab through his chest, and his jaw set tightly, hardening himself away from the pain.

What a fool he had been to be so vulnerable to an acquisition. He'd allowed himself to become soft and attached. He allowed himself to stupidly agree to hauling a liability farther than was necessary. The acquisition ended at the Way-ward, and he should have parted ways the morning after.

Twenty heads of gold, he reminded himself. Was it worth this effort? She'd get himself killed with how much of a burden she'd become.

Ysella wasn't the first to curse him for their fate. She wasn't the first to cast blame in his direction. But she was the first to make him care about his acquisition, and he hated himself for it. Ysella did not have the mind of a Lander. She did not know how to gauge risks.

The skin of her wrists felt like fire against his gloved fingers, and he removed them quickly. "If you want to wallow in what could have been, I will leave you to it," he said coldly, and turned towards the spider's carcass.

Ysella's knife rested on the ground, dirt flung atop the steel from the shuffle. Ilai swooped down, plucking the blade and stabbing it into the creature's flesh just above the fangs coated in leaking venom. Carefully, despite his rising anger, he extracted the chelicerae.

"Either you face what is your reality or die. That is the way of this land. Bastillos and its mountains make your people weak. You will never get back what you lost and either you become lost with it or you continue on."

"Having compassion and empathy does not make a person weak." Her voice held more venom than what he was harvesting. "Maybe I cannot slay spiders or worgs, but you are no less deficient in your coldness! You know nothing of what makes a life worth living, and I feel sorry for you!"

Her pity was a misguided attempt to direct her shame, he was sure. He did not feel sorry for himself, though he did feel shame for venturing this far with added burden. The fangs popped from their sockets with sacs in tact, slipping with considerable weight to the earth. He wrapped the fangs in the cloth of his cloak, tying them securely with rope. The exertion had warmed him enough for the travel back to Halvish.

"You exist, but to what end?"

Ilai closed his eyes, her words grating his nerves and testing his patience. Twenty gold heads. It was no longer worth the trouble.

Despite his silence, she would not relent.

"You really don't know, do you?" Ysella continued. "You can't see what you lack."

Pressure threatened to suffocate his lungs. It was as though a weight had been placed on his chest as he turned to look at the diplomat, willing his mind to feel nothing at the sight of her distress. A cold barrier formed between them, numbing his mind to her beauty. He slung the heavy chelicerae over his good shoulder.

"What I lack is a warm meal and a little more quiet," he stated flatly, and headed back towards Halvish. He no longer cared if she followed. He did not care if she tripped on a rock or fell into a ravine. All he wanted was to retrieve his reward and purchase a bed for the night.

She kept pace with him, furry balling her hands to fists. Now and again he'd catch her in his peripheral or hear her steps against the more rocky terrain. She followed him back into Halvish quietly right up to the door of the healer's hall. Ilai turned with a stony expression and hoisted one of the fangs from his shoulder. The bulk was large by comparison to her body.

He held out the knife first, which she hesitantly retrieved, anger still perching her lips to a frown. Then he set the large fang before her, holding out the rope for her to take. "Give this to Astrid. A gold fist will get you a horse."

"A horse?" She eyed him incredulously. "No. You do not get to walk away from this. We are going to find Rotheel and find out why this bounty was placed."

"You mock my way of living and then demand it." He scoffed and released his hold on the rope and let the fang fall heavily between them, his voice cold and terse. "Make up your damned mind, woman. Compassion and empathy is exactly what I give to you now at this very moment, and you spit it back."

She reeled back in shock as if he had struck her squarely in the face. "Compassion? To send me off alone? To return to my home a failure? And that is even if I survive such a journey!"

He rolled his eyes, turning to head back down the path to the road, but she quickly grabbed him by the arm. "First you rob me of my duty, then you would force me to return to certain exile by way of worgs and caravaners! What kindness is there in that?"

Her words wove through his heart, shared trauma driving her machinations. She was reminding him of the worgs to hint at the life debt, no doubt. It seemed she surmised the threat of caravaners was personal to him. Another part of her game of wits. Shera had not warned him of viperous women, but she had warned him to steel his heart.

"Whatever I give is never good enough for the likes of you," he said. "What happened was shit and that's life. If you cling to what has already happened, you die out here."

He turned from her again, boots settling into the wet mud on the road sloping downward. There was no point in continuing an argument with a diplomat trained in the art of debate. She would cling to her arrogance and disposition with her life.

With the second fang, he could meet with the facilitator to confirm the giant spider's death, and then go back to Astrid to sell the venom sac.

As he turned down the slope of the hill, Ysella rounded to his front, her hand outstretched to halt his tracks.

"You're a lot of things," she stated sternly, "most of them unpleasant, but I did not figure you for a coward until this very moment!"

Ilai groaned at her misjudgment, though his heart hadn't the energy to refute. He stared at her numbly, unable to halt her fury, his mind wishing for an end.

"If you will not help me save Rotheel, if you utterly refuse to redeem your decision, to impede my journey and deny me the knowledge of why I was taken, then I demand the satisfaction of justice!"

The knife was held in her hand in a sparring stance. Ilai quickly snatched her wrist, and with a strong grip, he pulled her to him, eyes glaring.

"You mistake apathy for cowardice," he growled. "I don't care about Rotheel. I don't care about redemption. I care about surviving, and with the way you act you'll get us both killed."

He released her hand and stepped back, arms outstretched to present himself. "Seek your justice, but weigh the cost."

"The way I act," she repeated in a hiss. "I saved your life. Or have you forgotten that as well?"

Her blatant reminder was the confirmation he needed to close his heart fully. All his grief snuffed to a numbness at his core. People were a selfish lot, and he lost sight of that.

Stepping back, tears streaming down her flush cheeks, a myriad of emotions waved over her features from anger to realization. "That's all you care about though, isn't it? The cost. The bounty."

He felt sick to his stomach, yet he couldn't move. She took the knife and dragged it across her palm, red blooming from her skin. She grabbed his hand tightly, pulling his glove from his fingers, the blood squelching between their closed palms. "There's your cost! Damn your apathy! And damn you, Ilai. My blood is on your hands."

Releasing him, she turned back towards the healer's hall, and he realized he had been holding his breath. He exhaled, the air returning to his lungs in a sharp, cold intake. His shoulder ached where the cold's bite was as hard as the worg's fangs. She was a clever diplomat, as much as it pained him to have been so easily manipulated by her. But he knew she had done it to survive and to save her friend. He couldn't fault her for being so cunning.

21
YSELLA

In the blink of an eye, the world suddenly seemed larger than she remembered. As distance formed between her and Ilai, she steeled her mind to her lonesome task, the cobbled path echoing with each calculated step leading to the healer's hall.

The pale ghost of the sun steeped lower in the clouds, each shadow cast from the rooftops deepening into an ominous stretch of darkness. It was a quiet reminder of the dangers they had faced, and those that now lay ahead of her.

Stooping down to pick up the discarded rope, she was quickly humbled by the incredible weight of the giant spider's fanged jaw. It was easily wider than her own body, its length half her height. She could only drag it over the threshold with Astrid's aid, who paid her with a gold fist as promised.

The gold was a large oblong sphere a bit larger than her own fist, its surface smooth and unpolished. Astrid gave her a pouch to carry it in, the weight of it pulling her belt downward.

Ilai had been insistent. She was a burden to him and he wanted to be rid of her. He would not see her safely to Ethyrnon Tower, and she had to accept that he had not changed as she once thought. He did not care. Astrid had been right to warn her, even Sabin had warned her weeks ago, yet somehow the pain felt deeper than it should have.

She should have felt relief parting from the bounty hunter. There should have been a sense of freedom, yet the further down the road she traveled, the more aware she became of her isolation. In the open streets, she felt watched, and the increasing paranoia streaked ice through her veins; a chill curling the length of her body.

Somewhere close by, a door creaked open, and Ysella looked toward the source. The wooden sign for The Boar's Bite wagged on its hinges in the chilling breeze, a rowdy pair spilling into the street with boisterous laughter. Drawing up her hood, she waited for the voices to fade and approached the establishment, slipping inside to a rowdy crowd and playful music from a pair of minstrels in the corner.

The warmth of the tavern surrounded her, the door shutting at her back. Shouts and laughter and conversations flooded overwhelmingly, merging into a cacophonous nothing. Something warm and savory was truncated by the pungent odor of alcohol, sweat, and something decidedly more foul than both.

Ysella caught only one other woman present in the patronage. The young barmaid flitted from table to table, golden curls piled high on her head, her cheeks red with exertion. Ysella's entrance came unnoticed, and she felt out of place. Nevertheless, she pressed on and approached the far counter and waited for the stocky, freckle-faced barkeep to turn her way.

"What can I do for you?" he asked, wiping his hands on the front of his apron. "Stew's down to dregs, but we've plenty else. Quieter tables upstairs as well. Or was it a room you needed?"

"Neither," Ysella answered, an unfamiliar edge of uneasiness in her voice. "Thank you. I'm in need of directions."

"Directions? Where you headed?"

"The Twisted Woods."

Curiosity touched the man's round face, a brow lofting as he scratched the wide, bristly mustache beneath his large nose. "That's a long stretch of lands, there. You'll need to be a little more specific. Do you know which laerd's land?"

Stumbling, Ysella quickly roved her memories for the name of the laerd. She did not wish to name the tower, lest it jog a memory of his own. He worked in The Boar's Bite, therefore he likely passed the board just outside the entrance every day.

"Laerd Valarad," Ysella recalled, and by the barkeeps long nod, she knew she'd given the right answer.

"Ah, that does make the most sense. He owns most of that tree line," he said. "But Laerd Gargas does own a lower portion of those woods. Not the best place to go, you know. Evil things come out of those woods."

"I'm aware." Ysella's shoulders rose in a shrug, her hands forming knots at her sides. "Yet that is where I must go. Only, I've never been there, and I don't know the way."

"Don't mean to eavesdrop, miss." The voice came from a man perched a few stools down to her right. Tall and lean, he came nearly to her full height sitting down, fixing her with a clear, green-eyed gaze. A noticeable scar ridged the end of his bony jaw partially obscured by long, dark curls. "You're headed to the Twisted Woods?"

Hesitantly, Ysella gave a brief nod. "I am, yes."

"My partner, Hamish, and I are headed that way ourselves. Could take you as far as Dournfast."

"I'm sorry, I can't pay you." It was a lie, but some odd instinct told her to hold fast to her metal. The tall man waved a dismissive hand.

"No need for payment," he assured. "It's only a few days travel if we stay clear of the weather. If you can cook, it's all the better. You look like you've got your own way handled."

"I can cook, yes. Some." While that was not a lie, it was a rare occasion where she had cooked a meal on her own. Her time in the kitchen was brief and intended for gossip with the kitchen staff while they prepared her family's meals. She watched, and was allowed to help in secret as long as her parents were away. The only time Ysella prepared a meal on her own was at the height of the rebel war.

The tall man grinned, pushing his mug aside and holding out his hand for her to shake. "Seems we can help each other on the long road ahead. Jonais. What can I call you?"

With a measure of uncertainty, Ysella looked to the barkeep who gave a shrug.

"Rowena," Ysella said as she shook the tall man's hand. "Thank you, Jonais. To Dournfast, you said?"

Jonais nodded. "Dournfast has a good lot. I'm sure you'll be able to find someone there to cart you all the way to Grey Point. We leave within the hour. Hamish is just getting supplies."

"And you'd do this free of charge?"

"Sometimes it's more about how we can help each other in the long run." Jonais finished the contents of his mug, motioning to the barkeep for another. "As long as you're no trouble, I don't see any hassle in it."

Hamish, as it turned out, was the squat fellow who had given directions to the healer's hut earlier that day. They met him just at the edge of Halvish while the sun still brightened the sky. He was two heads shorter than Jonais, but nearly twice as wide. His hair was too light for his olive skin, and his eyes were big and watery like he'd been exerting himself for hours. He met Ysella with a confused glance, which Jonais waved away.

"Didn't I see you with that surly looking fellow earlier today?" Hamish asked.

"He helped me get to Halvish," Ysella explained. "That job is done."

The two men exchanged a glance, then a nod, and Jonais gestured to a pack at Hamish's feet. "Do you mind carrying that one, Rowena?"

As Ysella leaned down to collect the pack, a familiar cold pressed against the back of her neck. In a fraction of a moment, confusion warred within her, panic swelling behind it as the familiar clack of a locking mechanism sealed her neck in metal, a rattling chain unfurling between her and Jonais.

Ysella bolted upright, Jonais firmly gripping the chain with an unnecessary yank to draw her close enough to smell the sour alcohol on his breath and see the dirt in his stubble.

"Here I thought a diplomat from Bastillos would be smart," he mused. "You know that portrait of yours has been in every town in the Grey for weeks now, right? Even in Halvish. Hamish recognized you immediately."

Ysella's heart raced, head whirling with fear and regret at her easy misfortune. She should have seen it from the start, and in her hindsight, she could see now these men were unsavory in appearance, their ill intent evident in their cold visages.

"Don't do this," she meekly begged. "Please."

The two men chuckled at her pleading, Hamish elbowing his cohort as he picked up the pack at his feet. "She's asking nicely, Jonais."

"What's a man to do in the face of such a nice request?" Jonais pulled the chain again, launching her forward in a stumble. Ysella scrambled for her footing to catch up to the pair. Hamish slowed his pace to watch her back.

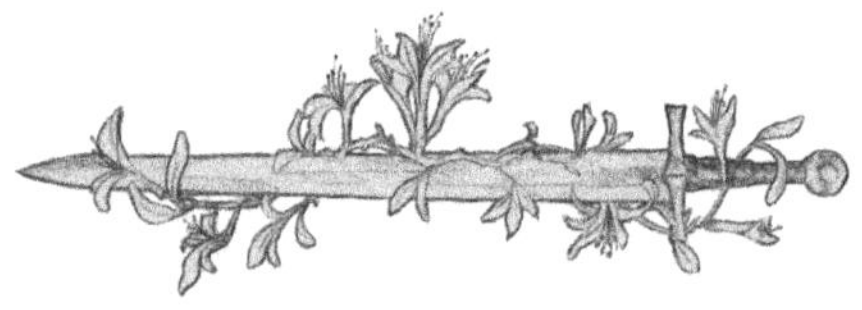

The road winding away from Halvish was well-worn, but the growing dark made it nearly impossible to see the rocks and stones beneath her feet. With each stumble, Jonais would give the chain a tug, the cold metal of the collar biting into her skin, irritating old bruises and creating new ones.

For all his initial harshness, Ilai had never been so cruel. Jonais and Hamish chuckled with each squeal of pain until Ysella bit her cheek to keep from crying out.

Copper filled her mouth, her eyes tearing, but over time their laughter dwindled. A spark of pride fanned at the surface of her mind, relishing in their diminished mirth at her expense. But it was as fleeting as embers once Jonais announced they were making camp. A new wave of fear welled within her.

We aren't people to them. We're just things that exist around them.

Astrid's words filled her mind like a broken nest of wasps, and her heart knit in her chest, eyes brimming with tears. Fear had been so prevalent the night Ilai had first taken her. She had anticipated the worst, but he had been shockingly honorable, and then he saved her life. They saved each other. Time and time again, they saved each other. So why had she doubted his ability to protect her with the spider? And why had he pushed her to leave? Now she was facing unknown horrors. The ones that Astrid had been wary of were her new captors.

And it was all her fault.

She had done this. Not Ilai. She had stubbornly refused to trust him. Looking down at her crudely bandaged hand, she grimaced at her painful reminder of her last words to Ilai. They were meant to hurt him. To wound him and appeal to that sliver of good in his soul.

Her words had exposed her, too. The hurt she felt in his apathy. That cold visage staring at her like a statue, indifferent and casting her aside so easily. He abandoned her without a fight.

She would have taken his apathy over the prospects before her now. These men showed little in conscience or a Lander's care for the individual. Regan seemed more savory than Jonais and Hamish, as much as she loathed to consider.

Hamish stoked a fire to life, and Jonais caught her emotional state in the firelight. "You know," Jonais said as he sat next to the fire, "we first got word of your bounty from a facilitator in Marvath. The postings had only just gone up that side of the Grey. Took a few days to get to where we planned to intercept, but we found a Bastillosi carriage ransacked instead, bodies splayed about like a worg attack."

Hamish chuckled. "*He* thought it was a worg attack."

Jonais swiped a hand through the air dismissively. "Worgs or not, we thought we were out twenty gold heads. I don't even think you understand how large a sum that is here. Even split fifty-fifty, Hamish and I'll be set for life."

"That's eight heads each," Hamish said.

"No I think it's nine and nine makes twenty," Jonais said.

"Odd numbers make odd numbers," Hamish said confidently.

"Ten," Ysella corrected, and the pair looked at her incredulously. "It's ten each. Ten and ten equals twenty."

Hamish scoffed, and Jonais rolled his eyes. "At least you're pretty. Anyway, we figured we could intercept the other diplomat, so we headed north for the job."

"Why are you telling me this?" Ysella asked. Her throat was parched, and she swallowed hard as she watched Hamish take a swig from his canteen. Ilai had at least offered her food and water as his acquisition. He was not like other hunters, it seemed.

"Everyone loves a good story," Jonais said.

"This isn't a very good story," she retorted.

"I'm getting to the good part, be patient." Jonais pulled a loaf of bread from his sack, tearing off a large piece and handing the rest to Hamish. The man continued his story, his mouth constantly half full with his meal. "We got word the other diplomat was killed back near Bavard—"

"Killed?" Ysella interjected, alert and straightening where she sat in the frosted dirt.

"Don't interrupt the story," Jonais said. Her heart sank, sorrow blanketing her soul as fresh tears threatened to fall. She couldn't believe Rotheel was truly dead. He was strong willed and clever and actually knew how to fight, unlike her. They had been close friends as children, but he had a cunning to him that she had grown to dislike as they grew older, which made it all the more complicated when their parents had announced their impending union. Still, she had cared for him, even if marriage had not been an appealing outcome.

"Anyway, we got to Halvish looking for another job to take and Hamish comes running down the road, face red as beets saying he found you. All this time and he found you wandering around with a bounty hunter who managed to convince you he'll protect you or whatever. Clever ruse. We hatched our plan then, you see. We were going to save you from him. Spent all day plotting, waiting for him to go to the facilitator with evidence of the spider kill. We figured he'd either die doing that, or he'd come back with the spoils."

Reaching out, his finger curled along Ysella's cheek, and she recoiled.

"Don't."

"Ah. Touchy." Jonais ran the pad of his thumb across the edge of her lower lip. Ysella slapped his hand away.

"I said *don't!*"

The back of his hand swung out, knuckle cracking against her mouth. As the taste of blood bloomed on her tongue, the chain drew taut. A tight grip caught her by the jaw, locking her head in place. Hamish whistled in amusement, chortling into his canteen.

"Out here, you don't make the demands," Jonais warned. Ysella's attempt to pull from his bony fingers only served to tighten his hold, his teeth clenched to mirror the vice. "I'll do whatever I please, you understand? You'll listen, or I'll make you beg Death will grant you mercy."

Shoving her to the dirt, he loosened the slack on the chain enough to return to his place by the fire. Hamish shook his head, silently reveling in the drama around him.

"She's not even the good kind of chatty," Hamish mused.

Testing her lip with her tongue, she found the split skin was already swelling. It stung, magnified by the cold air biting and drying her lips with each breath. Jonais chewed on his bread, his mood shifting away from his annoyances as he talked to Hamish idly about the weather. They heard it'd be clear for a few days. Enough to get them to Dournfast. Hamish straddled the chain as he placed a kettle near the fire.

"We'll sleep in shifts," Jonais said. "I wanna move out before first light. The sooner we rid ourselves of this useless bint, the sooner we're twenty gold heads richer."

Through all she had endured on her journey through the Grey Hinterlands, Ilai had always been there to protect her. First, he protected her as his acquisition. But then he protected her as an equal. He was always there. Always stalwart, saving her when all odds felt against her survival.

He wouldn't be here to save her this time.

Understanding threaded through memories and words as she felt the fibers weave blood into acquittance. Ilai wrapped himself in crimson blame, shrouding the man in the cavern from her guilt, pointing instead toward the needle of responsibility that laced through the loom of Death. She held that needle before he plucked it from her grasp and laid claim. Once again, she clutched the needle in guilt-ridden hands, trembling with the thought of dipping the thread in red once again.

Glancing between the pair absorbed in their conversation, Ysella found her opening, and with haste she gripped her chain and pulled. The links caught on Hamish's unbalanced back foot, the sudden momentum toppling the squat man forward, hands first, into the fire.

A scream exploded through the darkness around them. Jonais released the chain and pulled his friend free from the flames. He screamed, face blistered and eyes swollen shut, hair singed and hands shaking.

Bolting to her feet, Ysella ran. For the first time she ran. She made it no more than ten feet when a body collided with hers from behind. Powerful arms wrapped around her middle, air sucked from her lungs as she collided with the cold forest floor. A heavy weight settled on her throat beneath the metal collar as Jonais's hand barred her to the earth.

Hamish wailed in pain behind her, but Jonais held his gaze wildly, his free hand releasing a sliver of a blade with a flick of his wrist. Ysella tried to pull away with a soft whimper, the blade pressed against the soft flesh of her cheek following her movements.

"That was stupid. That was *really* stupid," he warned. "Do you want to be stupid *and* ugly? Maybe I'll carve up that pretty face a bit."

She flailed, hands swiping through the air, clawing at any part of his clothing she could reach. His head was too far away to reach his eyes. He was too tall of a man for such an endeavor, and he grinned at her futile attempts.

An arrow whistled through the night air, and with a heavy thwack! blood splattered against Ysella's face and arms as the arrow lodged in Jonais's throat. He clawed at the wound, groans turning to gurgling as fluid drowned him. And then Hamish's wailing was cut short, punctuated by a thud and crackling embers.

Slow footsteps walked up to Ysella as she coughed for air, coming to face another blade to her throat and a boot to her chest.

"Ysella of House Ronasin?" a woman's voice asked. She was pale and tall with dark hair that flowed around her shoulders like the mane of a horse. Across her cheek and down to her throat was a prominent scar.

Without moving, Ysella's breath exhaled in a soft sob, her eyes falling shut, the momentary flood of relief overwhelmed by the sinking weight of despair. Twenty gold heads. She would have given ten times that amount to undo her own foolhearty decisions to leave Ilai.

"What do you want?"

The woman lowered herself, boot still pressed to the diplomat's chest until she switched to her knee and pressed her weight into Ysella's sternum. "I want you to know-" She wrapped her hands around Ysella's neck, leaning in to whisper the rest. "-I don't care about the sum, you High Lumin scum."

Grimacing, fighting another bitter exhale, Ysella shot the woman a withering glare. "If you're going to insult me, the least you can do is not be a hypocrite about it," Ysella managed to gasp.

With a disgusted grimace, the woman's hands clenched tighter, leather gloves creaking with the strain, eyes boring into hers unwaveringly. Ysella struggled for air, the night growing darker around the edges of her eyes.

22
ILAI

Steam billowed from a bath house tub, the stone floors damp and musty as Ilai stared out at the cliff side view, bloody hand raised over the scrubbing bowl. Ysella's blood was smeared across his palm like the very Scar itself leading from wrist to fingers. He dipped the hand into the scrubbing bowl on the table next to the tub, scrubbing the hand clean with the cloth in the cold water.

It had been too long since he'd had a proper bath. The water was hot enough to prickle his skin as he entered, relief warming his muscles and bones. Staring out at the vista, the jutting cliffs served as a reminder of his failings.

Ilai scrubbed his body with soap and trimmed his beard with the provided sheers. Through the looking glass, he saw the mangled mess of his shoulder, the sutures holding steadfast. It looked like a map where portions of his skin healed in odd ridges where it was torn irreparably. Ilai cleaned the sheers of his beard hairs and cut each suture he could reach, pulling the threads free of his skin one by one.

Without the pull of threads, Ilai's range of motion improved. He no longer felt like he'd damage his skin further if he raised his arm too high. He slung the remaining spider's fang over his shoulder and made his way to The Boar's Bite.

Night would soon close on Halvish, the cloudy sky dimming. A woman clad in furs with a scar running up her neck to her jawline burst from the tavern door in a rush. Ilai immediately recognized her severity.

"Arjah?"

The woman turned, brow furrowing as she caught sight of Ilai. "Ilai?"

Their history defined their hesitation, Arjah only stepping to face him fully, one foot pointed to the road. Her wild hair had gotten longer since he last saw her. She always let it flow free, braiding only pieces to weave trinkets through the locks. Her blue eyes were as bright as a cloudy day and caught the light from The Boar's Bite like glass. She was once a slave of Bastillos, free now in the Grey, and he considered her a Lander.

"It's been some time," Ilai said. "Let me buy you a drink."

"I'm afraid I cannot tonight," she said. "I'm on the hunt."

Arjah was the fearsome sort of bounty hunter. She never captured acquisitions. She only killed them and took the lesser sum, often being hired specifically for assassinations. He pitied her prey, for he knew she was brutal and fierce.

"I understand," Ilai said. He would have liked to have a moment with her again. When last they parted, she disappeared in the night leaving only an apologetic letter. Her past still haunted her, and so she could not find peace enough to share her life with another.

"Perhaps our paths will cross again, Ilai," she said solemnly. "I must go."

She jogged off down the road to avoid further delay, and he did not deter her. Whatever distance was between her and her prey, she'd close it quickly.

The raucous patrons filled the main floor to capacity, Ilai weaving through the crowd as though he were pulling himself through a narrow cave. Eventually he made it to the barkeep, who nodded to Ilai in greeting.

"What can I do for you?" he asked through a bushy mustache.

"I'm looking for Branvas," Ilai said. The barkeep pointed up to the second level.

"He likes the corner overlooking the tavern," the barkeep informed. "Bald fellow with a big beard and ink at his temples that are tribute to Life and Death."

With a nod in thanks, Ilai headed up the stairs, the patronage thinning. It wasn't quieter on the upper level, the balcony wide open to the cacophony below. The patronage was significantly less rowdy.

Branvas sat in the far corner, chair leaning back against the wall, boots propped up on the railing. He was smoking a pipe as Ilai approached, brown eyes keenly assessing the hunter as Ilai rolled the cheliscera off his shoulder, the jaw thudding to the floor next to his table.

"Killed the spider, I see." Branvas sat up in his seat, motioning for Ilai to take the empty one across from him. "Was hoping someone would eventually get it."

"And payment?" Ilai settled in the chair, intent on keeping things strictly business.

Facilitators were the more social of the bounty hunters. They handled payments for a modest cut from the clients, preventing the unsavory business from darkening their doorstep.

Branvas did not look as approachable as he spoke. His deep set eyes were under heavy brows, his bald head gleaming from the firelight. Two tattoos stood out on his naturally darker skin. On his left temple was the symbol of the Patron of Death; a frayed chord, its edges weaving out like the roots of a tree tangled in the wax of a small, weeping candle. The chord was usually knotted in a frame around the skull, but for his tattoo, the chord snaked along the crown of his head to the an open eye of stars symbolizing the Patron of Life. The only hair on his face was his thick black beard braided at the chin.

His cloak and furs were draped on the back of his chair revealing a powerful, stocky build. He looked like he could still be a hunter himself were it not for his missing right arm. Digging through a pouch at his back, he produced a cinched sack that clattered against the table as he tossed it to Ilai.

There was more than the offered bounty in the sack, and Ilai counted the fingers twice. "This is twenty gold and ten silver fingers."

"Aye," Branvas said. "The silver fingers were added after the posting was printed. Locals pooled together after it started going after the livestock."

Ilai didn't question it further, stuffing the sack in his own secure pouch. The sum would fetch some proper equipment. He could afford a bow and a quiver of arrows on the silver alone.

"Do you have any unlisted postings?" Ilai asked. Facilitators were often given secret jobs to divvy out to inquiring and capable hunters. Branvas studied Ilai as he puffed his weed.

"I've got one that may interest you," he said. "Four Laerds' Lands have been plagued by a singular man who goes by the name of Wraith. Survivors say he's a blood mage. This one sounds old enough to be one of the ones involved in the Dark Calamity."

"They were all killed twenty years ago," Ilai said.

"He sounds just like them. No fresh marks on his skin to call on his magic. Feeds on the blood of his victims."

A mage of that caliber would be a difficult fight for Ilai, but a challenge he was willing to take. "Where was he last seen?"

"Western Grey," Branvas answered. "His trail of blood headed southward last I heard."

"He could be out of the Grey by now," Ilai remarked.

"Potentially, but survivors say he's searching for someone specific," the facilitator said. "I don't think he'll leave the Grey anytime soon. Laerds Fathgar, Wogh, Barmog, and Trevan request proof of death personally. You should be able to find a facilitator near their keeps."

Ilai followed the map of the Laerds' Lands in his mind, the eastern trail leading from Fathgar to Trevan's lands parallel with the Scar. It could have been a coincidence, but he couldn't help but notice the route starting where Rotheel had last been seen, and where Ilai and Ysella encountered the caravan. They even spoke to Laerd Trevan's watchers, who could have sold her information for a price.

"Do you know how far south?" Ilai asked. The Wayward was vulnerable, and he felt a surge of responsibility.

"Haven't heard of any attacks since, so I'm not sure what direction he's headed," Branvas admitted. Ilai stood, hauling the remnants of the giant spider back over his shoulder. "Oh, hunter, I've been meaning to ask. What happened to your earlier acquisition?"

He narrowed his eyes with scrutiny and noticed his table had a clear view of the window overlooking the posting board just outside the tavern. He must have been watching.

"The spider killed her," he answered flatly.

"Ah, I fear she might have pulled one over you," Branvas said. "Saw her leaving not but an hour or so ago with two other hunters from this very tavern. Headed to Dournfast, if I recall."

"Is that so?" Ilai feigned nonchalance.

"Had another hunter come in asking for her whereabouts," the facilitator continued. "She didn't seem to mind the competition. By the look of her, though, it won't be much of a fight. Those men were surly, but she has a look about her."

"Tall woman? Long hair?" Ilai asked, unable to contain his sense of urgency. If Arjah was going after Ysella, she would not be an acquisition.

"Yeah, deep scar from her throat to her jaw," Branvas said.

Ilai dropped the chelicera and darted from the tavern in a flash. The Grey's most dangerous assassin was on the heels of Ysella's new captors, and now he knew who she was hunting. Given her past, this was a personal hunt for Arjah. She'd stop at nothing to see Ysella dead.

Tracking in the dark of night wasn't impossible, but it was not Ilai's strongest skill. The overcast obscured details in the brush and dirt, the snow too much of a dusting to refract ambient light.

He knew the most direct way to Dournfast would require going up Death's Chord; a winding road carved into the cliff face beyond the dead spider's den. They'd have to camp for the night as the upward path was perilous and steep.

Given Arjah's hunt, he could not slow his pace for long, his lungs breathing in sharp, cold air that kept his anxious mind honed. Barely a thought raced through his mind as he focused sharply on his path, blind to everything but his own hunt.

An agonizing cry billowed through the woods. Ilai could barely make out the faint orange light dancing in the distance. He rushed forward, Arjah's silhouette unmistakable as she lowered herself to her knees before a cowering figure.

Ysella squirmed against Arjah's hold on her neck, hands raking through the dirt for retribution as she gasped for air. The hunter's knee pressed her weight into Ysella's chest, further straining her ability to breathe. Ysella's hand clenched a fist full of dirt, flinging it into Arjah's face.

Instinctively, Arjah shielded her eyes from the affronting dirt. It was his opening to attack. Ilai rushed behind her, lifting Arjah up by her shoulders and thrusting her across the woodland floor.

Sword drawn, he placed himself between Ysella and the feral-looking assassin, her pale skin beading with sweat and twisted in betrayal. She pulled a short sword from her side in an upward swoop, meeting Ilai's blade in a parry, swinging it back to keep her at a distance. Every attempt to flank him was met with swift resistance until she was backed further and further away from Ysella.

A heap of a man kindled the campfire to a heated roar as he fought against a capable adversary and once-friend. Steel clanged presenting an opening, and within a fraction of a breath his hilt impacted Arjah's head squarely. She fell backward in the momentum, body unmoving, but with quick observation, she was still breathing.

Ilai sheathed his sword and walked back to Ysella's side, gloved hands steadying her head to the firelight to check her wounds. He dug through the pockets of the dead man closest to her, producing the key and unlocking her collar.

"Ysella?"

As the metal slid free of her battered neck, Ysella stared at Ilai, tears leaving tracks in the dirt and viscera on her pale cheeks. There was a pause of silence, then wordlessly, her arms flew around his neck and she pulled herself to him.

"You came for me."

A rush of relief escaped his lungs at her embrace, and he returned it in kind. "We need to go. Do you still have your dagger?" He pulled back. "Are you injured?"

Sniffing lightly, her shaking hands brushed her cheeks dry by her palms. "Not badly, no." Fingertips testing her neck, she flinched. "I'll live."

Eyes wide, she kept her gaze fixed on him, firelight glittering against her tears as she gestured towards the roaring fire. "H-Hamish. My things."

The wounds she sustained crushed his soul. New bruises splotched against her skin, her lip split and swollen from a forceful impact. Ilai's thumb gingerly brushed over the split in her lip. He should not have let her leave.

"Stay here," he advised. "Don't look."

He turned toward the fire where the man once known as Hamish was now the main source to feed the fire. The portly man's upper body was charred and lapped in flames creating a pungent stench and dark smoke.

Next to the fire rested a pile of belongings, among which he found Ysella's medicine pouch and knife. He collected them, pilfering metal and weapons and bedding from the corpses. "Whatever our differences, I can help you hire a more suitable guard for the rest of your journey." He handed over the knife, and gave her Hamish's sword.

Tears freshly welled in her eyes as she scrambled to her feet. "Please don't leave. I-I'm sorry, I'm so sorry, Ilai. I was wrong. I was so wrong and I knew the moment I walked away. I was afraid."

Ilai set down the weapons, placing his hand back to her cheeks, and attempted to quiet her frantic regrets with a soft shush.

"I'll do whatever you need," she pleaded, his attempts to calm her unnoticed in her bout of fear. "I'll stay quiet. I'll learn to fight, to hunt, to build shelters and fires. Whatever you need, only please don't leave me."

"Ysella." He brushed the stray locks from her face and gently coaxed her gaze to his. "Do not compromise. I will help you, if that is what you truly want. But do not stay quiet if you don't want to be quiet. Learn if you wish to learn. Don't do it if you think I'll leave. I won't leave if you want me to stay."

Lip quivering, she managed a nod as she held back more sobs. She clasped her hands around his. "I can't do this without you, and I don't want to, Ilai. I need you to stay."

He was not a religious man. He did not believe in Elssar or the Patrons, but he swore to Oaths he would not leave her again.

"Can you walk?" He remained stalwart as she steadied her stance, then stooped down to retrieve the weapons and supplies. "We need to go."

Ysella held onto Ilai's arm as she steadied her stance, and she stared at the unconscious Arjah. "She was from Bastillos," Ysella said. "She didn't even want the bounty. She just wanted me dead. I've never even met her, but she hated me that much, and maybe she was right to."

Her fingers delicately touched her reddened neck. It was fortunate she did not know the full hatred of Arjah. "I never fully understood Lower Lumin's people until now."

"What do you mean?" Ilai asked as he slung one of the packs over his shoulder. He held one out to Ysella.

"We did our best to be kind to our servants. My family, at least. We tried to treat them right, but what we did was irreparable," Ysella explained. "They were still treated less than human. I could see that pain manifest in her eyes. I may not have been the one to hurt her, but I was a part of that society. I never fully understood their hatred, their rebellion, until I lived it. What does that make me?"

"Changed," Ilai said.

"I should not have fought back," Ysella said solemnly. "She deserved retribution. I've only experienced a fraction of what her life had been. No one deserves that. Well, they certainly don't. Maybe I did for not seeing it before. Elssar speaks of receiving what you put into the world."

"You don't deserve it either, Ysella." Ilai looked over his shoulder at the heap of the woman in the dirt, and ushered Ysella forward. Arjah would hunt for relief for the rest of her life, running from the anguish forced upon her childhood. "We are what our past made us to be."

23
YSELLA

"We're going back to Halvish?"

The hill town glowed in the dark of night, the slope littered with tiny orange dots of torchlight. "The safest place for you tonight is in the healer's hall," Ilai informed.

"You'll not leave me?"

"I will not," he assured. She clung to his arm all the same, the dark more frightening in the wilderness now that she knew the dangers on her own.

Astrid was asleep when they arrived, but roused and welcomed Ysella in without hesitation, a knife drawn and held to Ilai as he could cross the threshold. "Did he do this to you?"

"No, Astrid, he saved me from other hunters," Ysella assured, and placed a pleading hand on the healer's own. Astrid reluctantly lowered the knife and motioned for Ilai to enter.

Ilai offered to generously pay for two beds for the night. She took the silver fingers without argument, allowing the pair to take their pick of the seven remaining empty beds. The far bed still had its sick patient sleeping restlessly.

Astrid made little remarks as she cleaned and dressed Ysella's wounds. A healing balm on the lips soothed the sting. Ilai sat on the bed next to her and rummaged through the packs they stole from the dead hunters. One pack had proper cooking supplies with pans and a pot and dry ingredients for cooking. The other had blankets and clothes, a dagger, and extra metal.

"Clean this daily," Astrid advised Ysella. "I'll send some fresh bandages with you."

Astrid leaned in, her hand passing a small metal vial into Ysella's palm, her voice a whisper. "This is a poison. Coat your blade, or pour it in a drink. It won't take much. Keep it somewhere that won't be pilfered."

Ysella pitied the woman and her lack of trust. It seemed the cruelty of the Grey Hinterlands molded its people to eye each other warily. Astrid stepped away, leaving the two to their rest in privacy. Whatever concerns the healer had of Ilai, they did not seem threatening enough to forcibly pull Ysella away.

"Did you sell the fang I gave you?" Ilai asked.

"I did," Ysella answered. The gold fist was still in its pouch, and she handed it to him.

"That's a generous sum," Ilai mused. "More than killing the spider itself."

"Antivenom is highly valuable, and difficult to make, from what I understand," Ysella said. "Halvish was completely depleted."

He stuffed the gold fist in the pack of blankets. "We'll do well for the road ahead. Get some rest."

"Are we truly safe here?" Ysella asked, settling her head down on her pillow. She watched him do the same, and they looked at each other in the dim light of night.

"Safer than out there," he assured. "Attacking a healer's hall is a death sentence."

She pulled her blankets up to her neck, tucking herself protectively in their hold. Every movement, every step had allowed Ysella to focus on anything but her recent capture. She had shoved it aside and locked it away in the relief of true safety.

But she looked at Ilai in the light of the fire crackling in the hearth behind her, reality begging for its attention once again. This journey was more treacherous than she could have ever imagined, and the closer they came to Ethyrnon Tower, the more dangers emerged. She would not let this deter her, but she would be ignorant no longer.

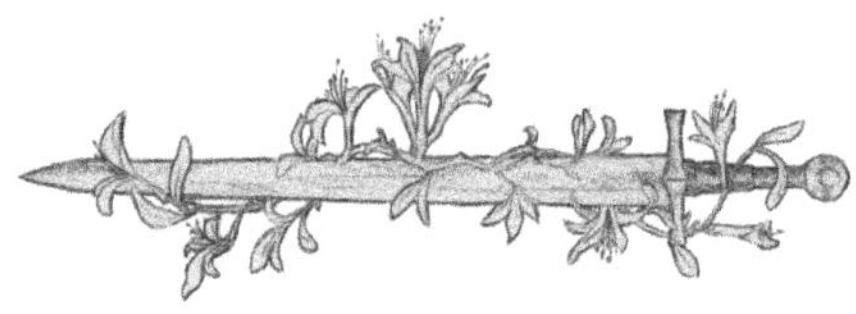

Their combined metal and pilfered weapons allowed Ilai to barter and trade for more equipment and supplies. He purchased a well-balanced longsword, even allowed Ysella to hold it to see if she'd like the weapon. It was far too heavy and large for her liking. The short sword was a different sort of heavy, but with two hands she could hold it aloft easier. They purchased a bow and a quiver of arrows on their way out of town.

"Will we get a horse?" Ysella asked as she tested the draw of the bow. It required a lot of power from her arm to pull back the string, and as long as she didn't hold it for long, she felt it would suit her well enough.

"I'd rather wait to get a horse in Dournfast," Ilai said. "Guiding them up the cliffs, even in the easier slopes, is still a challenge."

Ilai helped secure her weapons to a comfortable position. The sword hung heavily on her belt, and he had her pull it from the scabbard a few times to feel its resistance and how far she'd have to maneuver for its release. Each time, the heft caught her off guard, but she recovered quickly.

"Will you teach me how to fight?" Ysella asked as they journeyed down the slope leading northward from Halvish.

"Of course," he said. "We'll make camp early tonight and we can go through the basics."

The clouds overhead remained thick, wind picking up in strong gusts through the fields. They were nearly to the tree line, the rushing air singing through the dancing canopies.

"The clouds haven't parted in some time," Ilai noted. "A storm could be brewing. It's not uncommon for the skies to bring another thick snow to herald Spring. We'll want to get to Dournfast before then."

"How long until we get there?" Ysella asked.

"If we cut off a couple of hours of sleep each night we can make it to Dournfast in a couple of days," Ilai remarked.

Their course eventually turned eastward following a well-worn road that wound around the cliff to a deep ravine where the path continued. Snow fell intermittently in soft tufts, but did not threaten to bury them in a storm. Ysella's teeth chattered against the cold, the chill seeping through her bones.

Eventually, the ravine narrowed and opened and snaked through tall jagged rocks and mossy boulders. There was nowhere else to go but forward, and Ilai kept a trained eye above and below.

"What exactly does Bastillos hope to gain with your efforts?" he asked.

"We hope to avoid a war," Ysella answered plainly. "Tensions are rising in Nabannon and Ithrad, have you not heard? The Grey Hinterlands shares a border with both."

"I've heard, but it seems more of a precaution than a threat," he said.

"It's more complicated than that," she said. "Rotheel and I were dispatched to ensure it does not spiral out completely. Wars are expensive and costly, not just in lives, but it harms economies. Societies suffer."

"And that is all on your shoulders?" Ilai asked.

"Unfortunately, yes," she solemnly answered. "That is why it is my responsibility to determine who is behind the bounty on my head. Whoever it is wants a war. My absence in Nabannon may come as a further threat to the kingdom."

Ilai's boots crunched over the rocky terrain. He offered a hand to help her up and over a particularly precarious path with loose soil trailing down into the steep ravine. She barely managed to avoid stumbling into him, her feet skidding on a crumbling edge.

"Do you know who would benefit from a war in Edros?" Ilai asked, hands snatching her waist to steady her body. She reminded herself to breathe.

"Thank you," she murmured. His hand moved from her waist, remaining at the small of her back as he guided her up and over to more even ground.

"I don't know that anyone truly benefits from war," she continued. "None of the kingdoms would fare well with a war blocking most of the trade. Krei, Dradmida, and Nabannon at least have sea trade. Ithrad, Bastillos, the Grey Hinterlands, and Everyn are land locked. They'll suffer most, though the elves of Everyn always have their kin in Eversyth."

Once they made it out of the canyon, the land rolled with gently sloping hills and patches of woodlands mostly consisting of towering evergreens with thick trunks. There were clusters of smaller pines with wider branches that leaned down to the earth and created a natural shelter that would easily trap the heat from a small fire.

They stopped in a small glade and Ilai dug a hole for the fire to feed into the natural shelter while allowing the smoke to exit outside of its boughs.

"Pull out your sword," Ilai instructed. Ysella grabbed the hilt of her sword, hand on her scabbard to keep it steady as she pulled the blade free. It was difficult to hold it aloft with one hand. Ilai held his longsword with ease. "We'll go slow. Swords are different than knives. You've got more length. You can use two hands for now."

She held the short sword with two hands, alleviating some of the burden. He demonstrated a readied stance, first visually, then through guiding her form. At first, it felt silly and wide, but she soon realized she was balanced, and could step into or away from attacks with ease.

Slowly, he brought his sword down, instructing her to meet it. "Do you see how I had to move my body? Part of fighting is anticipating your opponent's next move. You can do that by watching their movements. Large weapons require more strength to wield, and thus they're more easily predicted."

He showed her how to parry, how to open her opponent to vulnerable attacks, and how to ensure her own attack would not leave her the same. Dodging was a bit more difficult for her. The weight of the sword was so cumbersome, it was difficult to move out of the way, even at a slowed pace.

They halted the lesson as the night darkened, Ilai stoking the fire as they sat. Ysella couldn't halt her smile. She'd learned something new today, and that felt like a rare occasion. Her mother would be aghast if she heard her eldest daughter, heir to House Ronasin, was learning to fight with a sword.

The air was still and windless, with snow falling intermittently. It was calm enough for it to gather in white patches, reflecting the covered moonlight to illuminate their surroundings. In preparation for their short rest, Ysella noticed Ilai's gaze drift her way occasionally. While it was hardly the first time the man had looked at her, it struck her differently, her heart taking on a new rhythm she could not quite understand. It wasn't born of fear, or even uneasiness. She knew that she was safe with him, and there was comfort in that security.

Her mind stilled with revelation as she spared a glance to the Lander with mirrored reticence. The brutish man had faded entirely, giving way to something that fluttered her heart within close proximity of her thoughts. She did not lean on him entirely for survival, though his skills were greatly appreciated. Her regard for him had surpassed every experience she knew, and had entered her into territory she was only just understanding.

As his voice broke the silence, he reached out to hand her a ration of flat bread, setting a small wheel of cheese between them on the cloth it was wrapped with. "Let's say you discover who issued this bounty on your head and take the information back to your queen. What then?"

"I've been wondering the same, to be honest." Taking the bread, she picked at the edge, fraying crumbs onto her folded legs.

"I can't imagine there's any good outcome from this." His voice was even, but his head turned her way, his eyes watching her closely.

"My only hope, and it is a small one, is to find evidence to explain this foul play and what they are attempting to gain. At this point, though, I'm not sure we'll return in time to prevent an escalation."

Ilai sat back on his elbows. "If war is inevitable, then we should prepare for it. I've heard if you can make it through the Twisted Woods, you can reach a town in Thallas that won't question your citizenship. It's right on the border. They'll take anyone who can work."

"I won't run, Ilai." She wasn't harsh. Her conviction was her own war pulling her between logic and emotion. "Even if I didn't have the weight of Edros on my shoulders, I have my family to think about. My sister."

"I understand," he said softly.

"Was Shera your only family?" Ysella asked.

"I had parents once," he answered, "and siblings. But they were not a part of my life."

"Why not?"

"Life is expensive," Ilai said with a slight shrug. "They had too many children. Too many mouths to feed, and metal was scarce. I was given to the church instead."

Ysella tried to fathom his lived past, but could not comprehend why parents would give up their child for any reason. While she was not close to her parents, they would have never given her away.

"The church couldn't help them with food?" she asked.

"The church fed most people in town when the orcs couldn't trade in the Winter months," he explained. "I wasn't the best child. I was difficult, so it made things challenging for them."

"I'm sorry you went through that," she said.

"I am not." He set a stick into the fire idly, eyes outwardly apathetic as he stared at the dancing flames. She could tell he'd had a bath. His curls were more evident, his beard trimmed and shaped and his skin clean. He was somehow still rugged and fierce and intimidating, though not in the same way as when he was her captor. Something had shifted between them. He was no longer a danger to her, no longer a hopeless reminder of her failings and a harbinger of impending doom. He was something else entirely, now.

24
ILAI

Ysella was more capable than Ilai had ever given her credit. He mistook her tears and empathy as a weakness when in fact they were her strongest driving force. She was free to cry, free to feel deep pain, because she thought of more than just herself. The war was on her shoulders because she feared for others, and whatever pains she endured, she felt in her heart it would be nothing by comparison to what is to come.

It was completely admirable. Ilai shielded himself from the pains of others. He hardened himself to protect his peace, and many in the Grey did so. Survival was keeping their heads down, their blades at their sides, and an eye of skepticism on everyone they pass.

Being vulnerable was not easy, yet she wore it well. It may have gotten her captured a second time, but it also likely kept her alive.

Ysella fell quiet, cheeks streaked with tears glittering in the firelight. He had seen so many acquisitions cry, yet none made him desire to wipe away the tears as she did. He fought the odd instinct by tugging at the end of his glove, the seams pulling into his fingers.

"I can't expect you to protect me forever," she said.

"You'll learn to defend yourself soon enough," Ilai assured. She eyed him and her palm brushed the tears away.

"That could take months," she said. "I need you."

His stomach turned to knots, and he thought perhaps a fist full of bread would quell the feeling. He had never been needed in his life. Only wanted for a job, and this was likely just that. Ysella could be manipulating him through semantics.

Ilai would like to think himself clever enough to know when he was being manipulated. He could no longer tell with Ysella, and it scared him.

"I could do that," Ilai offered quietly, his fingers tearing off a piece from the simple loaf idly. "Be your protector, I mean. I could do it for as long as you need."

What a stupid man he had become, but he felt perhaps even a working dynamic was better. She could get her way, achieve her goals, and his pockets would be filled.

And he could be in her company. Her infuriating and frustrating company. The one that made him feel for more than himself.

"I've done a few smuggling jobs. A few as a bodyguard," Ilai continued. "I'm not always on a hunt. I could help your family escape."

"Escape?" Ysella repeated the word, eyes distant as she directed them to the fire. Consideration fixed her perfect features, brow not yet knit, but firm, and her mouth relaxed. Her tears had dried, save for the wet streaks of what last fell. She did not move to brush them away.

And then she became distant. "The men that took me said Rotheel is dead."

"I'm sorry to hear that," Ilai said. He'd forgotten about the other diplomat and his importance to Ysella. The flames invited his mind to quiet in their hypnotic dance.

"I need to know who is behind it all," Ysella continued. "If you will stay with me and keep me alive, I can do that much at least."

"I will keep you alive," he promised.

It was an odd promise to make, considering the threats of the Grey. They were magnified by her bounty making a difficult promise to keep. The promise thoughtlessly passed through his lips, but she gave him no skeptical glance. She would hold him to that promise, and now he would have to as well. How could one keep a near impossible promise?

She remained contemplative and quiet for once, and it left him with an unease.

Gusts of wind tore through the trees throughout the night, the barren boughs clacking against each other as the trunks groaned. There were clusters of pine that danced between the netted canopy, and the air grew colder. The dense evergreens provided just the buffer they needed to keep the warmth of the fire surrounding them. Ilai watched the night through the silhouetted display. This weather was uninviting and meant most creatures would bed down and wait for calmer air. It also meant the storm was growing closer. They would need to wake before the sun.

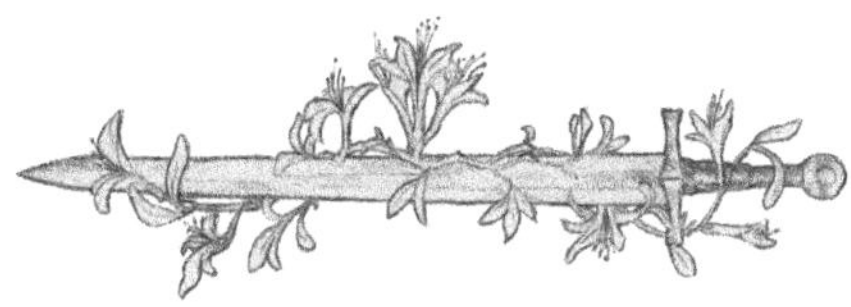

His light sleep allowed for a proper rise. The sky had lightened in a band on the horizon. The clouds thickened. Ilai covered the fire pit and collected what little items they carried and gently woke Ysella with a nudge to her shoulder.

Each day they traveled was similar to the last with rocky terrain, intermittent woods, whipping winds, and cloudy skies. The uneven paths slowed them down, requiring less sleep to stay ahead of the storm. Ilai could smell the air shift, the scent earthen and sharp. Snowfall came and went indecisively, though the further northeast they traveled, the more the rocks disappeared under white sheets.

The settlement of Dournfast was small and surrounded by thick woods and protected by sturdy fences made from the lumber sourced from their thick trunks. They breached from the woodland ravine, the towering walls barring entry unless through two different gates manned by watchers.

"Dournfast is under a kinder Laerd," Ilai said. "Laerd Godfrey. Don't let the tall walls or forest seclusion fool you. The people here are less afraid than most. Less paranoid. It's partially due to Godfrey's laws. It boils down to 'no violence, and you'll be treated well.' His definition of 'violence' is a bit strict, for my taste."

"What's would be crossing the line into a criminal act?" Ysella asked curiously. "Violence can even come in words."

"A threat can be enough here," Ilai confirmed. "If you threaten someone, it is considered a verbal contract. You'll not be exiled for it, but you'll spend time in a jail cell. Merchants are quite fond of the law. Makes their business safe."

The smile that proceeded was weak at best. Ysella was weary of mind, possibly due to the strenuous schedule he'd kept. She was the quietest she'd ever been, and for much of their travel he had to keep pace beside her just to make sure she was still moving.

He mirrored the strained smile and looked back through the opened gates as twelve men expertly carried a long trunk as thick as two men through the entrance. The leader, wearing a bright red cap, called out a command signaling a slight turn to the right down the wide road, and the men changed their stance and pacing accordingly. Merchants and traders looked up towards the sky as they dismantled their awnings and locked up their stalls. Lining the road was a long line of wagons pulled by oxen and horses, a few men loitering around them.

Ilai's hand quickly pulled Ysella behind the tall fence, and he peered through the slats to take a safer look. At first, he didn't explain himself. He had to confirm what he saw lest he caused his companion to worry.

It was a caravan, and judging by a few recognizable lackeys, it was the very same caravan Regan led. He watched as Cammon approached a group and leaned against one of the wagons with his tall frame, arms crossed. His bulk was magnified by pelts of fur and a thick grey cloak.

"We'll need to keep going," Ilai advised quietly. The snow fell more thickly and dusted their shoulders and the tops of their heads. Flakes powdered her lashes and the stray strands of hair framing her features. "If we head northward we can reach the next settlement tomorrow."

"Keep going? But you just said—" Ysella's words halted as she looked through the slats, realization stiffening her posture. "No..."

They were a clever lot despite appealing to the lesser intellect. Given they had a copy of her posting, they knew where she would be taken if she were still alive. It was either an unfortunate coincidence, or they planned their business around an eventual convergence. Ilai didn't like either prospect, and he cursed under his breath.

The storm would find them out in the wilderness, now. He'd been caught in one years ago that nearly toppled his shelter. He knew he could survive it.

"We have two options," Ilai said as he kept a wary eye on the caravan. "Option one: we keep going north and get caught in the storm. Option two: we go into Dournfast regardless. The caravan will learn we are here, but we will have shelter and protection while in the walls."

"We can't be seen by them," Ysella said thoughtfully. She undulated between calm and anxiety, her fiddling fingers giving away any shift in her emotional state. "They will not allow us to escape again."

Caravaners were led by a variety of people, their employees often the lowliest of men and women the Grey had to offer. It took a certain mind to carry out their business, and while they had unsavory trades, they had an unfortunate amount of goods sold at affordable prices. They always found a way to thrive and survive.

If they found Ysella this time, they were closer to the prize up north. They'd surely kill Ilai without a moment's hesitation to get rid of the liability.

"I trust you," Ysella said. "Where you go, I go."

He looked from the caravan to the sky as if a better course would reveal itself in the snowfall. It would not relent this time. They needed to find shelter, and he weighed each option carefully. Dournfast would be safe. They could find a room at the inn with protection from the law of the land. The caravaners wouldn't risk losing their business entirely within Godfrey's lands. But they could easily follow them out to the border and exact their plans there.

Right now, the caravaners were clueless to their presence. It was clearly safer to keep it that way.

"It's going to be a difficult night," Ilai warned. "It will be colder and harsher, and we'll have only what we have on us now."

Stepping from the tall wooden walls of Dournfast, they headed eastward a few miles. Laerd Godfrey's lands were mostly woodland, the lumbering operation calculated to ensure the forests are never cut back too far. Most lumber in the north came from Godfrey's forests.

The small footpath slowly curved northward, the snow hiding visible signs of previous wear. Ilai's familiarity with the northern lands aided him. He'd taken this path many times. Trees and brush always change, but rock formations and sturdy hills did not so easily.

They avoided the road on the off chance the caravan left town. They would still have time to travel north if they wished, especially with the speed of their wagons. Occasionally, Ilai looked behind them just to make sure they weren't followed. He noted Ysella doing the same of her own accord.

That eased his mind, especially as his belly ached for the warm meal he had been anticipating: a hearty roast with stringy greens and onions. Not that such a meal was guaranteed, but Dournfast did have many good cooks along the strip.

Hours passed, and the snow fell in thicker clumps, the wind picking up its pace as the sky darkened. "Look for tree wells or two trees close enough together for a shelter," he advised. They needed to prepare their shelter within the next hour, he guessed.

Ysella was already shivering, her cloak wrapped tightly around her as she nodded, jaw clenching. "T-tree... right..."

They found a cluster of trees with two close enough to fashion a shelter with surrounding sticks and pine fronds. Ilai kept Ysella moving by showing her how to tie it together, how to layer the fronds, and how to use the snow that had already fallen as a means of insulation. The shelter was built with enough room for them both, and he fashioned a fire within where the smoke would vacate from a vent he dug through the ground. The heat would collect inside and keep them warm.

Outside, the wind howled, but the shelter held fast. Inside, they were dry and warm with enough room to sit or lay. Ilai set his pack on one end, unfurling his bed roll and prompting Ysella to do the same.

It had been a long time since he'd slept on a bedroll. The comfort was welcoming, and would keep them warm throughout the night. Ysella had her palms to the fire pit, teeth chattering as she tried to stave off the chill.

He never realized how beautiful she was.

Surely, he hadn't. Ilai couldn't recall a moment where he was struck by her beauty. She was no Lander, after all. She barely had meat on her bones to keep her warm.

But somehow it struck him now. She was truly beautiful, and perhaps it was her determination as she refused to allow the cold to take her.

He huffed a small laugh as a chill ran down her spine and back up to her jaw, teeth clattering in an inhale. His hand reached out toward her arm to coax her to him, lips pressing to a line as he became perplexed by his action. He should have told her to focus on warming her core, not her hands.

Ilai could not ignore the flutter of his heart as she complied, curling into his chest gratefully. She was cocooned in her cloak, and he wrapped her in his own to share in his natural warmth.

She had a sweet smell to her. There was the lingering floral scent of soaps or oils she may have used from Halvish, but Ysella had her own warm smell, and he pulled his head upward to distract his senses.

As he rolled to his back, she rested her head on his shoulder, and he prayed to Elssar and the Nine Patrons for peace in his mind. She sparked chaos, conflict, and a haze of varying thoughts that pulled him in all directions. He wanted to run out into the storm, yet also bury his head in the curve her neck now exposed where she lay. He wanted to sit up, yet he wished to pull her closer to him.

"The caravan is limited to roads with their wagons," he said to distract himself. "Once this storm passes we'll have to continue on the lesser paths. Ethyrnon Tower is secluded enough to avoid settlements in the direction we're moving. If the caravan intends to intercept us, they'll have to go off the road."

"Promise me something, Ilai." Ysella curled herself inward, the shivering dissipating.

"If you want me to promise something stupid, I won't," he stated, and looked down at her with a small grin. "It better be a reasonable request."

She smiled in return, her eyes meeting his with uneasiness. "You should know me better than that by now. I know that you will do whatever you need to do to keep us safe. I've no doubt of it. But there have been so many variables along the way and there's no telling what may come. I need you to promise me... If they catch up to us, the caravaners, if we are overtaken, you will run. The bounty is on my head, not yours, and they will not hesitate to kill you. Not after last time."

He couldn't help but laugh, wondering if her wording was happenstance or intended. Now she asked *him* to run, after all the times she had ignored the very same command from him.

It seemed she had come to the same conclusion as he had, and he wondered how long it had been on her mind.

Surely she knew he would not run. It was odd she would suggest it, especially after Halvish. His heart was still bruised from the accusation of cowardice.

"You ask me to promise to run when you know I will refuse?" he questioned with amusement. "You'd have a better chance at survival if I stay and fight. I think it is you who should promise to run, yet I know you would not. You have demonstrated you will not. But, consider I could distract them or tear them down as you create distance. I think that would be better for Edros in the long run, don't you think?"

Ysella's eyes grew distant and solemn, glazing over with a consuming thought. "For Edros, perhaps," she said. "But not for me."

The softness of his heart, pained from bruising, drummed its pining beat. Such simple words, yet they filled him with a life unlike breathing. It was more than blood or food or survival. She held his heart and fed it directly with her soul. Did she know how he longed for their connection to be more than just his desires? Could she feel the connection too?

"Please reconsider my words, Ilai," she said. "If I'm caught and you're alive, there's still hope. If you perish, I'd have nothing to hope for. My chance of success diminishes."

Her words made no sense to him. She should know they made no sense. "I will stay and fight as you have with me," he said resolutely. His tone was calm, but his words were a declaration.

His hand rubbed her side idly. He wasn't sure how long he'd been doing it. She was resting her head on his uninjured shoulder allowing his arm to cradle her naturally. She was bundled up in layers yet felt too close to his palm.

She wasn't resisting against his touch.

"And what of your sword training?" Ilai added. "You've taken to it quickly."

"It's easy to go through the motions when your opponent is going so slow," she remarked.

"Oh, you desire it to go faster next time?"

Ysella looked up to him pleadingly. "Oh, not yet. I was only making an observation!"

Ilai chuckled and squeezed her against him playfully. "We'll go full pace in the morning to get our blood pumping."

"We will not!" She pulled a hand from her cocoon and lightly tapped his chest. "I wouldn't mind a bit more training, though. Do you think I could learn enough before we get to the tower?"

"Enough?" Ilai mulled over the prospects. They were days away from their destination, by his recollection. "I suppose it would depend on how quickly you catch on."

She propped her head on one elbow, warmth settling comfortably between them. Determination blazed like fire in her eyes. "Every day, before night's end, I want to practice, then."

"What do you expect to encounter?" Ilai asked.

"Those caravaners could still try to capture me for that bounty," Ysella said. "I'd like to make that endeavor difficult for them. And we haven't a clue what awaits us at Ethyrnon."

"I can hazard a guess," Ilai said.

"I wish I could say it would make sense for Shadow Casters to be waiting for me in that tower," Ysella said. "I've known Shadow Casters in Bastillos. Well, not known them. But I've encountered them, and they're nowhere near as frightening as men."

Ilai grunted thoughtfully. He'd never encountered a Shadow Caster in his life and had no frame of reference to pull from. "What do you mean?"

"Things are different out here," Ysella explained, and curled herself back into the crook of his arm. "The people are harsher. Meaner. Less trusting. Or just downright evil.

"I play it in my mind sometimes... Regan's words. The leader of that caravan. It wasn't so much what he said but it was the look in his eye. How anyone could so easily cast their humanity aside. How anyone could sit before a person and not see them as a person."

Was he no better than a caravaner in Ysella's eyes? Bounty hunters dealt mostly in criminals, though still acquired people with no history in exchange for a proper sum. Ilai had always viewed caravaners as a lesser evil. They helped in proper trade while dealing with unsavory transactions involving other people.

"Ysella." Ilai hesitated, unsure if he truly wanted to know the answer to the question lingering in his mind. "Do you view me as such? Do you view me as evil as a caravaner?"

"What makes you ask that?" She pushed herself back onto her elbow, brow furrowed in confusion.

"Bounty hunters distance themselves from their acquisitions," Ilai explained. "We sometimes deal with people."

"You said bounty hunters view their acquisitions as people," Ysella said. "Am I misremembering?"

"Well, no, but that doesn't mean you believe that," he said.

"I've lived as your acquisition," Ysella said, "and I've lived as a captive of a caravan. I am not saying I agree with how you bounty hunters conduct yourselves, but it is different. You still viewed me as a person. You just lacked the compassion to acknowledge what you were doing was wrong."

He grimaced, and cast his eyes away from her stare. "I don't know that I feel remorse for my past. No, I feel remorse for some of my past, but not my previous acquisitions. I had been part of a caravan once. Several years ago, now, though I've lost count.

I was young when they found me. No family. No guardian. Too young to swear to a laerd and join their army. I snagged the metal off of the wrong caravaner and they were going to take a finger for every finger I stole. But I was spared as long as I did work for them in towns snagging metal or sneaking into homes. I thought it was a mercy and enjoyed myself at first. They fed me and clothed me and protected me. But then I reached a certain age and the work changed."

Every transgression resurfaced in his mind. Every sorrowful look, every grip of guilt, and every mental brick he placed to close his mind from his crimes returned to judge him. It was Ysella's voice who broke him from the brooding spiral.

"Your life has not been easy, has it?"

"Shera had made it easier, but even before then with the caravan, I think I had it easier than most," he said. "Caravaners offer the highest level of protection and will do anything for food. The worst of it was merely staying above the things you captured. They tended to have it worse."

Twisting towards him slightly, her cool fingers brushed against his face, an odd warmth curling in his chest as her eyes met his. "But not always? How did this happen?"

His hand came up, curving carefully around hers in the pretense of touching the scar that ran the length of his eye. "A watcher gave it to me."

The steadiness of her gaze brought a thrumming beat to his throat and his own gaze lowered to her face, taking her in, her pristine, soft skin, the piercing blue of her eyes, the gentle slope of her mouth...

Gingerly, as though he were handling something fragile, his hand cradled her jaw, his thumb skimming the space below her lower lip. The split healed well, the former affront hardly present on her skin. He felt her tremble, heard a soft inhale, but her eyes were fixed on his, unyielding. With a cautious pull, he brought her closer.

Somewhere in the woodline, the wind gusted, branches clacking and snapping. Ysella lurched with a gasp, his hand falling away as her body went rigid. "What was that?"

"The storm," he assured.

The time for indulgence had passed, and he exhaled slowly to calm his mind. "You could say to some degree your life was not easy. I don't know much of Bastillos or diplomats, but I've heard many stories from many different people. Very rarely has one shared of an easy life. Even the wealthy and the nobility."

"Well, I suppose the last few weeks haven't exactly been luxurious," she teased. The dullness from his mind shifted, and color seemed more vibrant as the firelight danced with his heart.

"I suppose I never quantified my life in such a manner," she continued, and rested her head back on his shoulder. "It never felt like my life was my own. I knew my destiny before I was old enough to understand what it was. Every part of my life, everything I ever learned, revolved around becoming a diplomat to some capacity."

"Are diplomats of a high status?" Ilai asked.

"Bastillos is the center of Edros, both literally and economically," Ysella explained. "Diplomats ensure relations between kingdoms are kept civil and amicable. We're invaluable to the infrastructure of Edros. It's a high honor in Bastillos."

Ysella's vocabulary was broader than Ilai's. Half the words she used, he did not understand, but he could attempt to infer their meaning.

"You did not want to be of a high status?" Ilai asked.

"It's what my parents wanted," she said. "Even before the shame caused from the rebellion, my mother has had an obsession with elevating our status. She chose my outfits, my academics, my tutors and activities. I never had a say, though I also did not question it. My life wasn't difficult, per se. Not the same as starving in the wilderness or being hunted down by caravans. But now that I think about it, it wasn't the life I might have chosen for myself."

Her words slowed as the thought caught up to her, brow furrowing and eyes distant.

"We get to choose?" Ilai chuckled softly. "I know some choices were my own, and some were not. I chose to be a bounty hunter, but it was a logical path from the life I did not choose. Had my childhood been different I wonder if I would have been different. Do you feel that you could choose a life for yourself and it truly be the choice you would have wanted, or would it just be the choice you have to take?"

"I'm not sure," Ysella admitted. "Some things are a choice, or they should be. Until you pulled me out of that carriage, I had everything sorted. So much has changed now. My perspective on my life and the lives outside of Bastillos has changed. I'd like to believe you could make a life you want. I know for the last few weeks I've lived by my own choices. I've had to make my own choices and know what I want, and it wasn't easy. It was still necessary. I wish my first choices could have been under better circumstances."

"With the sum of your bounty," Ilai said thoughtfully, "it has been clear to me for some time that whoever turns you in is not expected to leave alive. I had wondered at the start. Twenty heads of gold is an incredible sum, but given your presumed status, there was always a possibility. High risk acquisitions often call for groups to work together. It was designed to entice the ones who wouldn't question it. Or people like me willing to take the risk."

The words halted as though it latched in his throat. Twenty gold heads was enough to retire and live out his days if he survived what lay ahead. He'd always known there'd be a fight at Ethyrnon. The pay was too good to be true, but even one head would be worth the trouble.

He had been a lonely man who did not know the loneliness had been eating away at his soul. He kept Sabin at arm's length so he wouldn't have to face what he faced with Shera's death.

Ysella had pulled the veil from his eyes, forcing him to face the old wounds he did not wish to acknowledge. Losing Shera hurt. She was the only caring family he had in years, and her loss was a reminder that life is fleeting.

In many ways, Ysella was completely different. She was no strong survivalist who could carry her own in a fight. She was no tracker or hunter. But she had the same sort of determination, the same loyalties to the people she cared about.

She was also beautiful to Ilai. He had felt the sting of lost love with Arjah, further hardening his heart from future connections. The compounded losses entombed his heart, and somehow Ysella chiseled her way through. He was starting to believe there could be more to life than metal.

"I have no intention of dying," Ilai said. "We may have no time to question whoever is at the tower. Or they may not let us. We won't know for certain, but if they've been there long, they may have something there that can offer answers. That is, if we don't have to run."

"We need a plan of action," Ysella suggested.

"What do you propose?"

She fell quiet for a moment. "The wanted posting said they wanted me alive. It means it's not just about what my disappearance could cause. They want information from me. Few people go through the trouble to allow for any variables. I suspect they could want me dead as soon as they get what they want from me."

"We won't let that happen," Ilai assured.

"That's the thing," she continued. "I have to get to that point to know what they want to know. They'll surely kill you before I'm interrogated."

"It will look suspicious if I don't take you in as a bounty hunter," Ilai said.

A heavy sigh escaped her. "I know. I don't have a plan yet, I'm trying to work through it."

"We have a few days travel left," he said. "We don't need to come up with a plan tonight."

"Tell me the truth," she said, lifting her head upward to look at him. "Do you think there's any point to it all?"

"A point to your bounty?" he asked, confused.

She shook her head. "No, I mean, with what I'm doing. With my desire for answers. Going through the possibilities, it seems like even if I did get the answers I was looking for, I'll be killed, and you'll be dead."

"We've come this far," he said. "It's natural to feel cold feet. But even if the chances of us dying are high, there's still a chance we will survive. It's not pointless as long as there's hope."

Ilai pulled her closer hoping it would offer the same comfort he felt from her touch. Her hand slipped out from her cloak to rest on his chest.

Quiet fell between them with only the crackle of fire and whistling wind to fill the silence. He knew their only option was to fight and kill the clients at Ethyrnon, and he was not sure Ysella would accept that.

Their shelter held through the night, Ilai only having to stoke and feed the fire twice. Ysella looked peaceful where she rested, orange firelight highlighting her resting features as beautiful as the paintings in a laerd's hall. He felt privileged to lay back next to her, cautious not to wake her each time.

The morning came with still air and snow past the shelter's door. Ilai carefully pushed through to let in the muted morning light and the chilly air.

As he crested the lip of the snow around the shelter, he froze in his tracks. In front of him stood a man cloaked in a thick green draped in a wolf's hide. On his back was a longsword fitted with a rune-etched crystal fixed at its pommel. He wore a severe grin towards Ilai's shock, and under the shadow of his hood were two glowing white eyes.

25
YSELLA

Whatever preternatural sense awoke her in that moment, Ysella would never fully understand. Perhaps it had simply been the absence of Ilai, of his warmth and the comfort of him beside her, or perhaps it had been the brightening of the sky as dawn pooled beneath the whitewashed heavens. Whatever it was, her eyes opened and caught sight of Ilai frozen at the opening of their shelter, and she felt her stomach turn.

Had he been an animal, no doubt she would have heard the growl, the hackles raised and full. Inching upright, her hand seeking out the hilt of the shortsword he'd given her, she eased behind him to peer out over his shoulder.

Ysella's heart drummed a frenzied beat at the sight of such an alarming presence. The stranger's eyes glowed ominously, like white fire, his blade dark and sinister as it barely reflected light.

"You know what I'm here for," the stranger said. The longsword was engraved with its own runes in a peculiar pattern down its length. "We can do this the easy way or the hard way. Either choice, I'll still have my fun."

Ilai reached for his own blade, and within the upward momentum, their steel clashed in an exchange of blows. Excitement pulled the stranger's face to a grin as they danced through the snow. They traded aggression and defensive maneuvers in a push and pull for the advance. The stranger, based on what little she could discern of his tactics, was purposefully prolonging the fight. He seemed reserved in his offense whereas Ilai was looking for the kill.

Anxiety and a lack of confidence stilled Ysella's resolve. Her sword felt heavier in her hand, the cumbersome weight refusing to raise as her heartbeat quickened. She was sure if she tried to enter the fray she'd either harm Ilai or herself in the attempt.

She would not run, but she could not sit idly by.

In their dance, Ilai had kept himself between the stranger and Ysella, but she rounded from behind him, sword held at the ready just as they'd practiced. Ilai had to double take, his parry blocking the stranger's advance towards her. She had managed to raise her sword, at the very least, her footing true as she continued to flank their assailant.

"You are surrounded, sir!" she warned. "You cannot possibly hope to come out of this the victor! Drop your blade!"

A hard thrum like muted thunder vibrated her core, punctuated by a shock of sudden pain. Daylight dimmed, and the stranger's form darkened as a wreath of unmistakable Shadow Magic swirled. Tendrils of darkness twisted, latching onto her form with an agonizing, wrenching contact.

Ilai's mouth moved, the sound of his voice merging with a high pitch churned by thousands of chittering whispers prickling at her psyche. Metal clanged and ground and whined as light was swallowed into nothingness.

The darkness clung to her senses like a web cocooning her form. Ysella's attempts to recoil, to struggle against the clinging abyss, were met with spikes of pain shooting through every perceivable part of her.

And then there was nothing.

No pain or concept of form. No cocoon enveloping her mind. Just her consciousness floating in an endless darkness and an incomprehensible silence stretching across a timeless expanse.

Fear escalated, pouring down her throat like a font ready to drown her. She couldn't cough or sputter. It was as though her body was not truly there. All she could do was beg for release in the recesses of her mind.

The silence was a crushing pressure that released with the sound of something dripping. Nothingness turned to chill, the air bright with minerals that struck down the darkness in mirrorlight. Ysella rose as if it were her first time on her feet, knees wobbling.

And then the air turned hot and acrid, the light dimming in a dusty veil.

The cavern city of Lumin was a cascade of rubble and crumbling structures roiling with curling smoke, a sulfurous scent burning her nostrils and stinging her lungs. Her eyes blurred from the ashes, and her skin glistened with perspiration. Not a single building stood, not even the palace at the Precipice. The statues had crumbled to their bases, pocked with rubble.

Tears fell in streaks she could not feel, an icy numbness enveloping her despite the sweltering heat billowing through the grand cavern. Merged within the roaring fires, a cacophony of screams rose with the smoke without source. She opened her mouth to call out to them, her own breath painful and raw, ravaging her throat until she realized the screams were her own.

Time was an odd passage drifting her consciousness through what felt like days as she wandered the ruins of caves and tunnels. Minutes felt like seconds, yet also felt like hours as time drew like a length of thread pulled from a spool without end. It never wove, never frayed or broke.

There were no bodies no matter how many rocks she moved. It was a never ending rubble with a complete absence of casualties. They were all eviscerated from reality leaving Ysella the last living Bastillosi.

Every turn she took to break free of the crumbling caverns of Bastillos, she was met with a barrier or an obstacle caused by the unknown chaos.

She was alone with nothing left but the knowledge of her survival. Tearfully, she fell to her knees, and light broke through fissures in the cavern walls. Golden rays turned red with blood that flowed down into the molten rock below. Sulfur struck her senses with each breath, sharp and affronting as heat rose to a swelter.

A loud crack shattered the air sending waves of agony searing through her skin, piercing deep into her core.

Darkness took her once again, slathering her consciousness in its ethereal web, dissolving into a cold wasteland. Time was more like swimming through water, Ysella struggling to orient herself in the sudden cold. It was bright due to the thick snow blanketing the forest floor, pine fronds heavy and coated in white. She was in the Grey Hinterlands.

As her eyes adjusted, she saw the stranger's wicked blade embedded in Ilai's chest. Blood seeped into the runes, activating them with a glisten of magic. His breath shuddered and hitched, and as he looked to Ysella with solemn finality, his body lurched as if pulled by an unseen force. For a moment his form appeared translucent, then translated into a wisp of white. The glowing wisp funneled into the blade and collected within the rune-etched crystal at the pommel.

The stranger turned toward Ysella, a grin spreading wide across his lips, savoring the fear that flashed in her eyes. "Shall we dance?" he asked playfully.

No sound passed through her throat. No fresh tears wet her cheeks. Despite the shock and disbelief, her mind racing to understand what she just witnessed, her heart was wracked by loss so incredible it felt as if it was her soul that disembarked, not Ilai's, carving a hollowness within her colder than the thick blanket of snow in the clearing.

Her resolve to stand strong did not steel her heart from his knowing. That damnable connection between them betrayed her, allowing the stranger to know her sorrow.

"Do I have a choice?" she asked.

Delight widened his sickened grin, pulling to bare his unnaturally fanged teeth. A chuckle escaped him in a low rumble. "I will allow you to make a choice," he said, his blade gripped in both hands. Ilai's blood lingered on the steel, small droplets staining the snow in red. "I see your soul as clear as moonlight on night's snow. I smell the scent of fear coursing through your blood. I will let you run if you wish."

The blood dripped as if the blade had been sated and was salivating for a new hunt. Ysella stood her ground, though realized her sword was no longer in her hand.

"I'm not going to run," Ysella said resolutely, though she felt hollowed out. "What do you want?"

"You will walk," he commanded, and pointed northward with his blade. "When I tell you to turn, you turn. When I tell you to stop, you stop."

He sheathed his sword behind his back, the glowing crystal resting just above his head in a soft blue ambience. The stranger moved his hand through the air in a gentle motion. The same dark presence at her core returned like a rope pulling taut between them.

"Now walk."

Hopelessness threatened to fill her hollowed heart, the numbness slowly relenting against the push of realization. Ilai was gone. *Gone.*

Why did it not feel so final? She had seen death years ago, witnessing life extinguish in a final breath. She knew the very pain of a life lost right in front of her eyes. Ysella recalled the blade jutting from Ilai's chest, the red blooming against the torn leathers.

But then his body *disappeared* into a wisp, sucked into the blade like a cloud in harsh winds. She did not understand that magic, and her mind could not decide between despair or hope.

The vision of Bastillos in rubble and fire felt as real as this, and she couldn't help but wonder if this was just a continuation of the nightmare. It felt so real, yet she couldn't quite grasp it.

"His name is Ilai," she murmured softly, almost as if she hadn't meant to speak at all. An agonizing ache filled her chest.

Their boots sunk deeply into the soft snow. It rose to mid calf causing their gaits to lumber.

"Ah, was he special to you?" the stranger asked in a melodious tone. "You must be heartbroken. Hmm, now I understand that last light in his eyes. That honeyed sorrow."

Ysella's steps faltered, a sharp breath spiking her lungs with cold air. The tree line slowly dissolved to an open white expanse, snow covering the Grey Hinterlands almost completely in a barren path to her demise.

Was Ilai truly gone?

She could not will the dream to release.

"He was a bounty hunter," she said, her feet moving her forward. "My captor. Nothing more. Where are we going?"

A lightning bolt of pain shot through her spine, white and blinding, her body tense as the stranger walked up to her, breath at her neck. "I did not say you could stop walking," he warned. The pain rose, and she was sure her body would break and tear into thousands of pieces.

With a twist of his hand, the pain subsided, and she nearly collapsed in the snow.

"Keep moving northeast," the stranger commanded.

Ragged breaths burned through her lungs, eyes watering as she wobbled forward. "Are you one of them, then?" she asked. "The ones who set the bounty."

"No, but I am their wraith," he said, chuckling as though he were admiring a child's innocence.

"Why? What possible purpose does all of this serve?" Ysella asked. "I know it's a war they want, but I don't understand why."

"I care not for their purpose," Wraith said. "I am their weapon sent to retrieve you; to ensure your arrival. I care only to taste the sweet, palatable fear that carries in the souls marching to their end. Did you see the glorious void?"

His mind was lost, his voice cracking in elation as he closed his eyes to revel in his self-made darkness.

Ysella scoffed. "There's nothing glorious about it. So you're their tool, then? Their pawn. It's curious someone with your abilities could be so content in servitude. Rather pitiful."

"Oh, how sad am I to be in such an arrangement," he replied mockingly. Whispers returned and receded, never fully leaving her psyche. They prickled like the chill of the wind against her crown. Some of the whispers murmured frantically, worried and hopeless, others were caught in an inaudible cacophony.

Through the hisses and hums, Ilai's familiar tenor sliced through the noise, calling her name in such clarity her stomach lurched. Her footsteps faltered, the emptiness within her too complete, too whole to afford her the emotions of loss and grief. Her tears fell with ease.

"The arrangement is exactly where I want it to be," Wraith said, and brought his head to her neck once again, inhaling her scent deeply. "Tell me more of what you think of my powers."

She froze, his fingers curling around her shoulders. "I think you're an abomination. I look forward to the day someone ends you."

"Despair is such a delectable thing," Wraith cooed. "I feel it. You try so hard to remain strong. You avoid the bitterness of isolation through delusions of strength, but I feel it all. I know it all. And I hunger."

Just as she moved to shirk from the man's touch, pain pierced through her veins, his teeth spiking through her neck and drawing hot blood. She relived the last month with Ilai in an instant, his death replaying repeatedly until guilt coiled in her gut and threatened to wretch.

Wraith pulled back, mouth bathed in her blood as he laughed in amusement. "If you stop again, I will drain you," he promised, and seemed delighted at the prospect. Ysella struggled to maintain upright, hand shakily rising to her throbbing neck.

"You need me alive," she reminded. "Your employers dispatched you to bring me alive."

His tongue raked the red from his lips, fangs glinting. "I care not. Now walk."

Blood oozed from the wound as she pressed her hand against it. She could feel the marks from his teeth where they dug into her flesh. Her feet moved with hardly a thought, shock filtering her thoughts to silence. They entered into thicket with its path barely visible. Wraith's hand lingered on her shoulder, directing her with soft nudges to keep her moving.

26
YSELLA

The storm passed gently overhead, the wind spinning thicker clumps of snowfall. Wraith would not allow Ysella to stop even as the snow proved more difficult to walk through. The ground below was uneven with loose small rocks Ysella stumbled over with wobbling legs.

To the east, three men covered thickly in furs rode up on horses and circled around the pair. "You there," one of them spoke. "Wraith. Regan wishes to speak with you."

Wraith groaned and commanded Ysella to turn eastward. The men on the horses walked alongside them as an escort.

Fate had been cruel, now it was derisive. Regan.

They had left Dournfast to avoid his caravan. They pressed on through the storm deep within the woods and away from the main roads only to cross paths with someone more merciless.

And now that person led him to Regan's caravan.

Ysella moved without protest, the invisible magical leash a tingle at her spine. They followed the caravaners to a small encampment next to a shallow cave made by tall jutting rocks. They were far from the main road, the wagons nowhere in sight. Regan had gathered a handful of his men to set out on his pursuit.

Regan placed another log on the fire as they approached, a brow lifting as he looked between Ysella and Wraith. He grinned widely, exposing his dark-stained teeth.

"Well, there you are," he said, and motioned to the stones around the fire pit cleared of snow.

Wraith looked to Ysella and pointed to one of the stones. "Sit."

Ysella ignored the instructions, moving instead towards Regan, striking out with a balled-up fist that collided with the edge of his jaw.

Not much of Regan moved, save the jolt of his head from the impact and the swift disappearance of his grin. The surrounding caravaners rose defensively, their hands curling to fists or reaching for knives as their leader held out a hand. He kept his gaze on Ysella while his crew regained their composure to a thin, taut line ready to snap at a moment's notice. Only when the last one sat back down did he look over to Wraith. who hadn't moved.

"If you're not going to keep her in line, I'm inclined to do so myself," Regan said. Wraith's head tilted, his tongue licking his teeth under his lips as he smirked.

"You will not," he stated, and Regan scoffed, stepping towards Ysella. Wraith made no move, at least not yet.

Ysella met the man's stare, unflinching and hardened with resolve despite the distance closing in between them. She could smell his sour breath and see the wiry grey hairs curling out of his peppered beard.

Amusement curled the edges of his lips, and he placed a hand to her throat in a gentle threat, calloused palm brushing against her skin as he situated his hold. She still did not flinch, and she could see a flicker of disappointment pull the edge of his lips downward.

"Not worried about keeping my skin smooth anymore, Regan?" she asked coolly.

His grin returned, widening to show his yellowed teeth. "Not in the slightest."

"Either do something, or let me go," she snapped. "I've little desire to be pawed at by a wet rat."

Regan's thumb brushed against her collarbone in contemplation, her senses plunging into a deep, dark cold as if she had fallen through ice on a lake. Over his shoulder, standing apart from the caravaners, she saw the vision of Ilai staring at her with empty, sunken eyes. He was bloodless, his skin pulled taut against his bones, waxy and sallow, lips a thin, bluish line. He was dressed in furs and leathers as he had been in life, but a gaping hole in his chest carved through the sturdy materials, his flesh exposed, ruined and stained by dark brown flakes of dried blood. Sharp pain coiled through her like a snake climbing from her toes along her spine, spiking through the back of her skull. Ysella's eyes squeezed shut as a scream clawed at the back of her throat.

"Sit," Wraith commanded calmly.

When she opened her eyes, Ilai was gone, the campsite devoid of his haunt, her lungs without air.

Regan was by the fire now, the other caravaners staring at her wide-eyed and pale. Silently, Ysella took a seat, digging her nails into her lap to keep from quivering.

The fire danced with her thoughts plagued by curious questions. How long might it take for a person to burn to death in a fire this small? It had not taken long for the flames to consume Hamish. His wallowing cries echoed in her memory, the heightened orange glow a lens to the pondered future. Could she make it into the fire fast enough before she was stopped? Could Wraith feel her intent as she felt his intrusion on her mind?

A quick flickering glance to Wraith told her the answer. The man's glowing white gaze was already upon her, staring at her like a feast, a smirk curling on the edge of his lips. Was he taunting her? His head lowered... Was that a nod?

She quickly looked away. Regan ladled a hearty looking soup from a pot over the fire, and handed a bowl to Wraith, who curiously took the offered meal. Perhaps he did require actual sustenance.

"They say this storm is going to last us another couple of days," Regan said.

"You risked much to share this bounty," Wraith stated. Regan feigned a laugh as he poured another bowl and offered it to Ysella.

"We made a deal, Wraith," he stated coldly. "The law of the land, foreigner."

A joyless laugh rose from her throat, softly at first, but grew louder as she looked between the two. "You're both complete imbeciles, aren't you? Bounties and laws and deals. Do you have any idea what will happen to these lands when this war starts? Do you think for one moment the Grey will be spared? You actually think you stand to gain anything. You'll be dead faster than Winter's bite. We all will."

The men surrounding her stopped and stared as she spoke. Regan set the offered bowl of soup down on the ground next to her, sitting back on his own stone to give her his undivided attention.

And then he laughed.

The caravaners joined in the chorus, some murmuring to each other to mock her words. Wraith smirked, sipping his broth.

Regan pointed out to the white landscape, the tall rocks breaching like a whale's fin. She'd seen the depictions in Lumin's library, the drawings of the magnificent creatures beautiful, yet terrifying. The rocks looked like the whales were stuck in a sea of white, very similar to the drawings on crisp paper.

"This land is no good for battles," Regan said boisterously. Under the thick blanket of snow would be the loose rocks she always tripped over, or the squishy mud that only hardened to ice in the right weather. "I don't give a shit about your war."

"When the famine hits and you're starving to death in your precious wagon, you will," Ysella said, her voice caustic. "Do you really think anyone will care about your trade then, Regan? About your chattel market? A maiden's virtue won't be worth much when men are killing each other in the streets for a meal."

She smirked dryly, sitting back with a scoff. Regan sat calmly, bringing his bowl to his lips to sip his soup. Not a single caravaner had utensils, their dirty fingers grasping their bowls at the edge.

"That is if you live that long," Ysella remarked. "My bet? You won't make it past the buyout for this deal of yours. You're an expendable waste of time."

Shadows cast from the firelight hollowed out their stares, some of the caravaners suspended in thought, their bowls hovering just at their chins as the steam rose across their features. Wraith inhaled deeply through his nose. He sensed something she could not.

But then Ysella noticed the shift in stances, the glint of eyes looking toward their leader who appeared to be unbothered by her words. The others were showing signs of doubt.

"You may spook the weak of mind, mountain lady," Regan said. He propped his forearms on his legs and leaned in closer to her. "Look me dead in my eyes and tell me if I care."

A small, dead smile lingered on her lips as Regan leaned in close, staring boldly into his hardened gaze. She'd debated worse minds in her time at the academy. There was a reason she was elevated to diplomat while most of them remain scholars.

"Come now, Regan," Ysella goaded. "I know you'd never show fear in front of your men. They would tear you to shreds the moment you flinched."

Something foreign within her welled with elation at her challenge. She tried to push it away, her heart pounding with manufactured adrenaline. "A war is a threat to your business," she continued, "and who do you think they'll blame when food becomes scarce? When profits lower as people hoard their metal? I'm sure you'd like to believe they'd be loyal as they have been since the start of their employment. You have a system to keep honorless men in check, do you not? Food. Protection. Metal."

A smile slowly spread across Regan's weathered features, a chuckle rumbling from his throat. Ysella felt a suggestion in the corners of her mind. Wraith had snaked himself into her psyche, attempting to influence her next move. In her brief pause, she dared to look at her captor, and when she did, his smile bore his fanged teeth.

"I think you believe you're good at hiding your fear, Regan," Ysella said, looking back to the caravan leader. He finished off his bowl of soup, ladling another portion, feigning amusement and apathy. "The thing about fear, though, is that it is all consuming. It lingers in your mind in doubts, and it shows itself in ways you might not consider. Your stalwart apathy, for instance, is a clear indication of your fear."

"Is that so?" Amused, Regan blew on his soup to cool it down.

"You have to keep yourself occupied," Ysella observed, "lest you fidget in more obvious ways. It serves to keep your mind busy with everything but the line of thinking your crew has already thought. There will come a day when they will look at you and see only one man... How many is it in your caravan?"

The caravaners hardened at her words, insulted by what she was insinuating. Ysella knew she was right, even if they displayed loyalty in the moment. They looked to Regan for when to move, how to act, what to do. One day Regan would give them a command that would test their loyalty, and it would be his undoing. A war would escalate that scenario.

"That reminds me." Regan slurped a mouthful of soup as he turned to Wraith. "Getting back to business. You owe me a finder's fee. I gave you his blood. It's only fair you let me turn her in. Now, I know you were headed off towards that tower without me. I'm willing to overlook that."

Regan pulled a knife he'd rested upon the embers next to the fire and tossed it in the air once for a bit of flare. The heated metal glowed briefly until the chill of the air swiped the color away.

The spin of the glowing blade swirled Ysella's consciousness into Ilai's swift dance with a sword, his graceful motions sending the steel singing through the air. Elegant. Perfect. Yet primal and aggressive.

Ilai had saved her time and time again. He saved her from the worgs, from the caravan, from the spider. He saved her from other hunters. Ilai was always there to keep her safe.

And now he was gone.

She had failed to save *him*.

"If you don't want to honor our arrangement," Regan continued, his words a muffled hum against the pounding in her head, "I'll gut her right here."

Consequences be damned. She grabbed his idle hand, and in the same momentum, she pushed the blade towards his middle, immediately met by the resistance of his strength. She could feel the tension and power in his forearm, and while it was likely he could easily overtake her, he allowed her futile attempt.

The hand holding the knife twisted against her fingers, his other hand grasping her throat. A familiar thrum like rolling thunder curled through her mind as the shallow cave dimmed.

Dark tendrils coiled around the caravaners, their bodies raised from the ground as their eyes rolled to the back of their heads. Regan's mouth hung agape as if to scream in agony, yet no sound pulled from his throat. They struggled to cry out, their breaths hitched with near suffocation.

Ysella rose from her stony perch aghast, eyes turning to Wraith questioning why she was spared. Wraith stood near what little light struggled in the fire, his hand raised as if pushing against a heavy, unseeable force. Faint glimmers pressed at her core that were not her own: elation, fear, pain.

"Do you want to know his fear, Ysella?" Wraith asked, basking in Regan's writhing form.

So this is what it looked like when he plunged her into that dark abyss. Ysella rounded to the back of Regan's form noting how his body bent and tensed. Was it her that delighted in whatever agony he faced, or was that Wraith?

She had never hated anyone, but in that moment, watching Regan's pain pull back and contort his face, she felt its weight pressing down on her, and she desperately desired to surrender to it; to let it consume her completely.

What would his fears manifest? Wraith's proposition echoed in her mind, pins driving down her spine as she considered them. Yes, she wanted to know. She wanted to know the horrors that drove a man into himself so she could wield it as a weapon. She wished to find what haunted him and leave him crawling.

She wanted to punish him.

And yet... It was not his fault. It was hers. She had forced Ilai to continue her mission. She dragged Ilai into her hubris when he had the better mind to leave. Her determination sharpened to its own weapon, guilting him into staying the course.

What had she said? Her blood was on his hands...

"Stop," she whispered, then repeated again, louder. "Stop it! Let them go. Just let them go." Her voice broke, a choking knot constricting her throat. "Please."

A shrill shriek whistled, funneling sharply through the air as Wraith raised his hand further, the dimness deepening as if it were a moonless night. The black tendrils bore into the caravaners' skin right to their very core, their exposed skin flaking like ash at the points of contact. Wraith's hand shook as if struggling against that unseen force, and with a swift motion his fingers closed to a fist with the sound of a drum strike on a hard edge.

Just as the illusion of night turned to pitch, the darkness dissipated. The caravaners fell in a state of shock as they fought to come to. Beyond the mouth of the shallow cave a fog had rolled through, eerily thick.

"Walk," Wraith commanded, and pointed towards the fog.

"A moment," Ysella asked softly, stepping closer to the throng of fallen men around the embers of the campfire. Wraith made no command to deny her request. She could still feel the ethereal tether of Shadow Magic between them, but felt nothing that was not her own.

Regan laid in a disoriented heap, his head lulling as his consciousness fought for clemency. She crouched carefully in front of him, staring at him with an odd mask of sympathy. "You're not a good man. I want you to know that I did not ask him to stop for your sake. These men that follow you? Many of them are not good men either, but when they recover from whatever hell they've seen, they'll have a choice: to stay here and become like you, so deeply rooted in their own disregard for human life that they cannot possibly crawl free of your hold, or to flee that grasp and become something better. Something like Ilai.

"Your power is but a thread, and I could have severed it. I don't know what frightens you, but maybe that will. Remember it." She rose with carefully composed movements, tucking his discarded knife into her boot.

Wraith watched her intimate interaction expressionless and cold, and as she rose, he twisted his arm outward, pinning Ysella where she stood with his Shadow Magic.

Agony struck once more like a harp's string, pronounced and reverberating. It was as if she was slowly crushed by an unseen hand, and as he clenched his fist closed, motioning towards himself, she floated toward him until she was face to face with his glowing eyes.

She could see the faint outline of what would have been his irises, now the brightest points of the glow. The pupil no longer existed, the whites of his eyes just a shade darker than the blinding white that stared through her.

"If you disobey me again," he growled, "I will keep you in the Forever until I deem it fit for you to return."

Gritting her teeth, jaw locked tight, Ysella glared. Somewhere in the powerful agony, she struggled against the desire to will the man's ire. They were connected by magic that revealed her emotions to him. Surely he sensed her own darkness welcoming his threat.

But then she remembered Odessa, head in the clouds, her arms wrapped around her in a loving embrace just before Ysella's mission. Ysella promised her she'd return.

"You must tell me of your travels," Odessa said, as she pulled from the embrace. "I hear Nabannon has the prettiest scenery. And all the outside houses are built with wide sloped roofs."

"Only in the north," Ysella corrected. Her sister had grown so much since the rebellion, yet even with her studies she had so much to learn. It was not entirely her fault. Her mother felt Odessa would be too free spirited if she knew too much. It would surely stifle her elevation, but then again, Odessa always did what she wanted to, anyway.

"Aren't you going to the north?" Odessa asked.

"No, the center of Nabannon is more to the mid-western region along the coast," Ysella said. "It's a city called Athranath, and it's surrounded by the thickest woodlands. Impenetrable, they say."

Wraith pulled her consciousness back to the cold bite of the Grey, a grimace pulling his lips as he awaited confirmation of her compliance. Pain rose like spikes through her bones.

She had to persevere. For Bastillos. For Odessa.

A tear streamed down her cheek like fire against the icy flesh, and she nodded.

His hand waved, dismissing the spell with such a sudden release, her knees nearly buckled. Ysella quickly recovered, rising upright as Wraith moved past her stopping just at the cusp of the thick veil of fog. He pointed into the grey shroud.

"If you do not run, I will ensure your survival through the fog. Run, and your soul is forfeit."

The fog was as like a layered skirt of thin fabrics moving in a breeze. It would not penetrate the entrance to the shallow cave and lingered like a wall of undulating smoke. Somewhere within its veil came the sounds of raking metal, groaning wood splintering and snapping, and the hiss of whispers.

The unknown was a horrible enough concept for Ysella to proceed with caution. There were things trudging through the fog, muted silhouettes so shrouded she was not sure what she saw. They stepped through in tandem, the fog embracing them as she kept her focus on pinpoints through the white sheet, heart racing at every awful, unfamiliar sound.

"This is not natural," she murmured. "What is it?"

A silhouette perhaps ten foot tall and arched, stood just mere feet from their path. Then, she realized, it was far, far taller, rising up into the mist like a tower adorned with multiple appendages and no discernible head. A chittering sound grew to a guttural, dual toned croak, the entity slowly flowing away from the path Wraith directed. The creature seemed indifferent to their presence.

Despite the magic tether between them, Wraith kept pace at Ysella's side through the fog, his hand on her shoulder to guide her through. He was not phased by the creatures marching past. Another silhouette lumbered in a bulk that had an indiscernible amount of walking limbs, and another that seemed to have no limbs at all and glided through the fog like a black, inky spirit.

The whispers hissed pleas of help, and through the noise a voice called through, at first like an echo, and then clearly calling to her.

"Ysella!"

Unmistakably, it was Ilai's voice, sharp in her mind but with no discernible location. She froze, rigid in place despite the quaking fear, her eyes darting about as she willed her body to move. "Ilai?" Her heart threatened to leap free, and she placed a hand on her chest as if to still its frenzied cadence.

She twisted free of Wraith's grip on her shoulder, stepping forward frantically. "I can hear him! Ilai?"

The fog drew in, shrouding her in gossamer with barely any sight ten feet in front of her. The chittering and lumbering of its occupants continued, creaking and groaning like metal hinges and wood splintering. She was alone, Wraith completely unseen, but his voice cut through just as clearly as Ilai's.

"Ah, to heed the siren's call. Such a caress makes Darkness loving, and eases the soul to its doom."

Ilai's voice carried once again, cutting through the whispers, aching her heart when she could not hear his every word. "I'm right here," his voice said, almost pleading. "Can you not see me?"

"I can hear you!" she called back. Tears came freely, her voice hinging on a sob that nearly choked her. "I can... I..."

Ilai was gone. That morning, she had watched as Wraith's blade lapped his blood into its runes, filtering his soul into its crystal pommel. The wound was mortal. The sword pierced right through his chest.

Ilai was gone.

Dropping to her knees, voice barely above a whisper, she wrapped her arms around herself. "Oh, Ilai... It's my fault. It's all my fault. I'm so sorry. I never should have made you come. You wanted to leave and I wouldn't let you and now you've gone where I cannot go. I never told you..."

A chill ran the length of her, disembodied from the last dredges of Winter's bite. Nails burrowing into the flesh of her balled fists, Ysella spoke to Wraith. "Why are you doing this?"

Wraith did not respond, and in his absence, the whispers grew. Ilai's voice struggled against the cacophony, but the sound had a direction now. It was as if he were kneeling right in front of her. She wanted desperately to reach out for him, yet there was nothing but wisps of an impossibly thick haze. Her hands remained tightly clenched.

"I'm here." His voice was earnest and undulated in and out of the whispers. "You need to get out of here...don't know where I am...back...do this."

Whirring and groans resounded like deep horns, and a massive silhouette reached out and clasped Ysella, its appendage wrapping around her form almost entirely. It was a wide creature made of ink blots that wisped within the fog. Bright glowing orbs dotted its form, and it wasn't until they blinked that they revealed themselves as its eyes.

Around its center, a maw-like cavern opened in a vortex of slowly funneling stars, and an appendage coiled from its center, wrapping around Ysella's head while embedding something sharp into her crown.

All at once, her mind was filled with a mass of horrific visions. Worlds colliding, ending, swirling into masses of light and dark, crumbling to dust, burning, tearing apart. She was thrown through the cosmos of starlight and stardust, and at the end of the vortex was a deep nothingness that grew in size. A final call of her name was ripped from her consciousness as sound became a deafening nothing.

A hand gripped her shoulder, pulling her from the chaos and into the clarity of grey clouds. Snow softened her fall, and Wraith appeared in her line of sight, crouching as his glowing eyes scanned her indifferently for any signs of consciousness.

Rolling over, Ysella swallowed hard, nearly losing the battle against rising bile in her throat, her entire body quivering without relent as her head burrowed in her hands.

I'm here.

Why had those words been so easy to believe? All that came after — the horrific thing from the fog, the visions — wove into her like every nightmarish thing she had witnessed thus far. They clung to her like wet clothes, heavy and stifling, yet the fear seemed like a distant, wavering darkness against a blinding, blooming light. She had seen his blood, watched him dissipate into nothing, but those words had filled her with an impossible feeling of hope.

Opening her eyes, she met Wraith's glowing gaze. Where she might have recoiled in the past, she only looked up at him with disinterest, determination clawing at the recesses of her mind.

27
WORG

The air was a stale, foggy expanse in a ruddy red. There was no source of light evident, but it was bright enough to see his own hands as he pushed himself from a muddy terrain. He couldn't see much past five feet in front of him. The foggy veil was too dense.

Pushing himself up to a stand, knees shaking as if he hadn't walked in years, he searched the nothingness for signs of life. It was an expanse of parched and dusty earth and rock veiled by a low hanging cloud. It wasn't dirt in the air. Whatever it was, it clung like fog, yet without the moisture.

His boots scuffed against the parched terrain. He couldn't remember how he got to this place or where he had come from or why he journeyed.

He couldn't remember who he was.

Each step forward looked like the last with the exception of a stray stone here and there in the small circumference he could see. Loose rocks clacked as his shuffling feet kicked them forward. The barren land would slope up or down, and sometimes he would find himself before a wall of tall rock, its peak completely obscured by the red fog. He followed the cliff side aimlessly, contemplating the sounds he could not place.

He was not alone in this land. There was an ever-present, mid-pitched hum that vibrated his eardrums. Accompanying it were inhuman calls and guttural groans and the cadence of crashing movement that shook the ground beneath him. An instinct within him knew not to call out or make himself known to whatever these creatures were in the fog. He drew more careful with his steps.

An odd sensation emanated from his chest, pulling him in a particular direction. Turning towards the sensation felt right. He shifted his stance and walked away from the cliff side. The further he stepped away from the rocks, the more it disappeared into the ruddy red fog.

Each step into the nothingness gave him time to contemplate his existence, grasping at thin threads of thoughts as some semblance of certainty took hold.

A thud hit the earth, rocks clattering from the proximity, and he halted. Another thud followed. And another. A laborious, bipedal monstrosity was silhouetted in the fog in front of him. It didn't see him as it passed, its height easily ten times his own. One thick, trunk-like leg nearly crashed into him. He stumbled away from it in shock, not just by its stature but by its visage. The creature was unlike anything he surmised he'd seen in his past. He knew it was otherworldly.

The entirety of its body swirled like a void of darkness, starry expanses distant and twinkling within its form. It was large in height and width, tendrils of blackness curling out from its back and lapping through the fog as if in search. Each tendril held an eye as white as stars, aberrations blinking as slits covered and retracted from each orb.

An involuntary gasp sucked into his lungs as an eye snaked past, starry pupil darting about in search. Three more of the tendrilled eyes turned swiftly in his direction, the creature pausing its lumbering. A low, groaning hum churned from its throat in a dissonant chord as the creature turned.

He instinctively reached for a sword at his hip, yet found nothing but an empty scabbard.

The creature's head jutted out from its torso like a skull covered in gossamer, the thin threads flowing in a breeze that did not exist. There were no eyes in its head, yet it searched, and as it turned towards his direction, he felt his head swim as though he were being repeatedly beaten by a blunt force.

Something grabbed the collar of his cloak and pulled him back just as an eye swooped closer. He was pulled further into the fog, away from the eye that twitched in its hunt, and as he scrambled from the hold, he looked up to see another man, his face ragged and worried as he held a finger to his lips.

The other man watched the creature search where they once stood, his body still, eyes wide and fearful. From this distance, the creature was shrouded by the ruddy veil to the point where it was merely a vague outline, its long appendages sweeping the dry earth. When it found nothing was there, it turned back to its lumbering walk and disappeared. Its crashing gait drew distant.

"You need to be more careful," the other man whispered. "Follow me. I have a shelter. Ask nothing until we are inside."

The man's form disappeared in the fog as he rushed forward. He rushed after the other man, eyes searching the dusty earth for disturbances to follow until he could keep the man in his sights. They traveled swiftly up a slope, the light brighter for a time, then dimming as they journeyed through a ravine. It was in the direction of the ever-present pull he felt at his core, and it gave him comfort.

Ducking into the entrance of a cave, the man waved for him to follow. The temperature was the same as outside, and that seemed wrong given the darkness. Light was supposed to be warm, he was sure of it.

"Do you remember your name yet?" the other man asked. He had abandoned his hushed tone as he walked more calmly through the natural tunnel leading up a gentle slope to a wider room. It had an opening looking out into the fog that was barred by man-made pillars of stacked rocks. Light was still allowed to bleed through and illuminate the space large enough to sit or lay comfortably.

The other man looked at him expectantly for an answer. He had dark curly hair that had grown out to his bearded jawline. His slender form was cloaked in a dark fabric and robed in once-elegant attire that looked fitting for someone more presentable.

"I don't remember," he said to the other man. "What is this place?"

The other man nodded and motioned towards a natural slab of rock a few feet above the ground. The man sat next to it like a table, and he followed suit. "My name is Rotheel," the other man said.

"I know that name," he said thoughtfully, brow furrowing as he tried to grasp at a memory dangling by a thread of Rotheel's name.

"I'm afraid I don't recognize you," Rotheel admitted, and cast his gaze out to the window. The fog looked like a sheet covering the view from the outside. "I don't know what this place is. I think it's a prison. Our jailer comes to visit. Usually, when he does, I remember everything, and then he leaves and it's gone with him."

A face, hollow and evil, grinned at him from a distant memory. Thin lips curled on pale skin, white glowing eyes stared at him hungrily. It was the face of a tormentor and an abomination, and his heart ached for something it caused. His hand reached to clutch his chest from the pain, his fingers finding the broken fibers of his shirt and shorn edges of leather.

He looked down to where his hand rested and found an angry, gaping hole that tore open his skin in a reddened fissure, glistening with stagnant blood. His hands pulled the fabric of his shirt further apart in disbelief, eyes widening at the mortal wound. He could feel it tunnel through him and open through his back, and his breath hitched.

"I should be dead."

Rotheel held out his hands. "Calm yourself," he said, and pulled back his own robes to reveal his similar wound across his chest. "I wondered if I were dead, too. I don't think we are, but I think we are stones from it. What comes after death is never described this way, from what I have learned of our religions."

There was more to the wound. He could feel it deep within him — the pull was connected to it. A face with eyes of a deep blue resurfaced in his mind as someone significant, but he could not recall the other features.

Resting back against the cave wall, Rotheel exhaled with a sorrowful smile. "It's felt like ages since I've been here, alone, with only my jailor to keep me company when he desired information. I can't help but feel some hope from your presence, friend."

"What if I am not a friend?" he asked.

"I've considered it," Rotheel said. "I think we are more alike than that. Something in me believes you are an ally. You have a look about you."

He found his own crook in the wall to lean against, and settled in as comfortably as rock would allow. The information provided wasn't overwhelming. It felt as though he understood to some degree, or perhaps he hadn't the capability to feel overwhelmed. Skittering clattered along the side of the rock face, loosing stones as something unseen moved downward. Rotheel steeled himself, posture stiffening as his eyes fixated on the window. He relaxed as soon as the unseen was no longer heard.

"That thing you saw earlier isn't the only thing out there," Rotheel informed. "They wander around this wasteland. Some hunt for things that should not be here. Sometimes when the light dims I can hear screams. Human screams. That's what we are. Do you at least remember that?"

He nodded his head. "Some things appear inherent," he said, his hand still pressed to the wound on his chest. It ached as if he'd been hollowed out like a gourd, but he could still feel the beating of his heart and the rise and fall of breath in his lungs.

"We should stick together," Rotheel suggested.

"Do you feel a pull?" he asked. His hand gripped the fabric over his wound. Rotheel nodded solemnly.

"Our jailer is connected to us," Rotheel informed. "It's just him. You don't want to go to him. He will punish you for it."

"Does our jailer have a name?"

Rotheel's head shook slightly. "I can't remember. I don't know if it is important either. Only that he has a terrible power over us."

"Ysella." The name parted his lips in a soft murmur as he grasped the familiarity. He saw those blue eyes again, and the slow reveal of detailing in the way her lips settled with determination, or how her hair fell in soft brown waves. The pull from his wound felt like an aching sickness.

"I know that name," Rotheel said, and sat up from his rest. His brow furrowed in confusion. "You're not Ysella. Do you recall how you know her?"

He shook his head. "I knew her well, I think. It seems fond. How do you know her?"

Rotheel sat back in disappointment. "I do not remember either. I know the name. I can almost picture her, yet it's just like all the rest." He placed a hand over his eyes and grimaced. His hands were shaking. "I'll tell you what I do remember. What I know. Perhaps it will help you remember something.

"My name is Rotheel of House Degent. I was on a mission when I was captured. I don't fully remember the mission. It was important. Something to do with a war. I think it was my job to help prevent it from happening."

There was a familiarity to his story as though it were somehow tied to him. Perhaps that explained his instincts when faced with the creature. War did not seem as important to him, though. Not enough to go on a mission to stop it. He felt like he did not have as noble of a name, nor one as long.

Rotheel looked at him thoughtfully as he paused, slight disappointment pulling his lips thin when no response came. "You need to remember more, friend," Rotheel continued. "If we can't remember we may risk losing ourselves entirely. Come."

As he rose, Rotheel leaned heavily on the rocks, his legs weak and shaky. He stood with Rotheel and offered an aiding hand. "It's an awful place, this prison," Rotheel said as he walked down the slope of the cave. "There will come a point where you will grow hungry. There is nothing for us to eat here. Our bodies will wither, but we cannot die."

"How do you know this?" he questioned as he followed. Rotheel stopped at the opening of the cave, his eyes searching through the fog, ears keen to every sound. Rotheel existed in this place long enough to survive despite the state of his weak body.

Rotheel motioned for him to follow, and they took the leftmost path following a narrow and tall ravine. He kept his voice low and his pace cautious, and he mimicked Rotheel's moves. "There's no way to count the days here. The light can dim, but it does not go dark. The dimming does not seem to correlate with our perception of time, but I know based on the growth of my beard and my hair it has been too long. I should have died long ago without food or water. It will be agony, friend."

A faint notion of a memory resurfaced. He knew the pains of starvation and the itch of a parched throat. As they continued up a path of loose rocks, careful not to disturb too many lest they loose, he recalled similar formations from a grey land where grass and moss grew alongside creek beds and waterfalls. There was no vegetation here. Only dust and rock.

Nearing the crest of the slope, Rotheel motioned for him to keep low and crept up to the edge. He slowly brought his eyes upward. The fog was less dense, the land more flat. He could see fifty feet outward, though the sky was still obscured.

Thousands of bodies stood, some slowly shuffling aimlessly with their heads low. Groans occasionally escaped a slacked jaw, teeth exposed and framed by split lips. Their skin had grown to a bluish hue, leathered and wrapped around the bones with no meat to give form. They were husks wandering a wasteland with no hope left in their eyes.

"Don't let them see you," Rotheel whispered. "They grow violent. I do not know why, but I think that is our fate the longer we stay here."

"We must act, then," he said resolutely. Rotheel turned to him with a small smile.

"I am glad to hear you say that," Rotheel said. A spark of hope glistened in his eyes. "I think with our minds combined we can come up with a plan."

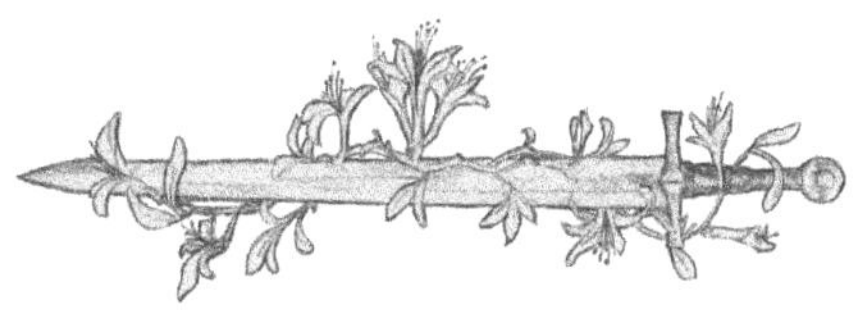

Time was an odd thing to recall in a place where time was not so evident. The light outside the cave did dim as Rotheel had mentioned, though it was like a passing cloud over the sun.

The sun... He knew of a land of grey clouds that shrouded the sun, and when the sun broke through, it was warm and welcoming. He couldn't fully recall the sensation of warmth, though he knew it to be good. The Grey. The Grey Hinterlands. How could he remember its name but not his own?

Rotheel had winded himself by the time they reached the safety of his hideaway. The man rested against a smoothed portion of the wall, head propped against the stone as if it were too heavy for his neck to hold. Despite his physical state, he looked alight with excitement and proposed ideas for workshop.

"That constant pull you feel right at your center," Rotheel said. "When our jailor comes it will feel like a command. It will no longer be just a sensation. It will be a compulsion. Lately he's come to me. I've been rather lethargic of late."

"We could set up a trap," he suggested. "We would know when he's coming if the pull feels different."

"Yes, but what sort of trap?" Rotheel motioned around the cave. "Nothing grows here. There are no vines or roots to thread or weave. There are just rocks and dust and creatures of the void."

"We have what's on us," he noted, and looked down at his body. His shoulders were draped with a heavy cloak lined with fur pelts, and his body was adorned in leathers threaded securely. Belts kept his scabbard at his side and a dagger to his back. "Where does he live?"

"What do you mean?"

"Does the Jailor live in this place?" he clarified. "We could go to him before he comes to us."

Rotheel's brow furrowed as if pained, his head shaking. "I do not think so. When he comes, the veil is called to him. This... fog. This haunting lack of sight breaks like water through a fissure. It's an affront to the senses. Overwhelming, yet has its own interest. He is within the fissures, but he can open and close them. I do not think he presides here unless he wants to."

Stepping over to the window, he inventoried his person as he thought. Rotheel was on edge, watching as he approached the window. He had a small dagger sheathed along his belt to his back and an empty scabbard where he likely once carried a sword. He wore a thick leather jerkin and leather greaves with studded plates. His left shoulder ached when he moved, a pull coming from his shoulder blade, and as he looked under his layers he saw fresh scars.

He remembered fire burning through the night held by a woman bravely fending off a pack of worgs. They gnashed their teeth as they backed away from her. It was Ysella. She was a brave woman, but she was no Lander.

What made a Lander? Her lips often pulled to a frown, he recalled. She called him a worg. A monster. A coward. His heart ached worse than his shoulder and pulsed out through the unseen tether binding him to his jailor. Her stern words sliced through his memory like the knife that painted the crimson on her palm.

You're a lot of things, most of them unpleasant...

He closed his eyes as if he could hide from the memory of her anguished features staring at him defiantly. He felt misunderstood, yet could not place why. The hole in his chest felt as though it widened.

"Are you well, friend?" Rotheel asked as he pushed himself to sit upright.

He shook his head. "Memories," he answered, and Rotheel nodded.

"They will do that. Do you remember your name yet?"

Placing a hand on his shoulder, he shook his head. "My name is Worg, for that is what I am."

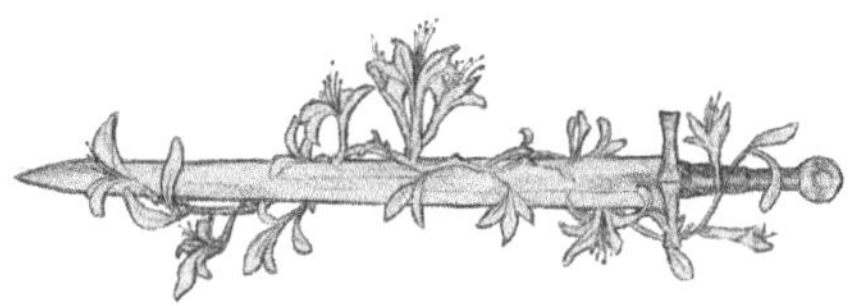

Time was a slow drift on Worg's consciousness. They slept for a time, though with the constant light he could not know how much had passed. Hunger plucked at his insides, dehydration prickling the back of his throat. Rotheel set up rocks on a grid drawn on the flat slab and played a solitary game he couldn't quite place. He knew the rules sometimes, but currently sat contemplating how the next move functioned.

Worg watched without any recollection of the game. He only wished to pass the time without thought towards his survival instincts. He needed sustenance to stay alive, to keep fighting. Without it, he would weaken by the day, whatever a day would be in this land.

"Do you feel a connection to darkness?" Rotheel asked. He held a finger on top of a rock that had been broken in half to reveal a smooth top.

"Here where it's always light?" Worg asked with a bit of amusement. Rotheel huffed a small laugh and shook his head.

"There is a muted darkness in here," he said. "But it is more than a visual sense. It's like... I can't explain it. It's a feeling. A connection. Almost like those creatures out there that lurk in the veil."

"You feel a connection to the creatures?"

"No," Rotheel answered, though he did not seem certain. He picked up the rock with a smooth top and placed it two grids diagonally from its place. "It's more like what they are made of. What they represent. I think I can harness what they possess."

Worg reflected on his own sensations churning throughout his body. He felt emotions, hunger, longing, and the pull he assumed was to his jailor, but he did not feel any connection with darkness. He wasn't entirely certain he'd know what to sense in himself that would suggest such a notion.

"Does it seem safe?" Worg asked. Rotheel's hand hovered over the rock he had just placed, and then he lifted it, setting it back in its former square as he shook his head.

"I don't know," he admitted. "I think I've always been wary of it. The Jailor can call upon it, though. When he uses it on me, it feels uplifting even through the pain."

Worg looked at him incredulously, and Rotheel shrugged. "It is strange to me, too. Not as strange as your name. It must have a story."

"It is just what I remember," Worg admitted. He knew he had a different name that was just out of reach of his recollection.

"So if I call upon it, you will answer?" Rotheel asked.

"If you never use it, I will never know," he answered. Rotheel smiled softly.

"Remember what I told you," Rotheel said. "Repeat your name over and over to yourself so that you do not forget it." He picked up a different rock, one that looked like a leaning tree, and placed it next to the smooth-topped rock and sat back once again. His fingers slowly scratched his chin through his haggard beard.

It was easy for Worg to remember such a name. The memories he recalled easily reminded him of how it came to be. He could remember the glint of the beast's eyes as they caught the firelight and how it stalked them through the night awaiting the perfect hour. He remembered the searing pain of his flesh being torn through and shredded as the creature thrashed him about like a doll. She had been so gentle with her touch, so desperate for his survival.

And yet she called him a worg for his beastly ways. What were those ways? A chain clattering in the cold air, biting at the honeyed skin of a neck that had once only known fine jewelry.

"Do you remember anything good from your life?" Worg asked.

"Define the word," Rotheel suggested rhetorically, and bleakly grinned. His demeanor shifted as he rolled his head against the stone he rested against. "That is curious. I cannot seem to remember the good. I remember things like brief moments of disappointment, of failure, of tribulations. Even my name is tied to something that weighs my soul."

Worg stood, his knees and back aching from the harsh seating. His head felt light as the room dipped, and he steadied himself against the wall. "We should scout the area. Look for fissures. Or at least study what we find."

"To what purpose?" Rotheel asked. "What if they find us?"

"We can be smart about it, but sitting here thinking about things we can't recall is doing us little good," Worg said. "We need to do what we can. What we know we can."

Determination set Rotheel's brow, and he pushed himself to a stand. He leaned more heavily against the wall, a hand to his head. "You're right. Perhaps it can help with planning our ambush."

Worg grinned at that and helped the man walk out of the cave.

Worg had slept three times since coming to this land. They decided to call it the Dungeon, though it was far brighter than any he could recall. His hunger grew from an annoying presence to a clawing in his gut he had to constantly push from his thoughts. Worg occupied his mind with other tasks like scouting and relaying thoughts with Rotheel.

Much of his strength was maintained. He kept himself moving even when in the little cave. Rotheel took to joining him in short spurts by pacing from one end to the other, the pair slowly walking back and forth as they discussed or thought. At points, Worg taught him how to use the dagger.

It was a small thing only about the length of his forearm from pommel to tip. Rotheel awkwardly followed his instruction as he thrusted the blade through the air. Then suddenly the moves flowed naturally.

"I think I know how to fight," Rotheel said.

"You should keep it," Worg suggested, and unclasped his belt to remove the scabbard. "It will serve you well to have a weapon."

"What of you?" Rotheel asked. "You have nothing now."

"I have my hands," he said confidently. While he could not remember how he knew his skills, something about it felt inherent and second nature. Handing the simple leather scabbard towards him, Rotheel hesitantly received it with trepidation creasing his brow.

"I hope I may never have to use it," he said, and sheathed the dagger. "I don't think I like fighting."

"Hide it under your cloak so the Jailor can't see it," Worg suggested.

A pull lurched him forward, Rotheel in tandem as the pair stumbled in place. The air grew thin, a clang resounding like a large sheet of metal struck by a hammer. Despite their staggering stance, no further pull heralded the coming of their captor.

"I don't understand," Rotheel murmured, and looked at his hands. "This is different."

A glimmer of something light welled inside Worg that was connected to the tether at his form. He placed a hand to his wound, the stagnant blood wetting his glove. It never seemed to heal, but it also never felt so pained as it did in that moment. It was as though the blade that made it had plunged through his flesh anew, no longer trapped by distant memories that failed to surface.

"Ysella."

He knew she was there at the end. Snow drifted around the memory of her soft features. Firelight illuminated a smile. She had a gentle touch when she placed her hand upon his chest, and he wanted to hold her closer to him in the night.

Wonderful recollections pulled him through the cave, Rotheel calling out the only name he could remember.

"Worg? What are you doing? Ignore it!"

The air swelled as the veil condensed to a thick, ruddy soup. Breathing was laborious, but he pushed through utilizing the unseen connection as his guide.

"Worg!"

He halted in his steps. "Rotheel!" he called out. "Come to me! Follow my voice! There's something to this!"

A groan croaked through the veil as a creature lumbered through the vibrating air. Worg felt a shift in his senses, his cheeks registering the prickling cold, his nose detecting the hint of smoke and spices.

"Ysella!" he called. The veil drew to a cold grey, thinning to reveal massive silhouettes towering through a fissure in the air. Each step caused a tremor through the snow-covered ground and left indentations the sizes of carts. The cold air sliced through his nose with each breath, and he exhaled as if the wind had been knocked from his lungs.

Through the thinning fog, Worg could see Ysella's familiar form being held by a man who wore an evil grin. The ethereal tether was bound to him and stretched taut. His icy-white eyes looked directly to him, perhaps through him, and it broadened his smile to reveal a set of fangs.

That was the Jailor.

Ysella looked behind her, hair trailing in waves of brown that fell about her face. "Ysella?"

She turned her head quickly, eyes frantically searching through the fog as she froze in place. "Ilai?"

Every forgotten moment flooded through him in an instant as his name returned to him. He was Ilai of the Grey Hinterlands. A bounty hunter. A survivor. He could remember Shera's wisdom and Sabin's warmth.

Ysella brought back the good he had forgotten, and he yearned for her closeness once again. Ilai closed the distance to her, but she walked past him as she searched for the source of his voice. "I can hear him!" she said. "Ilai!"

The Jailor chuckled airily as he watched, head shaking as if amused by a child's wanderings. "Ah, to heed the siren's call," the Jailor mused. "Such a caress makes darkness loving, and eases the soul to its doom."

Ilai quickly turned back to Ysella, hopeful she would not give into despair. "I'm right here!" he called to her. Her head did not turn to look at him even as he stepped into her desperate gaze. "Can you not see me?"

"I can hear you," she answered, eyes brimming with tears. Ilai dropped to his knees as she collapsed in front of him, his hands reaching out to touch her face only to find his fingers turning to dust at the touch. He recoiled, his appendages returning to their former state.

"It's my fault." Her voice was quiet and croaked in pain. "It's all my fault. I'm so sorry. I never should have made you come. You wanted to leave and I wouldn't let you and now you've gone where I cannot go..."

He shook his head in disbelief. She had such a strange way of casting blame. By forcing this false tragedy in her mind, she was hurting herself through the burden of blame. Ysella looked back towards the Jailor who only watched from afar.

"I'm here. I'll come for you, Ysella," Ilai promised softly. "You need to get out of here. Out of this place. I don't know what it is. I don't know where I am, but

I'll find a way back. I need you to keep fighting. Keep being stubborn and brave. You are a survivor. You can do this."

Agony ripped through his core, emanating from the wound in his chest, and the Jailor set his gaze squarely on his prey. His mouth did not move, but the Jailor's voice entered his mind through a cacophony of whispers.

Do you see the thread of hope fraying before your eyes? Do you see you are not living nor are you dead and can achieve neither? You cannot return to her, and even if you could, you will find yourself hollow, and her light will fade.

Pain tore through him like a thousand jagged shards of metal, piercing every muscle and shattering his bones, only to heal and shatter again. He was dragged through agony, as though his skin were being flayed to expose his raw flesh to poison. Blackness enveloped him, stretching into a vast expanse dotted with distant stars, so far out of reach that he couldn't tell if the light was even real.

The darkness blanketed him, muting the pain yet still allowing the suffering as it filtered through each pinpoint of torment. Then it flowed like a heavy torrent through his chest, and darkness turned to a grey expanse as he fell onto a cold, rocky floor.

28
YSELLA

Pushing up onto her elbows, Ysella rubbed her forehead, grimacing as her stomach roiled, the world spinning briefly. Wraith made no effort to aid her, and she was grateful for his lack of compassion, certain that if he touched her again, she would lose her very last shred of resolve. "Is it gone? The fog?"

The fog still lingered in a small haze surrounding the caravaners' camp, but she and Wraith had come out on the other side. Her captor chuckled, head shaking as if recalling a fond memory.

"Do you wish to return?" he asked, motioning back towards the eerie mist.

Ysella flinched at the pain as she stood, her head swimming. "He's not there."

But Ilai was somewhere. He had to be. She could feel it, and hope opened like a fortress door relenting to peace. The fury she felt toward Wraith muted as she watched him admire the fog. In place of that fury came pity. How horrible did one's life need to be to become such a perversely dark person? It didn't make her any less eager for his end, but she nearly felt sorry for him.

The pity dissolved with the pang of pain at her neck where his teeth marred her skin.

"We can move on," she answered tonelessly.

Wraith grinned and pointed away from the fog, prompting her to start their journey once again. The fog continued to hover in place near the caravaners' camp, falling out of view once they crested a larger hill. White tufts of snow drifted thickly through the sky, though this time without the bite of wind.

A tall tower jutted up from the blanketed earth in the distance, contrasted by a line of gnarled, black trees. The tower itself, walled simply with one gate, was still in one piece, its stone facade embraced by curling vines twining along the shell that belled outward at the top. A flickering orange glow emanated from the windows between the stonework.

The tower had no guard at its gate, and Wraith guided Ysella to the entrance, rapping his knuckles on the aged wooden door. Ysella felt the blade she stole from Regan resting safely in her boot, and she considered bending to retrieve it. Almost as if he could hear her thoughts, Wraith's glowing eyes fixed on hers, his smile a cruel dare.

Eventually, a man with eerily vibrant blue eyes opened the door, revealing a warmly lit interior. He met the pair with a cursory gaze, looking Ysella up and down, then turning to Wraith.

"She's upstairs." As the blue-eyed man pulled the door open further, Wraith commanded Ysella to enter, and tentatively, she stepped over the threshold.

The lower level of the tower had a wood stove for warmth, a fire softly crackling in its belly. There were a few cushioned chairs arranged near the stove, and on a small table between them was a platter of fruit and a book laid face down between pages. The stairs spiraled upward, nestled against the outer wall. The small windows that lined the exterior were covered in latched glass panes with frost around their edges from the snow along the sills.

They walked the spiraling stairs until her legs ached, eventually reaching the hatch leading to the upper level. It was open, and Wraith guided Ysella through.

The belled portion of the tower was far warmer and well furnished. It was sectioned into rooms in a circular layout, each room having its own cast iron stove humming with fire. Sconces of everglow crystals illuminated the majority of the space in an even, soft light.

"I thought I heard voices," a woman said as she stood from a desk intricately carved with geometric patterns, the wood stained darkly, but weathered with age. She had the same strange blue eyes as the man below, her presence more commanding. While she was perhaps a good decade or so older than Ysella, her skin was free of blemish and held only the faintest traces of age around her eyes and mouth. Her hair was braided and coiled into a bun at the top of her crown, and she wore thick garments lined with fur and adorned with gold embroidery.

She appraised Ysella with a cold smile. "I've been waiting for you. Will you sit with me?" She motioned towards an upholstered chair facing her mahogany desk.

Ysella lingered in the doorway, eyes keen to her surroundings. There came no sounds from behind closed doors, nor any indication that there were more people than just the two she'd seen.

Stepping into the room, eyes fixed on the woman, a recollection piqued her thoughts. She had seen others with oddly blue eyes in Lumin, very similarly to the woman before her. They looked like the hottest fire, almost with the same ferocious glow, but the color was the most vibrant blue she'd ever seen. The ambassador for the Edrosi Coalition of Trade came to mind. She remembered Elanath's assignment to Bastillos came after the end of the rebellion. The Coalition, while remaining neutral, negotiated with the monarchies of Edros for a representative to aid in every kingdom.

Ysella's focus steadily slipped, wandering as she did through the fog, Ilai's voice calling her name through the pale wash. In a moment like this, Ilai would not be afraid. He would know exactly what to make of these people.

She only felt helpless.

It was strange there were no guards, and the only watchful eyes came from the woman standing in front of her. Ysella contemplated action in the span it took her to close the distance, but in the end, she took the seat, folding her hands on her lap without hostility. The knife inside her boot shifted uncomfortably against her ankle as if to beg her to reconsider. Ysella swallowed the sensation, looking up into those unnervingly blue eyes.

"You speak as though we are long lost friends, yet I feel as much a captive here as I was in chains."

The woman rounded her desk, carefully collecting a small stack of papers to set them to a corner. With a quick flick of her hand, she waved off Wraith, and he complied, shutting the door behind him. The tension in Ysella's shoulders eased, grateful to see him go, yet her mind lingered on the woman on the other side of the desk.

For such a loathsome, evil thing as Wraith, what was the caliber of the ones who controlled him?

"Habit, perhaps," the woman said, "but make no mistake, Ysella, you are our captive. I require some information, and I hope you will oblige my request."

"And why should I?" Ysella carefully withheld the emotion from her voice, her tone even and clear, eyes focused, but cautious. Fear took root like fibrous strands coiling through her mind's soil, but she would rip them out one by one to keep it from bearing fruit.

"As your captive, I'm sure you think it is in my best interest to comply," Ysella continued coolly, "but what have I left to lose? Your lap dog has already taken from me what I cared for."

Taking her seat, the woman glanced to the door. "He's a barbarous thing. They all were. That's why they're dead, save for just the one. He's quite useful. His practices, however... Well, I apologize."

Her apology was cold and devoid of empathy, her words feigning authenticity. "I'd like to propose an exchange. You give me the information I request, and I give you something in return of equal value. You may set the terms."

This woman was practiced, at ease. Open, yet offering very little. Ysella had studied personalities such as these and how to combat them. It would be a delicate dance if she hoped to gain the upper hand. Allowing Ysella to set the terms of the exchange was just a ruse. Giving in to this woman's proposal would only serve her in the end.

"Is Rotheel here?" Ysella asked, redirecting the subject.

"Is this what you wish for the exchange?" The woman watched Ysella keenly.

"No," Ysella answered. The woman never broke her proper posture, her fingers lacing together as she set her palms on the edge of her desk. Her head tilted thoughtfully, studying Ysella with an even stare.

"Wraith. Come back in, please," she called.

The door swung open, Wraith dutifully approaching the end of the desk with a respectful incline of his head to the woman. The woman beckoned with two fingers. "Give me the crystals."

Wraith raised his head slowly, meeting her gaze with a challenge. His hand reached the pommel of his sword, and with a twist and a click! the glowing crystal pulled free from the hilt. He handed it to the woman with apparent hesitancy.

"Both," she commanded.

His jaw clenched, but he smiled, pulling another crystal from a pouch behind his cloak. The blue crystals were etched with runes, a soft glow emanating from within.

The woman's delicate fingers coiled around the second crystal, a smile straining as she thanked him for his compliance. Wraith turned, winking to Ysella as he passed, and exited, closing the door behind him.

Holding the second crystal aloft, the woman marveled at its make. "Do you know what this is, Ysella?"

"No," Ysella answered plainly. The woman set the two crystals down on the desk, a smile brimming her lips.

"Oh, delightful," she said. "Would you like to know?"

A set up. Ysella had not forgotten the woman's earlier proposal. Her attempts to prompt Ysella's inquiries were clever, perhaps devious, but Ysella was more clever now that she knew the game.

She had only a moment to shift her play. A lesser diplomat would rush in with a thousand questions, the first being the formality of knowing her name. It was improper not to ask, and perhaps this woman knew. Based on the way she waited for Ysella's response, this woman wanted her to think.

The runes on the crystals were a language of forbidden magic. Shadow Casters had been attempting to translate it for centuries, all of which lost their minds in the process. Elves use rune etching on crystals to house their natural magics, the most popular use being everglow. The language of elven magic was a beautiful script with flowing curves and brilliant threads of aether carved into the facets. What she could see on the crystals before her was an angry looking language, the ribbons of magic within the runes a coiling dark.

When Ysella had inquired into Rotheel's whereabouts, the woman called for these crystals.

Her mind drifted once again to the moment she broke from Wraith's nightmare, Ilai run through with his wicked blade. Ilai disappeared in a wisp of white that flowed to the pommel where the crystal was housed.

Ysella fought the lump in her throat welling with anxiety and hope, tears glistening. "Rotheel is here."

The woman smiled brightly, impressed. Her hand gently tapped the crystal to her left. "He is. And so is your previous captor." She held up the crystal to her right, turning it in her hand, the glow flickering. "A feisty one."

Ysella wrapped her arms around herself, suddenly and painfully aware of the chill in the air the little wood furnaces could not deter. Eyes fixating on the crystal in the woman's hand, her stomach threatened to heave, her heart aching with the worrying notion of what this woman was implying.

"I don't understand."

She was sure to make it a statement despite her desire for answers. All she could do was assume, and her assumption was sickening.

"I will give you this information freely with the adjustment of terms," the woman said, continuing without allowing interruption. "This is a Soul Vault. This crystal contains that of the bounty hunter, and the other contains the soul of Rotheel of House Degent. While they have no body to return to, you would have the power to lay one soul to rest. You may take only one so long as you provide me with everything I wish to know."

Agony wrenched her heart like a vice, and every breath felt like glass in her lungs. Ysella's throat closed and her eyes brimmed with tears as she clutched the armrests of her chair. Her head shook ever so slightly, desiring this new nightmare to end.

So she had assumed correctly. Ilai was removed from this world, yet denied death, and Rotheel had suffered the same fate. They were gone — truly gone, and she was being forced to choose only one to provide eternal rest.

Ysella could not relent. Not yet. "I know what you will ask of me."

"Do you?" The woman set Ilai's Soul Vault down next to Rotheel's, her hands resting upon them gently.

"What you will ask is worth both Soul Vaults," Ysella stated. "I will accept no less."

All of her strength, all of her focus held her resolve like a crumbling support column. She wanted to cry and wrap herself in comforts and let herself grieve, and she would once she found a way to win this game.

With a lofted brow, the woman collected the crystals, placing them within a drawer in her desk. With a light click of a lock and the jingle of keys finding their way to her dress pocket, the woman rose, rounding the desk as she kept a thoughtful stare on the diplomat. "Have you heard of the Tenebris, Ysella?"

"No." It was a careful, annoying game to ensure she did not pose anything close to a question, and perhaps that was part of her play. The woman wanted the proper back and forth of a conversation: a question posed, an answer, followed by a question to repeat the process. Ysella smirked in the silence between them.

She was winning.

The woman took in a sharp breath through her nose as her patience thinned. From her other pocket, she produced a smaller crystal held between two fingers. The facets had the similar angry runes as the Soul Vaults. "This is a Memory Vault," she explained tersely. "I'm sure that astute mind of yours can deduce its purpose. It's a shame you were born of Bastillos. You would have gone far with the Tenebris."

In a swift movement, the woman's hand grasped the top of Ysella's head, and the world spun into darkness. Memories flashed in bits and pieces as though her mind were a book, its pages thumbed through in a search.

The ruby necklace in her mother's hand, held out with such a warm, genuine smile, one she had only seen a handful of times on the woman's alabaster face. "We are so proud of you, Ysella."

"I don't understand, Instructor Dorneth. Why would you not try to appease both sides? Why are we to pick one? Could there not be a peaceful resol–" The older man's scowling face turned to a dark frown, his cane slamming into her desk, mere inches from her hands. "Because, child, if you wish to be a diplomat of Bastillos, you must have Bastillos's best interest in mind!"

Her sister, Odessa, so sweet and beautiful, her cheeks covered in tears as she clutched Ysella's hands. "You don't have to go, Essy. You and I... we could run. Leave Bastillos. Travel the world together. Imagine the adventures we could have! Oh, please, don't go."

Ilai on the edge of the pool, his arm around her waist as he pulled her from the murky water. His coarse hand gentle against her cheek, his words soft and encouraging. "We need to leave."

Each memory shifted to the next, some vanishing in the span of a sentence or the flicker of her surroundings. It felt as though the woman was searching for something specific, beyond Ysella's control. Her head was pierced by pain as if a knife were carving into her skull. Yet, the memories continued to unfold, indifferent to her suffering.

Then, just as abruptly, the memories faded and the room swirled into focus, the woman shouting out orders as she backed away from Ysella. Her skull throbbed with unspeakable pain shooting through her with every beat of her heart, but her hand dove instinctively to her boot, gripping the hilt of her stolen blade. The woman swiped her hands through the air, dark magic coalescing around her fingers. Her dark spell soared over Ysella's shoulder, the blast splintering the wooden frame that separated the rooms of the tower.

As the woman pulled back in preparation for a second strike, Ysella launched herself forward, burying the knife into the woman's shoulder. A shriek pulled from the woman in shock, her hands still working the spell into fruition, fingers aiming for Ysella's chest. She pulled the knife out from her flesh, arm raised and ready to strike a second time.

A figure collided with the woman. In his hand, he carried a familiar wicked blade, devoid of the glowing crystal upon its hilt. The woman gasped, the blade piercing through her middle deeply. Her eyes widened as her body pulled ethereal, then disappeared, a white glow coiling up the blade. Without a Soul Vault to contain her soul, it simply faded into nothingness.

29
ILAI

Ilai's body felt as though it were fused to the ground, as if his muscles could not hold up his weight. He shifted his body, shoulder and chest burning as he attempted to stand, but his muscles begged for respite, and he relented. His body fell heavily to the frosted dirt, cold stone scraping against his cheek.

A pair of boots caked in mud stopped next to his nose, and he looked up to find a wooden bowl next to his face, the contents within steaming. Regan stared down at him calmly, brow raised as he set the bowl down on the dirt.

"You look conscious enough," he said, and walked back towards the fire. A group of men pulled themselves up from the ground and sat around the fire, rubbing their necks and stretching their limbs. Some stared off behind Ilai, their gazes wary as they searched through the thinning fog. Two of them stared at Ilai cautiously, their hands on the hilts of their blades.

He recognized one of them as Cammon, his light brown hair pulled back to a high ponytail. He looked the least weary of the lot as he fixed his eyes on Ilai's every move. Ilai finally pushed himself from the ground with a grunt and smelled the bone broth and herbs from his bowl. A beef roast rested in beds of vegetables and potatoes, and he snatched the bowl to his lips. The broth had cooled significantly, but he did not care. It was needed sustenance, and it tasted amazing.

The more he ate, the more grounded he felt. The world no longer relentlessly held him to the stone, and the pain in his body lessened to a distant memory. The ache in his shoulder no longer felt like his wounds would split open again. Even the hole in his chest had muted.

"What do you know of Wraith?" Regan asked as he watched Ilai eat. Ilai shook his head in confusion. That name meant nothing to him, but another did.

Rotheel. Where was Rotheel?

He lowered the bowl as his mind sharpened, eyes scanning the cave of caravaners. Did this mean he was back? He turned his head quickly to the mouth of the shallow cave as a fog receded towards a cluster of woods.

"Rotheel!" Ilai called. He abandoned his bowl and rushed towards the rolling fog. "Rotheel!"

The fog dissipated completely, and he was left in the open, the snow disturbed from the foreign creatures that once walked the land. There was nothing left of the Dungeon's veil, and Rotheel hadn't come through. Ilai touched his torso where the wicked blade had struck through him. He could still feel the pull of an unseen tether. The wound was slick with fresh blood that would not flow or scab.

He knew who Rotheel was now that he had returned. His mind was his own again, no longer shrouded in mystery. Was this the fate that awaited Ysella?

Marching back to the cave, he looked at Regan squarely. "Do you want those twenty heads of gold?"

Regan sat back, brow furrowing incredulously as he measured Ilai's authenticity. The imposing man pointed to the bowl Ilai left on the floor. "Sit and eat. Seems like you have a proposition."

Despite his urge for immediate action, his instincts told him to regain his strength. Propositions had its own etiquette in the Grey. Ilai picked up the bowl and settled back onto the cold floor.

"No, come and sit by the fire," Regan said, and prompted his men to shift on the logs to give him room. Ilai rose and took the seat across from their leader. The others took a breath, eyes peeling from the mouth of the den to return to slurping down their stew. Cammon remained cautious as he used one hand to eat, the other resting at his blade.

"I recognize that name," one of the caravaners said. "Rotheel. I'm sure that's the other diplomat."

Regan nodded thoughtfully, feigning as if he hadn't had the same thought. He pointed his wooden spoon towards Ilai, its length wagging up and down in observation. "How'd you come to get such a nasty wound? You should be dead with something like that."

Ilai pulled his cloak over his form to hide the torn leather jerkin and blood-stained shirt. "I have a feeling you know the answer," he said, and Regan chuckled.

"I do," he admitted. "Daga, hand him a spoon, will you?"

The man called Daga reached into a sack that clattered with pots and produced a wooden spoon. He leaned across the two others between them for Ilai to take the smoothed utensil. It had a shallow bowl carved into it, but it would do. He nodded to Daga in quiet thanks that was ignored by the caravaner.

"Who is Wraith?" Ilai asked.

"The man who gave you that wound," Regan answered. Ilai paused thoughtfully as he scooped his stew to his lips. The action forced him to slow his eating and consume far less in his hungered state.

"You asked what I know of him," Ilai said. "I know very little. Only that by impaling me with his sword, instead of dying I was sent to the place where that fog exists. It also binds me to him. I know where he is and I want to end that connection."

"I'm assuming, given who we're talking about, that this connection works both ways?" Regan surmised. "He can likely feel the same about you."

"I don't care," Ilai admitted.

"What are you planning, bounty hunter?" he asked thoughtfully.

The plan in his mind was simple: to charge the tower and save Ysella. But even in the fraction of a moment he took to swallow his food, he knew he did not actually have much of a plan. "Join me in raiding the tower. I don't want any metal. Whatever you find is yours."

"You seek revenge?" he asked. The other caravaners nodded their heads in understanding, their stances straightening with the prospects of action.

"Does it matter what I seek?" Ilai asked.

Regan shook his head. "No, but there is still the issue of Wraith knowing you're coming. You'd be luring us into a trap. They have the advantage in that fortification."

"He can only tell I am coming," he corrected. "I grew up in that area. I know Ethyrnon Tower and its blind spots. It wasn't built as a fortification. It was built to observe and alert the threats of the Twisted Woods. I can lead us through its blind spots and we can have the upper hand. They'll be expecting me. They won't be expecting you. Do you know how many there are?"

"I only brokered a deal with Wraith when he threatened my caravan," Regan said. "I know nothing of what awaits you at that tower. I even question if the metal is real."

"It likely isn't," Ilai admitted. The caravaners shifted in disappointment, and they returned to their meals with half interest in the deal between the two. "My guess is they'd need some amount of metal for supplies given how long they might have been stationed there. The tower is usually unoccupied as there are no roads to it. You have to walk."

Regan placed his empty bowl next to his boot and scratched the edge of his groomed beard, eyes cast to the cracking fire between them in contemplation. "If we join you, we do it on our terms. We'll go to Grey Point first. Make inquiries. I want a head count of who is in that tower before we charge through."

Ilai fought back his impatience and irritation with a tight grip on his spoon. He briefly considered infiltrating on his own as he reached the tower knowing Wraith was waiting for his entrance. A sword was needed, at the very least. Going into that tower without the element of surprise or a weapon would be a sure death.

Do you see you are not living, nor are you dead and can achieve neither?

Wraith's words echoed in his memory. He wasn't sure if he wanted to test that theory. An unpleasant, dull ache radiated from the wound in his chest, the sensation roiling out his back, but it was manageable. How wounded could he become until it was too much to push through?

He'd rather have a sword to give him a proper fight and a decent chance. All the caravaners surrounding the fire had their swords and daggers securely in their scabbards belted to their sides. There was no blade he could easily steal, by the looks of it, and no surplus of supplies to spare.

"Do you intend to wait to travel to Grey Point?" Ilai asked. Regan looked out at the snowfall in the bright mid-day light. A smile crested his lips.

"You're after the diplomat," he noted. The other caravaners feigned disinterest, though glanced between the two from over the lips of their bowls.

"If you have no intention of leaving now, I will go on my own and leave you with no metal to scavenge," Ilai warned, but Regan laughed.

"You'd test fate with your odds?"

Ilai stood calmly and pulled open his cloak to better reveal the angry hole through his chest. "I cannot die. I will succeed."

He walked from the warmth of the fire out into the snow-covered field. The chill energized his senses, and he looked upward for signs of the sun. The cloud coverage was so thick he couldn't discern its direction.

Clatters of pots and murmurs merged with a few chuckles as he heard the crunch of snow from a pair of boots behind him. "Bounty hunter!" Regan called out. He had a smile on his face. "We're coming with you. Ride on my horse. We'll get there faster."

Ilai turned, stepping back toward the camp. "You have something of mine that I want returned," he said to Regan.

"Your sword?" Regan asked.

"And the band," Ilai added. Regan pursed his lips.

"That is good metal," the caravan leader said.

"It's a knuckle of iron, Regan, be reasonable," Ilai said. "You'll find far more in the tower."

"I have neither with me," Regan said, "but ensure I make it out alive and I will have them sent to Grey Point upon my return."

A caravaner's word was as honest as a thief's, but Ilai shook Regan's hand for the formality. "If you do not, I will hunt you," Ilai promised, and Regan grinned.

It was not a long ride to Grey Point. The settlement was built at the northernmost point of the Grey Hinterlands, its backdrop the towering mountains of Muldras partially obscured by the cloud coverage. The slope up towards the Laerd's Castle was steeper than Halvish, but better prepared for snow and ice with steps of wood and stone next to the roads partially warmed by torches. Most of Grey Point's residents were tucked away in the comforts of their homes built with sloped roofs to wait out the storm.

A Priest of Elssar, cloaked in thick white robes, approached them. "Greetings, travelers," he said. "Let me aid you in finding a place to stable your horses."

Regan deftly dismounted from his horse, Ilai following after him. The caravan leader stood a good head taller than the priest as he handed him the reins. "We need supplies and information."

The priest nodded and beckoned them to follow as he guided Regan's horse to the stable next to the monastery of Elssar. Ilai had never been devout, nor did he place much belief in the cosmic beings the world held in esteem. Despite his lack of faith, he knew the priests to be decent people willing to help anyone, even caravaners. Ilai had lived in their orphanage before he ran away and knew these men were good natured.

Time was more prevalent in Ilai's mind the more he spent in the Grey, and he drew more anxious by the minute. They would have to travel by foot from Grey

Point. It had been, at the very least, a half hour since he could recall being in this living realm. By foot, it would be another half hour to the tower, possibly more with the snow.

The caravaners had no sense of urgency about them. Their horses were stabled, and they talked amongst themselves as they followed the priest into the warmth of the monastery's halls. It was built from large stones with high ceilings and long tapestries and paintings hanging from the crown molding. Large pyres of fire were held by iron sconces along the walls, and Ilai contemplated the use of one as a makeshift weapon.

"Are you aware of the ones that occupy Ethyrnon Tower?" Regan asked as he tapped the snow from his boots against the corner of the wall connecting to another long hallway. The priest regarded the action briefly, face flashing with disappointment that was replaced with practiced calmness.

"Yes, they come here for supplies," the priest answered. Regan grinned.

"How many would you say are there?" Regan asked. The priest's brow furrowed in the first open display of his true thoughts, and he finally surveyed the men he'd welcomed into the monastery. Of all the Landers, caravaners and bounty hunters stood out as an unsavory lot, often with the sides of their heads shaved, their teeth decaying, or their skin marred with jagged scars. The priest quickly ascertained his present company.

"They're here under Laerd Valarad's protection as they study the encroachment of the Twisted Woods," the priest informed sternly. "I would advise against action against them. If you are not aware, the affliction of the woodland grows closer to our doorstep, and with it comes its monstrosities in the night. We need them."

Regan lofted a brow and gave Ilai a curious glance of amusement. Setting his jaw, Ilai stepped forward, and the priest sized him up. "They captured a diplomat of Bastillos," Ilai said sternly, and took another step closer to ensure the priest had to look up to his height. "Are you aware a war threatens Edros?"

Despite the imposing difference between them, the priest calmed his expression to mask his true feelings on the matter. "Laerd Valarad is not concerned with

Bastillos's war. So far north and so close to orcish lands, we are bound to never see any bloodshed."

"And what of the trade routes Grey Point relies upon for food and supplies? Can the fields of constant snow provide enough food for everyone here?" Ilai countered, and the priest tilted his head, intrigued. "I swore I would protect her. I will deal with the Laerd's law when I complete my mission."

"I have no intention of deterring you, nor will I report you," the priest stated. "If you can provide proof of their transgression, you will likely find pardon. There are more of you than there are of them, but the exact amount, I know not. Go with Elssar's Will."

"Peace find you, priest," Regan said with a chuckle, and lightly tapped Ilai's shoulder with the back of his hand. "Come, hunter, your lady awaits."

"I need a weapon. Anything you can spare," Ilai said. The priest shook his head. "We hold no weapons in the monastery."

Ilai bit back a curse. Wasting more time hunting down the blacksmith or convincing a local to give up arms plucked at his nerves, and he turned from the halls of the monastery. Regan stepped up beside him and kept pace as they walked down the steep slope of the snaking road.

"If you're quick enough with that scabbard, they'll be none the wiser," Regan suggested. It wouldn't withstand more than one blow, but it could serve such a purpose well.

"I'll bear it in mind," Ilai said, and then sized the rest of the caravaners that followed, a glint in their eyes. There were at least eight among them, including Regan. Ilai guided them into the forest walling the eastern side of the settlement, gentle hills undulating and then smoothing to shallow slopes the further south they traveled.

The tree line thinned and opened to an expanse of white where a tall tower stood in the clearing, its bulbous top aglow with light within. Ilai halted them just at the edge of the field and pointed to his right. They followed the path until no light could be seen from the windows of the tower.

"As long as you cannot see the windows, they cannot see you," he said, and pointed southward. "We head this direction to the back. There are windows that line the staircase on this side. It'll be their only way to view us, so we run fast to the base to lessen those chances. Let me go in first. Wait as long as you like. I'll leave that up to you."

He gave Regan a nod, who returned the gesture and brought his blade to his hand. "Lead the way."

Rushing out into the open, Ilai set the pace without looking back. He had to trust a caravaner at his word, though he hoped he could trust him at his greed. Certainly the people in the tower would have something the caravaners would want, even in concept. The snow fell around him in thick sheets that partially muted the tower's silhouette upon approach. The tether binding him to his jailor gave a stronger pull with each step.

His pace slowed, breath catching in his lungs as the air vibrated through him. A warning, perhaps. He brought his shaking hands to his belt and unclasped the scabbard from his hip, fighting against the sensation seeking to drown his senses. The sky turned ruddy for a brief moment, the air thick and accompanied by dissonant groaning.

Regan passed to his right, and as the man pulled him forward, Ilai plunged back into a cool grey sky divided by snow covered hills. The momentum the caravaner used to hoist Ilai from his stupor thrust him against the stone base of the tower. Regan looked at Ilai keenly.

"Are you still with us?" Regan asked quietly, his eyes searching the hunter's demeanor. Ilai nodded, taking in a sharp breath.

"Wraith knows I'm here," Ilai whispered, and then pat the man's forearm. "Whatever you plunder is yours to keep. No one touches the diplomat."

Regan held up his free hand in mock surrender. "She's yours."

The promise was trustworthy enough for a man of such low caliber. Ilai turned from the eager group of caravaners and headed up towards the only door at its southern end. It could lock from the inside, from what he could recall, but there was the chance they hadn't bothered given the lack of wind gusts in the last few hours.

Wraith's descent from above felt like the tower was slowly crumbling inward with each step. His jailor's ethereal rope inched him toward the entrance, and he heard a voice from behind the door. The door opened swiftly and Ilai slammed his boot into the body of the stranger darkening its frame.

A cackle fell from up a spiral staircase once Ilai stepped inside. There was only one man below holding his ribcage as he coughed and gasped for air. "Wraith! Damn you!" the man rasped. "Intruder!"

Regaining his composure, the man looked up at Ilai with bright, inhumanly blue eyes. His hands raised, and the firelight dimmed as a swift motion called upon a familiar sensation of near nothingness. Ilai slammed his scabbard into the man's forearms, smacking them from the act of coalescence.

Ilai was familiar with the stories of Shadow Casters and the tale of the Dark Calamity. The man at the door fit the descriptions of the mages that saved Krei from the crazed hemomancers. The mage's wrists closed together quickly as he turned his hands, tendrils of darkness closing around Ilai. The world tilted as he plunged off balance, and Ilai slammed the tip of his boot into the Shadow Caster's temple.

The dark tendrils dissipated in an instant as the man flew backward. From out of the corner of his eye, Ilai caught the glint of steel as it swiped down from above. Ilai rolled to the side and back to his feet as he came face to face with Wraith's broadening grin, a flicker of confusion and anger pulsing through their bond.

"What a delightful reunion, my pet," Wraith said as his dark blade swooped through the air. Ilai dodged its trajectory and lashed with his scabbard, eliciting a chuckle from Wraith. "The pet wishes to play. I see your wound bleeds with invitation."

The caravaners poured in through the doorway, three of them crowding the Shadow Caster just as he recovered. Wraith's grin grew. "And you brought friends for the feasting."

Swords plunged through the Shadow Caster's body as he released a spell that flickered to nothing, leaving Wraith the last to contend with in the tower's base. With the reach of his longsword, he kept them at bay, slashing through leather and skin with dark metal that bit harsher than mere steel. The runes glimmered as it soaked their blood, hunger flashing in Wraith's glowing eyes with every clashing blow.

Most men would be overwhelmed with the odds of nine to one, but Wraith reveled in it, dancing through the exchange. Each blow sliced deeper into their flesh, as though he were deliberately holding back. Blood sprayed across the chair, desk, books, and rug scattered at the base of the tower.

In a swift thrust, Regan tore through Wraith's cloak as his blade barely missed his center, and Wraith pulled a hand from his hilt and balled it into a fist. The caravaners rose as if pulled by an unseen rope tied at their center, their eyes rolling back into their heads. Ilai felt the demands of such potent darkness as it collided through his core in a lancing agony. He grit his teeth from the pain, recognizing the darkness and rejecting its call.

The tether snapped back, and Ilai realized a sensation still beckoned him upward. Reverberations from his rejection caused Wraith to falter, his hand dropping its spell that held the caravaners in a trance. Wraith stumbled on the stairs, the wicked blade clattering to the stone floor, and Ilai kicked him squarely in the spine to prevent his recovery. As he fell over the lip of the stairs, Wraith collided with Cammon on the rug next to the wood stove.

An irritated hiss pulled from Wraith's fanged teeth as he plunged into Cammon's neck. Wraith pulled back, ripping the neck flesh free, blood spraying his wild face as he swallowed the meat. The other caravaners were quick to act, eager to get Cammon out of harm's way, but in such close quarters, it was hard for each one to strike.

Wraith's body turned into a rushing cloud of inky black swirling through the hollow of the tower, crashing through the caravaners in a torrent of dark magic. Regan slashed his dagger through the black wake finding nothing but air and a cackle pulling through in an echo.

Ilai jumped down to the main level, reaching Cammon just as Wraith coalesced corporeal. Another command flowed into Ilai, urging him to take Cammon's life. The command released once the caravaners charged Wraith with their blades, their efforts drawing blood, but nothing mortal. He reveled in the red spilling from his wounds, hands swiping over them like a brush to ink.

With a fleck of his fingers, the droplets of crimson honed to long, thin needles, embedding themselves into the flesh of the remaining caravaners. The attack did not immediately incapacitate them. Just as the caravaners struck, their movements hitched, bodies writhing as they clawed through their leathers.

Balling a wad of cloth, Ilai placed it on Cammon's wound and pulled the man's hand up to hold it in place. "Keep pressure on it," Ilai instructed. Cammon nodded, his body trembling from the pain, but he would live.

At least if they could survive Wraith. As Wraith slowly raised his hands, darkness swirling around his form, Ilai grabbed the wicked blade from the floor. If he understood one thing, it was that a blade of this length would reach the man's vulnerability faster than he could react, and if he understood anything about his blade, it would send him to the Dungeon.

As soon as Ilai's hand touched the hilt, a gnawing hunger vibrated through his bones, longing for the taste of flesh. Wraith's head turned with a sudden realization, and Ilai quickly thrust the blade up through the man's rib cage, sinking into flesh, cutting through bone, and plunging out his chest in a dark, blood-soaked spire.

Air rushed from Ilai's lungs as the pain of Wraith's wound was shared between their link, sight darkening as a thunderous crack echoed in the cylindrical chamber. Wraith's body disappeared, pulled through the runes on his blade into nothingness. All that was left was his blood, the blade drinking it in gratefully.

A prickling thought traveled through the hilt and to his mind: a request for more. He could grant that desire. With Wraith gone, the caravaners recovered as the blood spell lost its potency.

The pull at Ilai's core remained, requesting his ascent to the upper levels of the tower, though devoid of a looming presence he surmised had once belonged to Wraith. What was above was entirely him.

Elation rose in remembrance of Wraith's demise, the wicked blade longing for another taste.

Regan stood at the base of the spiraling stairs, his face stern and cautious as he watched Ilai. "Your woman isn't down here, bounty hunter," he reminded, and gripped the hilt of his own sword firmly. Ilai hadn't realized how tightly he held the wicked blade, or how he stared at the caravaners like prey.

He could knock that sword from Regan's grasp in a quick flourish, and plunge his own straight through the caravaner's chest in mere seconds. They deserved to die. They were caravaners. Thieves. Slavers. A caravan could fall from power with their deaths.

Air swept through his lungs in a sudden, grounding breath. Ilai's mission returned to him, and he pushed away the blade's desire, running up the stairs toward the ever-growing pull at his core.

The blade pulled in the other direction as it longed, and he nearly abandoned it on the stairs. Whatever gave the weapon desire, it would be a nightmare in the hands of someone like Regan. He couldn't let it go just yet.

Just as he reached the opening into the top of the tower, Ilai could sense the origin of the pull. A closed door laid between him and his goal. He burst through the door, blade at the ready and hungering for another bite. A woman stood in front of Ysella, a hand palming the top of her head, fingers splayed as if clawing through her skull. Dark magic flowed from her fingertips. Ysella sat with a tense posture, eyes rolled back and teeth clenched.

The woman stumbled backward in shock, the magic releasing as her hand recoiled. A small crystal fell to the floor next to her feet. "No!" the woman said as she held out her hand. "Don't come any closer!"

Her hands swirled through the air as shadow formed and condensed into a sphere that, when released, clawed at the air like a mass of churning limbs. It collided with the door frame, wood splintering with a crunch.

Ysella's head rolled forward as she regained consciousness, her body lunging toward the woman with a knife in hand. It plunged into the woman's shoulder, and the wicked blade reveled as it sang through the woman's cries. Justice was sated by her blood as the steel slid through her belly.

Shock widened the Shadow Caster's eyes, her blood soaking and igniting the runes, her body pulling into a white wisp that became nothing in an instant. Wraith's blade clattered on the wooden floor, the boards creaking with Ilai's faltering footing. A haze lifted from his senses. Ysella's stumbled back into her chair, eyes wide and distant as she stared at where the woman once stood. His heart lurched, and within two steps he closed the distance, his hand hesitantly reaching out to cup her cheek.

30
YSELLA

Reality had become a fickle thing, teetering on the edges of her consciousness, pretending to be a dream. Ysella blinked away the blurry veil from
her vision, her senses slowly coming back to her with each breath. She could smell
the scent of aged wood, the spark of magic, and felt the gentle touch of a familiar,
calloused hand.

It must have been a dream. It had to be torture brought about by those mages.
Perhaps it was even Wraith toying with her sense of hope yet again. Ilai knelt
before her as though he were alive and well, his pale features twisted with worry.

He spoke, but the pounding in her skull muffled the words. Blinking several
times, trying both to clear the rush of pain in her head and the sudden shock of
all that had transpired, Ysella stared at the man in disbelief.

"Are you hurt?" he repeated, his thumb brushing over her jaw.

"Y-you can't—" Pulling back, she shook her head. "You can't be here. You
can't! You—"

He watched her sorrowfully as she recoiled. "It is me," he said. "Ysella, it's me..."

"Her mind's been played like a fiddle." Regan's voice carried gruffly behind them as he entered through the hatch and sauntered over to the desk. The large man looked down at the bloody sword, and then at the desk of papers. "Looks like everyone's been handled."

Regan yanked open a drawer, rifling around inside. He spared a momentary glance towards Ysella thoughtfully, but did not address her.

Eyes dancing wildly between Ilai and Regan, tears blurring her vision, Ysella's trembling fingers reached trepidatiously towards Ilai's face, but hovered in the air instead. "I watched you disappear. I watched you die. And you-" Narrowing her gaze to Regan, she bolted upright. "You're the reason that monster found us! You-" Dizzy and nauseous, she sank back into the chair again, her head dropping to her hands. "None of this is real..."

This was Wraith's game. He crushed her sense of reality piece by piece until she could no longer trust her own mind. It had come to that so quickly.

Lowering her arms, Ysella saw the blood soaked knife gripped tightly in her right hand and, flipping it inward, she held the pointed tip against her chest. This was her last act of defiance against that man's damnable mind games. Her hands quaked as she looked up at the pair. "Get out of my head!"

Dropping to his knees, Ilai curled his fingers around hers, halting the blade's plunge. With all her strength, she pulled the knife toward her, but he was stronger. Tears streamed down her cheeks as she struggled against the force keeping the knife from ending this torturous cycle.

"Ysella, please. It's me." He spoke her name, and she felt the depth of it. It was a pinprick of light in the welling darkness of her mind that grew with each syllable from his lips. Gently, his hands guided hers away, her grip loosening. "Look at me. Please don't. I was only lost, not dead. But I heard you, and I found my way out. I'm not in your head. I had to come back for you."

"I heard you in the fog," Ysella said. "I thought... I thought I was going mad." Pausing, breathing in, she shook her head again, uncurling her fists and letting the weapon fall to the floor with a clatter. "They were in my head. My mind. I want to believe it. More than anything at all, I do. But..." Her eyes flickered to Regan again. "Why are you here?"

Regan was busy fiddling with a locked drawer, nestling his sword between the seams to pry it open. The wood splintered against his strength, and the drawer pulled free, its contents clinking and jingling. The caravan leader grinned as he produced a large bag of what sounded to be metal.

"I'm here for what I'm owed," Regan said, his hand sifting through the bag's contents. It was large, and even as the man's powerful arms lifted it from the desk, it looked like he strained from the weight. "Pleasure doing business."

He gave a nod to Ilai, and then to Ysella, and walked back to the hatch. "We're moving out, men!" Regan called down the stairs. There were some shouts of praise and celebration far below, but Ysella barely registered them, staring at the glowing crystals that had rattled to the front of the broken drawer.

As the hatch closed, Ilai garnered her attention once again. "Ysella, I need you to concentrate. Is anyone else here?"

Rubbing her head, then drying her cheeks with the backs of her hands, Ysella looked around the room. The entrance had splintered, the door broken and hanging off one of its hinges. Blood splatters dotted the mahogany desk and dripped on the floorboards. "Wraith was here. The-the man who–" Swallowing, she recalled the woman's inhumanly blue eyes, wide with pain and horror as her body slipped into the ethereal. "There was one other like the woman when we first arrived."

"We dealt with him," Ilai assured. "No one else?"

Ysella shook her head in response, a silent stupor taking her. She watched Ilai pull the Soul Vaults out from the desk drawer, their insides aglow with life. "It's Rotheel," Ysella said. "The other. They killed him, too."

Ilai held both crystals, each the size of his hand. "Rotheel is not dead," he said, and pocketed the Soul Vaults, stooping down to pick up Wraith's sword and the little crystal on the floor. He crossed the room, opening the other doors cautiously, blade at the ready. Ysella didn't move and listened to the sound of his boots on the floorboards.

When he returned, he rested the sword on the desk and crouched back down to eye level with Ysella. He ran a hand gently through her hair, and her eyes flickered to him.

"I saw you in the fog," he murmured softly. "I called out to you. You couldn't see me, but we found each other somehow, and I knew we could again." He pulled her hand up and brought it to his lips, kissing her knuckles. The contact grounded her senses, and her emotions slowly trickled to fill the numbing void. "I couldn't touch you then, but I can now."

In that moment, every thought fled her mind, and tears burned against the backs of her eyes. She didn't care if it was a figment born from malicious magic. Let it be a dream, and let her stay there, trapped there forever.

"I thought I lost you," she whispered, a trembling hand reaching out, touching his cheek with the flat of her palm. "But I could not let you go. I would have gone with you into the darkness, Ilai. I would have followed you."

Wordlessly, his hands cradled her neck and pulled her to him, his lips seeking hers in an embrace galvanized with want and longing and connection, in celebration and triumph. She did not dare to pull away, her heart and mind racing, conflicted emotions mingling all together in a roiling mass of confusion, then melting away in their entirety until it was just him and her.

When at last they parted, and her eyes opened to meet his, she rested her forehead against his as tears resumed their tracks down her cheeks.

"I don't know if you're real or not," she whispered, "but I don't care. My heart has been forfeit to you since you came for me after Halvish. My mind may as well follow suit." Leaning back, the tips of her fingers brushed the line of his bearded jaw. "You found me again."

He kissed her forehead and brought his thumb to her cheek to wipe away her tears, and as he leaned back, he clasped her hands in his, his face fixed with solemnity. "I will always find you, Ysella. I would move mountains for you."

"You already have." Clutching his hand, she held it to her cheek, eyes falling closed, clarity warring with her desire to never leave that moment.

But it wasn't over. Not yet.

The tower was empty of threat, but filled with potential information. They would need to gather what they could find relevant to their cause to bring back to Bastillos. "We're not finished, Ilai. I have you, and I will not lose you again, but Edros is still at risk. Bastillos. My family. That woman was a small part of this.

The Tenebris want something, and they won't stop with me. I don't even know where to begin, but I have to see this through."

"Then we will see this through," he assured, kissing the back of her hand as he rose. Their journey would be a treacherous challenge, perhaps even more than before. But wherever they went, they would go together, even if it was to an inevitable war.

EPILOGUE

General Demonte stepped out onto the balcony overlooking Lumin's Cascade illuminated by mirrorlight. They had roofs in the cavern city, just like surface dwellers, only less utilitarian and practical. Some roofs were ornately designed with mosaic-like colored stones and glass that delicately refracted the light. Far beyond what the light touched was the darkness of the Low Lumin where its occupants used firelight to see.

Queen Zalette of House Iliume could sometimes see the faintest orange glow piercing through the void like strange stars. Given the closed spaces of the cavern, the use of fire was limited and required permits. It was evident some did not follow the rules, but the air still smelled fresh from the palace.

She did not have her adornments in place yet. Her long brown hair cascaded down her back, her youthful face wary and burdened as she watched merchants and civilians walk the ancient roads.

"Is it true?" she asked. "Are they dead?"

"We've only confirmed their escorts are dead," the general informed solemnly. They stood together quietly for a time. Zalette wondered if these people would know war again. There were still pock marks in the stone and scores of charred scars from their recent civil war. Bastillos could not withstand a war against anyone at this point, not even themselves. They still needed time to rebuild.

"How many ambassadors remain in Bastillos?" she asked.

"Only Dradmida, the representative for the Edrosi Coalition of Trade, and the druid," General Demonte informed. He was a powerful man standing a head taller than her, his long beard kept simple and groomed giving his jaw a stronger appearance. Despite his imposing demeanor, he looked at her softly, only just this once. The part of her still trapped as a young girl desired to favor the paternal display, but she pushed it away in favor of her duties. Her own expression remained strong.

"When did Ambassador Nin depart?"

"This morning."

"And she did not see it fit to speak to me..."

Krei had been a great ally all these years. Ambassador Nin had represented them since before Zalette was born, and it felt insulting she would leave so quietly. Bastillos aided Krei during the Dark Calamity twenty years ago.

"Should I be concerned with the nature of her departure?" Zalette asked.

"She said you were too burdened with the weight of Edros to be pandered to in formalities," Demonte informed. "Krei are intelligent people. I would not dismiss the nature of her departure, but I would not be concerned until I garnered my own information."

"Why don't we have a representative from the Grey Hinterlands?" Zalette asked.

"Each Laerd governs their own lands there," Demonte explained. "We would have to house a representative of each Laerd. I'm not sure they would be keen."

"I think we should propose it," Zalette stated. "We need allies. We need to focus on what we can do, and they're completely outside of the war. They border orcish lands. Perhaps they can help us bridge the gap where we once could not."

From her peripheral, she watched him contemplate her proposal, head nodding slightly as he leaned forward against the stone railing. "I will see to it. We will write letters to each Laerd with your proposal, but we should be cautious. Our own people were smuggled through their lands which in turn caused the catalyst of this potential war. Some could view this as threatening."

"Our people?" Zalette sighed as she looked back to the firelight specks in the dark. "You mean our slaves."

"They are slaves no longer," Demonte stated.

"But they still were when the incident happened," she said. Her vigilant mask was crumbling, and so she lowered her head, hiding her face in her hair. "Their lives are still no better, Demonte. Our mirrorlight does not even reach them. It is believed the Grey Hinterlands is comprised mostly of our lower caste fleeing oppression. The orcs were saving them. We suffered a civil war because of what we wrought, and now there is threat of another because of the same damnable thing. We are tyrants. Of course we would be viewed as a threat."

General Demonte softly exhaled and turned to the queen. "Then how do you wish to proceed?"

"I want to request an audience with the representative of Lower Lumin," she said. "He would have the best insight, I believe, as to how we could formulate our letters to the Laerds of the Grey Hinterlands. And bring me the remaining ambassadors. I need to request further insight into the impact of tensions on their people."

The general inclined his head. He was wearing a modest amount of plate armor that clattered in the motion. "General," Zalette said hesitantly. He raised to his full height inquisitively. "Do you resent the errands I task? And please, be honest. I do not see a need to placate me with lies."

"People offer platitudes to those in power because they feel powerless," he stated. "But also because honesty can often come across as a threat to those too weak to accept truths. I am not powerless, and you are not weak. I accept these menial tasks because I know they will be done honestly when in my hands. I accept these errands because it means I do not have to run my sword through a man's gut for a cause. I am a general of your army, yes, but I am also your grandfather, and that is a higher honor."

Zalette smiled and allowed the comfort in just for a moment. She missed when their relations were of a fireside story and horseback riding lessons. For the past six years it had been nothing but duty and business, and a great emotional distance had formed.

"I'm afraid to fail like my mother," she admitted.

"Your mother's decisions are what you can learn from," he advised. "I think a part of her thought she was doing the right thing. You should study her reign. And your grandmother's. Bastillos can yet be saved from a war that has not yet begun."

It would have been a good time to excuse himself, but he lingered, hesitant almost to breach what was on his mind. "If I may make a suggestion."

"Please do."

General Demonte inclined his head respectfully. They were no longer grandfather and granddaughter, now. "I would like to send a team in search for the missing diplomats. Both sites found were before the borders in the Grey Hinterlands. It could align with your efforts. I can send them in with the messengers."

"Do you think the Hinterlanders took them?" she asked with concern.

"I wouldn't rule it out," he answered, "but I do not see the benefit for them to have done so. We need to know who is behind this as their disappearance actively pushes us towards war. Their land is full of those who would do anything for gold regardless of the consequences. I would say that is more likely the case."

"I will make it clear we do not blame the Laerds for their disappearances," she said. "Let us hope that is the case."

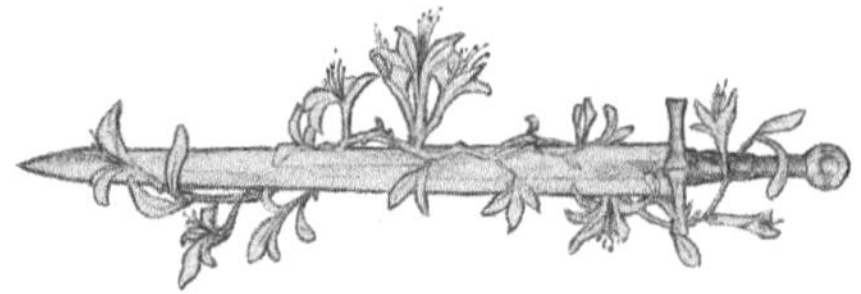

Heeled shoes clattered against the elegance of the long stone hallway in Lumin's palace. Elanath attempted to keep her gait calm, though quick with purpose. Her quarters were further down the western wing where the other representatives and foreign ambassadors were housed.

Apart from the druid. That man insisted on being outdoors, or what Lumin could grant as the outdoors, and slept within the greenhouse.

The hour was drawing to evening, the mirrorlight bathing Lumin in a golden glow. She missed the surface and the brilliance of a sunset. They only received a fraction of the colors through those mirrors. It was underwhelming.

Within her hand she clasped a crystal tightly to her chest. It was glowing intermittently signaling a request she knew to be urgent. They were never to contact her. It was always meant to be the other way around.

Her brilliantly blue eyes fixated on an imposing figure rapping against the doorframe to her quarters, and she hid her crystal from view. "General Demonte. What brings you to this side of the palace at such an hour?"

Stepping to face her, he inclined his head respectfully. "The Queen is requesting an audience with the remaining representatives of Edros."

"Well, that can't be good," she mused. "When is the meeting?"

"As soon as you are available," he informed.

"Oh, well, I need to write down a thought before it flitters away," she said. "I'll be over as soon as I handle my affairs. Will it be in the usual meeting room?"

"Indeed," he said. "I will inform her of your coming."

They bowed to each other in a dance Elanath did not care for. The cave dwellers had such strict formalities her patience struggled to handle. It was always a dance of heads and hand motions where the slightest turn one way or another could say more than words. All of it was intended to be accompanied by metal adornments which could only jingle or clink together in certain ways for certain emotions.

Elanath was grateful to close the door between them as she entered her room. It was a lavish accommodation of every want and need for a woman of status, including a secondary room for whatever she desired. It came with its own lock, making it perfect for her device.

It took nearly a year to acquire all the parts and assemble them. She couldn't have brought them with her, or had it pre-assembled as it would have called for too many questions. The contraption was half as tall as she was, with gears and wires all converging at the center where a pedestal was raised to chest height. She placed her glowing crystal into the apparatus in the pedestal, the metal locking it into place with a pull of a lever.

From what she discovered, it was of Krei design, though quite early in its prototype. Within the glowing crystal's facets were runes etched finely in precise locations, which were typically elven in nature. Hers, however, were Shadow.

Turning a knob continuously at the base, power from three other crystals interlinked within the mechanisms channeled through the machine and up into the apparatus. The glow ceased its undulation and became constant until darkened with Shadow Magic.

She waited and hoped they were still at their own device.

"Elanath?" The voice at the other end that carried through the crystal was unexpectedly Barthanox.

"Yes, it's me," she confirmed as she spoke into the crystal. "Where's Leinaux?"

"She's gone."

Gone? She couldn't decide whether to be angry or panic. That woman was like a sister to her, but it was unlike her to flee.

"Avrond as well," Barthanox added. "No sign of the pet, but we found blood. Too much blood. You know he likes that."

"Do you think Wraith could have killed them?" she asked, her voice wavering. Out of all the threats, he was perhaps the scariest to her. His existence was also illegal. The Tenebris had promised the wraiths were dead.

"He's not all there, so maybe." He sounded hesitant and uncertain. "There are no bodies, so it's possible."

"How did you get away?"

"I didn't. I wasn't even there," he admitted. "I went to retrieve some supplies in Kal'Katah with Harane. We only just returned."

"Rumors in Lumin suggest both of the diplomats of Bastillos are missing, possibly dead," Elanath said. "Did you find their bodies?"

"No, but Harane has been studying the aftermath," he said. "She thinks it was an attack. A robbery. Our gold stores are missing and some supplies as well. I'm going to remain here and cleanse the place. Harane is going to track who might have robbed the place. Get some answers."

"What of the directive?" Elanath asked. "Do we have a direction?"

"If the diplomats are presumed dead, we may still have some time," Barthanox said. "Make yourself invaluable to the Bastillosi queen. Figure out their weak points we can exploit during this war. For now, you're our last hope. Good luck, Elanath."

"May your key unlock the door," she said.

"May your key unlock the door," he repeated, and the magic faded.

A loud *crack!* echoed through a dense thicket within the Scar of the Grey Hinterlands. Fog billowed out from a fissure like smoke followed by the groans of shrouded, otherworldly beings crashing through the foliage in their lethargic lumbering.

Haggard and crazed, Wraith emerged from the fog with a weakened Rotheel grasped by a bloodied shirt collar. Wraith's lips were drenched in red that trickled in thick streaks down his chin as he cackled.

The cold bite of the Grey Hinterlands was as fresh as cold steel to his lungs, and he breathed in the damp earth and sweet pine. The bond between him and Rotheel gently rose with a sense of hope, weak, but ready to bloom through the frost of his mind.

"Yes, my pet," Wraith cooed. "Find your soul. Guide me to your fading light and I will make you whole once again."

Rotheel's cheeks wet with tears, his body coiling with anguish as the Shadowy spell spiked through his psyche. He could not resist Wraith's puppeteering being so far from his soul, but the wraith knew he'd break him completely by the time they recovered the crystal.

Wraith would make Ilai pay for his transgressions, and it will be delicious.

APPENDIX

This is a collection of lore within the world of Estyr as it pertains to Cohesion and Chaos.

The calendar year is 380 days. There are no months, so they define that time by Seasons instead. They have seven day weeks. Week days do not have names, but are referred to as Week Day One, etc., or Early Week or Mid Week. Or they will just refer to the day of the Season.

Lands of Edros:

- Bastillos

- Dradmida

- Everyn

- The Grey Hinterlands

- Ithrad

- Krei

Location: Bastillos

Bastillos is a kingdom built entirely underground within natural and man made caverns and tunnels that connect each city, settlement, and town. Natural light is brought into these dark spaces by either using a system of small tunnels fitted with mirrors, creating mirrorlight, or through natural fissures leading to the surface.

Lumin, the capitol, is separated into two sections: Low Lumin and High Lumin. Low Lumin is where the poor are housed, and as of the timeframe of Cohesion and Chaos, natural light does not reach them. Their use of fire is heavily regulated, requiring official permits, as fire "thins the air." But fire is their only source of light as everglow is incredibly rare and often stolen to be sold to High Lumin for food.

Bastillos is the capital of commerce in Edros as they control many of the trade roads crossing through and on their mountains.

A natural fissure cracks open one of the tall mountains that houses the city of Kelphern, which will later become a port city for airships.

Given the people of Bastillos have mined precious metals from their mountains, they are known for their fine jewelry. Women wear what is called adornments, which are headdresses or jewelry affixed to the head and ears. Chains, medallions, and gemstones cascade around braided hair or fashionable hats. Women of High Lumen have a culture around how their adornments move an jingle to signify their inner thoughts. Men wear caps with beads of metal and precious stone woven into them, and those who do not identify as either adorn themselves at their whim, sometimes combining the two.

The lower class has their own variation of these adornments, though not as garish. They weave discarded or repurposed metal chains in their hair or wear unbeaded caps if their hair is short.

Naming conventions vary between the upper and lower class of Bastillos. Women of high birth are given a first name with repeated consonants (Ysella), whereas men of such status have repeated vowels (Rotheel).

People of the lower class have names derived from the phonetics of letters and numbers (Arjah).

Location: The Grey Hinterlands

The Grey Hinterlands is not governed by one king, but several leaders known as laerds. The term "Laerds' Lands" refers to multiple governed lands in the Grey, and "Laerd's Lands" refers to one laerd's jurisdiction.

Some laws vary from laerd to laerd, and some laerds have alliances with others for the purposes of trade.

Because the Grey is not governed by one person, there is no capitol, but each Laerd's Land has one settlement where their castle is housed, typically occupying old fortresses.

People of the Grey come from all over Estyr. While some people's families have lived there centuries, some fled their homeland for a chance at freedom. The laerds of the lands rarely check citizenships or criminal records. All they care about is if a person swears to a laerd and agrees to abide by the laws. Freeloaders are frowned upon, but not uncommon. The locals will find a way to make them contribute to the economy even if they do not swear to a laerd.

To this, naming conventions are a melting pot in the Grey. The only indication they are a Lander is that you'll only find them in the Grey. They rarely see a need to flee the Laerds' Lands.

Location: Maldvir

Within the Southlyn Continent presides the largest and most varied region known as Maldvir. It holds the largest and oldest population of humans on Estyr. A portion of the starship that crash landed millennia ago now acts as the base structure for the capitol city of Starspire.

The battle between Light and Shadow originates in Maldvir. The people of Maldvir, known as Maldviri, tapped into the unnatural magic they call Inner Light, and built their culture around the practice of honing this magic.

They have one central ruler they call the Solasi. Under the Solasi are the Revered Houses that govern cities and settlements, and the heads of these houses are called the Revered, who are responsible for ensuring their lands provide food and trade and are required to train soldiers and house religious figures for protection.

Naming conventions often follow "bright" sounding names, or names that have an appealing cadence. They like when syllables punctuate when spoken.

Religion: Elssar

Elssar is a singular deity believed to be the god of everything. Priests and practitioners believe that they have to set aside their worldly feelings as an act of selflessness. They are there for others, not for themselves.

The concept of Elssar is similar to how we, in the real world, believe in "The Universe." If you believe it, truly believe it, Elssar grants it. Elssar's Will is the idea that you get what you deserve through your affirmations. You have to put in the work to believe you deserve it.

Religion: The Nine Patrons

The Nine Patrons is a specifically human religion revolving around nine divine beings known as Patrons. These Patrons are not gods, nor were they ever human or walked the earth. They are conceptual beings that embody their names.

A Giver is one who devotes their life to one or all of the Nine Patrons. Givers wear what's called a vav; a long drape worn over the shoulders weighted by bells. They wear simple, asymmetrical robes.

A Traveler is anyone who does not worship a Patron. They are considered "lost" and therefore a traveler in search for their Patron.

The Nine Patrons:

- Patron of Life

- Patron of Death

- Patron of Harvest

- Patron of Storms

- Patron of Oaths

- Patron of Night

- Patron of Day

- Patron of Seasons

- Patron of War

Rituals are performed for each Patron according to regional and societal beliefs. Some rituals remain constant across the world, others vary. For example, a common ritual at the start of Harvest is the slaughter of a pig before a burning effigy. They char the meat until the flames turn to embers, and then serve at the Harvest Feast. If the meat is overcooked, they will have a harsh Harvest season, but if the meat is succulent, their harvest will be good.

The Magic of Estyr

According to elven definitions, magic has two categories: natural and unnatural magic. Natural magic is that which one is born with, and to this, the only natural magic that exists is within elves and g'arm. Unnatural magic is what can be learned through study and practice, or in the case of Blood Magic, awarded later in life.

Natural magic is elemental and consists of Earth, Fire, Ice, and Arcane.

Unnatural magic consists of Inner Light, Shadow, and Blood.

Magic: Inner Light

Where Shadow corrupts, the Light rejuvenates. It is accessed from the caster's soul, and the "brilliance" or potency of the magic is dependent on the purity of the soul. Purity is defined by deeds, and over thousands of years Maldviri have learned how to measure deeds and transgressions to determine the path to betterment.

Thus the religion. It is based on a moral system and relies heavily on a good moral compass. Morals, however, are subjective, and this complicates the path.

Not everyone who wields Inner Light partakes in the religion, but those that do end up choosing a righteous path. The path of the Judicator is one who takes on the task of finding and determining the breadth of Shadow, or the potential for its path. A Vindicator is one who acts with any means necessary to cleanse the lands of Shadow. Luminaries are people who take on the passive path, seeking people in need and aiding with the idea of leaving every place better than when they entered.

The magic of Inner Light can blind foes with a flash of brilliance, burn the souls of its corruption, and even teleport their souls or their bodies across distances.

Those who practice the Inner Light are not easily afflicted by Shadow. While not completely immune, the effects of Shadow Magic is comparable to receiving a scratch where others would be brutally eviscerated. They are, however, immune to being corrupted by Shadow Magic and can even reverse the effects of corruption with enough time and energy.

When a practitioner of the Inner Light dies, Maldviri believe their soul transcends to the stars to continue the eternal combat against the Shadow. Eventually, their soul is "called" to the eternal battle to shine in the absence of the sun and provide light in the night.

Every practitioner is born without Inner Light, and through the teachings are taught how to bring it from within. This serves as a reminder that they are of the world and are equal to others, and that the Inner Light is a choice that everyone can choose.

Perfection isn't something Maldviri care about. Having the Inner Light is enough to them, and if people are at least good people but don't wish to partake in the religion, they are accepting. They believe everyone has their own calling, and that no one should be forced to do something they don't want to do.

Magic: Shadow

While most of Estyr shuns Shadow Casters, Shadow Magic is allowed in Edros under strict laws. Shadow Magic is tied to the mind and soul, feeding off of negative emotions to access its energy. Practitioners are encouraged to revel in their emotions, and groups like the Tenebris will perpetuate hostile or unforgiving environments to increase a Caster's potential.

Casting this form of magic is volatile and progressively corrupts a person's soul. Due to this, Arcane Mages can sense a Shadow Mage, and Blood Mages can see the corruption on their soul.

Those who practice shadow magic have a significantly shortened life span, apart from those of the Tenebris. The magic draws from their soul to sustain The Darkness within this plane of existence, effectively draining a Caster of their years without aging. Casters can drain from the life force of others to add to their own and gain back a few years, but it requires a significant amount of focus and is never done in battle.

Magic: Blood

Coming neither from Brilliance nor Darkness nor the World Tree's filtered Aether, Blood Magic is a form that is incredibly rare and illegal in Edros. Only humans can possess this type of magic after their souls have been plunged into the Afterlife, and they find their way back to their body, waking anew with the Sight of Souls and a connection to the energy that charges their blood with spells.

The Sight of Souls is a permanent affliction to the eyes, causing the entirety to glow a blue-white and allows them to see the souls of the living and the dead. The Sight of Souls can see Shadow Corruption, or the Brilliance of Inner Light, or the attunement of natural magic. Very few substances can block out the sight of a soul, though with enough thickness, any material can hide a soul.

Blood Mages can only manipulate their own blood, but they can merge their blood in another system after charging it with a spell. The magic requires the spell to be channeled from the heart, through the veins, and out of an open wound. The blood can be channeled through the air, but it must be charged with a spell before departing the body, otherwise it will take no effect.

Blood Mages became illegal in Edros after the Dark Calamity of 1200 where a group of Blood Mages learned to merge with Shadow Magic and become Wraiths.

Due to the corruption of Shadow and their souls constantly walking the veil of the Afterlife, they all went mad and nearly wiped out half of Edros.

* 9 7 9 8 9 9 3 5 7 7 6 1 6 *